A DEGREE OF UNCERTAINTY

Nicola K Smith

ISBN 978-1-912009-41-1

Typeset by The Book Refinery
www.thebookrefinery.com
Cover design by Josie Staveley-Taylor

Printed and bound by CMP Group (UK) Dorset

To Sheila and David
(AKA my much loved Mum and Dad)

To Nirola
A fellow Ascot girl!
And an inspiration!
Thank you.
Nirola /x

Chapter 1

Harry Manchester blinked at the red bulb flashing before his eyes. He squared his shoulders. The intense heat of the studio lights seemed only to fuel his confidence. This was his time, his moment. He summoned his ready TV smile and waited.

'And three, two, one… live.'

Jenny Trundle was even more attractive in real life, her skin smooth and her green eyes flashing, shapely bronzed legs elegantly arranged.

'We have Harry Manchester in the studio, one of the biggest estate agents in the West Cornwall town of Poltowan—'

'We are *the* biggest actually—'

'Thank you, Harry. Now you launched the Local Houses for Local People campaign that has been gathering momentum in Poltowan – a town which, I understand, is becoming increasingly divided by its rapidly expanding university?'

'That's right, Jenny. We need to cap the number of houses rented to students in the town before the balance tips too far.' Harry's voice gained deeper resonance. 'Without being melodramatic about it, the lives of many of Poltowan's long-term residents are being ruined by the change in its population, and the town itself, which is renowned for its charm, is turning into a ghetto…'

Jenny frowned, adjusting her earpiece, adrenaline starting to course through her. 'Sorry – we have just heard, live on air, that Poltowan University's Vice Chancellor, Dawn Goldberg, has this afternoon lodged a formal application to increase student numbers by fifty per cent – meaning an estimated three thousand more coming to the town next year. What is your response to that, Harry?'

Dawn Goldberg had a nerve. She had the previous week promised to work closely with Harry "to address any concerns", before fawning all over his new car in the university car park. They had met formally for the first time only after he had gone to some lengths to arrange a meeting with her, a stilted affair it had taken him two months to achieve. There had been no mention of any such development then. Her timing was characteristically impeccable.

Harry unfolded his long legs, balled his right hand into a fist. 'That is hugely disappointing, Jenny. I think it's also very worrying for the people of Poltowan, who are already struggling to adapt to living cheek by jowl with such a large student population.'

'I understand that the vote on the application will be held at the beginning of March. Does that give you sufficient time to mount a credible campaign against this increase?'

Harry sat forward, locking eyes with the presenter. He calculated the dates quickly in his head, realising the vote was about five weeks away. 'If there is one thing I have learned from many years of living in the town, it is that the people of Poltowan do not, and will not, give up easily. We will fight this – with everything we have.'

He pushed his glasses higher on the bridge of his nose. As he did so he felt a disconcerting vibration in his pocket, followed by the ugly buzz of feedback from his microphone. A high-pitched voice was asking Scaramouch if he could dance, if he could do the fandango, the tinny music playing jauntily from his trousers.

Jenny Trundle glared at him from behind her angular, pink

glasses, somehow managing a smile for the viewers at the same time. 'Apologies for the musical accompaniment there, I think someone has forgotten to turn off their mobile phone.' The noise came to an abrupt end and Harry felt the tingling sensation in his groin subside.

'My apologies. Don't get me wrong, students have brought some huge benefits to Poltowan, but we need to redress the balance and ensure that more residents are not pushed out. The news that has come to light today,' he paused, holding her gaze, 'has the potential to be quite devastating for the people of our town.'

'But not for the many local businesses who have seen an average uplift of twenty-three per cent since the university opened its doors three years ago?'

Glimpsing a man in the glass-fronted studio booth hold his hands aloft and begin to count down on his fingers, Harry made his sign-off as succinct as he could. 'There are two sides to every story, Jenny, but at the end of the day, living in Poltowan is about community, not personal gain.'

'Thank you, Harry Manchester, for joining us this evening. Sadly, we will have to leave it there.'

'The town's many beautiful houses,' he tried to add, inching forward in his seat as he did so, 'must be made available to locals and their families, not just a transient population—'

'Harry Manchester, thank you.'

He smiled and acknowledged camera three, then camera two, suddenly unsure which one he had been told to look at. Perspiration dribbled down his left temple.

Jenny Trundle windmilled her legs again for camera four's benefit and rearranged her smile. 'Now, if you have been hoping for some milder weather of late, you might—'

A hand took Harry's elbow and a skinny young man with

oversized headphones urged him from his seat and off set. 'Thanks, mate. All done here.' He reached up, unclipping the microphone from Harry's shirt with one deft move and pulling the battery pack from his back pocket. 'Cheers.'

Harry looked around, expecting someone to come and congratulate him on his performance, or at least offer him some refreshments in the Green Room. A short, rotund lady stood several feet away, clutching a clipboard to her ample bosom. She rounded on him.

'Sir, sir,' she said in hushed but urgent tones. 'If you could move off set, that way, that's right... quickly now!' She gesticulated as she spoke and suddenly Harry found himself in a cramped corridor, the studio door closing softly but definitively behind him, followed by the unmistakable sound of a key turning in a lock. The familiar closing tune of *News Time* started up as Harry began to work his way back along the labyrinthine corridors of the television station.

He had done well, he thought, mopping his brow with his Freddie Mercury monogrammed handkerchief. He had got his key messages across and even been able to think on his feet in the face of breaking news, not something everyone could handle.

He thought back to Dawn Goldberg's easy laughter during their meeting and the way she had tossed her hair over her shoulder when she was about to make a point. He had been prepared to challenge the prevailing gossip, to understand her point of view as Vice Chancellor of the University. And, if he was honest, he had also been more than a little impressed by her knowledge of the Mercedes V6 racing engine.

He felt used. But his disappointment in Dawn Goldberg was tempered by a touch of excitement. Now the people of Poltowan needed him more than ever. He pushed his way manfully through two sets of swing doors.

He thought of Mrs Coleman, who had only that morning

mouthed something incomprehensible but encouraging through his office window, holding aloft her fist as she disappeared up the hill. He thought of Dave Jose, who had popped in to shake his hand the previous day, turning as he left to say, 'You don't know 'ow important you are to us, 'arry, to this whole town.' He thought of Steph the bar owner, who had fallen into his arms after one too many gins the week before, bemoaning the fate of Poltowan. 'You won't let them do it to us, will you, Harry?' she had asked him, rhetorically.

They would all have tuned in tonight. They would be rattled by the latest news, of course, but they would be relieved that he was on their side; confident that he would fight their corner. They would be pleased that he had not allowed himself to be fazed by Jenny Trundle's slightly hostile manner. He had stood his ground.

He squeezed into the revolving door. He had even given his beloved Queen some air time, albeit unwittingly. That was twice his new iPhone had failed to respond to the mute voice command. He must get Ludo to look at it.

The January air was icy as Harry lumbered up the road in the direction of the multi-storey car park. A biting wind blew up Plymouth Hoe, screaming as it rounded each corner. Dustbin lids wheeled along the streets and tin cans rattled their way into gutters.

He felt his phone buzz several times against his heart and imagined the flood of messages following his TV appearance. He turned his collar up and bent his head towards the wind, clutching the Mercedes' key in his pocket. He muttered some words about being caught in a landslide with no escape from reality as he tried to ward off the cold. If anything, Dawn Goldberg had unwittingly given him a stronger platform for his campaign, a fixed point to which he could more tightly tether his cause. This was an opportunity, he decided, straightening his back.

On the corner of Saxon Street he saw something move in the entrance to a narrow alley next to Barclays. At first he thought it was an animal scavenging for food, but as he drew closer he realised it was a young woman, huddled in a blanket in the dark, a woollen hat pulled low over her brow. She tilted her face up towards him as he approached, shuffling into the glow of the streetlight. Her skin was almost translucent, eyes hollow.

'Any change to spare, please, any at all, just a…'

Harry continued past. The persistent cold was making his eyes stream and the frames of his glasses were digging into his sinuses. At the last moment he turned, retreating a couple of steps and pausing. He reached inside his jacket to find his wallet, his numb fingers grappling for the opening.

A hard blow rained down between his shoulder blades, expelling the air from his lungs, before an unknown force collided with the back of his knees, bringing him gracelessly to the ground. His glasses clattered to the tarmac and his wallet skidded away in the darkness. His eye socket slammed against the brickwork.

In seconds she was gone, rucksack on back, a shadowy figure disappearing towards the inky sea. Harry tried to call out as he struggled to his feet, a searing pain in his right kneecap, his breathing shallow and painful. His shout drifted away on the wind. He reached automatically for his wrist to check that his watch was in place and grasped his Rolex tightly.

Moments later he found his glasses on the ground, but his wallet was nowhere to be seen. He waved his iPhone slowly around the pavement, its powerful torch illuminating some old takeaway cartons and an empty cigarette packet. He plucked a fusty blanket between thumb and forefinger and shone the light underneath. Nothing.

Easing himself to his feet, he dialled the police, his chilled fingers first making several shaky stabs at the touch screen. The female questioner was brusque, her brevity reassuringly pragmatic. He answered her questions in the same manner, aware that his description of the female mugger was perhaps slightly exaggerated, her bulk greater, height more imposing – after all, it had been dark and he couldn't be sure. He completed the business-like transaction with his contact details. Only then did the call handler's voice soften.

'Are you OK to drive home, sir? Would you like an officer to—'

He could feel his knee already swelling from the impact, and his head ached with a dull pain. 'I'll be fine. Just doing my civic duty, alerting you so other less able persons aren't needlessly put at risk.'

'Thank you, sir. We'll be in touch.'

Harry limped towards the car park, out of the wind. Instinctively he called Sylvia. He didn't want to tell Jo, not yet.

'Yes?'

'Sylvia, it's me.'

'So I gathered.'

Harry sucked the cold air into his lungs, his ribs smarting at the effort. He leaned his weight on the car door. 'I've been mugged.'

'Mugged? In Poltowan?'

'Plymouth… It doesn't matter where. My bank stuff, the paperwork, it's in a red box file in the garage with the rest of my things. I need to cancel my cards.'

'Are you alright?'

'I'll pick it up on my way past… in about an hour and a half. Will you be there?'

'Are you hurt?'

He extended his knee slowly. 'No. But she took my wallet.'

'It was a woman?'

'There was a group of them,' he blurted. 'One was a woman.'

He could almost hear her disappointment in the ensuing silence.

'Have you rung the police?'

'Yes, yes. It's fine. Just some chancers. I need to cancel my cards.'

'Haven't you got your data backed up? Don't you still use that iPhone app?'

Harry stayed silent.

'You can pick it up later,' she said eventually. 'I'm not going out. Not tonight.'

He groaned as he slammed the car door shut, easing himself into the driver's seat. The silence and relative warmth of the Mercedes provided welcome relief. He placed his phone in the holder and pushed a button. The dashboard lit up before him, the engine simultaneously purring into life. Another button prompted warm air to start filling the car noiselessly.

Harry took his glasses off to clean the left lens but the mark proved stubborn. Peering closely, he saw a crack straight across the middle. He swore under his breath before placing them back on his nose, adjusting the angle so he could see through the fractured glass.

He began to make his way through the sea of lights towards the main road. When he flicked the radio on, haunting violin notes filled the air. He pushed the buttons, first on his steering wheel and then on the dashboard. Classic FM stubbornly refused to shift. He thought about using the voice activation but he didn't have the heart to talk to himself.

Chapter 2

Sylvia was tired. She had been awake since four o'clock that morning, listening to the crash of the distant waves and the cry of the gusting wind. She had momentarily forgotten that Harry had left but the other side of the bed was undoubtedly empty, the pillow pristine in its plumpness, the duvet unworried by the nocturnal thrashings of another body. It was what she had said she wanted – space, time, peace. But how could she really have known what that would feel like?

She had forced herself to get up, the freezing water on her face a sharp reminder of the day ahead. She had sought some sort of solace in routine, as she always did, pulling on jeans and jumper, descending the stairs, filling the kettle, stroking the cat as it stretched and yawned, putting the radio on. Then she had gazed out of the kitchen window into the darkness of the winter morning, the meaningless drone of the World Service just enough to keep her from her own thoughts.

Beyond the boundaries of her garden, still cloaked in its night shroud and just a little further than the neglected field beyond, the sea rolled and shattered on to Poltowan Beach, spewing great lengths of brown straggly seaweed onto the crescent of sand that glittered like gold in summer.

The day had dragged. There was little to do in the garden in January and everything lay exhausted and sodden after a night of heavy rain. She had slept for some of the afternoon, before watching the half-hearted daylight quickly submit to the weight of the evening; another day consigned to history. She had been contemplating embarking on her night-time routine when Harry's call had disturbed her.

His arrival was boisterous and dramatic as always, his large frame suddenly filling the kitchen, changing the shape of the house, bringing its walls alive with his energy. If only she could capture his vitality and suffocate this wretched black dog that had moved in almost permanently since he'd left.

Of course, it had toyed with her for years. It was why she had finally urged him to go. As much as depression had destroyed her, it had eaten away at his life, pushing him further into his work and doubtless helping to spawn his Local Houses for Local People campaign. It was a way of allowing him to sidestep the reality of her crippling illness after countless futile attempts to help.

She listened as he talked her through the assault, once again describing an attacker who was larger and more formidable than he actually remembered, and throwing in an extra kick for good measure. She watched impassively as he rubbed his knee, and then his head, a pained expression contorting his face as he did so. Sylvia wondered if the grimace arose not from the pain itself, but from his being unable to decide which injury was more deserving of her attention.

As it turned out, neither Harry's pounding head nor his wrenched knee received undue sympathy. After twenty minutes or so he emerged from the fog of victimhood and returned his attention quite suddenly to the kitchen of his former home and the pale face of his estranged wife, watching him intently with an odd mix of curiosity and boredom.

Nausea flooded him. He hobbled out of the kitchen door, across the hallway and into the downstairs toilet, having the foresight to flick on the exterior light switch before banging the door behind him.

Sylvia heard him retching and crossed the kitchen to the

sink to fill a glass of water. She handed it to him when he returned, his face now approaching the same pallor as her own, although she was unaware of quite how drawn she looked, not having thought to consult a mirror for several days.

'Must be shock,' he said matter-of-factly as he took the glass from her.

Harry's sips of water quickly became greedy gulps as an acute thirst gripped him. Sylvia had forgotten quite how much noise accompanied even the smallest of his actions; yet still she marvelled at the guttural sounds that issued from his sturdy anatomy.

'Thanks,' he said, placing the glass back on the worktop.

She waited in the cold draft of air by the kitchen door as Harry mumbled to himself in the garage, shifting and pulling at boxes before appearing with a red file. He came back into the kitchen and leaned against the door until it clicked.

'Did you lock it?'

He gestured to the key hanging off his finger. Sylvia took it from him and hung it on the hook in the corner. As they sat across the kitchen island from each other, Harry poring over old pieces of paperwork, it occurred to Sylvia that the physical tension that had been gripping her for weeks was dissipating. She felt her shoulders relaxing, a sense of calm beginning to ease itself under her skin, and the weight of her head became less of a burden.

Harry too was taking a certain comfort from being back in The Oaks, sitting on one of the stools they had bought together in Habitat not long after they had moved in. He settled into the familiar grooves, the foot rests exactly where he knew they would be.

Eventually he announced that he had found the piece of paper he needed. Sylvia straightened her back, folding her arms more tightly as he pushed an endless number of buttons to direct him through the virtual and unfathomable corridors of the bank's telephone network. Finally, a chirpy automated voice informed him that his call was important and that a human being would shortly be available to meet his every need. The pledge was quickly followed by the elegant violins of Eine kleine Nachtmusik, the brilliance of the composition marred almost irreparably by jangly acoustics and over-familiarity.

He pushed the speaker button and let Mozart fill the room, locking his eyes with Sylvia's. She raised her eyebrows ambiguously in response before shifting her gaze towards the Aga. Its hulking form stayed silent, as if deciding to remain non-partisan. Harry saw once again that faraway look steal into her eyes, like a curtain coming down across her thoughts as she retreated to that unreachable place.

'They only play this stuff because it's out of copyright,' said Harry, watching as she clawed her way slowly back to the present. 'It's cheap, that's all. You'd think they might be a bit more creative, a bit more original, a bit more *on brand*. It's an affront to Wolfgang.'

There was a muffled bang and Harry jumped while Sylvia watched Sting appear through the cat flap, his head tilted to one side. He paused in the middle of the kitchen and looked from Harry to Sylvia and back, as if expecting an explanation. None forthcoming, he leaped neatly onto Harry's lap.

Harry yelped as the cat's weight landed on his injured knee, swearing before nuzzling the furry neck and reverting to an affectionate jargon that was meaningful only to himself and Sting.

'How's he been?'

'Easily pleased, isn't he? Doesn't know he's born.'

'Spoiled.' As if in response, Sting jumped off Harry's lap and sprang on to Sylvia's.

'I miss him,' said Harry.

Mozart filled the ensuing silence. Sylvia focused on the comforting weight and heat of the cat in her lap, its eyes locked on hers. Sting was studying her, his green eyes intent. She bent to kiss him on the back of his neck, seized by a moment of pure love. Harry looked away, taking in the oddness of the familiar room, drumming his fingers on the work surface as the violins played on.

'Did you see the local news?'

Sylvia nodded, her hand working the cat's fur vigorously.

'Well?' said Harry.

'That dreadful ringtone,' she said eventually. 'It's awful at the best of times, let alone on live television.'

Harry shook his head, the dull ache around his skull returning. 'Need to get my phone looked at. But what did you think?' His foot tapped nervously against the stool.

'Nothing Dawn Goldberg does surprises me. She obviously timed the announcement to catch you off guard. Very clever. She certainly plays tough.'

Harry nodded, waiting for her to continue.

She noticed his eyes were shadowed underneath and watering slightly behind his glasses. 'You've got your work cut out.'

'And I'm going to step up the campaign. If she wants to fight dirty, so can I.'

'It's not your style.'

'What *is* my style?'

Sylvia thought for a moment. 'You're simple.'

Harry frowned.

'I mean, people trust you. You're upfront, you tell the truth. You do what you say you'll do.'

'Do you think so? You think people will trust me to stop

this rampage through our town? I mean, a lot rests on it – my reputation, the business…' He cleared his throat. 'Is it wise for me to keep going?'

Sylvia's gaze dropped. 'You're all they've got.'

'Oh, cheers,' he said, rubbing his swollen knee, which was now giving off a powerful heat.

Sylvia's pragmatism had often infuriated him, her dispassionate way of looking at things, her inability to view a situation in anything but the most commonsensical way, oblivious to the occasional need to speak half-truths in the name of duty or even kindness.

'But how did I come across tonight – was I OK?'

She knew what he was driving at, acutely aware of his need for frequent reassurance and liberal amounts of praise. She could barely muster the energy to be honest, let alone find the resources to be creative with the truth.

'Yes, you did OK. Not bad.'

Harry leaned forward on the island, his eyes trying to fix hers. 'How OK? What does OK mean?'

'Well, you asked if you did OK. I'm saying you did – OK.'

'But good OK, average OK? Where are we on the OK scale? Did I make my position clear? Did I—'

'Shouldn't you get your head checked? Call in at A&E on your way back?'

The violins ceased abruptly and a voice spoke. Harry clicked the speakerphone off and entered into a lengthy stream of monosyllabic answers punctuated by heavy sighs.

Fifteen minutes later he was leaving the house he jointly owned and thanking the woman who remained his wife. He hovered in the doorway, the hostile night air engulfing the two of them, figures framed on the threshold in the stark porch light.

'Are you alright, Sylve?'

'It's you that's had a shock. Not me.'

'You know what I mean. You look tired.'

'Harry, I'm fine.' She pulled her cardigan more tightly around herself, hunching her shoulders for warmth. 'You've got your life, I've got mine. There's no need for you to worry.'

'I can't help worrying.'

'Save your worrying for Jo.' Sylvia paused, narrowing her eyes and peering over Harry's shoulder in search of Sting, who had slunk out into the darkness. It seemed odd to say her name out loud, this other woman she could only imagine, a shadowy being, yet charming, witty, beautiful, all the same. 'She's your priority now.'

Harry was about to remonstrate but thought better of it. His wife's expression was hard to discern.

'It's early days, you know.'

She held up her hand sharply, as if by doing so she could stop, or even erase, his words. 'We agreed. You've moved on – we both have.'

Harry nodded. 'Thanks again for the file.'

Sylvia closed the door, turned the lock and put the chain on. She lingered in the dark hallway and watched through the frosted glass the tail lights of the Mercedes receding, heard the low hum of his engine retreating into the night. Then she switched off each of the lights in turn and made her way up the stairs.

❧

Harry glanced in his rear-view mirror as the house fell into darkness. He could almost hear the creak of the final stair as Sylvia stepped on it on her way to bed, the tread he had promised to investigate but never got around to fixing. She had not been angry with him towards the end; her paralysing depression left her no room for active resentment or festering recriminations. She had not moaned, just slipped into a state of quiet resignation as he became swallowed up in the politics of Poltowan, the demands on his time, on his influence, growing incrementally until they absorbed his every waking hour, came to monopolise his every thought. When she told him to leave, over and over, he finally realised that maybe this was her only hope of getting better.

He passed the winding drive leading up to the Chyangwens Hotel. It was where he and Sylvia had held their wedding reception on that windy September day all those years ago. The sign looked a little tired now, the once proud Cornish wall where they had happily posed for the photographer crumbling slightly, unable to hold up its end of the bargain.

Harry had thought he knew it all then. At twenty-five years of age, he had the woman he loved on his arm and big plans to take over Maycroft's estate agency. He would be successful and wealthy, but just as importantly, he would be liked, combining the three things in a way that many before him had seemed incapable of doing.

Dawn Goldberg's face returned to mind. She might have a PhD and a lengthy CV but she lacked soul. She didn't understand what made Poltowan special, or how its delicate societal mix made for a rich and thriving community. She had marched across the Tamar clearly expecting the Cornish people to capitulate as her shadow lengthened. But no academic qualification could prepare her for this fight. Sylvia was right: the people of Poltowan needed him to lead them to victory.

He opened the window to let some of the briny night air blow in, shifting in his seat as he turned down Bosvennen Avenue. He swore suddenly as he recalled his phone call to the police, banging the steering wheel in frustration. He should never have reported the incident. He could already picture the front page of the *Poltowan Post*: 'Local Businessman Mugged in City', a picture of his bespectacled face grinning out, blow-up guitar held aloft. They always seemed to dig out that shot from last year's carnival, even though he had sent the newspaper's editor Dennis Flintoff at least two professional portrait photos since.

He swore again, this time louder, taking pleasure from the release it gave him. Harry rarely swore. He found it unbecoming in others and was of the opinion that it very rarely added impact to an argument or helped to articulate a point – it was unimaginative, lazy. Yet in the isolation of his car he experienced a strange thrill. He pulled into a parking space just along from Jo's apartment and turned the engine off. He repeated the obscenity, this time shouting it as loud as he could, his headache pounding now as the word reverberated back at him.

He sat for a moment, rehearsing the words he would say to Jo. He didn't want to alarm her, he didn't want any fuss. Just some quiet sympathy, an understanding hug, a cold beer.

'Darling, what's wrong?'

Harry jumped at the unexpected voice, raising his hand with the keys pointing outwards, poised as if to attack.

'I could hear you at the end of the road, effing and blinding. What is it?'

Jo was shivering as she looked in through his half-open window. She was dressed in pyjamas, her thick white dressing gown clutched tightly across her generous cleavage. He closed his eyes in relief.

'I forgot it was open.' He pushed a button, the window drawing silently up between them. He eased himself out of the car, angling his knee carefully as he stood up.

'Just letting off some steam.' He exhaled noisily. 'Sorry,' he said, almost to himself.

'I don't think I've ever heard you swear. What have you done to your leg?' Jo was unused to him being anything other than dynamic and positive. Now his every movement seemed fraught with uncertainty, slowed by some invisible force, while even his face looked different, his glasses sitting clumsily.

He touched her arm, summoning the calmness she would expect from him. 'Honey,' he said, 'go on up, it's freezing. I'm right behind you. I'll explain in a minute.'

She retreated along the path and into the building. Harry could see the man in the ground-floor flat peering through the gap in his curtains, unconcerned about being observed.

The flat was warm, lit with a welcoming glow, a smell of vanilla drifting from the tiny lounge. Harry had not yet told Jo of his dislike of incense sticks. He placed his leather briefcase down by the door, loosening his tie.

Jo stood on tiptoe, throwing her arms around his neck, the sweet smell of white wine on her breath, her lips pressing against his. He winced, trying to disengage himself.

'You look done in.' She eased his jacket from his shoulders and led him by the hand to the lounge, encouraging him on to the sofa and rubbing his solid, sinewy neck, kissing his head. 'You were brilliant tonight, Harry. You showed that high and mighty so and so who's boss.'

He eased her down next to him. She studied him, removing his glasses and frowning at the broken lens, then at the deep red indentations on his nose. She believed his thick glasses obscured possibly his best physical feature: brilliant blue eyes, framed by long dark lashes.

She remembered the first time she had noticed them. He had stood chatting to her while removing his glasses to wipe away a speck of dust. His eyes had quite taken her breath away, and it was as if in that moment he had revealed himself to her; the strong physique, concealed slightly by the extra pounds he carried, thanks to his liking for good food; the dark hair that had once been thick and plentiful, now teasingly revealing his temples; the kindly smile that radiated amiability; and those blue eyes, paired with a telling network of laughter lines that only underlined his lust for life. It had been like seeing him for the first time.

'Don't be alarmed, Jo, but I was attacked after I left the TV studio.'

She cupped his face in both her hands. 'Darling! Oh, God, are you OK? What did they do? What did they take?'

She noticed the bruise that was rapidly appearing around his left eye. He looked more vulnerable than she ever remembered seeing him.

Harry ran through the details again, almost starting to believe that there had been a group of attackers, and feeling anew the impact of the parting blow to his knee that the attacker may or may have not have delivered after he fell.

She held him close. 'How am I supposed to look after you properly if you're not wholly mine? Not really. Not until you're free of—'

Harry groaned, his body growing suddenly rigid, a sharp pain shooting from one temple to the other. Jo knew better than to continue down that particular path tonight. She would revisit the topic tomorrow. Her more worldly friends had advised her that a drip-feed approach was the best way to expedite his divorce proceedings, coupled with some judicious references to making a proper home together. Soon they would be out of her poky flat, perhaps enjoying a house by the river, and Harry would be truly hers.

Jo pressed a cold beer into his hands, removed his shoes, placed ice on his knee and massaged his temples until his eyes closed. He could see why young boys with scraped knees and grazed knuckles sought easy solace in her arms at Poltowan

Primary School. She oozed compassion and warmth, her voice soothing to the soul. She'd made caring her life's work, at first looking after her disabled mother at the expense of most of her own youth, and then belatedly training as a teacher. Caring was the very essence of Jo.

At times her maternal ways would irritate him, force him to withdraw into himself. On other occasions, like this one, he readily gave himself up to the tsunami of tenderness, playing his part willingly and well.

Thoughts of Sylvia slipped slowly from his mind, and even Dawn Goldberg's face became less distinct, her features starting to merge with those of Jenny Trundle, and then legs swam into his mind, lots of legs, as Jo tended to his every need, his beer sitting unopened in his hand.

Chapter 3

Dawn Goldberg took four deliberate paces towards the corner of her well-appointed office, overlooking the gardens between her and the digital animation studios. In the middle of the lawns, white-tinged under a thin covering of frost, stood a huge statue of a naked man, paint brush held over an imaginary easel, chin angled, deep in thought.

She had commissioned it the year before from a former student who had recently won a prize from some well-respected arts body looking to recognise future talent. It had caused quite a stir, and not only within the walls of the university. *The Poltowan Post* had featured it on its front page under the headline 'Naked Ambition?', and run it alongside a photo of a smiling Dawn Goldberg with the quote, "It is art, not porn." The furore that followed had only served to highlight the ignorance of so many people, she thought, who worked themselves into an irrational frenzy when presented with the magnificent male form.

She looked at it, a seagull perched audaciously upon the statue's head, and smiled. She liked to call it Michael, for reasons she could not now recall. The statue was angled in such a way that she could fully appreciate his ample manhood, almost as if he were standing there for her pleasure alone. She would often practise her speeches on him, looking to him for some sign of endorsement, which he invariably gave.

She twisted around to face the three actual men sitting before her, tossing her head in the shaft of winter sunlight and imagining how the newly applied golden-red colours – "burnished gold" her hairdresser had called the shade – would be lending her an almost angelic hue. Her father's photograph gazed up at her from the wooden frame on her desk, his characteristically ambiguous expression suggesting that he too thought the men in front of her were buffoons, hardly worthy of her time, and certainly not deserving of her patience.

Slowly she began to launch into what she called her "future strategy", outlining her plans to win over the people who mattered, changing hearts and minds. It was, after all, only a matter of time before her plans for the enlargement of the university received the go-ahead.

Andy Hornblower shifted in his seat, mouth visibly twitching, occasionally opening for a few seconds before slowly shutting again like a soft-closing bin. Each time his fat lips threatened to utter a sound, Dawn raised her voice slightly, sometimes lifting her finger in the air as if leading a dog obedience class.

The other two men listened enraptured, the angle of their heads mimicking hers as her curls danced around her bespectacled face. Andy cleared his throat during one of Dawn's rare pauses for breath, summoning the courage to speak.

'I've prepared some detailed plans along the lines of the actions you suggested, Dawn.' He raised the carefully bound document he had been clutching in his lap. 'I'll leave it with you, but I think you'll find it adds a bit of meat to the bone, shall we say, dots the i's, crosses the t's. And I've provisionally scheduled a meeting with Carrie Menhenick at Poltowan Council, she's—'

'I don't think that will be necessary Andy.' Dawn spun around to see the seagull hop down to Michael's nether regions, its tiny eyes darting left and right as if it knew it was pushing the boundaries of social acceptability.

'I have just outlined exactly how the manifesto will take

shape, and we needn't waste our time on the local Council. It's the County Council who will have the final say. Luke, you get on to the local press, gauge the mood, see what they're planning. Jowan, you research every possible line of objection and find a rebuttal as to why it's unsound. Andy, you oversee both and report back to me once we have a watertight strategy. I, meanwhile, am leveraging my contacts in the national press and at the County Council.' She rolled the l seductively and brought her hands together as if in prayer when she'd finished speaking.

'I really do think you should reconsider holding a meeting with Harry Manchester...' muttered Andy.

'I saw him last week,' said Dawn, her voice rising an octave. 'And I don't need to see that loathsome gawping man from that snivelling little industry again.'

'But, Dawn, we should remember he wields considerable local influence, and after contriving to let him find out about our expansion plans on live TV, I think it might be wise to...'

Dawn crossed the office floor quickly, her sturdy legs striding into the shadows where Andy sat. Her painted finger was held aloft, her eyes wide. 'And I rather think that this meeting is closed.' She paused for a moment after she'd made her announcement, relishing her ability to bring instantaneous quiet upon the room.

'One other thing—' Andy said, exhaling as if a captor had finally removed tape from his mouth. Dawn glared down at him, her finger still raised. He seemed unaware of quite how close to the wind he was sailing. 'Dave White has written an open letter to Kernow Click. It's online now. Might be a good idea for you have a look – in case you want to respond?'

She glowered at him.

'When I was in the police,' he continued, 'it was always considered best practice to—'

'You are not in the force now, PC Hornblower.'

Jowan coughed. Luke studied the worn-down heels of his shoes.

'Well, I wasn't actually a PC, as you know, I worked—'

'Off you go, gents. No time to waste.'

Dawn sat behind her desk as the last of them filed out. It pleased her to see Luke and Jowan's admiring glances, their eyes dipping towards her cleavage as she spoke. Sometimes she wondered if this was how an actor felt, strutting across the stage in front of a worshipful audience, everybody hanging on their every word, eyes unable to disguise the marvel they felt at the genius before them.

She slid open her left-hand drawer and eyed the miniature vodka bottle inside. Sucking in her breath, she retrieved a packet of chocolate biscuits instead, forcing one into her mouth whole. She closed her eyes in momentary rapture, the chocolate melting on her tongue, the sweet sugary sensation pleasingly spiking her bloodstream.

A tentative knock at the office door forced her to attempt an ill-timed and painful swallow, and for a terrifying moment she was rendered speechless. The knock sounded again a few seconds later, this time with slightly more commitment.

The apparent impatience of the interruption, not to mention the inconsiderate and presumptuous timing, would ordinarily have made Dawn set her jaw and flare her nostrils slightly. It was a look that could strike terror into her colleagues, unsure quite what ruthless affront would follow. But with her upper and lower jaw currently unable to meet, she dared not attempt it. She slammed her desk drawer shut and brushed the cascade of crumbs from her Apple Mac.

'Yes,' she said eventually, shifting her laptop slightly so as to screen off the glance of her father, the enigmatic smile having somehow morphed into one of disapproval.

The door creaked open. Andy entered the room as if someone had pushed him from behind, the bound document still clamped under his arm. He had vowed to enter with conviction and stride towards her. He had even envisioned tossing the document down on the desk in front of her before thrusting his hands casually into his pockets and telling her exactly what was on his mind, just like Jonathan Seaman used to do.

Jonathan had seemed to get away with it, although he was, admittedly, taller than Andy, with an angular jaw and a mop of dark hair. He had been spotted on numerous occasions enjoying intimate lunches with Dawn where several bottles of wine had, by all accounts, been consumed. Andy had often wondered why a man of his standing had left so suddenly.

Instead, Andy hovered uncertainly while Dawn contrived to frown down at the blank screen in front of her, her tongue working hard to dislodge the remaining biscuit.

He grew in confidence as he spoke, taking her silence for a sign of acquiescence. He deigned to place the document on the desk in front of her, not quite tossing it, but placing it with considered casualness, before slipping one hand slowly into his pocket.

'... and I think the detail in there will be hugely valuable in fine tuning some of the PR actions we discussed earlier. We do, after all, need to be careful not to ignore the student audience, who will play a key role in helping us shift public opinion and nail this thing.'

Dawn sat back in her chair suddenly and fixed her eyes on him. 'Andy, I've got cuts to make. And the comms department is, frankly, bloated.'

'But I'm the most senior person in comms. I—'

Dawn swivelled round to face the window, training her gaze on Michael, the seagull absent from his manhood now.

'Perhaps we need some young blood, new ideas, people who will think more laterally, challenge convention.' She swung back to face him.

The document sat untouched on the table between them. He retrieved it decisively, using it to gesticulate as he ransacked his mind for the right words. He glanced briefly at the sculpture outside the window, taking momentary heart from the man's bold and certain stance. 'And that is what you will get from me, Dawn. I'll use this… as a platform for change.'

'There will plenty of that to come, Andy.'

He nodded, marching out of the door, unsure what had just happened, but galvanised all the same.

Dawn scrolled down the Kernow Click news site, her contorted features lit by the ghostly bright light of the screen as she scanned Dave White's letter. Then she started again, her finger stabbing at the air as she did so, as if popping each word like a bubble.

She had never liked Dave. Apart from his over-enthusiastic penchant for the ladies, exacerbated by a deluded sense of his own attractiveness, he had always been one to question everything, to resist any change instinctively, and to try and cause constant low-level unrest among the staff. She remembered him cornering her at a drinks evening for the opening of the new film centre, telling her that not conforming for conforming's sake was healthy, adding, 'When you stop looking, listening and asking questions, it's time to die.'

She had asked him to consider if such curiosity could actually be a cause of death, before attempting to drain her already empty glass of wine and disappear into the throng, her loud laughter prompting others to look at her, then at him, before politely turning away.

His letter certainly bore all the hallmarks of his arrogant and vociferous Northern manner. It claimed that he had been forced out, his hands tied, and that he was simply the tip of the iceberg with all the problems mounting at Poltowan University:

> *I am not the first experienced and respected member of staff to be booted out overnight, told to go quietly or else, and I won't be the last. There is a culture of fear and loathing at Poltowan and few will be brave enough to speak out about it. For some unfathomable reason, Dawn Goldberg has the board eating out of her hand, no questions asked, and this rotten state of affairs will continue until someone stands up to her. She might be ticking all the right boxes now but she will bring the university to its knees given time.*

Dawn read on, the chunky rings on the fingers of her right hand rapping against her mahogany desk as she scrolled down. The truth was, Dave had dug his own grave by constantly challenging her pay and expenses instead of getting on with his own job. Leading the protest against lecturers' 1.5 per cent pay rise by comparing it to her 12 per cent rise was, frankly, infantile.

'I'm the bloody Chief Executive of this business,' said Dawn out loud, as she had at the time. 'My pay is commensurate with the responsibility I bear – get over it.'

Dave White's blatant attempts to fuel the disquiet of the students, urging them to rally against the rumour that their numbers would soon be increased, had been the last straw for Dawn. She had paid Celia, her friend Diane's leggy daughter, handsomely to execute a honey trap, contriving to snap him sharing a tipsy snog with the girl while leaving a bar before threatening to tell his wife. He had resigned quietly, and his desk had been cleared before nine the next day. Dawn wondered why he felt he could start voicing his opinions now – she didn't, after all, have a short memory.

'Imbecile,' she said out loud as she read the final paragraph attacking her recent pay rise. 'I thought you might regurgitate that tired old chestnut. How predictable.'

She swivelled around in her chair, her eyes meeting Michael's. 'Well, he has finally exposed himself for the cretin that he is. And I was forgiving enough to give him a reference, for God's sake! Bloody delinquent. No one will believe that bilge.'

Chapter 4

Harry loped slowly through the park on his way to his office, squinting into the high winter sunshine through his broken glasses. He was unusually oblivious to the day's charms: not hearing the rise and fall of the blackbirds' trill, not seeing the brave, nodding daffodils emerging prematurely into the January dawn, unaware of the presence of another person hurrying behind him, his heavy trainer-clad feet quickly gaining ground.

Harry was entangled in a trying medley of thoughts from which he couldn't break free. At the very second the hand was clapped firmly down on his shoulder he was ruminating over how Dawn Goldberg had come to have so much self-confidence, frowning at her brashness and wondering why she had so many people in her thrall.

At the touch of Ludo's hand Harry spun round, instinctively raising his right arm, fist clenched, heart hammering hard within his ribcage.

'Fella, calm yourself. It's me. I've been calling you from over there.'

Harry stopped walking, shaking his head at Ludo and drawing a deep breath.

Despite Harry's not inconsiderable height, Ludo was two inches taller than him, his thickset frame and mop of blond curls lending him a commanding presence.

'You OK? You seem a bit jumpy.' Ludo placed his arm back on Harry's, this time cautiously, as if ready to defend himself against a blow. 'Is that a shiner you got there? Harry Manchester, have you been fighting?'

He took another steadying breath and cleared his throat. 'Not quite. I was jumped a couple of days ago. They nicked my wallet.'

A look of genuine concern crept over the younger man's face. 'I had no clue. Are you OK? If I'm honest, I thought you were looking a little ropy, limping along.'

'Stiff knee. Fell on my kneecap – bang – then they kicked me a couple of times.'

'And a punch in the face?' Ludo held his finger an inch from Harry's face, tracing it around the outline of a yellow-tinged bruise.

'Knocked my glasses as I fell.'

Ludo tried to scrutinise Harry as they walked but he kept his head down, embarrassed by the attention. He had lain awake all night, anger rising within him that he hadn't reacted quicker, been more aware, struck out in self-defence. He kept replaying the incident in his mind.

He had been so submerged in thoughts of his TV appearance, so self-congratulatory about the way he had countered Jenny Trundle's barbed comments, that common sense had deserted him. Ludo's almost palpable pity irked him further and he steeled himself for more such remarks as the day wore on. Harry lengthened his stride, bracing himself against the persistent pain in his knee.

He and Ludo continued together through the park, weaving in and out of the chill canopy of trees until they were shielded from the unforgiving glare of the sun. Harry strode more purposefully now, his suit lending him an industrious, businesslike air, while Ludo galumphed alongside, each stride covering more ground than seemed humanly possible, his low-slung jeans revealing the bright yellow waistband of his boxer shorts as he moved.

'Time for a quick coffee?'

Harry looked at his Rolex. On the underside was the inscription: "All my love, Sylvia x".

He had not looked at the words lately, although he was all too mindful that they were there, a twenty-eight-year-old message pressed against his flesh. He had some time ago considered the irony of the watch's longevity, the message on the underside as neatly engraved as if it was done yesterday, the watch's bold face barely aged but for a couple of everyday battle scars.

Its ticking endured, continuing to stand the test of time in the way their marriage had failed to do. How he wished he could help Sylvia recapture that all too fleeting lightness of soul now, help to drag her from the mire of despair and into the sunny morning, but he knew from years of gentle cajoling, earnest beseeching and everything in between, that only she could save herself. His leaving had been an act of weary resignation, of desperation. And then he had met Jo.

'Just a quick one?' Ludo repeated in his soft Irish lilt.

All at once Harry could almost taste the cappuccino, its rich flavour filling his mouth and energising him from the feet up, firing him for the crusade that lay ahead. He wriggled himself partially free from the clutches of irascibility and clapped Ludo on the shoulder in a show of positivity that took even himself by surprise. Caffeine was exactly what he needed.

'I need to pick your brains as it happens. Let's do it. My treat.'

Ludo protested in a half-hearted way but was cheered by the thought of a free coffee and Harry's company, and he knew Harry would be affronted if he, an impoverished student, even made to get his wallet out. Besides, he had spent nearly half an hour fixing Harry's iPhone the week before, expertise for which he could normally command a respectable sum. Harry meanwhile remembered that he didn't have a wallet, or any cards, just a £10 note he had borrowed from Jo that morning. He was sure Ted would put it on the tab.

Cappuccin–oh! was typically busy, its seven irregular tables and chairs variously populated with a mix of chatty students and lone workers, tapping away at laptops as the coffee machine hissed violently away in the background. Cappucin–oh! was situated on the hilly spine that ran between Poltowan's town and park, and while it was often frequented by takeaway customers on hot summer days, when people flocked to the beach a twenty-five-minute walk away, it thrived in the frequently inclement weather, providing a cosy sanctuary away from the unpredictable Cornish elements.

Ted tightened his neatly ironed barista apron and gestured at Harry to sit down, raising his eyebrows in acknowledgement of his usual order and winking at him. Harry thought he mouthed 'Great stuff' but couldn't be sure.

'I've a bone to pick with you.' Harry placed his iPhone on the table in front of Ludo.

'This wouldn't be about your performance on *News Time* the other night, would it? Gee, I'm sorry, fella. Are you telling me that feckin' mute button is playing up again?'

'I could have looked a right prat.'

'Not at all, you dealt with it well. Very well as it happens.'

Ludo frowned at the device, flicking through screens and pushing buttons one-fingered as Harry looked on.

Ludo's mouth twitched involuntarily at the recollection of 'Bohemian Rhapsody' resounding from Harry's nether regions. At the time Ludo had rolled on the floor laughing, his abdominal muscles aching for respite, tears rolling down his face as he pushed the rewind button and played it over and over. But now he felt chastened. Harry was one of the good guys. It offended Ludo that someone could have considered it acceptable to make an unprovoked attack on him.

Now he sat solemn-faced, eyes trained on the iPhone, focused on the task in hand, genuinely baffled as to why the problem had occurred. Harry waited, watching in awe as Ludo's agile thumb navigated the screen with the dexterity of a human joystick.

'You were ace, Harry. Ace,' said Ted, putting two steaming cups on the table. He placed his fingertips on Harry's back. 'Very well done.'

Harry adjusted his tie. 'Thanks, Ted. It went OK. Not that I haven't still got work to do – I've picked up two messages this morning from people wanting to know if I'll let their houses for them. One even went to the trouble of saying what a fantastic time it was to "cash in on the student boom". If he calls again, I'll have trouble keeping my mouth shut.'

'What have you done to yourself?' Ted stood back from Harry in dramatic fashion, arms held wide. 'That eye, Harry. What happened?'

Ludo glanced up from Harry's iPhone. 'He doesn't want to talk about it, Ted. Got jumped so he did. Nasty business. Poor fella. He needs his coffee this morning, that's for sure.'

Harry shot a warning look at Ludo before rolling his eyes. 'If anyone asks, I did it kick boxing.'

Ted's eyes widened momentarily. He tapped his nose and moved away to serve the growing queue of people, some casting sly glances in Harry's direction. He paused midway and called back, 'But it was a dominant performance last night. Coffee's on the house.'

Ludo slid the iPhone back across the table and uncrossed and recrossed his long legs before speaking.

'So I'm sitting there, watching you on the big screen, thinking: how can I help Harry? How can I help Harry's campaign? I mean, we have to keep the cap, right? It's no good for you, for the locals – hell, or for us students, that's for sure – if it's raised. In fact, from where I'm sitting, I'm pretty hard pushed to see how it helps anyone except The Goldburger and a bunch of greedy landlords.'

Harry was suddenly buoyed by Ludo's genuine enthusiasm. He looked him in the eye a moment to check for traces of irony, but found none. Two earnest green eyes were looking back at him, eyebrows slightly furrowed under Ludo's unruly thatch of curls.

This was just what Harry needed. A student champion to galvanise the others into action, to engage them with the cause and encourage them to stand up and be counted. He dribbled coffee very slightly in his eagerness to speak.

'You certainly can help,' he said, dabbing at his chin. 'If you're serious, you could be a huge boon to the campaign. In fact – ' Harry leaned forward ' – you already have been. Keep the Cap is exactly the slogan we need: simple, punchy, meaningful. And it will fit neatly on a placard.'

Ludo took Harry's hand and shook it with an enthusiasm that took him by surprise. 'Well, I've been thinking,' said Ludo, the words issuing from his mouth at the same rate at which they were forming in his brain. It was one of his strengths – his mind worked with impressive speed, processing and interrogating information while many people would still be absorbing the words.

It was why Harry had commandeered him as his IT specialist, calling on him to address any digital conundrums that couldn't be fixed by simply switching a device on and off. It took just minutes for Ludo's dexterous brain, and equally dexterous fingers, to overcome the frequent and impenetrable challenges posed by technology. He was well worth a bit of cash in hand here and there.

He had even persuaded Harry to create a Facebook page for his estate agency, convincing him that it was a perfect platform for the business – and its owner. Harry's initial reluctance had been quickly overcome by Ludo's blandishments and he had recently begun to see the merit in it, although he remained baffled by the mass of vapid nonsense shared on the site and refused to be drawn into it. He was a busy man, after all.

'Facebook,' Ludo continued. 'It's the perfect medium to muster the troops. Have you, for example…' he began flicking through his own mobile screen as he spoke '… seen the response to your TV appearance?' He turned the screen around to show Harry, who peered over his glasses at it.

Ludo proceeded to read out the stats – the fifty-eight people who had liked, loved and laughed over his TV appearance, as well as those who had been inspired to post messages of support, and those who were simply amused by his musical faux-pas.

'That damn' phone thing—' said Harry, starting to wonder if he hadn't handled it as well as he had thought; if the comic incident would overshadow the important messages he had tried to impart.

Ludo fell silent as he began to read a string of comments further down. Jo McCloud had made reference to her "hero" in one of her responses to a friend, before attacking the "cowardly bastards" who "had it in for Harry" the night before. The ensuing wave of curiosity – masked mainly as concern – had prompted her to write, "Aww, thanks, all. He is just battered and bruised but it could have been worse!!!"

Careless, thought Ludo, twitching. Harry's bird had been careless. Why didn't people think before they shared intimate details with the world? Facebook was a platform that required an almost anal level of care, yet people increasingly broadcast their whole lives over it, impetuously sending their innermost thoughts out into the universe in the hope of… what? A sea of equally meaningless and banal replies.

Ludo flicked over the comment and continued to the numerous posts about Harry's lively TV appearance.

'So you turn it to your advantage, Harry,' said Ludo, as if stating the obvious. Once again his brain was whirring, giving birth to multiple ideas in quick succession, the resulting notions seamlessly articulated.

'Look at this one. She calls herself Rockstr.' Ludo rolled the r with relish. 'Clearly a student-cum-aspiring musician.' He paused, zooming in on her picture: the wild blonde hair with red streaks, the nose stud, the large brown eyes, the petite, curvy figure photographed against a sandy backdrop. An unsettling feebleness suddenly flooded his body, interrupting his usual poise and making his mind swim.

Harry waited, drumming his fingers on the table, struggling to summon his patience as he waited for his adviser's train of thought to materialise. He watched as Ludo's eyes widened, Adam's apple bobbing wildly in his stubbly throat, eyes trained on his mobile screen.

'And?' said Harry.

Ludo recruited the synapses in his brain again, forcing his gaze away from the picture to the words below:

Way to go, Harry Manchester, love that you plugged the legendary Freddie Mercury and caught that sly presenter off guard! Agree with all you said – Goldberg has her head up her arse and is driving Poltowan and its uni into the ground. Something needs to be done!

Harry straightened in his seat, screwing up his nose to nudge his glasses a little higher. Ludo stabbed a button requesting to befriend Rockstr, before slipping the phone back into his jeans pocket.

'You see what has happened here? You have engaged with the youth. They get you. They see that you're human – you're like them. Not the most polished performance but you're authentic. You are articulating their thoughts, but you have the power, the experience, the local standing, they lack. We need to harness this.'

Harry leaned backwards, tilting his chair onto the back two legs and rocking several times before a sharp pain in his knee forced him forward with a jolt. He steepled his hands on the table. 'Ludo, gird – your – loins.'

Ludo was unaware that his leg left was jigging up and down under the table, the two coffee cups vibrating with the repetitive movement. His loins were now well and truly girded, and not just as a result of Harry's nascent campaign. He sensed that he was teetering on the summit of real purpose, something he had been seeking since his arrival in Poltowan. He was going to make a difference, put the mind his mother had always described as "overactive" to good use. He was going to save his university, and this town to boot. He and Harry Manchester were an unstoppable force, and Dawn Goldberg would be foolish to try.

'Oh, and tonight if you're free, there's a meeting at the Church Hall,' said Harry.

Ludo stared back at him, mentally trying to locate such a place.

'It's in the street directly behind the big church. In the square.'

'Ah.' Ludo recalled the church, of course, with its looming clock tower watching over the people of Poltowan. 'I'm supposed to have five-a-side but what time is it? I'll try and get there, bring some of the boys.'

'Seven o'clock. It's just to raise awareness and inform people, get the conversation going.'

Ludo nodded. 'One thing though, Harry,' he said as they stood to leave. 'Your girl has been a bit of a flute.'

'A flute?'

'She's kind of gone and lost her head on Facebook, made some indiscreet comment about you being her hero.'

Harry rubbed his chin, considering whether the term was a worthy one. Perhaps it was a little premature.

'She's told people you were attacked is what I'm kind of saying. It's not necessarily the best strategy here, we'd have done better to keep it quiet.'

The realisation hit Harry like another kick in the stomach. 'She's said what?'

Harry pulled his phone out of his pocket, only for Ludo to take his wrist and stop him. 'No need, Harry. She's not said much but... have a word, will you? See if you can't get her to lay off the oversharing for a bit.'

Harry nodded. He was beginning to see that Ludo had his finger on the pulse when it came to social media. As he left the cafe, he recalled the words of Theodore Roosevelt, albeit a little sketchily: 'The best leader is the one who has enough sense to pick good men to do what he wants done, and self-restraint enough to keep from meddling with them while they do it.' When it came to technology and social media, he was happy to take the same approach.

Harry stepped outside the coffee shop and was about to call Jo when his mobile alerted him to a voicemail. It was Dennis Flintoff, asking after Harry following his "trouble" and suggesting they ought to catch up. Harry bristled slightly and inwardly cursed Jo. He knew she would have meant well but, not for the first time, eagerness to talk had got the better of her.

❧

Harry called Dennis several times that morning but was each time met with the almost magisterial tones of his voicemail, politely but firmly instructing him to leave a short message. Harry deemed the subject matter too delicate to commit to the intangible vaults of a mobile device, instead clicking off in frustration each time he received the greeting.

He picked up his jacket and attempted to sweep out of the office, once again forgetting the limitations of his injured leg, which forced him into an ungainly limp as he crossed the floor. He was just stepping out when Diggory appeared, ambling past with his hands in his pockets. He paused, grinning at Harry.

'I thought you'd be up at the BBC doing *The One Show* or something by now?'

They shook hands. 'You're a funny guy, Diggory,' said Harry. 'How's things?'

Diggory took a step back, frowning. 'What have you done to yourself?'

'Mugged. In Plymouth. After last night's recording.' Harry removed his glasses and tentatively rubbed his nose.

'Oh, mate. What's the damage?'

'Lost wallet, broken nose, gammy leg… think that's all.'

Diggory scrutinised Harry's nose. 'Broken?'

'Probably not. Just feels like it.'

'Did they get the guy who did it?'

Harry shuffled closer to his old friend, dropping his voice. 'It was a woman actually. A right bruiser, but a woman. Took me completely by surprise. I wasn't concentrating, just minding my own, then *bang* from behind.'

Diggory's jaw dropped as he listened. 'An even greater insult to injury. What a bitch. And they didn't get her?'

'Dunno. I left it with them.'

'Need to borrow any cash?'

43

'You're alright. I borrowed some from Jo. I'll get my new cards through tomorrow. I'll survive.'

The two men stood in silence for a moment.

'How's it going with Jo?'

'She's great, Dig. Yeah, it's alright.'

'I bumped into Sylvia last week.' Diggory rocked back on his heels, his hands deep in the pockets of his designer jeans. His greying hair was slightly unkempt but he managed to cultivate a year-round tan from surfing most days, and his body remained fit and firm.

In Harry's eyes he had barely changed since they were at school – always in possession of a quiet composure, always adopting new trends effortlessly with Harry bringing up the rear. They were unlikely allies, their chosen paths having veered in opposing directions. Diggory ran a business building and repairing boats and surfboards, but the overheads on his boat shed were cheap and he had no great drive, preferring instead to be on the water whenever the surf allowed. But despite their disparate lifestyles, their friendship had been easy and constant for forty years and continued to endure.

'How did she seem?'

'Said she was OK but, you know, I could tell she was putting on a brave face. She looked tired.'

Harry glanced away. 'I called in yesterday. Just not sure what I can do.'

'Not much you can do, mate. Except stay in touch with her, I guess.'

'Appreciate it if you could keep an eye on her, though, look her up once in a while?'

Diggory nodded. 'Chloe said she'd call her next week for a coffee. Anyway... take it easy. No more heroics – you've got enough of a fight on your hands.' He made as if to leave and Harry stepped in his way.

'What did you think? Of last night?'

Diggory whistled through his teeth. 'Well, I like Queen almost as much as you but, you certainly pick your moments.'

'Seriously. Come on – what did you think?'

Diggory studied Harry's blackened eye, his slightly uneven glasses, the earnestness in his face, and a rush of affection rose up from somewhere deep inside, taking him by surprise.

'Mate, are you sure you want to take this on? I mean, you aren't just taking that woman on, you're putting the cat among the pigeons in Poltowan too. Times have changed. I just wonder if you're fighting a losing battle.'

Harry smiled. Diggory's apathy was another trait that had not changed since school. He wasn't lazy, as such, but he was unlikely to engage in anything that met with any resistance, quietly retreating instead to find another way, an easier path.

'Times have changed too much, pal. Do you want to wake up to a whole road of neglected student lets, not to mention the noise, the rubbish, the constant parties?'

'Actually, Chlo and I went to a student party up the road last week.' Diggory laughed. 'It was great – like being twenty again. And I don't hear any noise. I've usually got my headphones on and I'm never in bed before about two a.m.'

His friend's easy detachment frequently exasperated Harry, and while he sometimes felt a strong urge to shake him, to provoke some latent emotion to rise to the surface, he envied Diggory's ability to step outside of the fray, to observe rather than to feature. He knew Diggory was the wrong person from whom to seek reassurance or encouragement. But he could rely on his honesty.

'Just be careful. I mean, you've got this place.' He gestured at the bold Harry Manchester sign above their heads. 'You've worked hard to build this up. Don't throw it all away for some whimsical cause.'

'Whimsical? It's far from whimsical, Dig. Soon Poltowan as we know it will only exist as a fringe community serving the university – serving Dawn Goldberg. We will even lament the loss of the tourists if we're not careful, much as we often moan about them.'

'You've got to take your hat off to her drive and ambition – she certainly seems to know how to get whatever she wants.'

'But only to line her own pockets, to embellish her own CV. She doesn't give a toss about Poltowan. She doesn't even live here - she's holed up in some swanky pad twenty miles away! A converted farmstead of some sort, out in the sticks.'

'She's a bit of alright, though, isn't she?' said Diggory. 'I mean, she has something about her—' He waited for Harry's explosive rant to gather pace, knowing he had pushed the right buttons to trigger a lengthy diatribe, widening his stance as if in readiness to physically absorb the attack.

As Harry opened his mouth to speak, a lady with a toddler and a pram paused next to him, her head cocked slightly to one side. She was softly spoken, her voice melodious. 'I just wanted to say – and sorry to interrupt – that I'm so glad you are doing what you are doing.'

Her toddler squirmed away from her and she grabbed his arm, prompting a squeal. 'I absolutely agree with your concerns about more students. I want my kids to grow up here, I want to keep my family home here. If they lift the cap, I can't see any way we could stay. So thank you for doing what you're doing and speaking out. It's very brave.'

Harry smiled, her words acting as a balm to his ruffled feelings. He thanked her for her support, seeing her glance at his black eye as she spoke, before hurrying on with her whining child. Harry raised his eyebrows at Diggory.

'Brave, you see,' said his friend. 'She said "brave" but she might as well have said "foolhardy". You're putting yourself at odds with other traders, some of whom have been here as long as you have.'

Harry eyed him for a moment. 'Am I at odds with you?'

Diggory looked away. He knew that trying to remonstrate with Harry would only increase his obstinacy, forcing him further down the wrong road. 'Well, you know, sometimes you have to go with it. Ride it.'

'That theory might work when you're surfing but it won't in real life.' Harry shook his head. 'Where's your fight? There are times when you have to stand up and defend what you care about.' He projected the final sentence more loudly than he had intended, a surge of Churchillian spirit rising up within him. Across the square, the clock tower struck eleven.

The boyish smile returned to Diggory's face. He saw Harry's scowl, and held up his hands as if in surrender. 'I admire it, Harry, I do. But don't say I didn't warn you.' He nodded towards the shop front. 'Don't cut off your nose to spite your face.'

They parted with the barely audible murmur only old friends understand.

Diggory's unabashed scepticism served to fuel Harry's determination. He would show him, and any other doubters, that he could effect change. Ride it indeed, he thought, shaking his head as he made his way to his car.

Chapter 5

Harry had braced himself for the comments about his black – and fast-yellowing – eye, and his limp. It was unfortunate timing, of course, to turn up to a key meeting looking like a thug, but he had planned the event some weeks before as the climax to a month's leafleting and door knocking, with the intention of capitalising on the frenzy he had whipped up. The invitation to appear on News Time had at first appeared fortuitous, falling the night before the meeting, and he had decided that, black eye aside, the gathering still presented a timely opportunity, particularly given Dawn Goldberg's sudden announcement. It was news that would surely swell the audience, perhaps persuade the undecided to turn out.

Harry estimated in excess of two hundred faces as he stood at the front on his makeshift platform, waiting for Bob Chase to close the huge doors at the back of the hall. Ludo had dashed in at the last moment looking sweaty and athletic, his pale sinewy legs exposed to the January air. He had brought with him a group of similarly dishevelled student mates, who looked far less enthusiastic about being there. Harry smiled at his young friend's powers of persuasion.

He was pleased to see a number of people grasping copies of the leaflet he had spent most evenings and weekends delivering over the past few weeks. 'Local Houses for Local People' seemed to have chimed with residents, and he was emboldened by the fact that the words he had spent several hours writing, had not only been read, but were being kept for reference.

Jo sat in the front row beaming at him. She was flanked by two work colleagues who both lived in the town. Jo widened her eyes at Harry, looking as delighted and eager as if she were at the Old Vic for a first night. Harry thought how effortlessly stylish she looked, how attractive. He stood a little taller.

Harry quickly got into his stride, speaking fluently and engagingly about how the town had changed since the university had opened three years ago. He was keen to stress the benefits of the institution: supporting local businesses, boosting the economy, creating jobs and putting Poltowan on the map.

'But there is an uglier, more worrying side to this change,' he said, pausing for dramatic effect. A collective exhalation laced with fear and trepidation emanated from the audience.

'A town like this can only support so many people – a finite number – if everyone is to live in harmony, side by side, and a happy equilibrium is to be maintained.'

He laid his notes down on the table and lurched off the platform, only realising as he did so that this was an imprudent move since he would struggle to step up again unassisted. He moved quickly on, talking from the heart, his bullet points forgotten, his large frame owning the small space at the front of the church hall, his voice commanding, his left eye sparkling with enough passion to distract from his swollen and discoloured right eye.

'But the balance has tipped too far, and as many of you will have seen or heard, Dawn Goldberg's proposal to lift the cap on numbers and increase the student population here by fifty per cent – or three thousand in real terms – poses a threat to many of us who have made our lives here.'

When Dawn Goldberg's name was mentioned there were growls and hisses not unlike those used to greet a pantomime villain, followed by an outbreak of muttering.

Harry paused. 'I know that the sheer number of students,

coupled with the lack of accommodation provided on campus, is already causing problems for many local people.'

He gazed over at his notes on the platform and thought better of trying to retrieve them. Instead he counted out on his fingers as he spoke. He knew there were five key points he wanted to state. 'House prices are going up as stock diminishes, with private landlords buying up properties to rent to multiple students; these houses are frequently falling into disrepair as neither students nor landlords feel themselves accountable for their upkeep; noise is keeping working people and their families awake through the night as students return from pubs and clubs, or hold all-night parties; a number of well-used bus routes and timetables have been changed to favour the university; and—'

Harry made his way across the floor, head bowed as if waiting for people to absorb the impact of his words. In truth he was desperately trying to remember his fifth point. Jo's shiny patent boots came into his line of sight as he pondered, triggering a memory. 'And shops and local businesses are changing, gearing up, not to the needs of locals, but to students. In the last twelve months alone we have seen a popular wool shop become a tattoo parlour; a renowned restaurant turned into a late-night shots bar; and a greengrocer's become a mobile phone shop.'

'Are you saying it's only students who have tattoos and mobile phones?'

It took Harry a moment to locate this voice before realising it belonged to Steve Kent, his bulldog features easily recognisable under his shaved head as he stared at Harry from the back of the room. Steve ran the local general store and had done for some years after making the unlikely move to Poltowan from Peckham. Belligerence was his natural state. While Harry was familiar with him, he often gave him a wide berth.

'Hello, Steve. Thanks for coming.'

'Lighten up, can't you? Students ain't the only ones inking up and enjoying the latest technology – it's the way of the world now. Get over it.'

Harry inwardly counted to three before answering. 'I am certainly not suggesting that students have a monopoly on tattoos and mobile phones.'

'Well, it sounded like that to me!'

Someone laughed and Harry spotted Kevin Teague, owner of a carpet-cleaning business, sitting just along from Steve. He was grinning at Harry.

'My point is that these new… amenities have arrived at the expense of arguably far more useful outlets – '

'Like a knittin' shop?' said Steve. 'I've 'eard it all now.'

' – far more useful outlets that have a greater contribution to make to the lives of residents of Poltowan. Now—'

Harry happened to catch Jo's eye; her earlier enthusiasm had been replaced by a look of alarm. Had he been wrongfooted? 'Now, if we took a quick and very unscientific poll among the hundred and fifty or so people in this room, of which I think we have a handful of students…?' Harry raised his eyebrows as he searched the room.

'Ten of us, I think, Harry,' said Ludo.

'… so ten students. Please can people raise their arms – inked or otherwise – if they have a tattoo?'

Six of the students raised their pale arms skywards while Ludo stood up, revealing a star-shaped marking halfway up his lean thigh. Two women in the row in front twisted round to see what the fuss was about and one lady further along emitted an appreciative noise.

'Thank you, Ludo, we don't necessarily need to see the tattoos in question.'

Another hand was raised in the middle of the audience. It belonged to Jack Rowe, who was a few years past seventy. He looked startled when Harry's eyes rested on him. 'I was in the Navy when I had it – stupidest thing I ever did,' he said, by way of explanation.

The audience murmured.

'Mine's on my thigh too but I'd have to take me trousers down,' said Steve, his burly arm thrust into the air.

'That won't be necessary.' Harry waved his hand again to silence people. 'So, sixty per cent of the students present this evening are sporting tattoos, compared to less than two percent of non-students. Anecdotal, I know, but I would suggest it gives us a good idea of how student needs differ from those of other residents.'

Steve shook his head in disgust. Harry continued talking, while just in front of him Jo beamed at her colleague.

'I am not, of course, saying we shouldn't cater for existing students, but if this means long-standing residents start to lose essential services and conveniences, we have a problem. And, ladies and gentlemen, I put it to you that we are currently only seeing the tip of the iceberg.

'It is down to us to make our voices heard, to spread the word, to lobby local Councillors and ensure that Poltowan remains a wonderful place to live – for both residents and students – but that the population numbers stay as they are so that we maintain the balance that is essential for us all to thrive.'

Harry didn't attempt to silence the keen applause that followed. He looked at Jo and nodded hopefully towards his notes. She jumped up and took his elbow, placing her ear close to his mouth before passing him his sheets of paper together with a squeeze of his bicep.

Just as the clapping began to peter out, Harry became aware of unusually persistent applause towards the back of the room, a slow, loud slapping noise that superseded the polite patter that had now died away. Harry saw Steve's smug face looking at him as his hands came together with a thunderous sound, again and again. The rest of the audience turned to look at him but he kept his gaze fixed on Harry, undaunted by the eyes boring into him. Eventually the ironic clapping stopped.

'Thank you. Now, if I can open the floor to questions, as I'm sure you all—'

Steve's hand shot up at the same time as he declared, 'Yes, I 'ave one.'

Harry paused, drawing on his patience. 'Yes, Steve?'

'I want to know what gives you the right to push these things through people's doors, littering our 'ouses?' He balled up a leaflet as he spoke before letting it fall to the floor. 'Standing up there, shoving your opinions down people's throats, when it's a free world and everyone has the right to make their own mind up.' He wriggled back in his seat, a self-satisfied smile on his face.

Silence fell over the hall as all eyes turned to the front. Jo rummaged in her pocket for a tissue, her gaze trained on Harry.

'That is a fair question,' he said, wincing as a jolt of pain travelled from his bruised eye to the back of his head. 'Steve, as many of you probably know, owns the general store in the square.'

''Ave done for fifteen years,' he interjected. 'Business has never been better.'

'I'm a local businessman too,' said Harry soberly. 'I care deeply about this town and its future—'

'What's to say I don't? I 'ave seen an upturn in trade since the university opened, it fair saved me from going down the plug 'ole, and many other local businesses will tell you the same thing.' He stood up, his face slightly flushed. 'I know you'll be quick to get on your 'igh 'orse and tell me I'm an emmet in your speak, a DFL. Well, I'll tell you, I've given a lot to this town, and I've made it my 'ome, created a business 'ere, and I put back into the economy too. I 'ave every right to speak up.'

Harry closed his eyes for a moment, willing Steve's voice to stop. People began tutting in the audience and shifting in their seats. 'Thank you, Steve. As I was saying, I care deeply about this town. I was born and brought up here—'

'There, you see? Always 'avin' a go.'

'—and I feel a responsibility to help spread the word, give people here a voice.'

Steve worked his mouth soundlessly for a moment, as if chewing an invisible match.

'Surely you have a vested interest though,' came another voice, from a lady Harry didn't know. 'I mean, you run an estate agency and you need availability of housing stock – that's your product, without which you can't run your business.'

''Xactly,' said Steve, leaning forward to see the speaker and repeatedly nodding his bald head as if she had just articulated the sentiment he had intended to convey with his earlier words.

'So people could be forgiven for thinking that you are scaremongering and jeopardising real economic progress in order to safeguard Harry Manchester.'

Harry stepped sideways, getting the speaker in his sights. 'Thank you. And, sorry, would you mind introducing yourself, madam?'

'I'm Stella Maycroft. I've lived here for five years... since the university first opened actually.' She hesitated, taking in the curious faces around her. 'I don't work as I suffer from a chronic health condition. But I love the life and energy the students bring to the town, and I welcome what they add. Surely it's better than a bunch of old folk in a sleepy, dying community?'

A small chorus of voices murmured agreement, followed by Steve shouting: 'At last someone's speaking sense.'

'Thank you, Stella. I take your point, and people may construe my campaign as one driven by commercial concerns, but I can do no more at this stage than reassure you that this is not about my business. One key point that I hope will help to convince you of my motivation is the fact that Harry Manchester's only deals with sales and purchase – not rentals, and not sales to private landlords. I can assure you that, as a businessman, if I were driven primarily by money, I would've opened a lettings arm some years ago, when the university opened.'

A murmur of approval rippled through the crowd. 'But I don't believe in it,' continued Harry, raising his voice. 'I am a man of principle, and I can see for myself that student lets are damaging the very fabric of our society – pushing house prices up, driving residents out and resulting in whole roads of once sought-after houses falling into disrepair.'

A woman stood up, her hand raised for good measure. 'No disrespect to the individuals here tonight, but I don't understand why students have attended this meeting. This is the residents' fight, right? It's about us, the long-term residents of Poltowan.'

Harry limped across the front of the hall. 'Mrs Collins, hello. I'm very glad indeed that you have raised that point because I think it's a common misconception. Our student friends here tonight,' Harry gestured at Ludo and his cohort, lounging at the back of the audience, 'stand alongside us in wishing to prevent an increase in student numbers. This isn't about students versus residents. It's about what is best for Poltowan. Ludo, perhaps you'd like to…'

Ludo shot to his feet, his gangly frame looking boyish in his football shorts, his shin pads drooping out of his socks. 'Mrs Collins, first, we don't want to spoil your pretty town – the self-same town that attracted us here in the first place.'

Mrs Collins frowned at him, distrusting his unfamiliar brogue.

'Secondly, we didn't pay a shed load of money to come to a university that was bursting at the seams with people – we were offered a boutique experience if I remember rightly. We all need a bed to sleep in and a seat in the lecture theatre, both of which are already proving hard to come by with so many students enrolled. It'll only get worse if The Goldburger gets her way.'

Mrs Collins smoothed her hands over her skirt.

'And, to be honest, we chose Cornwall as a place to study so we could live alongside good Cornish folk like yourself, to study here but to enjoy all that your rich culture has to offer too. We want to get along with local people, and we understand that can't happen if you feel we have bowled in and taken over the place. So we stand shoulder to shoulder with you, Mrs Collins, as us Irish say, to stop this crazy expansion.'

Harry cleared his throat before putting the microphone back to his lips. 'Thank you, Ludo.'

Some of the residents looked around, mirroring each other's scepticism. 'There's got to be more to it,' whispered one in a loud voice.

'There's not really,' said Ludo, overhearing. 'I come from a little town in Ireland called Cobh, maybe half the size of Poltowan, and I love that sense of community. It's important, I get it. Hey, we don't want to be the enemy here.'

Mrs Collins stared at him a little longer, her eyes travelling over his long frame before resting on his bare, blackened knees.

'Steve, you ask why I feel I have the right to, as you put it, "shove my opinions down people's throats",' said Harry. 'Well, I am making it my business to furnish people with the facts, so that they can reach their own conclusions. Dawn Goldberg has well-documented plans to expand the university – to open specialist research buildings and such like – so she is under pressure to increase student numbers in order to fund such ventures. She is very ambitious and no doubt sees it as her legacy. But, ladies and gentlemen, at what cost to other people? I ask you to consider that very carefully: at-what-cost?'

This time thunderous applause broke out and Harry saw Steve Kent and Kevin Teague leaving by the back door, followed by a handful of others. The majority seemed content to linger, including Stella Maycroft, who sat stock still, not clapping but not rushing to escape, as if still processing all that had been said.

Harry tried to flex his knee surreptitiously, a gnawing pain persisting behind the swelling.

'Wonderful. You were wonderful,' said Jo, standing on tiptoe to plant a kiss on his cheek.

Harry found himself feeling fleetingly like a war hero at his homecoming as people gathered around, their eyes flicking from his right eye to his left and back again. But his thoughts had begun to drift towards a large G&T, the cucumber garnish curling elegantly and enticingly around the rim of the glass.

❧

Some twenty miles away Dawn Goldberg rang Andy Hornblower, who placed down his fork, gulped his mouthful of salmon, and obediently answered.

'What news, Hornblower?'

'Sorry, Dawn?' He stood up, as if better to address the Vice Chancellor.

'The meeting… what happened? You did go, didn't you?'

Andy cleared his throat, wiping a piece of spinach from his plump lips. 'You did say – we did agree – that it wasn't necessary for me to go to this meeting Dawn. If you remember—'

'Remember? I remember very well, thank you. I specifically asked you to go and listen in, gauge the mood.'

'But you then said not to bother as, I think your words

were, "Harry Manchester is full of hot air and the people who go to those sort of things are hardly likely to change the world".

Dawn made a strange hissing sound down the mouthpiece. She could not now recall exactly what had been said, although the words did sound vaguely familiar.

'You didn't think that, after our major announcement yesterday, it might just be advisable to go along and listen in to hoi-polloi, just in case one of them managed to string a half-coherent sentence together? And to put paid to any misconceptions, quash any false rumours about our intent? No, Hornblower, you obviously did not. Of course, it was too much to ask that you might use your initiative.'

Andy thought for a moment, his jaw sagging. 'I wonder now if you should have attended, Dawn, given your standing, the respect you command? You'd have had far more clout than—'

'Me? In a draughty church hall? A woman of my authority? You never cease to amaze me.'

Andy picked at his teeth. 'I can find out, Dawn. I'll do some probing.'

'Oh, you can certainly do some probing, and I think you know where.' Dawn jabbed at the red button with one long painted fingernail, tossing her phone down on the sofa in disgust.

Chapter 6

Harry was walking towards the rather underwhelming offices of Cornwall Press, home of the *Poltowan Post*, when he heard the purr of a sports car across the car park. He turned to see Dawn Goldberg's red MX-5 draw to a halt some hundred yards away. She was mostly hidden behind large dark glasses – undoubtedly a wholly necessary accessory on an overcast Cornish day – but her mane of blow-dried waves gave her away. Perched beside her was Dennis Flintoff.

Among other things she had been giving him an unrequested sneak preview of her plans to open a specialist impact centre on the campus. When he had looked at her blankly, she had explained rather impatiently that such a facility would make a "hugely valuable" contribution to achieving higher safety standards on roads, allowing Poltowan's engineering graduates to simulate car crashes, measuring things like moment of inertia and centre of gravity, and equipping them with world-leading skills.

Dennis had sipped his small glass of wine as Dawn continued to explain her intentions for the centre to become an approved consultancy for the Vehicle Certification Agency and, ultimately, an FIA-approved site for crash-testing Formula One vehicles. He had been about to ask how such an expensive facility could be funded with little public money available for such projects, but Dawn had begun to suck an olive from a cocktail stick, her eyes taking on a faraway look as she imagined the stream of state-of-the-art racing cars parading onto the

Poltowan campus. Dennis had sat captivated, quite losing his train of thought.

Harry barged in through the entrance to the newspaper offices, hoping he hadn't been spotted. Minutes later, as he loitered unattended in reception, the red sports car glided past the door, followed seconds later by the breezy arrival of Dennis.

He hesitated as he entered. 'Harry,' he said, in a formal tone that betrayed none of their forty-year acquaintance. He held out his hand in greeting.

Harry shook it. 'Dennis, good to see you.'

'It's been a while.'

'Well, you're looking good, very fit indeed,' said Harry, admiring Dennis' muscular frame. He looked as if he had been working out, his chest appearing to protrude slightly from under his winter jacket. He looked solid.

'A bit better than you unfortunately.' Dennis scrutinised Harry's eye, his onion and wine breath wafting under Harry's nostrils.

Harry stepped backwards and thrust his hands into his pockets.

'You got my message, I assume. That eye looks nasty.'

'Something and nothing,' said Harry, forcing a smile. 'I tried to call you back a couple of times but to no avail so I thought I'd swing by and say hello instead.'

'As you gathered…' Dennis guided Harry ahead of him into the open lift '… I was otherwise engaged.'

'The perils of being a newspaper editor, I'm sure. Always being wined and dined. I only wish I could say the same about being an estate agent.'

Dennis smiled, smoothing his hand down his tie and checking his hair in the mirror. He caught sight of a fragment of green in his front tooth and stealthily tried to tease it out with his nail. It must have been that blasted lemon and chive vinaigrette Dawn had insisted on pouring over their shared potato salad.

Suddenly the lift doors slid shut and it jolted clumsily into action.

Harry looked at himself in the mirror, the purplish hue under his right eye looking even more pronounced in the clinical light of the lift. He adjusted his glasses and took in Dennis' square shoulders.

'You look in good shape.'

Dennis looked down at himself as if seeing his own body anew. 'Oh, you know. Trying to lose a few pounds and fight the flab. A bit of running, a few push ups. At our age…' He sucked his teeth.

'Don't forget I'm a couple of years younger than you,' said Harry, holding two fingers in the air to make his point.

'… it's a constant battle. And how could I forget that, Harry?'

'I'm sure Dawn Goldberg cast some admiring glances your way.'

Dennis looked down at his feet before cocking his head at the panel of lights and frowning as the lift continued its shaky upward trajectory. The doors finally opened, revealing a bare-looking corridor with putrid pink linoleum peeling off the floors. Harry followed Dennis to his office where they were met with a cold rush of air. The open window inched to and fro on its hook before Dennis slammed it shut, rubbing his hands together.

'Sorry, Harry. It's brass monkey in here. Not sure how that came to be open. Take a seat.'

The two men faced each other over the desk. Harry resisted the urge to talk, instead putting the onus on Dennis, holding him quietly with his steady gaze.

'So, any idea who they were – these attackers?'

Harry shook his head. He had the feeling suddenly of being under police questioning, imagining the presence of his brief next to him, shooting him looks and shaking his head cautiously. Moving a few feet from the intimacy of the lift to the more formal surrounds of the office, the large desk placed squarely between them, had suddenly altered the mood. He almost expected Dennis to click his voice recorder on or start scribbling notes.

'And did they take much? You must have been…'

'Just my wallet, but it was pretty much empty. Look, it wasn't premeditated, just some goons trying their luck.' Harry drummed his fingers on the desk. 'There really isn't a story here, Dennis.'

He rocked back in his chair. 'Oh, I wasn't thinking of a story, Harry, at least not until you just mentioned it. I was merely interested to know how it happened. I can only imagine it was very frightening indeed. You certainly seem a little… less jovial than usual. Understandably, of course. Coffee?'

'The only reason I reported it was to stop anyone unable to look after themselves becoming the next victim. Not because I felt it was a serious offence. It wasn't. And look,' Harry leaned forward, 'I'd really appreciate it if you didn't put anything in the paper, Dennis. I don't want any fuss.'

He raised his eyebrows. 'I hadn't considered it being a story until you…'

'Oh, come on, Dennis.' Harry stood up, his imposing frame suddenly filling the small office. He blew into his cold hands. 'I don't think you called me for purely altruistic reasons, did you?'

'I wanted to know how you were. We go way back. I was concerned.'

'Well, that's kind, and I'm sorry if I seem a bit paranoid but there's a lot going on with the university campaign and I'm keen to keep people focused on the issues that really matter – not the gossip.'

'And as you well know, the *Poltowan Post* doesn't deal in gossip, Harry, just in news that matters to residents. If it affects our readers,' he held both hands in the air resignedly and blew a raspberry, 'it goes in the paper.'

It was a favourite saying of Dennis' that he often found himself repeating to staff and readers alike. He had left school at sixteen and completed his journalist training on the *Poltowan Post* before securing a senior reporter's job on the *Western Morning News* aged twenty-one, an opportunity that saw him move eighty miles away to Plymouth. It was just eighteen months before he was coaxed back to Poltowan by his childhood sweetheart, Barbara, who had fallen unexpectedly pregnant during a particularly amorous weekend in Mevagissey.

He promptly married her and returned to the *Poltowan Post* as news editor. While he relished coming back to the town paper as a senior member of staff where once he had been tea boy, he had never stopped wondering what he could have been if his life had not been rudely interrupted by that twist of fate. Not that he didn't love his daughter – he did, very much – but it was her unplanned entry into the world that had expedited his marriage to Barbara and abruptly applied the brakes to his dream of progressing to a national newspaper. He gazed out of the window, sighing at his lot.

'How did you hear anyway?' asked Harry.

Dennis spun round, his mouth beginning to form a word that faded away unspoken.

Harry rolled his shoulders, trying to shake his gruff demeanour and rouse his more amiable self. He was, after all, here to ask for a favour. He tried to erase the image of Dennis sitting like a pet chihuahua beside Dawn Goldberg and focus on more pressing matters. Ludo would be urging him to grasp this opportunity, turn the tide in his own favour, Harry knew.

'One of my team actually alerted me this morning. They had, I think, seen something on the Oracle that is Facebook.'

'Ah.' Harry thought of Jo again, frowning at her apparent failure to consider the ramifications of her actions given his standing in the local community. Ludo had later reassured him that she hadn't been the one to break the news, but even so, allowing herself to be needlessly drawn into the conversation in such a public domain was naive.

Frustration quickly gave way to leniency born of tenderness. Apparently, she had used the word hero. Of course, she wasn't used to being associated with someone with such a high public profile.

Harry planted himself back in the worn swivel chair.

'What did the police say?' said Dennis. 'I hope they took it seriously.'

'Oh, you know. They asked all the right questions, said all the right things. Who knows how these things get followed up?'

'They damn' well better give it some attention. You could have been really hurt.' Dennis screwed up a piece of paper and threw it a little too hard across the room. It bounced off the side of the bin and rolled back across the floor. 'I can call my contact at the regional HQ if you like? Chivvy them up a bit and see what that lazy lot have found out.'

Harry smiled at Dennis' apparent eagerness to act on his behalf. 'Really, it's fine. I'm sure they have more urgent matters to deal with.'

'They spend too much time hiding out to catch motorists who dare to go two or three miles over the speed limit, instead of pursuing the real criminals.'

'Oh, I don't know if she was a hardened criminal. More someone down on their luck and looking for a break.'

'She?'

'Sorry?'

'You said "she". It was a woman?'

Harry adjusted his position once, then twice. 'Well, there were a few of them. The one whose face I managed to glimpse was a woman.'

A look of surprise etched itself onto Dennis' face and stayed there.

'Her and a couple of burly guys.' Harry raised his arms in an ape-like pose, fists clenched tight.

'That's really tough luck. Being set upon by a gang. Plymouth, was it, seafront?'

'One of the side roads.'

Dennis shook his head. 'You were very lucky to get out with just a black eye. And you held on to your wallet, you say?'

'No, they took my wallet, cards and all.'

'Phone?'

Harry shook his head.

'I bet Sylvia was pretty shaken up as well, you coming home in that state.'

'She was pretty good actually. I mean, we're separated currently, but I had to see her to... sort some stuff out. My cards...' Harry swiped at the air with his large hand before tailing off and looking around the sparse room for something of interest.

'I'm sorry to hear that. I had no idea.' Dennis frowned and nodded in a kindly way.

'So... Dawn Goldberg. How was she?' Harry straightened his back in the chair, lifting his chin slightly as he posed the question.

Dennis insisted that it had been a routine lunch to stay up to speed with the university's plans.

'What do you make of her? She seems pretty switched on, very ambitious.'

Dennis folded his hands on the desk in front of him. 'I don't know her very well, to be truthful. We catch up occasionally, on a business front. She is certainly very competent, very...' he pulled at one ear lobe '... very able.'

'And pretty ruthless, timing her latest announcement for when I was live on the box.'

'Perhaps that was just fortuitous.'

'Oh, come on, Dennis, You and I both know she planned that to a tee. She might be many things but stupid she is not.'

Dennis nodded. 'You may be right. I suppose she's quite a fiesty character. Knows exactly what she wants.'

'And where do you stand on this – this proposal to increase the number of students coming to Poltowan. Are you in support of it?'

'Oh, we like to stay neutral, as you well know, Harry. Our job is not to take sides but to do all the information-gathering and present the facts, clear and simple, so readers can make up their own minds.'

'But what about you personally? You've lived here most of your life too.'

Dennis manoeuvred a paperweight around his desk, avoiding Harry's gaze. 'There are benefits to the community and the local economy too, Harry. It isn't all doom and gloom as you seem to think.'

'I agree – some benefits, but they are already being reaped. I really fear any more students will tip the balance irretrievably.'

Dennis smiled. 'I don't think it's as drastic as some are making out. Many students will be housed on campus. Some of the numbers quoted are misleading – they won't all be studying at Poltowan but at various satellite campuses, not to mention some online.'

'Where on campus? There are no signs of any accommodation blocks being built and the existing ones are packed to the rafters as it is. It is only first years currently being housed on campus.'

'There are plans, Harry.'

'But no date?'

Dennis stood up, turning to look out of the window, his shoulders rising and falling slowly.

'I do understand your position. You are the biggest estate agent in town and you have worked hard to build your business, hats off to you. But you can't run a campaign rooted in your own business interests – change and competition are just two of life's certainties. Like death and taxes - hackneyed but true.'

Harry sat up a little straighter in his seat. 'You think this is about my business?'

Harry felt anger surge in his chest. He glared at Dennis. 'This is not about my business. That will continue regardless, thanks to the loyal local following I have built up over years. Some people steadfastly refuse to deal with other agents – they will only bring their business to us. That feeling runs through generations. I have no worries on that front, I know how well we serve people. No, this is about the town, its people.'

Dennis continued to look out of the window. He was thinking about the glittering array of jewellery that adorned Dawn Goldberg's fingers, and the immaculately painted nails. For a slightly larger lady, she had very beautiful hands.

Harry stood up, his knee cracking as he did so. He grimaced. 'Do you really think this is about self-interest?'

Dennis turned around slowly. If he'd been wearing a waistcoat, he would have thrust his thumbs into the arm holes.

'I do know a lot of businesses welcome the university's proposals.'

'But not all, and only those that are thinking about their own bank balance and not the future good of the town.'

'I really think they might have a case. More students, a higher profile, more public funding, job creation, a greater proportion of students staying in Cornwall to live and work and bring up families.'

'But that's just it,' said Harry, dropping his hand firmly on the desk with a low thud. 'They won't have a hope in hell of doing that if every house is bought up by some merciless London landlord who has never even visited Poltowan, let alone taken an interest in what the town is all about.'

'And your business?'

Harry pushed at his glasses, trying to see over the fracture in his lens, which had begun disconcertingly to separate Dennis' head from his neck. 'If I was all about money, Dennis, don't you think I would take the easy route and start doing student lettings, start selling to landlords, build on my reputation and slip seamlessly into a new and growing market? It would be the easiest thing in the world.'

'Tell me the same thing in two, three, four years' time.'

Harry shook his head in disbelief. 'I thought you'd get this, as a local and a newspaper editor. I thought you'd see this as a great chance to campaign, to draw the community together.'

'Is that what you're after, to get the *Poltowan Post* backing your latest PR stunt?'

Harry drew a deep breath, swallowing back some of the words that lingered on his tongue with ill intent. 'It's not a PR stunt. It is a campaign with a lot of substance and a lot of sense.' He held his hand out. 'We'll leave it there.'

Dennis shook his hand somewhat reluctantly. 'Don't be angry, Harry. I just think you should regroup and rethink before you embark on this. I can see both sides of the argument. But

Dawn Goldberg has a lot of influence, a lot of big ideas. They could break you.'

'That woman might be capable of breaking other men, Dennis, but she will not break me.' Harry twisted the door knob and swung the door open, the resulting breeze causing a proof of one of the week's pages to float lazily to the floor. They both watched as it skidded across the lino, landing face up. Harry stooped, narrowing his eyes to read the headline now laid bare at his feet. **'Don't Stop Me Now'** read the bold inky letters, alongside a grainy photo of Harry, his air guitar raised above his head, glasses glinting in the sunshine.

Local businessman, Harry Manchester this week swore to fight an increase in student numbers with everything he has, as news broke of Poltowan's University's proposal while he was live on television.

Dennis folded his arms and said Harry's name wearily.

'Is this your idea of delivering the essential facts – an outdated and inappropriate photo under a flippant headline?'

Dennis rocked on his heels, his eyes cast downwards at the sheet of paper between them. 'Harry...'

'Is this what you deem to be good journalism, Dennis? Telling the public what they need to know?'

'It's not been approved. My sub wrote it. It's a first draft.'

Harry dipped his head to see Dennis clearly through his glasses, like a schoolteacher eyeballing a child with a frightening level of disapproval. But so great was the sense of frustration and injustice burning within him that words failed. He turned and left.

Chapter 7

Nell knocked at the door of The Oaks a second time before letting herself in. 'Hello? Sylvia? It's me.'

The house had a hollow air about it, as if even the inanimate objects had let any remaining spirit escape without trace. The woman in the painting in the hall stared blank-eyed, where before she had followed visitors with her gaze; the huge plant in the kitchen sat weary, still; its leaves used to sway and dance a little in welcome.

Nell called again. Some seconds later Sylvia appeared through the back door, her long face and wide eyes bearing all the signs of a sleepless night.

'Sorry, I was in the garden. All that rain overnight. Everything sodden. I need to cut it all back when we get a dry day – if we get another dry day.' Her voice tailed off.

'Tomorrow's supposed to be sunny.'

Sylvia pulled her boots off one by one and stacked them carefully by the door. Slowly she dragged off her coat, its sleeves matted with dirt, the hem slightly torn. She washed and dried her hands thoroughly, before standing still for a moment in the middle of the kitchen. She was vaguely aware of Nell's voice.

'… so all in all, I'm not doing too badly. I'm looking forward to my coffee at Dufflin House. Shall we?' Nell's voice intruded on her thoughts.

Sylvia pulled on what she called her 'public' coat, a bright fusion of colours that seemed immediately at odds with her mood, and her walking boots, before following Nell out of the door.

Nell chatted intermittently as they drove, leaving the hilly streets of Poltowan and skirting the coastline before heading inland and climbing up onto the wild and barren moorland. She knew better than to probe, or to try and fix things.

Nell had once tried to suggest that Sylvia return to work, not in the pressured environment of before, as a finance director for one of the West Country's biggest building firms – a cut-throat climate that had doubtless contributed to her first breakdown – but in a more gentle part-time role, perhaps leveraging her horticultural knowledge at one of the National Trust sites. Sylvia had dismissed this out of hand and was clearly upset that her friend appeared to have so little understanding of her struggle. It was an exchange that had distressed Nell for weeks afterwards. She had decided she would let Sylvia warm up in her own time.

By the time they were half an hour into their walk, Sylvia's mood had lifted. She was not swinging from the trees or doing cartwheels, but she had an air of animation that had been lacking before, a passing interest in the information Nell was imparting, and if not a spring in her step, then a slightly more deliberate stride. She even paused at one stage to point out granny's toenails, smiling to herself before looking at Nell, inviting her to ask for an explanation.

'Bird's foot trefoil,' said Sylvia proudly. 'We used to call it granny's toenails when we were children.' She raised her voice to counter the rising wind. 'It'll flower in late April, maybe May.'

As they crowned the hill they paused for a moment, savouring the view of both coasts. 'We're on top of the world, Sylve,' said Nell, holding her arms wide in defiance of the wind. Sylvia's gaze rested on the distant north coast.

They began to head back down the path to the main house,

their voices dropping as the wind fell, and Sylvia started to tell Nell about the attack on Harry. She was impassive in her telling, detailing only the facts, but was clearly absorbed in the tale, her mind suddenly engaged in something outside her own world.

'So he's OK?'

'A bruised ego. His glasses were a bit of a mess. He's probably got a black eye by now.'

'Poor Harry. That must have been quite traumatic.'

Nell recalled Harry's jocular disposition, his warm embrace, and tried to picture him battered and bruised, his familiar smile gone, blue eyes sad. She had always had a soft spot for him, sometimes even allowing herself to wonder about what could have been. After all, he had met both Sylvia and Nell at the same time all those years ago, at a local night club in a country house just outside Poltowan. Inwardly she maintained that he had perhaps shown a greater interest in her during the first half of the evening, but she had sprained her ankle making her way along the cobbled path to the entrance, preventing her from accepting his invitation to dance. Naturally, Sylvia had stepped in – almost literally – to fill her shoes. If Nell had only been allowed to demonstrate her superior dance steps – Sylvia had never had much rhythm – who knows what would have become of her and Harry?

Yet Nell was the first to concede that he and Sylvia made a good couple, even if they did harbour different interests and lead largely separate lives. They always seemed to put up a united front, to have that unspoken togetherness that seasoned couples share.

Nell had felt wretched when Sylvia started to talk about separation. In the depths of her despair, Sylvia had decided that Harry was better off without her, that she was holding him back. He had resisted for quite some time and had even spoken to Nell privately about it, opening up his anguished heart about how helpless he felt. But even Harry had eventually come to accept that Sylvia could be right. Somehow she had worn him down and he had reluctantly walked away, convincing himself that it might be the only way out of the mire they found themselves sinking into. Perhaps Sylvia's pragmatic view did trump his romantic one – perhaps love wasn't, after all, enough.

Then Jo had walked into his life, making Harry question everything he thought he knew. Nell had been outraged when Sylvia first told her that he was seeing someone else. Yet she sensed a certain relief from Sylvia, as if this was a problem that had been taken off her hands. Nell still nursed a hope that the whole sorry episode would come to a close soon and that normal service would be resumed. So far it looked unlikely.

'You've not been in touch since then?'

'Oh, no. We don't – we don't tend to see each other now. He only called round to sort out his credit cards. He's still got boxes of paperwork in the garage.'

'I'm sure it wasn't just that, Sylve. He probably wanted to see you after such a shock.'

'He's got someone else now. We're moving on.'

Nell fell silent for a moment. 'Is it what you really want?'

'We're both happier. Not rowing all the time. I'm not playing second fiddle to his estate agency work and his community work, his music – someone else can do that. I know where I am now. I've got my garden, I've got Sting…'

Nell nodded. Who was she to remonstrate that it wasn't enough? She also lived alone with her cat, as she had done for years. And she was happy with her lot. But somehow it didn't seem to suit Sylvia. Somehow it had seemed appropriate that she had a significant other, and she and Harry just seemed to fit. It was the natural order of things.

Nell had felt their separation with an almost physical anguish. Visiting the house since then had made her feel uneasy, the happiness and security it had always offered disappearing with Harry's departure. Now it felt sad, as if the walls were grieving for him, the eaves sagging a little in his absence.

They took a seat in the window of the high-ceilinged drawing room in Dufflin House, an open fire burning nearby.

'So, I start on Tuesday,' said Nell. 'I feel a little daunted if I'm honest, taking on an office job after all this time, it's—'

'Where? Start where?' said Sylvia, blinking quickly as if trying to see through a fog.

Nell inhaled deeply. She had thought Sylvia seemed underwhelmed by the news when she told her earlier.

'At the university. I've got a job as Administrative Assistant for Student Affairs. I did mention it. It sounds much grander than it is, and it's only part-time, but the pay is OK and it seems quite interesting.'

'Well done, Nell. Sorry, I—' Sylvia dabbed at her mouth with a napkin, leaving her scone untouched on her plate.

'It's a bit like being a PA to the directors as well as other stuff – you know, helping to organise events, some reception duties, assisting with student housing. It's a little bit of everything.'

Sylvia nodded. It was as if Nell's news was trickling through a thick mesh, each word falling separately upon her ears before eventually reaching her brain for processing.

'It sounds quite demanding.'

'And the money will be very handy. I can give up the office work I was doing at Langham Pascoe, and the books at Morgan's; just have one job. And they all seem very nice up there.'

Sylvia looked at Nell, their eyes meeting properly for the first time that day.

'I think it'll be good – a bit of a challenge, keep the grey matter working.'

Sylvia didn't respond.

'Oh, and they are kindly introducing a new bus route next month, which just happens to go from the end of my road to the university campus in just over ten minutes! Almost like a personal chauffeur!'

'A student charabanc more like.' Sylvia sipped her tea. 'Will you be working directly for Dawn Goldberg?'

Nell spread a small dollop of bright red jam on her scone. 'I expect so. She's the bigwig, isn't she? I get the impression all roads lead to Dawn. I met her briefly when I went for my second interview. Lovely she was, very attractive. She took my hands in both of hers and welcomed me to her empire. She was being flippant, of course. She even told me she was sure we'd become good friends. She seems very switched on, very dynamic.'

'She's certainly got a very clear agenda.'

'Well, she seems to have done her homework. I'm afraid it's all in the name of progress, isn't it? Poor Harry. I know he means well but...' Nell tried to think of a kindly way to word it. 'I'm a little afraid that he might be stuck in the past. Things change, you know, and sometimes it turns out for the better.'

Sylvia pushed her uneaten scone away and looked out of the window, her shoulders sagging once more. She said something Nell didn't catch. Nell asked her to repeat it.

'I didn't think,' said Sylvia, with some effort, 'that you agreed with more students coming to the town.'

Nell clasped her hands in front of her. 'I think we're all guilty of it – a kneejerk reaction to change. But the more I've thought about it, the more I think it could be a great opportunity for Poltowan – something that will really give the town an economic boost and put us on the map.'

Sylvia couldn't help but smile. 'It sounds like she did a good job on you. Is spreading the gospel part of your remit too?'

Nell coloured slightly. 'Look, Sylvia, I know it's hard, what with Harry's position, but I genuinely can see the good it will do to Poltowan.'

'You don't think it's just a few thousand people too many for our small town?'

'That's just it. Our small town often struggles for business out of season. Yes, we get summer visitors and the – what do they call it? – halo effect from St Ives and what not, but in winter the shop owners and local businesses have a very hard time making ends meet.'

'Not since the university opened they don't. Business is up by twenty per cent since then, according to Jenny Trundle the other night. Surely that's enough of a fillip – a happy medium?'

Sylvia watched as Nell twisted the napkin in her hands without answering before slumping back in her seat.

'It's more complex than any of us know, Nell. But I'm pleased about your new job.'

Both women looked out of the window, allowing the hum of conversation and the occasional clatter of crockery to fill the silence. Nell worked her ring around her finger.

'Maybe Harry will come to see that fighting it is futile,' she said eventually.

Sylvia's eyes followed an elderly couple as they walked slowly down the drive towards the house, arm in arm, swaying slightly as they went, their bodies moving in timeworn unity.

'He'll soon come round, like lots of the other businesses,' Nell persisted.

Sylvia's elbow jerked outwards, sending her knife clattering to the wooden floor. She watched it with indifference before bending to pick it up. Her voice came from under the table: 'Harry is not for turning.'

Nell drained the froth from the bottom of her coffee cup and placed it back on its saucer before fumbling in her bag for her purse. Sylvia was right. He seemed to have set himself on a collision course and he was not one to back down.

The pair of them ambled slowly back to the car, Nell trying to change tack with talk about Sylvia's garden and what spring might bring. But Harry's ghostly presence seemed to loom over each sentence, his physical absence underlining any mutterings about pruning the wisteria and cutting back the shrubs. Sylvia couldn't bear even to think about preparing the vegetable seed beds the following month.

Harry had never involved himself in the garden, it was Sylvia's domain. Yet without his uninformed but well-meaning comments and forced phases of interest, everything seemed so futile. She needed to get out and prune and tidy but it was as if the garden itself had given up hope of ever seeing another spring, surrendering to winter with a complete disregard for its appearance.

That morning she had simply stood and looked at the unruly vegetation all around her, its forlorn air mirroring her own. She had remained unable to tackle it, even to hack at one sad shrub in passing. Instead she had stood and looked at it, paralysed. A light drizzle had started falling; her hair grew lank, her hands chilled. Still she had stood and stared, until the sound of her friend calling her name had roused her.

They were waiting at a red light when Sylvia next spoke. Nell was wondering if perhaps she could orchestrate an apparently chance meeting with Harry, try to sow some seeds to dissuade him from embarking on this particular battle. She had the impression that Dawn Goldberg would stop at nothing to get her way, and Nell's growing unease was accentuated by her creeping belief that Dawn was right. Surely thwarting growth for the town was short-sighted?

If she could only see Harry she could perhaps help him to adopt a more sensible position. And she could gauge how serious it was with this Jo and try and steer him towards a reunion with Sylvia.

'I'm thinking of selling up.'

Nell looked sideways at her friend before a gentle toot from the car behind alerted her to the green light.

'Selling the house? Whatever for?'

Sylvia watched the oncoming traffic drift past.

'Why, Sylvia?' repeated Nell, gripping the steering wheel harder than was necessary.

'I'm rattling around in there. It's far too big for one person. Expensive too. And the garden is a lot of work.'

'But you love your garden. It's your passion. And one of your many talents.'

Sylvia pressed her lips together. She appreciated her friend's attempts to make her feel better, but it was as if the words skimmed over the surface and quickly disappeared. They didn't have the power to penetrate her mind, her soul. She heard them, and she could make sense of them. She even agreed with them – she was a good gardener. She had accumulated a lot of knowledge over the years and she had given a lot of time to it.

But right now she could take no pleasure in it – it was a burden that taunted her every morning when she opened the curtains, and every afternoon until the light began to fade; a reminder of another life. She couldn't see a time when the simple enjoyment and satisfaction she had derived from deadheading roses and butchering shrubs would ever return. It was a pointless exercise: the flowers bloomed and died, the vegetables were picked and eaten – those that didn't wither, neglected, forgotten, their one chance wasted – before beginning their circle of life again. On and on and on it went, and it would do so long after she left the earth. How could her fleeting interference in nature ever matter?

'At least don't make a decision now, Sylve,' urged Nell as they rounded a corner slightly too fast, both women veering to the left. 'It's a rotten month – the worst. Things will look a lot brighter in a couple of weeks, as we get into February – when your crocuses start to pop up. And your cornflowers.'

'Cornflowers don't bloom until June.'

'My point is,' said Nell, making every effort to soften her voice, 'that things look bleak at the moment. Just give it a couple of weeks. If you still feel the same then, well, let's talk again.'

She turned off the ignition. 'Anyway, what would Harry say? You never know. You might patch things up.'

Sylvia opened the door sharply. 'That ship has sailed, Nell. Longer ago than you know. Thanks for the walk. You probably don't want to come in, do you? Things to do, I'm sure.'

Nell started the engine and backed out of the drive, admiring the handsome house as she did so. It was large for one person, of course, but surely Sylvia didn't think things with Harry were terminal? Jo was clearly just a flash in the pan, a sop to his ego. For all Harry's virtues, even he had one of those.

Chapter 8

Ludo sat on the roof of the houseboat, his rangy legs swinging, trainers thudding against the window beneath. The January air had crept just above freezing and he sat listlessly puffing on his electronic cigarette, watching the morning haze slowly drift above the stillness of the River Poltowan.

He often got up early on cold winter mornings, when ice began forming on the insides of the windows. He would pull on his fleece and jacket and sit on the roof, where the temperature seemed ever so slightly warmer than within his Baltic quarters.

He had spent his first year in Poltowan on campus, when the students numbered a fairly small and intimate group, and they had easy access to state-of-the-art technology, being able to call on their lecturers for a chat unannounced. Ludo had written home to his parents in his first term telling them what a "full on collaborative culture" it was, his film-making maturing quickly under the tutelage of Dave White. He had arrived with lofty aspirations to be a documentary film-maker, having grown up devouring Ken Loach's early work, inspired and moved to make a difference through film.

But as student numbers had swelled under the suspect stewardship of Dawn Goldberg and lecturers continued to disappear overnight, resources became stretched and the once happy-go-lucky atmosphere that had permeated both staff and student lives at Poltowan, one which had encouraged creativity, had leaked away.

Now accommodation on campus was creaking under the sheer weight of numbers. Other students were scattered across myriad areas, with many crammed into once-beautiful town houses, some even sleeping in baths, tents and garden sheds. Some welcomed the unending sociability, the fast-tracked relationships, the enforced intertwining of limbs. More studious and reserved types were horrified by it.

The promise of a "boutique university offering a highly personal experience" had lured many people to the Cornwall town, yet Ludo had seen the change almost immediately before beginning his second year, when he was advised that he would have to find his own accommodation in town. He ended up in a three-storey townhouse, which came to house twelve people in four bedrooms by the time he left. The landlord was eventually forced to sell up in order to pay the not insignificant fine imposed on him for renting out the illegal extension of a property in a neighbouring road.

It was not that such crowded living conditions were a shock to Ludo – he came from a family of nine, being the third-youngest of seven siblings, and they had lived in a farmhouse in the wilds outside Cobh, reconfiguring their arrangements every time another baby came along. He was used to sharing beds, bedrooms and baths, and had learned to be first to the table to ensure his elder brothers didn't eat his share. But at first Poltowan University had offered him the space he craved – the room to think, to create.

He had taken on two part-time jobs in order to help pay the ludicrous rent on the townhouse, jobs that had sapped his energy and stolen valuable time from his film-making. Jobs were easy to come by, given his size and stature, with nightclub and pub owners assuming he was a dab hand at throwing punches and physically manhandling drunks. It couldn't have been further from the truth.

Ludo hated violence and would much rather solve disputes with his well-honed powers of negotiation than his fists. He had calmed some potentially explosive situations in exactly that way, only once being punched in the face by a lowlife who had the ingenious idea of leaping off a chair to overcome the height difference, striking Ludo clean in the mouth and splitting his lip. Even then it had not crossed Ludo's mind to punch his aggressor back, only to insult him with a string of inventive and debasing names.

In his third year, fed up with overcrowded houses, extortionate rent and little time to pursue his film projects, Ludo chatted up the owner of a houseboat in the pub one night, securing a year's tenancy at a mooring on the beautiful Poltowan river, which snaked around the eastern edge of the university campus, a fifteen-minute bus ride from the town. In truth, Ludo had been completely unaware what a 1938 gentleman's cruiser was, but his Irish spirit was drawn to the romantic possibilities of such a life and, fuelled by several pints of Guinness, he'd agreed to the lease there and then.

The boat itself wasn't huge, particularly for someone of his exceptional height, but it had enough space for a bed, toilet, sink, galley kitchen and a lounge-cum-study area, while a Heath Robinson contraption on deck served as a shower, although Ludo mostly completed his ablutions at the gym. For the first time he could remember, he felt he could breathe.

In better weather he had the small deck at his disposal, which had served him well for some impromptu summer parties that spilled on to the riverbank. Compared to some of the student houses he had experienced, the boat was positively luxurious, and despite having to spend much of his time with his head carefully bent, he felt rather smug for having orchestrated such a home for himself.

His phone pinged, bringing with it a promise that was invariably disappointed. He pulled it awkwardly from his pocket and squinted at the screen through the strawberry vapour. Rockstr had accepted his friend request, even messaging him an accompanying smiley face.

He bent his head in concentration, tapping a response. He had spent the previous evening scanning through her photos, finding mutual acquaintances, trying to piece together a fuller picture of this beautiful stranger. He could see no sign of a permanent other. In fact, he struggled to find any revealing history on her at all, as if she had carefully curated her posts to reflect only her current status as an aspiring musician. Most of her timeline was characterised by images of her playing her guitar and singing, alone and with her band. He had replayed one shaky video of her singing 'Cry Me Out' without any musical accompaniment thirteen times, before forcing himself to hit the stop button.

He had then spent a fitful night in his cramped bunk, images of Rockstr playing havoc with his usually reliable circadian clock. Lying there in the dark with the soporific lapping of water as a soundtrack, Ludo had tried to force his mind down other less stimulating avenues but could only turn his thoughts to Harry and his cause. These ultimately delivered him helplessly back to Rockstr in an unhelpful loop of wakefulness.

Her reply popped up with jaunty promptness, and the ensuing conversation was pleasingly fast and flirty. She was in the halls nearest to the river. Maybe they could hook up sometime? Ludo inhaled deeply on his electronic cigarette and looked up at the icy sky, exhaling slowly into the blanket whiteness as he pondered the infinite possibilities.

His ruminating was interrupted by the shrill call of his mobile, and he answered with the joviality that Harry often inspired in him.

'Top of the morning to you, sir, how can I help?'

He heard Harry sigh. 'How are you, Ludo?'

'Very well indeed. And yourself?'

'Not bad, not bad.'

'How's the eye? The knee?'

'Oh, fine, fine. Listen, I've got nearly two hundred people following me.'

'Come again?'

'There are one hundred and ninety-eight young people following me.'

'What are you, the feckin' Pied Piper?'

'I haven't got time for your comedy act, Ludo. What do I do with them all? They're on my... page. And we need to round them up!'

'Ah, I get you now.' Ludo stifled a laugh. 'So on your Facebook page, you've got one hundred and ninety-eight people who have liked or loved or engaged in some way with the news story about your recent TV appearance?'

'Exactly – as I just said.'

'Gotcha. So I'm thinking—' Ludo ran his nail along the paintwork on the side of the boat, watching as some flaked off and fell to the deck. 'We'll have a concert.'

'A concert? What sort of concert?'

'A music concert. Pop music, if you will. We invite all the kids who have engaged with you, plus all their friends, and we lay on a free concert. It gives you a platform to speak to a captive audience. Think Jeremy Corbyn at Glasto.'

Ludo clicked his rubber heels together with satisfaction at his own spontaneous idea.

Harry made a hmming noise. 'And who will we get to play? These things take time to organise. And money.'

'So here's the genius part. We get an up and coming act – a really hot act – who has a bit of a profile, a bit of a following, and who will absolutely relish the chance to perform live in front of her peers. So much so, in fact, that she will do it for free – perhaps we throw in some expenses – and everyone's a winner, baby. Now do you get my drift?'

Harry mulled the concept over. His eyebrows had risen a little more with Ludo's every word and now they sat high on his forehead, so stupefied and impressed was he by the seeming brilliance of the idea.

'But who is this rising star who would be ready and willing to play for free at the drop of a hat?'

'Leave that with me, Harry Manchester. I have a very talented feek in mind. I will report back forthwith.'

Ludo hummed to himself as he peed in a perfect arc over the side of the boat. His two current favourite things were going to come together in beautiful harmony – and he had masterminded the scheme.

∽

Rockstr seemed to float up to the bar, her eyes burning with an intensity he couldn't quite recall seeing in anyone before. Yet, despite her beauty, she had an impatient air about her – almost as if she was only passing through. He had the immediate impression that he would have to snare her quickly otherwise she would be gone, disappearing like the ineluctable setting of the sun.

Ludo remained slouched on the bar stool so as not to alarm her with his height. He had seen it happen before. Countless perfectly amiable girls with a bit of chat had suddenly reeled back in horror as he had stood up to his full height, staring up at him as if a full-blown skyscraper had spontaneously materialised in front of them. He had learned that it was something that needed to be handled sensitively.

He tried to take in all of her with one sweeping gaze but found himself not knowing which part of her to focus on, such was the deep brown of her eyes, the blonde wildness of her artfully styled air and the intricacy of her outfit. Finally he thrust out his hand.

'You must be Rockstr, I'm guessing?'

'Ludo?'

She hopped up on to the bar stool next to him, her fishnet-clad knee abutting his. Instinctively, he looked down.

'Ah, sorry, man. I'm in your space.'

'No, no. I'm just admiring your outfit. It's… sweet. Cool.'

He winced. He never used either of those words, and now they had tumbled out one after the other as if they were part of his everyday lexicon. He felt like a fifteen year old again.

'What can I get you?' He gestured to the bar.

'Just an orange juice. Thanks.'

'Sure?' Ludo took a deep draught of his beer, wiping his mouth on the back of his hand and suppressing a hiccup.

She smiled at him as if signalling that he now had her full attention. His leg began to jig up and down and he launched into some small talk about the pub and its supposedly artisan beers. All the while her eyes watched him with an amused twinkle in them. He hauled himself back on track, as if coming to the end of his warm up act.

'So, what brought you to Poltowan? Shouldn't you be at the Royal College of Music or… somewhere equally as suitable for a lady of your talents?'

She dropped her gaze and in that second Ludo's confidence returned. He had harnessed the momentum once more, the ball was back in his court, and it was his to win or lose. He sat back against the pillar, shoulders relaxing, leg slowing, and began to seize the moment.

'I flunked my audition.'

'Seriously? You had an audition?'

Rockstr nodded, her impish smile returning. 'Yep. But I blew it.'

'Why? What happened?'

She shook her head and flicked her blonde fringe simultaneously.

'Long story. Short version is, I got distracted by a boy. Thought I could manage both, got complacent, let him talk me out of spending enough time practising and – bang. The life I was going to have went up in smoke.'

'Wow. But you must be pretty good even to get an audition?'

'I play a couple of instruments and I sing. I'm still set on a music career, I've just got to take a more roundabout route to get there.'

He seemed genuinely interested in her and her musical talent rather than her looks. It had been a long time since that had happened.

'Maybe it's better that way. Maybe you weren't cut out for the Royal College – or maybe it wasn't cut out for you?'

She stirred her juice with metronomic precision.

'But why Cornwall, and the west of Cornwall at that? You couldn't have gone much further away from the capital. Is that where you're from? Your accent sounds pretty—'

'You're very curious.'

'Only if someone catches my attention, Rockstr. How do you say that by the way – do you roll the r or what's the deal here? Did I get it right?'

'Is it important? My name doesn't define me.'

Ludo searched her face for irony before clearing his throat and raising both hands as if in surrender. 'Hey, none of my business. I didn't mean to pry.'

She re-crossed her legs. 'You know, it's not my real name.'

'No way! And I thought it was, like, number one girls' baby name in 1998 or whatever the hell year you were born!'

She smiled despite herself, starting to take in his casual blond curls and his almond-shaped eyes, the long legs folded under the bar stool.

'So what is it – your real name?'

'Guess.'

'Oh, I'm not going to play that game. Reeling off the name of every woman I've ever known as my life ebbs away before me. Come on!'

'It's Moira.'

Ludo nodded slowly. 'Well, like I said, Rockstr is a great name.'

She laughed properly this time, showing her near-perfect white teeth. Suddenly she seemed younger than when she had first walked through the door, her air of blazing self-confidence starting to melt away.

'So, what is it? Scottish?'

'Indeed. Two Scottish parents.'

'Two parents? Wow.'

She angled her head. 'Two Scots, is my point.'

'I got you.'

As Ludo's second pint found its way into his bloodstream he began to relax. Rockstr's steely edge was still visible just below the surface, but Ludo was increasingly confident that his natural charm was breaking down any resistance.

'But you're not from Scotland, by the sound of you? You're a bit...' He smiled at her over the rim of his pint glass. 'A little bit mockney, little bit North London?'

She lowered her eyelids before reaching for her drink.

'Don't get me wrong,' said Ludo. 'It's just the way you said "point", it sounded almost—'

'Did you get me here to talk about regional dialects?'

Ludo held up his pint in mock surrender before broaching the topic of the concert, leading her in by way of the comment she had made on Harry's news post.

'So what's the deal with The Goldburger?' he asked. 'You seem to have pretty strong feelings about the direction she's taking the university.'

'Is that what they call her?' Rockstr twisted her nose stud. 'It sounds very fitting.'

'It's what I call her.'

'The bottom line is that she swans about, treats her staff like shit, wants to break her deal with us – having lured us here with the promise of small study groups and "unprecedented access to experts and facilities" or some such crap – and seems to be only interested in herself. Everyone seems to kowtow to her face to face, but behind her back I haven't met anyone with a good word to say. Well, barely anyone.'

Ludo nodded, frowning. 'I hear you.'

'I haven't a clue what I am going to do next year. There are, like, so many students without anywhere to live. We only got rooms on campus because we're first years and we applied early. Second years are expected to find their own accommodation but the rent in town is ridiculous and most of the houses are filthy squats with hundreds of people living in each room.'

'That does sound crowded.'

Rockstr held his gaze. 'I know I sound, like, neurotic, but it actually is a serious issue. Some of us don't have money to throw around like that. How are we supposed to live and study? How do you manage it?'

'Don't your folks have a country pile somewhere?'

'I'm paying them back every penny of my degree, that's the deal.' She lowered her eyes, giving her drink undue attention.

Ludo whistled. 'My folks are paying most of the basic fees if I'm honest, but I'm mostly working to pay my accommodation and beer. But good for you, girl – not many eighteen year olds will commit to paying all that cash back – not if they can help it.'

'I'm nearly twenty-one.'

Ludo swallowed his beer hard. 'Wowzer. Sorry, I just thought, as a first year and all, you were that bit younger. You're the same age as me, man.' He began to tap his foot on the stool again as he waited for her to elaborate.

'So, like, where have you been all my life?' His eyes widened with the intended humour of the line but Rockstr's head remained bowed, her cheeks a fetching pink hue.

'Just… you know,' she said eventually. 'Generally screwing things up. But I'm here now so, onwards and upwards.' She raised her glass of orange juice at him and he raised his beer in return.

'You're not a drinker?'

She shook her head.

'Wow, first you say you're not eighteen and now you say you're a teetotaller – what sort of student are you?'

She began to look around the room, fingering her mobile in her pocket.

The Guinness must have affected Ludo's brain more than he had believed. He pushed the glass several inches away from him in a show of sobriety and sincerity.

'I'm sorry. I'm an arse. Sometimes I think I'm this great witty guy and – ' he waved his hand ' – I'm just a spanner, particularly after some of the black stuff.'

Rockstr pursed her lips in an effort to suppress the smile that threatened to break out on hearing the word 'spanner'. The absurdity of the word used in such a context appealed to the frivolous side of her nature. She pulled her phone from her bag and began to swipe at it furiously.

Ludo continued undeterred, telling her about himself, about growing up in Ireland with so many unruly siblings, about learning to drive a tractor as soon as his feet could reach the pedals, and about escaping to Poltowan to find space to conceive pieces of filmic work that would make a profound difference to the world.

Rockstr looked up occasionally with studied indifference, working hard to keep her mouth from betraying her amusement at his lyrical Irish anecdotes, his endearing turns of phrase. When he stopped to draw breath panic set in: he was pretty sure he had lost his audience now.

'Listen,' he said, straightening his posture, 'I have a proposition for you. It will help you to address the problem that is The Goldburger.'

Slowly Rockstr looked up at him, phone still in hand, her brown eyes flashing as they met his. 'How?'

This was Ludo's moment to shine. As he began to outline his idea for the concert, displaying his inimitable enthusiasm and energy, Rockstr's already wide eyes grew wider. Ludo continued to embellish the idea until he knew he had her undivided attention.

'That Harry sounds like a legend.'

'Oh, he is, no question. You wait 'til you meet him.'

'I feel like I have. Tell the truth, I didn't see that item on *News Time*, I just heard about it and I loved his daring, the way he'd carried it off. And I'm a big fan of the Queen rock gods… so, it was all good.'

Rockstr fiddled with her phone for a moment before holding it up to her face and focusing on the screen. A tinny noise sounded.

'What is it?' said Ludo, before hearing the unmistakable voice of Jenny Trundle.

Rockstr turned the screen round and shuffled closer to Ludo. As it played, he could feel the hysteria beginning to rise inside him again and his efforts to suppress it were making the back of his neck sweat. He had not laughed like this for a long time, and as disloyal as it felt to Harry, he could feel another bout of paralysing and undignified mirth approaching.

The pair of them sat with tears streaming down their cheeks, Ludo barely able to stay on his bar stool, a challenge exacerbated by having consumed nearly three pints of Guinness. Meanwhile Rockstr wiped at her eyes, her imperturbable front gone and her girlish underbelly revealed.

It took Ludo several attempts to speak, each effort aborted by an infectious outbreak of hilarity that threw Rockstr into an equally unmanageable fit of laughter. Finally, he managed to regain his composure.

'So. What I'm saying is – it is, undoubtedly, one of the funniest things I have seen in a while. But I'm not laughing at Harry. He is, as you rightly pointed out, a legend in his own News Time, and is deserving of our utmost respect.'

He swigged his pint, gaze still fixed on Rockstr's laughing brown eyes.

'I'll do it, anyway, and I'm pretty sure the band will too. For Harry, for me, for you… for all my fellow students. And, of course, the residents of this great town. I can play some of our new tracks, get them out there.'

'You're a sound girl. We'll sort a venue fast and I'll get cracking on spreading the word.'

She slid off the bar stool quickly and elegantly and turned to go, her aplomb restored. 'Nice meeting you. I'd better run – I've got, like, a mountain of work to do and I need to get some study space. Let me know the deal.' She turned back a moment later. 'And by the way, Ludo is also a Scottish name, don't you know? At least I had the sense to change mine.'

She winked, the light briefly catching her nose stud with a flash, then disappeared from the bar. Ludo finished his pint in one greedy swallow and slapped his hands in a short, loud, celebratory rhythm on his lean thighs.

Chapter 9

Dawn Goldberg angled her car around the narrow country lanes, flicking between blasts of pop music on Radio Kernow and bouts of serious debate on Radio 4. She felt she should be tuned in to the latter, but when she was at the wheel of her sports car she felt compelled to have punchy tunes filling the air, demonstrating her voguish taste for music as she wended her way through campus to her office.

It was a fifty-minute drive from her village to Poltowan. Her route took in the boundless bucolic beauty of Cornwall as well as a couple of inoffensive A-roads. As she crested the hill, the south coast revealed itself slowly like a lover, before she plunged down a series of increasingly leafy lanes towards the university. She enjoyed the journey. It allowed her to psych herself up for the day ahead on the morning leg, relishing the changing moods of the sea – at times blue and inviting, shimmering in the sunshine, at others a foreboding grey, jagged waves leaping as if boiling. It often reflected her own moods, giving her reassurance that her rich and varied spectrum of humours was not, after all, extraordinary. The same journey enabled her to wind down on her return home, liberally discarding work-induced resentment and anger as she went.

Today she was feeling particularly fired up. Her PA, Janice, who also happened to be her best friend, was returning from two weeks away, and Dawn was keen to brief her on progress on the application to increase student numbers. She had teased her with brief updates in a series of WhatsApp messages, but was relishing the chance to embellish the sketchy headlines with a riot of colourful detail, not to mention copious amounts of coffee and doughnuts.

The sheer anticipation of the meeting – coupled with a particularly lively Ed Sheeran number – impelled her to press her foot slightly harder on the accelerator than she had intended. Suddenly she found herself being propelled towards a sharp bend. For a fleeting moment the world seemed to spin around her, the roadside trees nearing her windscreen at terrifying speed. She was being thrust towards the woodland. She righted the car with an exaggerated jerk of the wheel, rescuing herself from almost certain death at the last second. The bloodcurdling screech of rubber on tarmac was so deafening, so surprising, that she glanced in her rear-view mirror in full expectation of seeing another car careering towards her. The road was empty.

Dawn wrenched the car left and flicked the music off, plunging herself into a stark and sobering silence. She sat motionless, still gripping the wheel, her eyes staring straight ahead. She closed them and tried to focus on the breathing techniques she had learned, but her breaths came ragged and shallow. *Fill your lower lungs; then your upper lungs*. She said the words out loud to herself. She pictured the red armchair she used to sit in as Marie talked in her soporific, heavily accented way, urging her to float on her breath, to banish the rising panic. For a moment she was back there, in that musty, windowless room, her Thursday morning sessions from some forty years before as clear as day.

It was some moments before she started the engine again, her trembling hands turning the wheel slowly to pull her back onto the road. She approached the final turning to the university with exaggerated caution, suddenly aware of an intense heat rising up her neck and into her cheeks.

It was not often she dwelled on the circumstances of her father's death, or allowed herself to consider the finer details of what may or may not have occurred that Tuesday morning, but very occasionally, when at the wheel, she experienced a stark reminder of how quickly life could become death; of how we all hover uncertainly between this world and the next.

Her memory of that day was a blur, almost to the point that she sometimes questioned whether she had been in the car with her father at all. He had been taking her to her entrance exam at the nearby girls' school, something he had perceived as a formality for the brilliantly academic Dawn – not that she possessed the same level of confidence in herself. Until then she had been unduly tainted by her mother's unrelentingly gloomy outlook, believing that her father was, in contrast, overly ambitious on her behalf, riddling her with a desperate anxiety that she would fail him.

Bramley Hill was a twenty-five-minute journey, along roads that her father had driven numerous times. He loved to drive his green Cortina Mk4, purchased from his savings when it rolled off the production line the year before. She often helped him to wash and polish it on Saturday afternoons, and sometimes he would let her top up the oil and check the water. On occasion she would lie under the car next to him as he worked on the underside, revelling in the dark intimacy they shared, her mother tutting and berating her from the kitchen window. It was during these times that his faith in her began to permeate Dawn's mind, nourishing her self-belief and feeding her courage; letting her dare to dream. He was a man of few words, often quiet and reserved, but he chose those few words carefully, and she treasured every one of them. How she had longed to know all his thoughts.

Other times he would stand with his head under the bonnet for hours, removing parts and replacing them, humming to himself. It was when he was at his happiest; it was when he was at his kindest.

She had insisted on sitting in the back seat that day. She wanted to do some last-minute, uninterrupted revision on her French verbs. Her father had sat silently in the driver's seat, his oversized brown suit jacket looking faintly ridiculous on his narrow shoulders. He had bought it when he was promoted to factory manager some two years before. It had always been slightly too big for him, almost as if he thought the higher rank, the improved status, would in itself take up the slack. His hair had been slicked across his head in the way he wore it on important occasions. His very demeanour suggested he had finally arrived, that his life's journey had been about this moment.

Dawn sometimes thought she could remember the sirens, the ugly twisted wreckage of the green Cortina, the windscreen missing, its bonnet screwed up like a used tissue. She had sat on the grass verge at the roadside in her best skirt as she repeated, *'Je suis, tu es, il est, elle est...'*, while the chaos unfolded around her.

But she could also be persuaded that this was simply the product of the numerous accounts she had heard over the years; an inauthentic narrative created and recreated so many times that it had lodged in her brain as a false memory.

The one thing she did recall was the sound of the breaking windscreen. It had started with a violent crack before shattering unhurriedly yet with certitude, a symphony of sound all around her, tinkling and crunching as it settled like snow. She was sure she had watched it for a long time, mesmerised as it fell away, not comprehending the speed with which such huge devastation could be wreaked.

Dawn had insisted on sitting her delayed entrance exam less than three weeks later, four days after burying her father. She passed with flying colours and was immediately offered a place, only to be unceremoniously removed before the end of the year when her mother announced that she could no longer afford to pay the fees.

Dawn had greeted this statement with grudging acceptance at first but had soon come to realise that her father had left them suitably well off, certainly if her mother's growing wardrobe was anything to go by. The truth was that her mother had never believed Dawn either capable or worthy of a private education. She often repeated the fact that Dawn's older cousin had not "demanded" a private education and had instead been quite content with her Pitman touch typing qualification, which would see her through until she married. Dawn had often wondered which of these two fates would be the most tedious.

It had been an ignominious and premature end to what she had quickly come to believe would have been a brilliant career. As captain of her year's debating team, she had allowed herself to believe she might one day even rise to become Prime Minister, although she was unsure if she would have wanted to live in that house with its austere railings and unprepossessing black door. It was the only consolation she could think of as she walked out of the gates of Bramley Hill for the last time.

It had been clear her father had believed that she could achieve great things – after all, he had been the one to encourage her school career, to accompany her to the library on Saturdays, plucking weighty tomes from its shelves and thrusting them upon her purposefully. And, of course, he had insisted on taking a day off work to drive her to the pivotal entrance exam. She had heard him say on more than one occasion that Dawn would not fulfil her potential if she continued to study alongside any old Tom, Dick or Sally, a comment that invariably prompted one of her mother's blackest looks.

Dawn had come to believe this too. She struggled to fit back in on her sudden return to state school and was bullied for the hubris she had adopted almost as part of the uniform at Bramley Hill, propelling her into a state of precarious limbo as she hit puberty. Delayed grief had collided with a disorientating sense of alienation both at home and at school. She had eventually been referred by her GP for counselling with Marie Durand, an ageing French lady who conducted her sessions in a dark panelled room that reeked of stale lives and ageing wood. Dawn would sit in the large red chair disgorging occasional thoughts and feelings while Marie looked at her with her kindly, sad eyes. Dawn stopped going after five weeks, instead spending the allotted time in the nearby library, an activity of which she knew her father would have been far more approving.

Dawn's immortalised father continued to be her unerring ally. His vividly remembered presence inspired her towards ever-greater things, unfailingly supportive yet, somehow, never quite satisfied with her achievements.

❦

Dawn had taken a moment to apply her lipstick and waited for the end of a sobering news item on Radio 4 before she crossed the car park to her office, her calm demeanour almost fully restored. She was cheered to see Janice faithfully back at her desk, already shuffling through post. She greeted Dawn with a warm hug, her skin nut brown from the Caribbean sun, her eyes alive with renewed vigour.

'What a time for me to go away… so much going on. Tell all, and don't spare the details!'

Dawn hugged her friend back, holding on to her for a moment longer than usual.

'These are not things that can be hurried, Janice,' she said eventually. 'We need to address them properly, give them due time and attention.'

Dawn continued into her office and placed her oversized bag and laptop case on her desk. She leaned casually in the doorway.

'So. How was Barbados? You certainly look bronzed and relaxed.'

'Wonderful. We did nothing, it was absolutely wonderful!'

Dawn rolled her eyes. 'Well, welcome back to the real world, where "nothing" is a swear word and only "everything" will do!'

The two women laughed.

'How are you? You look a bit – pale, dare I say?'

'Damn' right I'm pale. I've been in stuck in Cornwall while you've been in the bloody Caribbean sunning yourself. You wait until I go on my jollies.'

'Are you shaking?' Janice frowned and reached for her friend's hand, and Dawn hurriedly snatched it away.

'I just need coffee. You know the drill, Jan.' She tossed her hair over her shoulder. 'Give me fifteen minutes and I'll be ready for our debrief. Oh, and doughnuts, of course – the custard ones. Best get four.'

Dawn closed the door softly and leaned against it. She watched Michael standing alone in the garden outside. Somehow he looked cold and forlorn today, his paintbrush raised more in hope than expectation.

'We can but carry on,' Dawn said softly to herself before adjusting the photo frame on her desk, catching her father's eye before firing up her laptop.

In her eagerness to reconvene with her friend, Janice forgot to knock, barging through Dawn's office door some ten minutes later laden with two large coffees and a generous-sized pastry box, a stash of documents tucked under her arm.

She was just in time to see Dawn hastily sealing the lid on her miniature vodka bottle and slipping it inside her desk drawer. Janice spun round, closing the door slowly in exaggerated fashion before expounding on her short walk to the university canteen, the unbroken stream of chatter only ceasing when she had quite literally run out of air.

'I think perhaps he needs a clean,' said Dawn. 'A little male grooming.'

Janice placed the coffees on the desk and followed Dawn's gaze towards the statue.

'He does look a little… grimier since I last laid eyes on him.'

Dawn continued to stare at Michael. She was savouring the sensation of the vodka slowly reaching her knees, a sense of calm gradually enfolding her.

'Yes. I'll call… whatshis face this afternoon. Get him on it.'

Dawn paused before turning to face her friend, now with her customary smile on her face, and taking her seat. She was starting to return to herself.

'I can't tell you how lovely it is to have you back, Jan. This place is the pits without you.'

Janice sat down, her pleasure at Dawn's compliment apparent in her wide grin. She pulled a newspaper from the pile and held it aloft.

'"Don't Stop Me Now"', read Dawn out loud, narrowing her eyes slightly at the sizeable photo of Harry Manchester on the cover of the latest *Poltowan Post*.

She snatched it from Janice's grasp, her heart sinking.

'What the – I took Dennis out for a very nice lunch last week to ensure that man doesn't get this sort of exposure. And here he is!'

'Read it,' urged Janice, reaching for her first doughnut.

Dawn was momentarily torn between retrieving her own doughnut and reading the front page of the paper, eventually deciding to do both. Her sugary lips began to part in undisguised mirth, her white teeth gleaming as she tilted the paper to let page two fall open, consuming the words as eagerly as she consumed the doughnut.

'Oh, Dennis,' she said eventually. 'You have done me proud,' she muttered, licking jam from the corner of her painted lips.

Janice felt a glow of satisfaction. 'I thought the same! Harry Manchester's pompous statements about how he will keep fighting, like he's leading his troops to war! It is all written with a steadfastly ironic hand. The *Post* is having a clear dig at our local hero.'

Dawn sat down, re-reading the article in silence, considering the story in more depth.

'It is certainly ironic… My concern is that the people of Poltowan, God love 'em, are not worldly enough to appreciate the irony. I wonder if Dennis hasn't credited them with a little too much intelligence.'

'Surely even the people of Poltowan are not stupid enough to listen to a man who not only wanders around town with an inflatable guitar but has a Queen ringtone on his phone?'

Dawn spluttered, wiping sugar from her mouth with the back of her hand before spotting a napkin.

'It's a shame they didn't run that photo. It would have been much more fitting than a posed shot of him splayed across his desk. Did you actually see the TV clip?'

'Someone posted it on Facebook. Funniest thing I've seen for a long time. And perfect timing on your part, if I may say.'

'It worked out pretty well, although he did his damnedest to take it in his stride. But it wasn't my doing to have him jumped on his way out of the studio door – on that charge I am definitely not guilty, m'lud.'

'What?'

Dawn filled Janice in on the attack, although she had only gleaned sketchy details from Dennis, and had heard another vague account from someone who had seen a reference on Facebook. She'd filled in any blanks herself.

'Well. You wouldn't wish that on anybody,' said Janice deadpan. Seconds later they were doubled up in fits of laughter, the remaining doughnuts taunting them from the desk top.

When the laughter ceased, Dawn's gaze drifted back to her father, sitting quietly observing her from his corner of the desk.

'I suppose you heard about Dave White's letter to the Kernow Click website?'

'He's not worth it, Dawn.'

'Oh, he's worth silencing – I've still got that photo on my phone and I'm not afraid to use it.' Dawn began scrolling through her photographs. 'I was waiting for your return to get your advice on how best to go about it. Get a canvas printed and deliver it by hand to his wife? Or post it on Facebook? Or we could get really creative—'

'He's left his wife. I guess that's why he felt he could finally air his grievances. Nothing to lose.'

A sudden darkness stole over Dawn's face. 'He left her?'

Janice lowered her gaze. 'Actually, he has been seeing Celia.'

Dawn stood up and turned to face the window. 'Bloody hell.'

'I know. You couldn't make it up – actually running off with the honey trap herself. But it'll be short-lived, I'm sure.'

'Diane never said anything.'

'She's probably embarrassed of her daughter. He's hardly a catch. Anyway, who reads Kernow Click, for God's sake?'

'I've got Hornblower on the case, demanding they take it down. It's litigious drivel.'

'Is all this stuff about the student proposals getting to you? You do seem a bit out of sorts today.'

'What? Oh, no. I've just been thinking about my old dad. Wondering what he would do in my shoes. Wondering quite how hardball I play it.'

Janice thought for a moment. 'He'd be so proud of you, Dawn.'

'Oh, I know,' she said, staring intently into her father's eyes, pushing away thoughts of his final moments, the terror he must have felt.

'So proud,' repeated Janice softly.

There was pride in his eyes, for sure, thought Dawn, but there was also that suggestion of slight uncertainty, that hint of vexation she had seen so many times in him when she was a child. She had done well. But she could always do better.

'Anyway, you have to fight fire with fire, Dawn,' continued Janice. 'Sounds like Harry Manchester is going all out for maximum publicity, dead set on rallying the residents and, in his vainglorious words, "working with other local businesses to get a clear picture of what this might mean for our community". He's a businessman, albeit an estate agent. He won't have any scruples about what he has to do to get his point across.'

Dawn drained her coffee cup and lifted the second doughnut onto her napkin in readiness.

'It's not like you to worry about playing hardball anyway. That's how you got to be Vice Chancellor – it's survival of the fittest, particularly where people like him are concerned. The university needs you if it's going to grow and thrive.'

Dawn let her friend's flattery wash over her, hoping she would continue her steady stream of encouragement, but Janice tucked into her second doughnut and the adulation came to a sudden end. Its powers had been sufficiently restorative though. Dawn could already feel her old daring returning, her momentary self-doubt ebbing away, replaced with the familiar heady rush associated with a challenge.

A faltering knock at the door interrupted them. She held Janice's gaze for a moment before inviting the unknown visitor to enter.

Andy Hornblower shuffled in, raising his hand in greeting as the two faces turned dispassionately towards him.

'Sorry to interrupt, ladies.'

'Don't apologise, Andy – not unless you're wasting my time again.' Dawn sat back, licking her sugary fingers in readiness for her Head of Communications' latest pearl of wisdom.

He laughed, the noise sounding slightly strangulated, before taking a moment to compose himself. 'I have an idea...'

The two women continued to stare at him.

'I know you said you were looking for something slightly left field, a bit different, a bit—'

'I don't recall using those words but carry on,' said Dawn.

'Well, I think perhaps what we need is some sort of university event that brings the whole community together – students, residents, business owners – establishing some common ground and giving us a stage on which to position our messaging and actually start to bring alive how we see the increased numbers working and why it will benefit...'

'Like a fete, you mean?' said Dawn.

'Not as such, no,' said Andy, hovering in the doorway, looking as if he was unsure whether he was arriving or leaving. He continued blindly along his obstacle-strewn path.

'More a festival – think music, literature, film, science – celebrating all the courses we do so well here and giving students from each faculty the chance to showcase their work to the public, bridging that divide between town and gown and also opening up opportunities for local businesses to identify partnership opportunities, like the—'

'Firstly, it is not students, it is customers. Secondly, we do not supply courses, we market products. And how much exactly would such an extravaganza cost?'

'Well, I haven't done any costings yet, Dawn, I thought I'd—'

'That's the trouble with you, Andy.' Dawn spun around to seek Michael's approval. 'You think too much. All thought and no substance.'

'Of course, I can go away and do some sums—'

'Just do the first bit, Andy,' said Dawn, swivelling back to face him.

'Which bit is that exactly?' he said, venturing to lift his chin a little higher and smile at her.

'Go away.'

Andy waited for her to laugh, for her to appeal to him to share in her dry sense of humour, but deep down he knew better than to think her caustic words were meant any other way than literally.

'Right. Well, it was just a thought.'

'For the last time, I do the thinking, you do the doing. Goodbye.'

The door closed softly behind him.

Dawn leaned her head on one hand. 'That man,' she sighed.

Janice shifted uncomfortably in her seat. Dawn was definitely out of sorts today. Janice had heard her speak to staff derogatorily numerous times but she was usually more clever about it, wielding her contempt with skill and grace and delivering withering put downs that simultaneously offended and puzzled the recipient, the full force of the insult not being felt until they were able to give it greater consideration. By then, Dawn was long gone, and the realisation of their own dull-wittedness was an additional source of shame.

'He was in the police, would you believe?' said Dawn.

'A policeman?'

'Good God, no. Can you imagine him on the beat, tasked with keeping the community safe? He'd probably stun himself with the TASER gun before he caught anyone.' Dawn's laughter was short and sharp this time.

'Actually,' ventured Janice, 'I wonder if there is something in what he says? I mean, holding a community event to show off what we do and get the nay-sayers on board. As you alluded to earlier, Dawn, most of the local residents don't have a clue what we do here – they think we sit here with our fingers up our noses, dreaming up ways to spend their money.'

'Then they don't deserve to know!' bellowed Dawn, taking her friend by surprise.

'But, Dawn, they need to know,' said Janice, trying to appease her. 'We may not like it, but it is the only way we are going to reduce resistance to the university having more students.'

'I am going to go straight to the people who matter, not the peasants,' said Dawn, standing up and pacing across her office.

'Every audience matters.'

'The Councillors matter, Jan – the strategic planning committee at Cornwall Council. They will be the people voting on lifting the cap. Ultimately it is only their views that count. And they will be chiefly moved by the press, and by me. They trust everything they read in the *Poltowan Post* – it's their bible. No amount of costly open-house events and pandering to the bloody public will influence the final vote. We must not allow ourselves to be distracted by all the furore. What matters is my reputation – and that of the university.'

Janice felt chastened. Dawn had never cared about being popular. Success to her was about winning, about achieving, and that was something she did well. It was never about being lauded by people who were, to all intents and purposes, extraneous. Dawn knew exactly who to ingratiate herself with to get things done, and troubled herself little with those who fell outside that remit.

'You know what we need, Jan,' said Dawn, her face brightening. 'An after-work livener. Fancy a cheeky one at the Wild Grape?'

Janice hesitated. 'I'm a bit bushed to be honest. How about Friday? I can do Friday. Tonight's – Tony's expecting me.'

'I might go on my own anyway, see what's going on. I can have one double stiffy, if I have some of their tapas. Those chilli prawns are to die for.'

'Or hold fire until Friday – wait for me?' Janice knew it was dangerous to stand anywhere between Dawn and her vodka particularly in this mood, but she had been increasingly worried by her friend's drinking lately, and while she was sure that the miniature bottle of vodka in Dawn's desk was rarely recruited, she was all too aware that secreting alcohol in the office was a slippery slope.

'No chance. The day I'm having? And it's only eleven o'clock. Come with me. Tony can wait. You've just spent two weeks with him. You and I have lots of catching up to do. And I still haven't updated you on the progress of the impact centre.' Dawn pressed her hands together like a small child. 'I have been exchanging some very promising emails with the FIA…'

Janice looked at her, mouth slightly open.

'The FIA, Janice – the governing body for motor sport, who will hopefully be helping to fund the facility.'

Janice got the distinct impression she had been told about the FIA's involvement in Dawn's pet project before. She nodded and muttered in agreement.

'And if I have my way, they will also be sending all their extremely handsome cars here for testing.'

'How exciting. It sounds like quite a coup.'

'It will be worth all the work when it finally gets signed off and the hugely inconvenient matter of funding is sorted out.

Engineering students from all over the world will be happily giving their right arms to study here – particularly when we increase the numbers.' Dawn spun round in her chair. 'So, yes, vodka after work, lots to catch up on.'

Janice grappled for the right words to postpone Dawn without causing offence or upset.

'That's settled then,' she said. 'Ring and tell Tony you'll be a teensy bit late.' She emitted her raucous laugh, already cheered by the thought of her five o'clock tipple, any memories of the mangled green Cortina pushed firmly to the back of her mind: or 'compartmentalised', as Marie would have said.

Chapter 10

Harry had reluctantly agreed to join Jo for a drink at the Wild Grape. In truth, he wanted some time to himself, ideally wearing his oversized headphones in the comfortable office at his old marital home, rock music blaring while he relaxed in his recliner and mulled over the problems of the world.

While he'd had the foresight to take his headphones with him when he left – along with fifteen carefully chosen vinyl records and his Bang & Olufsen portable speaker – the close confines of Jo's flat didn't allow for the luxury of isolation. Not unless he drew his knees up to his chest and sought peace in her pea-shaped bath. Jo didn't even possess a record player, but somehow Harry felt comforted by having some of his vinyl stacked against the wall in her lounge.

He shifted uncomfortably on the bar stool, trousers pulling tight around his crotch. His fingers drummed in time to the music and he whistled under his breath, picking out the chorus of the Def Leppard song.

Sylvia's face returned to his mind. His whistling was one thing that had come to annoy her over the years. In the early days it had made her smile, quietly pleased her. But his almost incessant cheeriness had evolved into a source of bewilderment to Sylvia, highlighting her own increasingly joyless outlook on life. It had slowly but surely driven a wedge between the two of them.

Harry's fingers fell silent and he pulled his phone from his pocket. He was standing at the bar, frowning at the screen of his mobile, when Steph approached from behind and threw her narrow arms around his waist. He had been preoccupied by the alarming rate at which people – mostly young people – were following him on Facebook.

'Harry Manchester, TV star!'

Harry turned around and prised Steph gently away, giving her a customary kiss on the cheek at the same time as he scanned the half-full bar for any familiar faces. He raised his eyebrows at James Cowley, with whom he used to play in a band in his teenage years. James was now considerably fatter and balder but with a sizeable bank balance to make up for it, thanks to his ownership of the town's butcher's shops, not to mention the burger bar that he had recently opened as a natural extension of his business. James nodded at him before muttering something that made his companion laugh. Harry simply smiled in response.

Steph looked up at him, a wide grin on her face. 'I was so proud!'

'Very kind of you, Steph, but let's not get carried away. There's a long way to go yet, I fear.'

'But you were –' Steph made a lip-smacking noise as she rounded the bar to prepare Harry's usual gin and tonic ' – so good.'

Harry tugged at his crisp white shirt sleeves and adjusted his Rolex watch. He watched her as she prepared his favoured cucumber garnish: one slice in the glass and one slice artistically straddling the rim. Steph had always been quick to fight his corner, even when she was ill informed about quite why he was embroiled in a heated discussion, or what had – very occasionally – caused him to suffer a spell of the blues. This time, she not only threw her slender form energetically behind his cause, but she cared passionately about it herself.

She had made Poltowan her home ten years before, leaving

behind a successful career in interior design in London to pursue her dream of running a wine bar, funded largely by a surprise inheritance from a distant relative. Her offering reflected her penchant for all things beautiful, elegant and striking, and the resulting establishment was an exquisite sanctuary for those seeking good wine, classy cocktails and stimulating conversation, far away from student nights, ten per cent off vouchers and happy hours. It was a powerful USP in a town that increasingly pandered to pre-loading, free-loading students.

Indeed, as a growing number of more mature residents moved out of Poltowan, hastened on their way by intolerable noise in the early hours, increasingly rubbish-strewn streets resulting from both landlords' and students' unwillingness to invest in buying proper dustbins, and an inexplicable trend for old blankets hung in place of curtains, Steph had started to see her customer base decline. It was not yet too damaging to her profits, but she feared that if the same momentum continued, fuelled by the possible arrival of another three thousand young people, the Wild Grape would struggle to survive, its discerning regulars driven out of town by an intrusion of fly-by-nights.

'What's the plan, Harry?'

He straightened his back and broadened his stance, adjusting his new glasses before placing his splayed hands flat on the bar.

'Well, we are kicking off our awareness campaign with a concert.'

Steph remained silent, cocking her head at him in anticipation of further news. She was grappling for words of encouragement but was momentarily baffled by the announcement.

Harry tapped his fingers on the wooden surface. 'It's Ludo's brainchild – you know, my student friend? He's quite a boon to the campaign, Steph. The idea is to use the support I've drummed up on Facebook, get everyone together and give us a proper platform to communicate why this is so important.'

She began to nod. 'Harry, that sounds like a bloody great idea. It's exactly what you need – a platform from which to address people. And a concert! It's a stroke of genius – it's very you.'

She raised her hand to high-five Harry and slowly he lifted his arm, his large palm dwarfing hers. As their hands met, Jo appeared in the doorway. She stopped, pausing for a moment unobserved. She knew Harry had known Steph for years and they often engaged in banter with each other, but this evening she felt a tremor of something approaching jealousy. It was an odd, alien sensation that shot something akin to an electrical charge right through her.

It was these unfamiliar stabs of spite that had first made Jo realise the extent of her feelings for Harry. She had never before truly wanted or expected anything much for herself. From the age of seventeen she had spent most of her time being a primary carer for her mother, who suffered from a host of complex, severe and regressive mobility problems. Her father had worked long hours, changing his job to be more available when the time came for Jo to go to university. But instead of making an overdue bid for freedom she had plumped to study just thirty miles away, never quite trusting her inept but well-meaning father to deliver the level of care she knew her mother needed.

Two months after she graduated from teacher training, securing a job at a nearby primary school and moving back into the family home to help with her mother's care, her father left. He moved across town to live with another woman, claiming that he still loved her mother but that their marriage had changed. Jo never quite forgave him and had continued to juggle her increasingly demanding job with looking after her mother, until her death two years before. Relationships had simply eluded her.

At the age of thirty-five, Jo had met Harry. At last, she knew what love was: it was as if she had finally been invited to the party that everyone else had long been talking about. So enamoured was she that she struggled hard against her instincts to speed the relationship to what she saw as its inevitable conclusion. While mindful that Harry's decision to move in with her was born more of convenience than careful consideration, she had seen it as a God-given opportunity to prove their compatibility and cement their future. The depth of her feelings had also prompted her to subconsciously dismiss the idea of him having a wife, deciding it was a temporary state that would soon be resolved.

But it struck her now, as she began her descent from the darkness of the entrance into the light of the bar, that perhaps other women found him as attractive as she did; and that perhaps he saw the demise of his marriage as the start of a whole new chapter, of which Jo was just the first page.

She cleared her throat and cautiously negotiated the three narrow steps down to the bar in her high heels. She waved her hand in exaggerated greeting to Harry and then Steph, before giving Harry a lingering kiss and running her hand down his arm.

'Sorry I'm late. I got held up, but it's all very exciting,' said Jo, slipping her large handbag off her shoulder and on to a stool. She unwound her indulgent scarf several times from around her neck and Harry took her coat and hung it on a nearby hook.

'I thought you looked a bit sly.' He drank her in: shiny bobbed hair, slightly flushed cheeks, smiling eyes, pronounced dimples at the sides of her small mouth.

She was slightly breathless from a mixture of excitement and nervousness and her feverish state contrasted with Harry's habitual calm. He took her hand and tried to search her face for any clue as to the reason for her apparent animation. She ordered herself a drink and looked around the room, trying to buy time to compose herself.

'Isn't that your old band mate over there – the butcher?'

Harry nodded.

Jo fixed her eyes on something across the room before she narrowed them at Harry and leaned forward. 'I think he's talking about you. Or me. Or us.'

Harry didn't allow himself to look. He paid Steph for their two drinks and winked at Jo. 'You, no doubt. Why wouldn't he? So—' He twisted the stem of the glass around in his hand. 'What is your news?'

Jo inhaled, placing her hand on Harry's knee. She entwined her fingers with his and looked beseechingly at him. A friend from work had announced that she would shortly be handing in her notice on her penthouse apartment overlooking the river.

'It is to-die-for,' said Jo. Harry could see the excitement in her eyes, observing the tiny orange flecks that appeared there whenever she was particularly happy or enthused, the pink hue rising in her cheeks.

'She said for us to go and have a quick look round, you know, to get an idea of what's on offer. Oh my God, Harry. It would be just perfect for us – it's immaculate, great big windows, open-plan, gorgeous view over the river, a sunken bath – can you imagine? A sunken bath. It is heavenly.'

Harry glanced over at James Cowley before returning his gaze to Jo. 'Well, let's have a chat about it later.'

'It will be snapped up like that, Susie says,' said Jo, trying and failing to click her fingers. 'There's no time to waste. I said we'd go and have a look tomorrow evening, get first dibs if we want it. Harry, it's so beautiful. What parties we could have! You'll love it!'

He released his hand from hers and adjusted his watch.

'I'm sure it's lovely. But we have to think practically.'

'That's just it. It's so cramped with the two of us in the flat now. I mean, it was fine with just me, and it's a lovely place, but with the two of us there's hardly room to swing a cat, which is fine in the short term but, you know, as time goes on...'

She found his hand again and stared down at their fingers, once more interwoven.

'I thought you'd be pleased,' she said. 'You know, after the attack and with everything. You haven't been yourself lately. It would be something to look forward to. We can start to—'

Harry stared at their hands too, his broad long fingers next to her elegant hands that were almost as small as a child's. Sometimes, lately, he wondered if he would feel relieved if Jo decided he was too old for her, too fat, too boring. It was often tiring, trying to live up to her image of him as the perennial joker, the life and soul, the happy-go-lucky optimist to whom everyone warmed. 'The rent on a place like that will be extortionate. When I say practically, I really mean financially.'

'That's the beauty of it,' said Jo. 'I almost forgot. The landlord lives abroad and just wants it let long-term to professional, responsible people. That's what I was discussing with Susie. He gives them a discount because they're good tenants and he can trust them. If she recommends us and gives a written reference, he has pretty much said that he'll charge the same rent – save him having to vet new tenants. It's a six-month contract, because of the rent reduction, but what's six months?'

Jo was beaming again, her face flushed. Harry sipped his drink, eyeing the cucumber suspiciously.

'I think we might be getting ahead of ourselves.'

'Not when you sort everything else out.'

Harry shot her an involuntarily warning glance and watched her smile melt from her face, the sparkle disappear from her eyes in that moment. All of a sudden, he wanted to walk out of there and keep walking, yet her crestfallen face also awoke in him an urge to wrap her in his arms and restore her smile. These conflicting feelings rendered him immobile. The pair of them sat in silence watching Steph deftly prepare a trio of rum cocktails.

'Would you like another drink?' said Harry, tipping his glass to savour the final splash of gin.

Jo was silent for a moment before dropping her voice to barely more than a whisper.

'I would like to start a life with you, to plan a future, for us to be properly together. That is what I would like, Harry.' She took a hurried mouthful of her drink. 'Another gin will not help.'

He examined his fingernails for a moment before looking back at her.

'I'll see you back at the flat,' she said.

'Wait. Jo…'

'You can't have it both ways, Harry.'

She wound her scarf back around her neck with dizzying speed and reached for her coat, draping it around her shoulders in one flowing movement before sweeping away across the room. She walked up the stairs. Harry stared at the space where she had been, inertia gripping him.

'Still busy on the campaign trail, I see?'

Harry turned to encounter the familiar pink-flushed face of James Cowley, his breath fragrant with gin.

'How're you doing, James?' said Harry, unfolding himself to his full height. The two men shook hands.

'Not bad at all. Have you tried my new burger bar yet? Can't say I've seen you in there.'

Last time they'd met, nigh on a year ago, James had regaled Harry with his ambitious plan for his new venture, which involved bringing gourmet meats to Poltowan and changing the face of fast food.

'I'm sorry to say I haven't yet had a chance.' Harry adjusted his watch. 'How is business?'

'You must pop in. One hundred per cent prime beef, handmade sauces – we've just introduced a gluten-free menu too. It's doing well. Come down, have one of our thirty-day dry-aged steak patties – on the house.'

James broke off to place his drinks order with Steph, repeating his question to her and reiterating the virtues of grass-fed beef from locally raised cattle.

'I think you're barking up the wrong tree here, James, I'm veggie.' She shot a knowing glance at Harry.

He smiled, clapping James on the back before settling back on to his bar stool.

James widened his stance. 'You might well laugh, but we cater for all tastes – bean patties, falafel – you name it.'

Steph conceded defeat and promised to pay an imminent visit as she poured two double gins for James, nimbly chopping and adding a sprig of mint to both.

He turned to Harry, clutching the drinks to his ample belly.

'So the campaign – you're not serious, are you?'

Harry assured him that he was.

'Do you know, I thought, good old Harry, he knows an opportunity for a bit of self-promotion when he sees one. But I didn't think you actually believed in it. I didn't think for one minute you would be anti-progress, anti-capitalist...'

Harry exhaled through his nostrils, unsure which point to tackle first. 'I wouldn't go on regional TV if I didn't believe in it, James. And how can putting the good of Poltowan first possibly be construed as anti-progress?'

James looked into Harry's eyes for a moment. 'Well, you've changed, mate. There was a time you'd have welcomed a bit more life in this town, a bit more going on.'

'There's quite enough going on.'

James placed his two drinks back on the bar one by one. A lesser man than Harry might even have felt a quiver of fear at the deliberateness of the act.

'Holy Cow has been open almost a year. Over half my business is from students who appreciate a decent burger when they see it. I'm not alone. The pubs, the coffee shops, the stationers — in fact, I can't think of another business owner who doesn't welcome a lifting of the cap. It's the future.'

Harry shook his head. 'It's short-sighted.'

James shrugged. 'I know you're in the property game but this is not just about houses. If businesses aren't making money it means there's no job creation and locals don't have an income. You need that foundation.'

Harry eased his glasses higher on his nose. 'You've said yourself your burger bar is doing well, and the butcher shop too, I'm sure, so why not be content with that?'

A look of disgust travelled across James' face. His lip curled, eyes darkened. 'It's business, Harry. You see an opportunity, a market, an opening, and you exploit it. It's what any good entrepreneur is about. Has been since time immemorial. You've done it yourself – set up a business, tapped into a need, serviced a community. It's a bit hypocritical to stop others doing the same.'

'It's – greed. When it's at the expense of the community, it's greed.'

Harry felt bold and strong as he spoke, but quickly braced himself for a verbal onslaught. James had always had a short fuse, forever smashing his guitar up and walking out of practice sessions, even leaving them in the lurch in the middle of a gig once.

'You can't see the bigger picture, can you, Harry? That always was your problem. It's all about you.'

Harry was saved by James' companion, who called across the bar just at that moment, enquiring loudly what had become of his drink.

James picked up the two glasses again, his cheeks a deep red, his eyes bulging. He put his face close to Harry's, eyes level with Harry's chin, his confidence boosted by his own generous girth. 'You're on your own, mate. And who knows? Maybe I've got another business idea up my sleeve that relies on this expansion because I don't see it as greed.' A tiny globule of spittle exited his mouth and landed on Harry's glasses. 'And I'm not done yet.'

Harry took off his glasses and slowly wiped the left lens. 'Nor am I, James. Nor am I.'

Steph appeared at the bar, her arms folded.

'We're not talking to you, sweetheart,' said James, allowing his eyes to rest on Steph's cleavage. 'You stick to what you're good at – serving the drinks.'

James turned to walk away, muttering under his breath.

Harry touched his arm lightly, but firmly enough to stop him in his tracks. 'I'd be quick with an apology if I were you.'

James stared at Harry, his eyes burning with indignation, his fat hands gripping the two now warm glasses of gin, the ice long-since melted. 'Sorry, love,' he said eventually, still eyeballing Harry. 'No harm meant.'

He pushed his face close to Harry's. 'Don't let all that TV

stuff go to your head, will you?' He smirked, rejoining his companion, blaspheming as he got to the table.

'You didn't have to, Harry,' said Steph. 'I'm more than capable of dealing with his sort. He's harmless.'

'I know, I know. Sorry, Steph. I couldn't help it. The man can be an arse.'

She swept his glass up and smiled at him. 'You've got enough battles to fight without fighting mine as well.'

؆

As Harry left he heard her unmistakable voice carrying along the corridor. His heart sank and he hesitated a moment, wondering if it would be wise to retreat to the gents until she had passed. But he was too late, her voice growing louder, her laughter more cacophonous. He could even smell the waft of her perfume. She came into view just as he reached the doorway.

'Harry Manchester, good evening to you.'

'Dawn.'

He stood back to let her and her companion past but she took it as an invitation to talk.

'It's a shame we missed each other. Like ships in the night.'

'It's probably not, Dawn, all things considered.'

She rested her fingertips on his arm, a look of grave concern stealing over her face.

'I hope we aren't going to let professional differences get in the way of our friendship Harry.'

He looked her in the eye, searching for what he assumed to be irony.

'I think it's too late for that, don't you? Civility, perhaps. Friendship? I don't think it was ever that, Dawn. Excuse me.'

He nodded in acknowledgement of her friend and left, the sound of Dawn's laughter echoing behind him in the narrow space. Janice urged her friend towards the bar, embarrassed by her unnecessary impudence.

Harry stepped out into the cold night, closing his eyes briefly as if in silent prayer.

Chapter 11

The bus was almost empty apart from a man at the front who sat devouring a pasty like he hadn't eaten for days. Nell settled into a seat at the back, concerned about turning up smelling of beef and potato, a combination she was sure would not please Dawn.

It pulled away from the end of Tremaine Road and embarked on its short journey to the university campus. She revelled in being able to drink in the familiar from a wholly unfamiliar vantage point and relished the opportunity to peer into her neighbours' gardens in a way she had never dreamed of doing before, raising an eyebrow at a neglected flowerbed here, tutting at a badly pruned bush there, before admonishing herself.

It cheered her that they all looked as bereft as her own after the cold January frosts, each one mirroring the next with their shrunken appearance and bedraggled foliage. Only a line of hardy daffodils brightened the picture, standing to attention along the grass verge near the junction, as if in defiance of the weather.

There were only five other passengers on the bus by the time it reached the campus, each of whom got off at the university. Nell filed off last and walked slowly towards the main building, aware that she was fifty minutes early, yet quietly smug at the efficiency of her new commute. New bus routes were another benefit of a growing university, something she had at first failed to appreciate in the instinctive dread she'd felt at Dawn

Goldberg's announcement. Now she was starting to see, and reap, the advantages.

Nell hovered in the canteen, watching a group of students gathered around a small screen, laughing in unison at a video. She marvelled at their apparent self-assurance, their confidence as they strutted around dressed in what she deemed to be outlandish clothes, with no hint of self-consciousness as they called out to each other, exchanging banter, alive in the moment.

But most of all, she envied them their endless opportunities, the time that stretched yawningly ahead of them. Whoever said youth is wasted on the young was right, she thought wistfully as she sat down with her coffee.

She allowed herself to wonder once again what might have been between her and Harry if her sprained ankle hadn't scuppered her chances, spun her life off in a different direction, the same twist of fate simultaneously delivering Sylvia into Harry's arms.

She finished her coffee, butterflies starting to dance in her stomach, and began her amble across the square to the building that housed Dawn Goldberg's office. Her high heels made a reassuringly professional clip-clop on the paving stones as she approached, her new handbag hanging daintily on her arm.

The poster arrested her as soon as she rounded the corner. It was a picture of a smiling Dawn Goldberg, yet the bright red letters making up 'Poltowan' were being squeezed so tightly together between her superimposed oversized fists that the T and the O were non-existent. The tag line below, in a matching font, read: 'Dawn Goldmine – squeezing the life out of Poltowan'.

Nell stopped, unsure what to do. As she examined the poster a second time Dawn Goldberg's red Mazda cruised into the car park, a rapid beat reverberating from within before coming to an abrupt end as the engine halted. Nell reached a hand towards the poster. Janice appeared behind her then, a bunch of keys jangling noisily at her hip. Her greeting was cut short as she too absorbed the impact of the image plastered in front of them.

With Dawn now marching towards them across the car park, Janice made a stab at one corner of the artwork, attempting to rip it free, but it had been painstakingly laminated and secured with a staple gun. She tugged harder, urging Nell to grab the other corner, but even with the two of them pulling, the poster would not budge.

'Ladies, is there a problem?' chirped Dawn as she arrived level with them, her tone intimating that any issue would surely be a trifling one that she could almost certainly deal with, single-handed and without fuss.

Dawn fell silent for a moment as the reluctant parting of Nell and Janice revealed her own image looking back at her, her hair slightly unsatisfactorily curled on the left-hand side and her mouth too wide for her liking. Then her eyes fell on the cartoon hands and the damning tagline.

'We've been trying to remove it, Dawn, but it's stapled very securely.' Janice shook her bunch of keys purposefully. 'I've got a staple remover inside,' she added, defiantly.

Dawn swanned straight past and through reception before disappearing into her office, just a luxurious waft of Chanel No. 5 lingering behind her. It certainly beat beef and potato.

Nell edged into the building behind a bustling Janice. She placed her handbag on the more modest desk she knew was hers and stood inspecting her newly painted nails. Dawn's office door clicked softly shut while Janice charged outside, staple gun in hand, to remove the offending item.

When Janice didn't return promptly Nell followed her outside, only to find her red-faced and tugging roughly at the corners of the poster, the lethal-looking tool clasped tightly in her fist.

'Can I help?' said Nell.

Janice glanced up at her. 'Bloody thing. This is not a good start, not a good start at all. Dawn will be going absolutely ballistic in there – quietly, granted, but absolutely bloody ballistic.'

With that the final corner came free and Janice went bowling backwards, Nell reaching out to catch her arm just as she was about to pivot off into the perfectly tended flowerbed.

'Whoever did this…' Janice's empty threat tailed off into the cool morning air and she straightened her jacket before marching back inside.

'What can I do? Make coffee?' Nell ventured.

'Good idea, Nell. It is Nell, isn't it? But don't take Dawn's cup in – I'll do that. It's best that I handle her when she's like this.' Janice widened her eyes as if warning of all the possible horrors that could befall them when Dawn Goldberg was in just such a mood.

Nell made her way down the corridor to the small kitchen she had seen when she came for her interview, pleased to extricate herself from the decidedly odd atmosphere in the main office. On her last visit, Dawn and Janice had appeared almost like a double act, firing off each other with quick quips and finishing each other's sentences while bustling around the office. Nell had sensed that it would be a very jolly place to work, and she had missed being part of a tight-knit team.

She made a pot of coffee and carried it through to the office with three bone china mugs and a jug of milk. No sooner had she placed it down on the desk than Janice arrived at her elbow, picking up one of the mugs and disappearing back to the kitchen.

'She won't drink out of that one. She's very particular. You weren't to know.' Janice returned seconds later with a large mug and began to pour the coffee. 'This should help a little. At least, I hope it will,' she said, more to herself than to Nell, before tapping on Dawn's door. Nell didn't hear any response but Janice crept in anyway, the door closing behind her.

It was some twenty minutes before she re-emerged. Nell sat at her desk, sipping her coffee and flicking through a university brochure from the year before, thinking how attractive the campus looked in the photos, how impressive the facilities, how alluring the golden beach and expanse of blue sea.

'We have recently invested in a new green screen and motion-capture studio, designed for shooting actors, practical special effects and miniatures, in addition to motion-capture data acquisition.'

Nell raised her eyebrows. She had no idea what a green screen was or what miniatures might entail, but she was sure it sounded like state-of-the-art technology and nodded approvingly.

'Poltowan prides itself on being a small but thriving community, differentiated from city universities by its homely vibe, where students and residents enjoy a harmonious and symbiotic relationship. The emphasis here is on quality, not quantity, with every student valued for their individuality and unique input.'

Nell sighed and flicked over the page. She glanced up at the discarded poster of Dawn squeezing the life out of Poltowan and marvelled at the work that had gone into creating the monstrous hands and achieving the seamless effect of Dawn appearing to rise up out of the poster. It was laminated so precisely too – hardly an impromptu act of rebellion conceived in a fit of rage. Whoever had worked it up was clearly a gifted creative type who had invested both thought and time. Perhaps they had used the green screen to make it? Now that would be ironic.

'So your first job, Nell. It is Nell, isn't it?'

Dawn Goldberg appeared next to her, a sheaf of paper in her hand. She didn't wait for an answer before launching into a dizzying set of demands for her new office furniture, complete not just with specific tones but also favoured materials plus artwork from a noted artist.

'Just prints, mind,' she said, waving her finger. 'I've got a tight budget to stick to for this office refurb, even if it is long overdue. Anyway, I've already got a couple of his originals at home.'

Dawn began to retreat into her office before spinning around.

'Welcome on board, by the way. You'll be happy here.'

She snatched the laminated poster up from Janice's desk on her way past and bolted once more into her lair.

In the sanctity of her office, Dawn stood and stared at the poster before placing it calmly into her shredder. The machine began whirring enthusiastically before grinding to a noisy halt, Dawn's smiling face staring back at her as her impressive if slightly unruly mane of hair vibrated violently with each judder of the machine. Dawn switched it off at the mains before retrieving the image awkwardly from its teeth, a pathetic gnawing at the bottom of the laminate the only sign that it had been anywhere near a shredder. She opened her desk drawer and shoved it in, hesitating as she closed it.

Seconds later she opened it again and retrieved a miniature vodka bottle, swigging from it before replacing it carefully in the drawer. She turned to face Michael, who looked sympathetically back at her from the garden. He understood that a little artificial lift was needed at such a traumatic time. He didn't judge her, not today.

She took a deep breath and turned back to her desk, eyeballing her father. He was as she had anticipated – looking less understanding, one eyebrow seemingly raised slightly in disapproval. She flicked the photo frame over and sank into her chair, bringing her laptop screen to life with the touch of a button. She would get Hornblower on the case. She could trust him to find the perpetrator; put his relentless search for truth and honesty to good use for once.

'Andy. Not interrupting, am I? Good. My office, please.' Dawn replaced the phone and licked the taste of spirits from her upper lip.

Nell knew nothing about interior design, and while she had obediently written down the various hues Dawn expressly liked and disliked, she was unsure what most of them were. She had asked Dawn to repeat one shade, Clunch, three times before deciding that she had, after all, heard her correctly, even if it did sound like an inebriated attempt at a midday meal. Another, Smoked Trout (firmly on Dawn's favoured list), had severely tested her ability to maintain a poker face, while Elephant's Breath had finally seen the collapse of Nell's hitherto inscrutable features, revealing her slightly protruding teeth and a wealth of laughter lines.

Dawn's stern gaze had prompted her to regain her composure rapidly, her head dipped slightly lower than was necessary as she continued with her list.

'And chairs… for god's sake, no cheap plastic. I'm of a certain age and I need good support. Perhaps one of those HÅG Capsize swivels, although I've no idea what they sell for. But you can't put a price on spinal health.'

By lunchtime Nell's head was spinning with lockable tilts, retardant polyesters and wipe-clean arm rests, not to mention a veritable rainbow of colours and sub-shades, but by mid-afternoon she felt she had a handle on her first task, even beginning to relish the process as she created a shortlist for Dawn's approval.

It was during their afternoon tea break that Nell managed to chat to Janice alone in the kitchen. She dared to ask how Dawn was after her shock this morning.

'She's tough. She'll bounce back in no time. But it's so upsetting when something like that happens. It takes a bit of time to get yourself together again, as it would for any of us.'

Nell agreed, lowering her voice before she asked, 'Has it happened before, this sort of thing?'

Janice heated the teapot with boiling water, swilling it round several times before watching as it spiralled into the sink. She took four tea bags from the jar and dropped them into the pot, one by one.

'She's in such a high-profile position, that's the thing. Would you pass the teacups, Nell?'

Nell passed three china cups from the cupboard. Janice handed one back and nodded towards the draining board at the large individual cup turned upside down.

Nell swapped them over.

'And what with this proposal to increase the number of students,' continued Janice. 'Poor thing, she's doing it for the good of the university, she knows what's best, of course she does, but it puts her right in the firing line.'

Janice paused to look directly at Nell, shaking her head vigorously. 'I couldn't do it, God forbid. And she's got that estate agent trying to undermine her cause every step of the way, much good it'll do him. I don't think he quite knows what an unstoppable force our Dawn is. Although—'

A sudden anxiety gripped Nell as Janice mentioned Harry's name, a palpable fear of what she might say, what unkind words might be spoken, unable to be unsaid.

'I know Harry Manchester actually.' Nell picked up a crumpled tea towel and folded it over her arm before placing it back on the work surface.

'Oh, I see. Well, I feel sorry for him if I'm honest, Nell. Dawn can be quite ruthless.'

'I've known him for years. He's no pushover himself.'

Nell paused to consider the possible imprudence of her own words. 'But he does seem to have underestimated what he's taken on. I mean, as you say, Dawn is quite a force to be reckoned with.'

Harry's vivid blue eyes swam back into Nell's mind with readiness and clarity. A sense of his voice, his height, his gentle manner rushed through her.

'I suppose Dawn isn't happy about this concert,' she said, a note of concern in her voice.

Janice stopped pouring the tea and stared at her. 'What concert?'

Nell's cheeks began to burn with an unfamiliar heat. She wracked her brains for a swift response, quickly considering whether ignorance, deafness or plain stupidity would wash, but she was not one to dabble in untruths and she knew she was rumbled. Ambiguity was her only friend.

'Oh, well, I don't know the details – and it may not be happening at all – but there was talk of a concert in Poltowan to, you know, raise awareness of Harry's campaign to keep the cap.'

Nell repeated the slogan in a slightly embarrassed way, conscious that it sounded a bit lame when not shouted with gusto while waving a homemade placard.

Janice stirred the teapot, crashing the spoon against its ceramic sides. 'Right. Thank you, Nell. That is very interesting indeed. Biscuits are in the cupboard.'

She scooted out of the kitchen with Dawn's special teacup in her hand, a slightly oversized version of the others as if it was itself head of the teacup hierarchy. As she emerged into the main office Andy Hornblower appeared, slightly breathless, falling through the main door with his trademark look of hope. Janice's patience with Andy had long ago worn out. She had willed him to give up on trying to change Dawn's mind on certain issues, or impose his own suggestions on her in his constant quest to please. She had felt almost sorry for him. Now she took a certain pleasure in seeing him crushed by Dawn, again and again, so oblivious was he to the way of things. If people couldn't learn from their own mistakes, why should she waste her pity on them?

They greeted each other in a rather perfunctory fashion before Janice asked, 'Is Dawn expecting you?'

'She summoned – that is, called me a moment ago. I came straight here.'

Janice glanced down at the teacup in her hand and back at Andy, taking in his crumpled suit.

'One moment.'

She returned seconds later and nodded for him to enter, hovering by the door as it closed gently.

Dawn was straight to the point. She handed the poster to Andy and told him to find who'd made it, and fast.

Andy held it in his hand for a while, frowning.

'They've certainly got talent. It's very – professional.'

Dawn picked up the photo of her father and placed it back the right way up.

'Let me know as soon as you've found out.'

He hesitated, as if readying himself to unleash another incisive remark or penetrating question, his forehead creased with concern.

'Goodbye,' said Dawn, swivelling around to face Michael, her iPad in her hand. She waited until she heard Andy shuffle out and the door click to behind him.

∽

Janice stood next to Dawn, the two of them looking out at Michael as a light rain fell. He looked back undeterred, muscles glistening under the damp sheen. If anything, a little rain added to his appeal, thought Dawn, almost as if he had been lathered in oil, the sinewy definition even more pronounced.

'It'll be a spoiled student, unhappy that Mummy and Daddy can't run to a penthouse suite on the river,' said Dawn. 'Well, welcome to the real world. When I was at university, I shared a number of awful dives. It was just the way it was. The student life. Little bastards today don't know they're born.'

'Some other news has come to my attention, Dawn.'

She detected a note of nervousness in her friend's voice. Dawn narrowed her eyes at Michael and waited.

'It seems that Harry Manchester might be planning a concert of sorts. Some sort of music event to get his point across.'

Dawn remained impassive, eyes trained on Michael's right thigh.

'Nell told me. Apparently she knows him – has done for years.'

'Well, who knew our new recruit could be so useful?' said Dawn, finally turning to look at Janice. 'That said, if she is indiscreet about that man's news, she will be indiscreet about our plans. Who knows what information she might carelessly drip feed him, given half the chance?'

'Oh, I don't think it's like that, Dawn. I don't get the impression they're close. She says she hasn't seen him for some time. I think she's actually more friendly with his estranged wife. Sylvia, is it?'

'Well, we need to be mindful. You know my motto, Jan. You can't trust anyone except yourself. And even that's debatable sometimes.'

Janice laughed, placing her hand fleetingly on Dawn's arm.

'So when is it, this concert?'

'I don't have any details yet but I'll do some digging.'

'Not that I'm particularly worried. What does he expect a concert to achieve? As I said before, it's the Councillors who matter, and the press, not the masses – not that I'd expect him to understand that. He's an estate agent after all, not Isaac Newton.'

Janice laughed obligingly.

'And on that note, I'm seeing Jason Redthorne next week.'

Dawn paused a moment before pre-empting her friend's next question.

'He is only the second-in-command on Cornwall Council's Strategic Planning Committee. A much better use of time than putting on a bit of music in a church hall. I mean, what's Harry Manchester going to do – ask everyone to gather round his mobile phone?'

After Janice had left the room, Dawn trained her gaze once more on Michael's firm buttocks, and pondered how such an event could serve, not to communicate Harry Manchester's grand vision to the community, but to show them what a foolish and deluded man he was.

Chapter 12

Sylvia had read the front page of the *Poltowan Post* several times before texting Harry. The flippant tone of the article had stirred something within her. The strength of the feeling pierced the apathy she usually felt. Sylvia was angry and the urgency of it took her by surprise.

Her text was deliberately casual, merely checking that Harry had seen that week's paper and offering a couple of fittingly barbed comments about the editorial team. He had responded with a phone call half an hour later, cheered by the contact and touched by her obvious exasperation on his behalf. He'd had time to get over the lazy journalism and Dennis' apparent deference to Dawn Goldberg, instead focusing on listening to the concerns of the stream of community members who kept appearing in his office, and imagining the success of the concert that would allow him to galvanise local people into voicing their support to the Council.

Harry was pleased to hear the rise and fall in Sylvia's voice today, the tonal range consistent with an 'up' day rather than the depressed monotone he had come to dread.

'I'm surprised they've shown themselves to be so biased,' she said, watching a blackbird peck fruitlessly at the waterlogged earth.

'Dennis is in thrall to Dawn Goldberg, Sylve. She's been schmoozing him – I saw them together last week. He's a sucker for a bit of feminine charm.'

'Show me a man who isn't.'

The blackbird fluttered up and away into the grey sky.

Harry cleared his throat, waving to a man who was frowning through the office window.

'Justice will prevail, don't you worry,' said Harry. 'I've got a couple of tricks up my sleeve to cut straight to the heart of the community, really make the Council sit up and take notice.'

'A concert?' said Sylvia, reverting to her world-weary tone.

'How do you know?'

'Nell mentioned it.'

'How does Nell know?'

'You know what Poltowan is like, Harry – tell the right person and word travels fast.'

He wracked his brains. This was Ludo's doing. It was probably all over Facebook by now and even Harry didn't quite know the full plan yet. His idea for a venue had been acclaimed by Ludo as mind-blowingly simple. But it relied on Sylvia's co-operation.

'Thing is, Sylve, we need a venue.'

His words were met with patient silence but he continued, unfazed.

'We were gunning for the town square – you know, under the Council offices, centre of the action yada yada, or failing that the beach, but we can't get the right licence in time and there's some confusion over whether it is deemed to be a political event – ridiculous, I know – because it can be seen as a protest of sorts, so...'

The man who'd been hovering outside on the pavement finally came in. Harry put his hand over the mouthpiece.

'One minute, sir, I'll be right with you. Please, take a seat.'

He returned to the call, sounding rushed.

'We were thinking perhaps our two-acre field would fit the

bill. One night only, of course, and there's the access gate at the back. It would finish at eleven o'clock. And the beauty is that it would be a private event – we wouldn't need licences or permission from anyone.'

The silence continued. Harry caught the eye of the man sitting in the corner of the room.

'That's what we're proposing, if you're amenable to it.'

Sylvia's struggling spirits sank lower. She looked beyond the garden to the trees lining their two acres of land at the back. It had until recently been rented out to horse owners who used it for grazing, but now it lay fallow and overgrown, forgotten. She used to like seeing the horses over the hedge.

'I think we should sell up, Harry.'

'What?' He stood up quickly, overturning his pot of pens with a crash. He turned his back on the waiting customer.

'I'll be amenable, as you put it, to your concert, as long as you're amenable to us putting the house up for sale. It's time, Harry.'

He finished the call abruptly. He clapped his hands together in a gesture of over-exaggerated glee and turned his attention to the new arrival with Sylvia's words still playing over in his head. The man spoke at length about what he was looking for, about downsizing since his wife had died, about how the town was changing and how he had seen Harry's support for the community.

Harry nodded and murmured but the words fell like snow around his ears, each floating lazily towards him yet eluding his grasp. He scribbled some notes on his notepad but at the end of the conversation all he could see was 'sell up', scratched over and over in the bottom corner of the page, underlined three times.

He put a note in the diary to visit the man the following week, scribbling down his address and phone number as if in a trance, shaking his hand too hard and for too long when he left the office.

Harry grabbed his keys and shouted to Aaron, who was doing battle with the photocopier in the back room, before striding quickly down the hill towards his car.

Just as he started the ignition his phone rang, Jo's name flashing up on the screen. He cursed under his breath, debating for a moment whether to answer it.

'You OK, honey?' he managed eventually.

'How's your day?'

'Oh, you know. Listen, I'm just dashing off to meet Ludo – is it important, can I call you later?'

'Just a quick one, baby, I'm on lunch duty. Susie said can we make it six o'clock instead of five-thirty tonight – she's going to be a bit late back. I said it was fine but thought I'd double check?'

Harry looked up, the ominous grey sky even more threatening through the tinted sunroof of his Mercedes. He had completely forgotten about viewing the penthouse apartment. He had agreed to it to placate Jo after their disagreement in the wine bar, confident she would soon see that a place like that, overlooking the river, was beyond their means. After all, he didn't want to seem intransigent. He just needed more time.

He flicked the conversation on to hands-free and began to reverse. 'I suppose so. Look, I've got to go, see you there at six o'clock.'

'Love you.'

He accelerated up the hill, eyes narrowed in concentration, sensing that everything he knew – the foundation of his life – was slipping away from him at high speed, and he had no idea how to stop it.

❦

Sylvia was surprised to see him standing at her front door. She had fully expected a call back and a lengthy and emotional monologue. She hadn't expected him to turn up.

She stood back to let him in. Harry strode straight into the kitchen, dropping his keys noisily on the work surface. Sting leaped off the stool and on to the floor, rudely awoken by the interruption, before eyeing Harry sleepily, then fondly, and rubbing against his leg. Harry bent to ruffle his fur perfunctorily.

'Tea?' Habit compelled Sylvia to begin filling the kettle.

'I haven't got time. Sit down. Please, just talk to me.' He lingered close behind her as she stood at the sink, the stream of water from the tap running painfully slowly into the spout of the kettle. He reached around her and turned the tap off.

'Sylvia. Please.'

Harry removed his glasses and swiped his thumb and forefinger over his eyes, meeting at the bridge of his nose. His glasses remained in his hand, naked blue eyes seeking Sylvia's. She tried to avoid his gaze yet something about those deep, kind pools that she knew so well tugged uncomfortably at her heart. They stood facing each other for a moment.

'I don't know what you want me to say, Harry.' Sylvia's words were measured, soft. She clasped her hands in front of her, her eyes now trained on Sting.

'We are no longer a couple, we're married only in name,' she continued. 'It seems the most sensible course of action. I don't need all this.' She gestured to the room around her, the house beyond that, and in her mind saw the gardens extending further, the sprawling town around them, the unknown stretching away beyond.

Harry scratched his forehead. 'But it's early days. Such early days. We haven't made any final decisions. We haven't even discussed us, not really.'

'You're with someone else, Harry.'

Sylvia looked up at him for the first time. His eyes were pained, the blue turned to grey suddenly. She looked quickly away. Sting was licking at his paws, oblivious to the tension.

'I don't know if it's serious. I don't know—' He turned away. 'I left because you told me to. It was you who pushed it… who pushed me away.'

'Because it wasn't working. You don't need me. We want different things. And you stayed out of kindness, we both know that.'

Harry shook his head in exasperation, gripping the work surface with his free hand, words failing him. He replaced his glasses.

'Jo is testament to that. You wouldn't be living with her so – so quickly if things had been right between us.'

Sylvia wished she'd put the kettle on in spite of Harry's protest. The stubborn silence that followed was almost unbearable, rapidly expanding to fill the room and creaking under its own weight. Right on cue, Sting began to lap noisily at his milk. They both turned to watch.

Harry suddenly felt as if he was observing the scene from above, the two of them standing in their once shared kitchen, unable to voice the sentiments that could transport them back again to that once happy place. Yet everything she said was true, her logic, as always, sound. So why did it feel so wrong? Why did he feel so desperate?

The kitchen clock struck 3.30 p.m.

'I've got to go. I'm meeting Ludo. Look, Sylvia, we need to talk properly. Can—'

'We don't, Harry. It's too hard.'

She made as if to lay her hand on his arm but diverted its course at the last moment, instead smoothing her skirt repeatedly downwards.

'We know what needs to be done – well, I do, even if you don't. Please put The Oaks on the market next week. You're moving on, I'm stuck here. I need to move on too. This house—' She hesitated. 'It's swallowing me whole.'

◦§

Ludo stood up, his long arms outstretched in welcome. Next to him was an attractive young woman with wild blonde hair tinged with bold red streaks. She had big brown eyes. She wore tight black leggings and a multi-layered lacy top. She was strikingly beautiful with a calm demeanour, an air of quiet confidence. Harry had been impressed by her video on YouTube, and genuinely moved by her effortless mastery of the guitar. Now, in the flesh, he could see she had presence too. A shiver ran up his spine.

She remained seated, letting Ludo make the introductions.

'This is the legend that is Harry Manchester. Harry – this is the ridiculously talented Rockstr.'

Harry bent to shake Rockstr's small hand and she smiled up at him, suddenly bashful.

'So sorry I'm late, guys,' said Harry, rubbing his cold hands together.

Ludo led the charge, enthusiasm evident in his deployment of a barrage of lengthy words, his arms flailing along with them. It was agreed that Rockstr would headline the concert, such was her fledgling but loyal following, and that Josh Toddington and his band would support.

Harry was summoning all his mental resources to keep his mind firmly on track, continually hauling it back from thoughts of Sylvia, but he could not recall having heard the name Josh Toddington before.

'Oh, he's quite a find actually,' said Ludo, puffing out his chest. 'Rockstr here suggested him as an up and coming talent and I thought the name rang a bell – you know… Toddington. Anyway, did some digging and it only turns out he's Darren Toddington's son!'

Harry frowned at Ludo.

He laughed, smile wide, eyes alight with enthusiasm.

'Come on, man, he's only one of the main guys on Cornwall Council! His boy is a budding musician, lead singer of The Drones.'

'They're pretty good,' added Rockstr, encouragingly.

'Doesn't even matter if they're any good,' said Ludo, wiping froth from his top lip. 'Point is, we get him to get his old man down to his first proper gig and – bingo. One key target onside. Who knows? Maybe Dazza will bring some mates as well?'

Harry nodded and winked at Rockstr. 'He's pretty good,' he said, gesturing at Ludo. 'But don't tell him I said so.'

'So, the venue, my friend, is it all sorted?' asked Ludo, his eyes wide, expectant.

Harry placed his hands on his knees, massaging his tender kneecap. 'All sorted. The concert will be held at mine. Well, ours.'

He turned to address Rockstr. 'We've got a couple of acres at the back of the house being put to no good use at the moment. A mile or so out of town. Not a bad spot. We'll need a marquee, of course, but that's easily sorted.'

'We're thinking maybe three hundred people,' said Ludo. 'Two bands, a chat from the one and only Mr Manchester in between, bring your own beers, and Bob's your uncle. And we have a twenty-one-day countdown… bring it on!'

He pumped his fist. 'I love it when a plan comes together.'

'I can't even tell you how massive this is,' said Rockstr over the rim of her teacup. 'It's going to be the goat.'

She held Ludo's gaze for a moment and Harry suddenly sensed the chemistry between them. Their limbs had been continually colliding for the past half an hour, knowing looks sliding easily from one to the other. He felt like an onlooker.

He also had no idea what the "goat" referred to, but no explanation was forthcoming. It was time to leave. He confirmed a fee with Rockstr and thanked them both, clapping Ludo on the back.

'Don't worry, fella, it'll come together like a dream, scout's honour. You just get working on your words. It'll be like Corbyn on the Pyramid Stage all over again.'

'I trust it'll be better than that,' said Harry, waving his hand aloft as he left the bar, and feeling as if at least one troubling weight had been lifted from his shoulders.

It was more from habit than need that Harry scurried to his car through the rapidly darkening January afternoon. He lowered his large frame into the leather seat and sat for a moment while his breathing slowed, daring to close his eyes. Sylvia had looked even thinner today, her shoulder bones protruding slightly from her jumper, her face surely more gaunt than before. He replayed the scene in his head, picturing her apparent detachment, her dispassionate assessment of their situation.

His voice resonated within the car's void and his phone lit up in response. It began dialling Nell, who answered within a couple of rings, sounding slightly startled as if distrustful of the device in her hand.

'Is it Sylvia? Is everything OK?' she asked instinctively.

'Everything's fine, Nell. How are you? It's been a while.'

She had missed Harry's deep voice, the comforting quality to it. It was as if, whatever happened, Harry could make it alright. Nell placed one hand on the banister and closed her eyes, letting his words wash pleasingly over her.

When the call ended she placed her mobile back in its customary position on the hall table. She had promised to pop the kettle straight on, but first she hurried upstairs to the bedroom and changed into her red cardigan, before applying some lipstick and squirting her favourite cologne into the air, stepping through the mist with a coquettish smile.

Harry arrived in Tremaine Road moments later, his big car cruising noiselessly to a halt outside her house. She felt a flicker of excitement at the unfamiliar sight, checking the alignment of her bobbed hair once again in the hall mirror before opening the door.

'Harry Manchester, come on in.'

He bent to kiss her on the cheek, inhaling the reassuring womanly fragrance that greeted him.

'It's good to see you. I'll make some tea,' she said.

Harry didn't want more tea. He had just drained two cups and was starting to feel the pressing discomfort in his lower abdomen, but it was easier to agree to the social nicety. He sat awkwardly in the narrow wingback chair by the window, Nell settling herself opposite on the sofa next to the warm glow of the corner light. The fire flickered in the grate and Harry watched the flames trance-like for a moment.

She could not recall him visiting her at home before. Sitting bold and upright in her mother's old chair, he looked almost too big, too grand for her modest house. It had been a while since she'd had a male visitor. His burnished brown leather shoes and navy suit looked incongruous against the pastel pinks of the lounge, his large hands and long fingers dwarfing the cup and saucer.

He had always dressed well, thought Nell, her eyes travelling up over his outstretched legs to the bright white cuffs of his shirt and the starched collar, the precisely knotted tie. For a moment her usually easy flow of chatter deserted her. It was Harry's rich tones that brought her back to the present moment, that and the crashing of his teacup against his saucer as he misjudged the distance to his lap.

'Sorry, Nell. I'm used to a plain old mug.' He placed it on the coffee table between them. 'The thing is, I'm worried about Sylvia. She's been going through one of her black periods and seems to be deteriorating, not getting better. But it's as if she's shut me out – even more so than usual.' He frowned, running his hand over his clean-shaven chin. 'Does she talk to you? Has she said anything?'

Nell cleared her throat, shuffling slightly in her seat.

'Oh, I don't want to compromise you, Nell, that's not why I'm here. I'm not asking you to share confidences, I just —'

Nell shook her head. 'Don't you think I've known you long enough to realise you wouldn't do that? I've no concerns of that sort. Sylvia hasn't really said much to me. She's withdrawn into herself. The shutters have come down since – well, since you left.'

Harry drummed his fingers on the arm of the chair.

'Did she tell you why I left?'

'That's between you two. But I know you're with a young lady now.'

'This isn't about Jo. Sylvia told me to leave, many times. Until finally I did. I didn't want to go. I wanted to stay and help her but she seemed to have given up on us. She said we wanted different things. Left me with nowhere to go but away. I thought it was what she wanted.'

Nell sighed. 'But this Jo – is it serious? I mean, you're already living together.'

Harry watched as the fire spat and crackled suddenly.

'I had little option. My hand was forced. I couldn't stay at Diggory's forever. Jo's was an obvious solution when we started seeing each other. It just happened. She had the space and, well—'

Nell tried to bring the conversation back to Jo, to find out more about this mystery woman, but Harry wouldn't be drawn, sticking doggedly to his own agenda.

'Has Sylvia mentioned she wants to sell the house?'

'Yes, but I don't know how serious she was, Harry. Just a fancy maybe, a whim.'

'I don't know. She seemed pretty dead set on it to me. It's such a big decision to take when I'm not sure if she knows what she really wants. I don't think she's in the right frame of mind to decide on selling our home, not at the moment.'

'You being with Jo has hit her quite hard,' ventured Sylvia, looking down at the cup and saucer in her hands. 'Perhaps she feels she needs to move on from all those shared memories. I mean, that house... it must be a constant reminder of you, of the two of you. And now you've found someone else it must seem quite final.'

'We've been together five minutes. I mean Jo's lovely, she's great, but who knows? Technically I'm still a married man.'

Nell crossed her legs, a thrill in the pit of her stomach as she saw Harry's eyes on her bare calves. Yet Harry barely noticed, despite appearing to watch intently as she placed one slim leg over the other, her skirt falling back and exposing her knees as she did so. He was at that moment fighting an inner battle between his concern for Sylvia and his loyalty to Jo, their two opposing claims giving rise to a dull ache at the nape of his neck.

He stood up, suddenly feeling smothered by the narrow chair, the small, stifling room. 'I won't keep you. I just wanted to see if you knew any more than I did. If she was OK.'

Nell stayed seated, Harry towering over her. She patted the seat next to her. 'Don't rush off, Harry. Stay a moment longer.'

He hesitated slightly before sitting heavily down next to her, the cushion compressing beneath his bulk. Nell wondered if he too remembered their first meeting at the night club, the way he had looked at her, his blue eyes then free from thick-lensed glasses, his face a little thinner, his body firm.

Harry shifted his weight, Nell rising quickly up and down on the cushion next to him in equal and opposite reaction to the changing force.

'If you get a chance, Nell, please try to get over to Sylvia that I am still here for her. I don't want her to feel she has to move, or that Jo has anything to do with this – she hasn't.'

Nell nodded wearily, feeling the familiar sense of frustration towards Sylvia. Despite Jo's presence, Sylvia still had it in her power to rescue her relationship, to recover this man. It was all easily within her grasp. Yet she was blind to it. And the longer she refused to see it, the more likely Harry was to slip away.

Nell watched him staring out of the window into the twilight, as if trying to make sense of the fast-falling darkness. 'I'm at the university now, Harry,' she told him, picking at a loose thread on the cushion as she spoke.

'I hadn't realised. What have they got you doing there?'

'Oh, it's just part-time, three days a week. I'm a general dogsbody. I'm in Dawn Goldberg's office, a sort of PA cum admin assistant.'

Harry studied her face carefully. It was only inches away from his. 'Is that your title?'

'Technically I'm Administrative Assistant for Student Affairs but it sounds a bit grand for what I'm doing. It's a bit of paperwork really.'

Harry massaged his knee thoughtfully. 'Well, you know my

position, Nell. We're on opposing sides at the moment, me and Dawn Goldberg. She's not my favourite person, not in the least. Just watch your back—'

'She seems alright, her and Janice. I'm not there much. They keep me at arm's length.'

Harry frowned and smiled simultaneously. 'I did meet Janice fleetingly. She seemed to be in Dawn's thrall. She'd do well to get out while she still can.'

He stood up, letting the heat of the fire warm his legs for a moment before turning to leave.

'Just give Dawn Goldberg a bit of a wide berth, Nell. She can certainly turn on the charm but she can just as quickly turn it off again.'

Nell stood up to join him, twisting her hands together. 'She knows about the concert you're planning. I accidentally—'

Harry looked blankly at her, battling to suppress his annoyance.

'—told Janice.' Nell screwed up her eyes as if she was in physical pain. 'I didn't mean anything by it, Harry, I just didn't think. Or rather, I assumed she would already know.'

He caught a sudden waft of her perfume, a scent that transported him back to a host of places, a lifetime of shared memories. 'Oh, I shouldn't worry. Ludo's probably let the cat out of the bag already. And we have to start publicising it imminently, we're just finalising some details.'

Nell's expression remained pained.

'Will you come? The girl we've got lined up to sing – she's quite something. One to watch, I think.'

Harry brushed his lips against Nell's cheek at the same time as opening the front door. As he did so 'Bohemian Rhapsody' began to play from his pocket. He turned to her and rolled his eyes, mouthing sorry and stepping back into her hallway again.

Nell stood admiring his authoritative and purposeful air as he took the call, answering brusquely before cutting the caller off.

'You're always in demand.'

'Ha. Another woman calling to see if Harry Manchester does lettings. Well, no, he doesn't.'

Nell laughed.

Harry slipped his phone back into his pocket. 'You will call me if you think I can do anything to help Sylvia?'

'It's probably just time she needs, Harry. And space.'

'You're a good friend, Nell.'

He retreated down the driveway, tapping his key rhythmically on his thumb. Nell pulled half-heartedly at a weed on her front doorstep as Harry stepped away into the evening, the glancing impression of his lips still on her cheek.

৵

Harry wished he'd used Nell's facilities but despite the squeeze on his bladder he had not considered the possibility until he neared the end of her road, the growing discomfort exacerbated by seeing a Graves' For Sale sign outside one of the larger terraced houses. Graves didn't even have their own office in Poltowan yet they had led the way in selling properties to out-of-town investors and, by all accounts, had quite a list of interested landlords on their books.

Harry fidgeted in his seat, flicking a switch to fill the car with an early Genesis track. He hoped a bit of prog rock would take his mind off his screaming stretch receptors, but he had almost passed the point of no return and nothing could distract him. Despite driving a little quicker than he knew he should, he pulled up by the apartments overlooking Poltowan River at 6.10 p.m. He could see Jo's restless silhouette against the entrance hall as she hopped from one foot to the other to keep warm.

The wind was up and the river made a menacing sound somewhere close by in the darkness. The warm glow of the apartment windows looked increasingly inviting.

'Sorry, Jo. I got held up,' Harry half shouted as he disappeared in the other direction, towards the sound of the heavily flowing water.

'Where are you going?'

Harry unzipped his fly and closed his eyes against the bitter wind, relief flooding through him as he emptied his bladder slowly onto the shadowy river bank, deaf to Jo's increasingly exasperated questioning.

'Harry!' she said finally, standing slightly breathless behind him. 'We're already late! What are you—'

Harry continued to pee, eyes and ears closed to any interruption. When he finally did zip up and turn around she had retreated, back across the dark patch of grass and inside the lobby where she was waiting impatiently for the lift to the third floor.

'Sorry. I was desperate,' he said, joining her.

'Surely you could have waited ten minutes. We're late as it is.'

'You might want to wipe your shoes off, looks like—'

Jo looked at her muddy Gabors and gave him a look of distinct displeasure as she stepped away to lean against a wall, taking a tissue from her handbag and dabbing at her earthy heels.

The lift announced its arrival on the ground floor. Harry stepped across the threshold, arm held out to stop the door from closing. He winced at the tinny muzak filling the lobby, sure that he wouldn't be able to abide being assaulted by that every time he stepped in and out of an apartment. He resisted the closing of the lift doors three times before Jo reappeared, pink-cheeked, her mouth set in a stubborn line.

Upstairs the landing was opulent, light and creamy with a wide-open square of space bathed in carefully angled spotlights. Their shoes clicked on the tiled floor.

'Number six,' said Jo, eyes wide as she pushed the bell and took his arm, her annoyance clearly eclipsed by the promise of what lay behind the imposing front door.

Susie was stick-thin with a wide smile on her not unattractive face. She hugged Jo and shook Harry's hand enthusiastically. Jo apologised profusely for their lateness and Harry murmured in agreement, looking over Susie's shoulder at the cavernous lounge and huge flat-screen TV. It even had Sonos multi-room speakers, which streamed music from the wi-fi. He began to drum his fingers against his thighs.

This place was impressive, Harry had to admit. Even on a dark January evening with the allegedly splendid river views and Poltowan skyline swallowed up by the night, the apartment had a luxurious feel.

Jo had leaped ahead of him and was stroking the heavy curtain fabric and marvelling at the high ceilings before yelping with delight at the huge bathroom with its sunken bath. She could already picture herself and Harry up to their necks in bubbles, a bottle of champagne sitting on the wide shelf behind.

'Don't get carried away, Jo,' he told her. 'It's lovely, undoubtedly, but we do need to have a think and do some sums.'

He smiled at Susie in a way that he hoped managed her expectations. When he turned around Jo was standing in the open-plan kitchen, her hands spread proprietorially over the shiny work surface.

'Isn't it amazing, Harry? Imagine when the sun is out and we can see the river too!'

Susie opened the door to the balcony, a blast of frozen air whipping through the toasty room. The three of them stepped outside briefly. Harry began to imagine how it would feel to get home on a summer's evening and come out here, letting the gentle chattering of water wash over him. To his left were the lights of Poltowan, peppering the night sky like jewels. He could make out the church spire against a street light and the row of houses where his grandmother used to live. To the right he could see the roof of the Chyangwens Hotel. It still cut a handsome and imposing figure on the skyline, almost as if it was hewn from the granite beneath. Beyond lay the potent force of the ocean, its presence palpable as it brooded quietly under the night sky.

'Come back in, Harry, it's freezing,' said Jo from the lounge. Susie's hand was poised on the door handle. He stepped reluctantly back inside.

'It's very quiet too, as you can hear,' said Susie. 'Just the sound of the river really, and the odd car. Occasionally people on the footpath but nothing to speak of.'

'The other tenants, do you have much to do with them, Susie?'

'Only to pass the time of day. We all seem to come and go at different times but they seem very pleasant. Professionals, you know, although a couple of them aren't here all the time. Second homes, I think,' she said, dropping her voice to a whisper.

'Don't mention that to Harry,' said Jo, entwining her fingers with his.

'I've seen your campaign, in the paper and on the telly. I think it's great.'

'It's something I believe in very strongly,' he said.

'If it's about saving beautiful Poltowan from ruin then I'm all in favour. We're only moving because we've found a bigger place with a garden. It's on the edge of town so we'll still be around. I wouldn't want to leave Poltowan – we've got it all here.'

'We've a concert coming up actually – end of February.

Perhaps you'd like to come? It's a bit of a marketing event to raise awareness of the campaign and engage with our supporters.'

Jo beamed up at Harry, a suffusion of feelings surging inside.

'I'd love to. Let me know the details. My other half loves his music too.'

'I noticed the sound system.' Harry nodded at the sleek black speakers in the kitchen and lounge. 'That's a good piece of kit.'

'It's what finally sold this place to Gus to be honest. The sound quality is amazing and it follows us wherever we go – even in the bath! He's getting the same kit put in at the new place - apparently!'

'Oh, that bath,' said Jo once again, the image of her and Harry submerged in it swimming back to mind.

'Did you see the wine rack built into the kitchen unit, Jo? Come and have a quick look,' said Susie, disappearing back into the living space.

Harry said his goodbyes while Jo gushed over the apartment a little longer before reluctantly stepping back over the threshold.

'I'll let you know once we've chatted, Susie. I don't want anyone else snapping it up until we decide.'

'Listen, you've got a week or so before the owner comes back to sort it out so no rush – well, not much of one.'

Susie's laughter reverberated around the landing as Jo and Harry glided down to the lobby in the lift, Harry bracing himself for Jo's entreaties when the door shut. But the onslaught didn't come. He looked down at the top of her head, tipping her chin up towards him when she stayed silent. He saw that her eyes were brimming with tears.

'Jo, honey, what's wrong?'

'I just love it. And I love you. I want us to be together there. I can see us together there, properly together.'

Harry wrapped her tightly in his arms, his chin resting lightly on top of her head as they quickly descended to the ground floor. The doors slid open and he gestured to her to step out.

'It's a chance for a proper start, Harry,' she said, pulling a tissue from her handbag.

He smiled at her and rubbed his hands together. 'Let's go and get some dinner. I'm starving.'

Chapter 13

Rockstr was trying to immerse herself in researching a paper on the development of hip-hop and the culture wars in 1980s New York. She had given up trying to work in her room when her neighbour's music began vibrating through the thin wall. She didn't have the energy to knock again.

Downstairs in the communal kitchen there had been five strangers lounging around the table, including two with their heavy black boots resting on the table top itself, while three bodies were still slumbering in various parts of the shared lounge. She had tried to book one of the individual study rooms Poltowan University had made so much of on her induction day, but they were all fully booked until the following week.

When she arrived in the university study centre there was only one desk free, situated under the rumbling combi-boiler in the darkest corner of the room. She began to wend her way over, only to be beaten to it by a woman who seemed to appear from nowhere, swiftly settling into the chair and laying her books, tablet and coffee in front of her in a manner that suggested she would be some time.

Rockstr retreated across the large concrete square and up some stone steps into the library itself.

'The library closes in forty-five minutes,' said a voice from behind the reception desk, enunciating each word with great precision as if fighting with their local accent.

Rockstr sighed and swore very quietly under her breath.

'Early closing on a Friday,' the disembodied voice continued sternly.

Rockstr headed up another flight of stairs to the free desk area. She had to get the paper finished by Monday lunchtime, giving her less than three days to research and write it. She had already had one abortive attempt to read up on the subject the day before, when she had been unceremoniously kicked out of a vacant study room by a lecturer who insisted his tutor group had nowhere else to go. She had ended up sitting in the corner of a corridor against a warm central heating pipe, her papers propped up against her knees. The Student Union had been trying for some time to push for opening the library twenty-four hours a day, but they were constantly rebuffed with cries of lack of funding. Rockstr eventually found a corner desk and slammed her laptop bag onto the table.

She was just nearing the end of the first page of reading when she heard raised voices outside. Through the window Rockstr spied Dawn Goldberg talking to one of the music lecturers, Phil Pullen. His hands were dug deep into his customary low-slung jeans, and he shook his head slowly, repeatedly, glancing around periodically in a vain search for support. Every so often his neck would jolt backwards, his eyes widening, followed by more head shaking.

Rockstr jumped up, her chair scraping backwards, before descending the stairs two at a time and exiting the university building at the top of the stone steps. She had been hoping to catch Phil Pullen about the paper she was working on, to pick his brains about the angle she had chosen. She had emailed him the day before but knew from past experience that he would be unlikely to respond for a couple of days, such was the demand for his attention.

She watched from the top of the steps for a moment, instinct telling her that it was not a good time to interrupt. The conversation continued in the same way for another minute before Dawn Goldberg delivered her parting words, head tilted to one side, that sanctimonious smile on her face, and walked away. Phil Pullen stood stock still for a moment, his eyes still trained on the space where she had been standing moments before. It was a while before he continued on his way, eyes downcast, the familiar slouch even more pronounced.

Rockstr skipped down the steps and jogged after him, calling his name. Eventually he turned around, his pale face even more ashen than usual.

'Phil, have you got a minute? I wanted a quick word about my hip-hop paper.'

He looked blankly back at her.

'It won't take long.'

He guided her into the lobby of the library out of the chill wind, finally finding his tongue. 'Sorry, Rockstr, of course. How can I help?'

Rockstr explained her dilemma, her uncertainty about whether to concentrate on the lyrics and how they reflected the culture or whether to widen her focus.

At first he nodded as if he was in tune with her thinking, but when she'd finished speaking he continued to nod – automatically, it seemed.

Rockstr shifted her gaze momentarily to the doors, still sliding open and closed mesmerically. When she glanced back his head nodding had come to a stop, and he delivered an articulate and precise answer of the sort she had come to expect from him, reassuring her about the angle she had taken and encouraging her persistence. Then he took her elbow and lowered his voice, telling her what a great student she was and how much potential she had shown in the first part of the year.

'You excel at all the practical aspects – you are a very gifted musician – but don't neglect the theory, you are more than capable of excelling at that too. Don't lose focus. Whatever happens, stick to it.'

Rockstr returned to the library through the sweeping automatic doors.

'Library's closing in ten minutes,' came the voice from beyond, a note of boredom creeping in.

Rockstar paused to peer at the reception desk but still couldn't identify the source of the words.

She packed her books up and joined the exodus of bodies into the wintry late afternoon, a hint of bonfire smoke drifting in the dank air. As she made her way across the square and up the path towards her halls she saw Dawn Goldberg again, swanning along the route perpendicular to hers, their paths set to cross.

Rockstr steeled herself, one hand gripping her bag strap tightly. The Vice Chancellor was striding along at quite a pace, her top-heavy frame almost bouncing along the path. Her head was bowed, eyes fixed on the ground. As she pivoted at right angles on to the new path, Rockstr was forced to lunge onto the wet grass, Dawn Goldberg completely unaware of her presence, let alone the emergency diversion she'd had to make. Her blatant disregard fuelled Rockstr's determination to speak up and be heard.

'Excuse me? Dawn?'

The VC whirled around, a smile finally forcing its way on to her features, its falsity permeating her face. She shifted her large bag from one hand to the other, pushing the memory of Phil Pullen's face with its barely visible ginger eyelashes – blinking with incomprehension – to the back of her mind.

'When I chose to study at Poltowan, Vice Chancellor, it was because we were offered a boutique experience, easy access to lecturers, individual study rooms and, like, a more personal experience than we'd get at the larger universities.' Rockstr's voice suddenly sounded like someone else's. 'That hasn't been my experience so far.'

She twisted her fringe in her fingers, hoping her breathing would soon return to normal. She was unsure how to interpret Dawn Goldberg's poker face, the fixed smile now more of a gurn. She seemed to be swaying slightly, her eyes with a faraway look.

Rockstr was aware that a small group of students had slowed to a halt just behind the Vice Chancellor, watching with interest. She raised her voice slightly.

'Last week I had to study in the corridor and I have just been turned out of the library at four o'clock. I've nowhere else to work – the study rooms are fully booked and my halls are, like, totally chaotic. When I tried to find a lecturer to talk to last week my—'

'What's your name?'

'Rockstr.'

Dawn stared at her, eyebrows raised.

Rockstr kept her eyes fixed on the Vice Chancellor's. 'It's what people call me.'

Dawn Goldberg smiled, this time flashing her teeth. 'Far be it from me to question the follies of others,' she said, as if to an imaginary audience seated somewhere slightly beyond her field of vision.

The ensuing silence left Rockstr wondering if she had missed something. But she was not about to waste her chance. A bespectacled man in the assembled group mimed a slow and exaggerated fist pump at her from behind Dawn's left ear.

'With the plans to bring so many more students here next year – well, there are already too many. It's hard enough for us to study. And rent is already extortionate in Poltowan. I've got friends who—'

'Why did you come here?'

'To get a music degree – a first-class music degree.'

Dawn rolled her eyes. 'But why? Why do you want a first-class music degree?'

Rockstr was tempted to explain how it would make her parents proud, how she could redeem herself for throwing away her opportunity to study at the Royal College of Music, and how she could prove to herself that she had it in her to achieve something.

'To be a musician.'

'Ah! *Finally* she has a clue why she is here in the farthest reaches of darkest Cornwall!' Dawn threw back her head and laughed, a gold filling briefly exposing itself.

Rockstr glanced around at the other students now making their way out of Friday afternoon lectures.

'And do you know the employability ranking Poltowan has?'

Rockstr shook her head.

'It now stands at a mighty ninety-five per cent, meaning the vast majority of our graduates are in employment or further study within six months of leaving us – six months! What does that tell you... Bash Street?'

'Bash Street?' repeated Rockstr, frowning.

'What did you say your name was?'

'Rockstr. People know me as Rockstr.'

The group behind her sniggered. 'And what does that say to you – Rockstr?'

'But I won't even pass my degree if I can't have access to somewhere quiet to study – if I can't, like, even get to speak to my tutors without booking a slot two weeks in advance; if I can't have time in the music studio to record. I'm not worried about finding a job after graduation – I'm worried about even getting that far.'

Dawn Goldberg pinned her with a gaze that was no longer vague and unfocussed. 'Poltowan graduates have a reputation for strength and stamina, for resourcefulness as well as academic brilliance. If they don't have sufficient gumption – ' here she paused momentarily, taking delight in how the word sounded as it rolled off her tongue ' – then they, *like*, don't deserve to be here. You won't be spoon-fed in the real world, you know. It's dog eat dog out there.'

The smile slid off Dawn Goldberg's face as quickly as it had appeared and she turned to go, her limited reserves of patience spent. 'And you may be interested to know that we are investing in some very exciting new facilities indeed, but they are currently under wraps, so watch this space.' These last words rang out over her shoulder. 'Sorry, I've got to be somewhere.'

'I am here because I want to make it work,' cried Rockstr. 'But we aren't happy about the university having more students. It isn't what we signed up to!' She was surprised by her own persistence.

'We?' Dawn shouted back, her stride quickening.

'Yes, we,' said Rockstr, legs slightly astride now, voice raised, a strange rushing sound in her ears. 'Most of us students, most of the staff and most of the people who live here. And we will not let you ruin everything.' The final words were, she was sure, disregarded by their target.

Rockstr watched as Dawn Goldberg lurched away down the path before crossing the square, pausing only until the group of students, standing ill-advisedly in her way, parted to let her through.

'Finally! Someone speaks the truth. Well said,' shouted one of them.

Rockstr stood staring after the figure marching off into the distance, her pulse still galloping, her cheeks hot with rage.

Jemima, a fellow student from her classical music module, appeared silently at her shoulder.

'Did I just see that right? You were having a ding-dong with Dawn Goldberg?'

Rockstr waited a moment before emitting a strangulated yell. 'She is an ignorant, stuck-up cow!'

'That seems to be the commonly held belief. Although I haven't been in such close quarters to her as you have. What did you say to her?'

'I was letting her know my – our – feelings about the overcrowding here; about the fact that we are totally not getting what we were promised.'

'And?'

'And she doesn't give a shit. She seemed to think it was funny. Told me Poltowan had a ninety something per cent employment rate—'

'Like that means anything.'

'Exactly – as if that was an answer in itself.'

'She gets paid too much to care. It's all about league tables.'

'Too right.'

'How much do you reckon she gets?'

'Too much. And it's clearly where our ridiculous tuition fees go – to line her pockets. And the higher up the league tables she climbs, the more she gets.'

Chapter 14

Dawn pulled into the car park of Cornwall Council's offices, perched high on a hill in a Georgian manor forty-five minutes along the coast from Poltowan. The beautiful architecture was ruined only by an ill-conceived sixties concrete extension jutting out from the back, peeping around as if in embarrassment. She hesitated a moment before edging her red car into a space next to a sleek convertible Bentley. She shivered. It was the GT V8 S, with the heady thrumming engine.

She climbed out of her Mazda and peered inside the Bentley's windows, almost salivating at what she knew its salespeople described as the 'piano black' veneers. She ran her finger slowly over the bright wing vent while admiring the slender seven-spoke alloy wheels. Bending over once more, her rear in the air, eyes shielded, she groaned softly as she drank in the interior.

'Muscular yet graceful, powerful yet aesthetically superior...' she muttered. How her father would have marvelled at such a machine.

'Can I help at all?'

She righted herself quickly, tossing her hair over her shoulder in futile defiance of the gusting wind. A tall, slim dark-suited man was standing next to her, hands thrust casually into his pockets, his curious eyes trained on Dawn, not without a hint of distaste.

'I am just admiring this gorgeous beast. You don't know who it belongs to, do you?'

He looked it up and down for a moment. 'As a matter of fact, it's mine.'

A short, high-pitched laugh escaped from Dawn. 'Well, it's a very sexy creature. You're one lucky man.' She held out her hand to him. 'I'm Dawn Goldberg.'

He looked her up and down briefly before holding out his own hand. Dawn enthusiastically pumped his cool fingers up and down, willing his blank face to register some recognition.

'VC, Poltowan University?'

'Yes, yes, of course. Jason Redthorne. We have a meeting scheduled. Apologies. It's been a busy day.' He knew all too well who Dawn Goldberg was, and she looked almost exactly the way she did on the television, if perhaps a little older. He'd discovered that feigning ignorance often helped to give him the edge with particularly challenging people.

'When did you get her?'

He turned to look at the Bentley, as if seeing it for the first time. 'Six months maybe? Come in.'

He began to walk towards the building but Dawn hesitated to follow. 'What's she like to drive? Reaches one hundred and ninety-one miles per hour, I've read. Does she?'

He paused, turning back to look at her with his head slightly tilted to one side. 'I haven't had the chance to test that particular claim.'

She hurried a little to catch up with him. 'I bet she's impressive – all those pistons firing, all that power.' As Dawn spoke she made a strange thrusting motion with her hips, taking even herself by surprise.

'Come through to my office,' Jason said, without commenting further. He led the way down a gloomy corridor and into a large room, inviting her to take a seat with a barely perceptible gesture.

Dawn began to tell him about her tireless work to achieve her vision of an impact centre that would attract the world's most ambitious and talented automotive engineering students. 'That's confidential at this stage, of course, but I'm sure you're a man of discretion. And I have a strong inkling this project will float your boat.'

'So... to the matter in hand.' Jason shuffled some papers on his desk, determined not to allow himself to be lured into a distracting byway, while inwardly conceding that the plan did sound very interesting indeed. He picked up a print out of their email correspondence.

Jason had long been a supporter of increasing student numbers at Poltowan. He had grown up on a farm just outside the town and, thirty years ago, had been forced to leave his beloved Cornwall in order to train as an architect. He saw Poltowan University as representing a massive opportunity for local students to study on their home turf, then hopefully remain in the area to work rather than adding to the brain drain to London.

He believed Poltowan could be a leading light in the UK's higher education system, and predicted that the benefits to Cornwall of its further expansion could be huge. 'Critical mass,' he had preached to many of his colleagues. The university needed to attain critical mass before it could really establish itself. Branding itself as a boutique university was all very well but it would not deliver results in the long term. The university needed a continued expansion programme. Jason took his position on the County Council very seriously and was acutely aware of the need to make strategic decisions for the good of Cornwall. He prided himself on not being limited by the sometimes parochial views of his colleagues. He was forward-thinking and expansive in his vision.

The stumbling block for him was Dawn Goldberg. He'd read about her, seen her speak, and watched her TV interviews.

He disliked her intensely, believing she was driven by her own vanity, and had heard too many stories about her poor treatment of fellow staff to warm to the woman. Yet he also knew she was very adept at using her femininity to charm the right people – a tactic which, by all accounts, knew no bounds. By virtue of his own carefully guarded sexuality, it was highly unlikely to have any impact on him. He acknowledged the fact that she hit the targets that mattered, making her tenure as VC virtually incontestable. He wanted to see student numbers increase, but he also wanted to see someone else at the helm.

'Increasing student numbers at Poltowan,' he said, gruffly.

'A hugely important matter, I know you'll agree,' said Dawn, undoing the top button of her blouse and loosening her jacket as Jason narrowed his eyes at the piece of paper in front of him before quickly discarding it. She crossed her legs and carefully arranged herself in the chair, tilting herself slightly forward, hair drawn over one shoulder. She noted the day's Guardian sitting folded on his desk, half-obscuring that week's *Poltowan Post*.

'Obviously this will go in front of a meeting of the Strategic Planning Committee,' he said, folding his hands in front of him. 'I can only listen to what you have to add today and take it back to the committee.'

'Of course, and I do appreciate your taking the time to chew the fat with me, Jason – it's lovely to have the opportunity to get to know one another a little better.'

He frowned, scratching his chin. Her voice was already grating on him.

'So, you will doubtless be well informed of all the debate the proposal to lift the cap has prompted.' Dawn shifted from one ample buttock to the other as she spoke. 'There's been no end of hysteria from local people – and certain local businesses – who have leaped on it without a clue what it really means and how, actually, it is the saviour of the local economy, their community, their business, their future. In truth, I have never witnessed such ill-informed histrionics, Jason.'

He continued to watch her from under his lowered brow. Under the table his foot tapped rhythmically in its Italian shoe.

'Under my leadership the university has made a significant contribution to the local economy, creating over two thousand jobs and giving Cornwall's young people the opportunity to study and work in the county they grew up in.'

Dawn dropped her voice to a husky pitch. 'The facts speak for themselves, Jason, as I'm sure a man in your position will be well aware. We simply want to build on the sturdy foundations we have already put in place.'

'More of the same?'

'Exactly! I knew we'd get on, you and me, Jason. As soon as I saw that beautiful machine parked out the front, I knew we'd have an understanding.'

Jason cleared his throat as an assistant swept in with a tray of tea, nodding his thanks and waiting until the man had left before he resumed the conversation.

'I suppose the people of Poltowan do have some excuse for being a little parochial in their views. They are, after all, perched almost at the end of the county in what is a more rural spot than most, and the town itself has never seen anything quite like the university before, in scale or concept.'

'So true. And parochial is an understatement!' Dawn slipped her hand inside her blouse and pulled out her gold necklace, twisting the warm metal slowly around her fingers. 'They are positively backward-looking, opposed to progress of any sort.'

The first signs of a smile played across Jason's lips. 'It's understandable, I guess. The university came as a shock to them and it has grown very quickly – with you at the helm.'

'Well, I won't deny that our growth has been exceptional. The figures back it up. Any other town would be desperate to have a burgeoning academic institution on their doorstep – generating jobs, creating opportunities, driving innovation. But not Poltowan. There it's like pulling teeth.' Her hearty laughter seemed out of place in the austere wood-panelled room.

'I suppose the benefits haven't yet filtered through to the majority of people – not in any way they can easily quantify,' said Jason. 'All they see are the downsides of change: the shifting of priorities towards this new, younger generation, the accommodation shortage, the chaos that comes with the student population. They feel threatened.'

'Exactly – they have tunnel vision, they are completely irrational. But those who are complaining about a housing shortage and chirping about having to move – well, they're better off moving if we're honest, going somewhere quieter and freeing up the housing stock for the people who are our future. We need a good injection of positivity, not gripers and grumblers holding us back.'

Jason nodded, starting to take the measure of the woman sitting in front of him. 'And more students are necessary to achieve this vision of the future?'

'Certainly. More students will bring in more money, give us greater clout, really put us on the map. We'll attract better staff, invest in more innovation, create more jobs, and bring more of the world's best brains to Cornwall.'

'You aren't worried that we've already reached tipping point? That all the excellence you have achieved will be unsustainable with another three thousand students crammed into a small town? I mean, less is sometimes more.'

'Not on this occasion. More is more, Jason! Poltowan can become a Russell Group university, a centre of excellence in so many disciplines, able to charge top fees and attract greater funding. The impact centre is just one example of my vision – imagine being the go-to place for testing on F1 cars; imagine the kudos! We will become *the* place for automotive engineering students.'

Jason tapped the point of his pen slowly on the desk top. 'Well, it's definitely food for thought. And, as I said, the committee will give it full consideration before a final decision is made on March the second.'

'I can see you're in agreement though, Jason,' she ventured.

'My job is to take a countywide strategic point of view – look at what's best for Cornwall as a whole.'

Dawn leaned closer to him, pausing at a forty-five-degree angle and looking up at him from under her false eyelashes. 'But surely you can see – this will boost the county's economy in so many ways. There are untold benefits.'

'There are other considerations too – like infrastructure, housing, taxes, sustaining a balanced community.' He glanced out of the window at the now darkening sky, subconsciously taking hold of the orange stress ball on his desk, gripping it tightly in one fist. 'Do you know, for example, that we missed out on more than one million pounds in council tax last year because of all the multiple-occupancy properties in Poltowan? It astounds me that they aren't obliged to pay it like other residents. That revenue would have saved us from making the budget cuts we announced at the end of last year. There is no government funding to compensate for that loss.' It was a point some of his colleagues made to him frequently in their strenuous efforts to argue against increasing student numbers, and he repeated it to Dawn with gleeful insincerity.

'But I can trust you to see that the pros outweigh the cons?' she said. 'I mean, it's swings and roundabouts, isn't it?'

He looked at her sternly. 'Where do you live, Dawn?'

She held his gaze for a moment. 'Not very far from Poltowan

at all. You and I, Jason, we are very lucky to live in Cornwall, it's the envy of—'

'But not *in* Poltowan itself? How far away exactly?'

'No one wants to live on their office doorstep, Jason. It's a glorious forty-five-minute drive.'

He bounced the stress ball repeatedly on his desk. 'If the cap is lifted, the number of multi-occupancy homes will grow and the county will lose more money. In short, the rest of Cornwall will be subsidising Poltowan, and not the permanent residents of the town but the students who come to study here temporarily. Your customers.'

'With respect, Poltowan University contributed forty-one million to the Cornish economy this year. I think that far outweighs any shortfall in council tax, don't you?'

'Those are spurious figures.'

'Spurious? Spurious, Jason? They come from a study conducted by Oxford Economics.'

'I am not suggesting they are wilfully spurious, just open to interpretation, hard to pin down.' He stood up. 'Anyway, as I said, the committee as a whole will decide. And first we will listen to the Poltowan Councillors.'

Dawn gazed at him in horror before rearranging her features into a more becoming expression. 'But you are second-in-command of the county, Jason – the co-pilot as it were?'

'Yes, but the point of a committee is that we work together, share views and opinions, pool our expertise to come up with the best solutions for Cornwall. I suppose it's not dissimilar to your board of governors. You work together for the greater good. We don't deal in egos here.'

He rounded the desk and stood next to Dawn, the orange stress ball still clutched in his right palm. She got to her feet, stepping closer to him and touching his arm. 'You don't know how much I appreciate talking to a like-minded person – it's so refreshing.'

He placed the stress ball pointedly on the desk and looked out of the window, watching evening start to settle over the sea.

'Here's my card, Jason, I've scribbled my personal mobile number on the back. Call me, any time. Perhaps we can do lunch. Who knows? I might even be invited for a ride in your Bentley!'

'Goodbye, Dawn.' He placed her card on his desk and showed her to the door, his cool hand once more being grasped by her strong, warm one as she left.

She cast an admiring glance at his well-cut Burberry suit as he began to push the door shut. 'Lovely suit by the way – I haven't seen many Council workers so well dressed, I have to say.'

He managed a half-smile, continuing to push the door, but Dawn held it open momentarily with her hand. 'And the car, of course – you have done very well. The Council is lucky to have you.'

He rubbed one eye. 'I care deeply about Cornwall, about how it develops.'

'And I'm sure you have great experience, great expertise to draw upon from previous roles – I mean, you can't always have been a Council worker?'

'I'm an architect by trade. Sold my practice. This is more of an altruistic occupation for me.'

'As I said, Jason, we are very lucky to have you on side, a man with your wealth of experience. You have a safe drive home in that beast. Do you have far to go, back to your family?'

'Goodbye, Dawn.'

Jason flicked the office lights off and stood at the window in the gathering gloom. He watched as Dawn Goldberg crossed the car park, eyes narrowed against the fine rain. As she passed his Bentley she ran her index finger lightly all the way up the boot and over the convertible roof, lovingly tracing its outline. He shuddered.

Chapter 15

Harry was sitting at his favourite window table in Cappucin–oh! trying to catch up on some admin, but he couldn't think straight. Within the space of fifteen minutes he had received a text from Jo urging him to agree to the penthouse lease – followed by a row of ridiculous emojis that he couldn't even make out – and a phone message from Sylvia asking if he had yet valued the house and when the photos would be taken. His right temple was pounding and his heart was racing. He was on his third Americano.

He had just heard that the three valuations he had carried out that week had not come to anything. The owner of the last one, a terraced townhouse in Saltings Road, had told him he was somewhat reluctantly putting it on the market with Graves. He needed a quick sale and knew they had buyers waiting. 'One specific buyer from London, I think,' Mr Bolt had told him rather sheepishly when Harry called to follow up.

Another one bites the dust, he'd thought to himself. He knew it was a perfect family house for his clients the Pardews but they were unlikely to be able to match what an investment buyer would be happy to pay.

He rested his head in his hands for a moment.

'You still plotting the downfall of Poltowan?'

He looked up. Steve Kent was standing half in and half out of the door, a takeaway coffee in his hand. With his trademark crew cut and black polo-necked jumper he looked like a convict; the scowl on his face didn't help either.

'Steve. How are you?'

Steve shifted his weight from one stocky leg to the other and hauled himself back into the shop, placing his cup squarely in the middle of Harry's paperwork. 'I'm alright as it happens, Harry. But I'm 'oping for better times.'

Harry lifted his eyes towards him, examining his savagely pockmarked skin. 'Aren't we all, Steve?'

He sat down opposite Harry, their knees bumping. 'All this nonsense about "Keep the Cap" and "Say no to more students". Tell me it's a stunt to get your mug in the paper? You don't really believe holding back progress will 'elp anyone, do you?'

Harry massaged his throbbing temple before looking up to meet Steve's deep brown eyes. 'No, it's not a publicity stunt, and yes, I do believe it is the right thing for Poltowan. I am simply doing what I – and most of the residents, not to mention the students too – believe is right.'

Steve sat back in his chair, a smirk on his face. 'Do you know how much I turned over this year? Two hundred K. Just three years ago that figure was less than one hundred. Why? Because of the growing university, because of the student trade, and I ain't afraid to admit it. It means I've bought a proper nice house locally, and I spend my bangers and mash here too – straight back into the local economy. Completes the circle.'

Harry cleared his throat. 'Just the one house, Steve? Or a nice little investment too?'

Steve stared back at him impassively, as if struggling to process the question. 'So I 'ave a buy to let gaff as well, thanks very much. What are you, some kind of raving communist?'

'Let to students, by any chance?'

Steve jabbed the tip of one finger on the table in front of Harry. 'I get three times the rent from that lot as I would from a professional, and that's a fact.'

'I know it is.' Harry deliberately kept his voice at its usual volume. 'But that's exactly the trend that means local people can't afford to buy here anymore.'

'You're like a broken record. You ain't gonna win! Not a cat in 'ell's chance. People here want progress, they want profit. Whereas you want your head seeing to. You call yourself a businessman yet—' Steve shook his head and stood up, the table tipping slightly under his weight. He swept his coffee cup up with a move not dissimilar to a right hook. 'Nothing personal, mate, but you're gonna get a thrashing if you carry on like this. It's not gonna be pretty, not in the least.'

Harry raised his hand, large fingers splayed, as if to warn him against uttering another word. The door banged shut and he watched Steve pound down the road, his short legs pumping, his knees slightly out-turned. He even walked like he wanted a fight.

Harry's phone bleeped with another ambiguous set of emojis, the only clear ones being a small house with a red roof and a bottle of fizz of some description. He turned it to silent, replacing it a little too firmly on the table, and took his glasses off, rubbing the bridge of his nose.

A car pulled up a few yards from Cappucin–oh!, opera playing loudly from within, incongruous in the quiet of the morning. The driver got out of the car and hurried across the road to the post office, engine still running, music still blaring. Freddie Mercury's unmistakable voice exploded through the slightly open window and the words of the chorus hit home. 'Who *does* want to live forever?' said Harry quietly paraphrasing the song. 'And as for who waits forever...' he whispered the words before accompanying Freddie in the final line, his voice barely audible. He felt a shiver run down his spine. The driver returned, accelerating away before the next song began.

Harry drummed his fingers purposefully on the table and

picked up his phone. 'Let's do it then. Tell Susie yes and let me have the landlord's details so I can sort it out.'

He was glad it was Jo's voicemail he was speaking to. He knew she would be teaching now and wouldn't pick up the message until lunchtime. He wasn't ready to withstand the full force of her joy.

He opened his notepad and tried to decipher his half-hearted notes about The Oaks. It was odd having to value his own house and try to see it dispassionately through the eyes of a possible buyer. It was simple enough on paper – four bedrooms, three reception rooms, kitchen diner, own driveway and double garage, three acres of garden, mature trees and amenity land. Harry could still see Sylvia in the garden, her hand on her lower back, surveying her work in the morning sunshine, or wandering around the perimeter deep in thought, coffee mug in hand. He could imagine himself back in the office – it was what they called it, although new owners might have other ideas – lying back in his recliner, his oversized headphones delivering him to another world, while Sylvia listened to the radio downstairs, the smell of cooking eventually drawing him to the kitchen.

He remembered the two of them decorating the hallway, varnishing the parquet flooring, ripping out the old lino, assembling that blasted dresser that took two days instead of two hours, hanging the huge Kurt Jackson landscape on the landing. Images passed through his brain like a film reel on fast forward and palpitations kicked uncomfortably in his chest as the frames streamed past his mind's eye.

He picked up his phone, trying to slow his breathing in rhythm with the ringtone. 'Aaron, how are things?'

'Good, good. A bit quiet but – how are you?'

'Listen, have you got time to do a valuation in the next couple of days?'

There was a faint scuffling sound as Aaron flicked through the office diary. 'Yes, boss. Any time.'

'Can you pop round to The Oaks?'

'Your house, Harry?'

'The same. Keep it under your hat but we're just keen to know the value. I've got a figure in mind, but it's hard when it's your own place, when you've lived there and – well, a fresh pair of eyes would be useful.'

'I understand, no problem. What time?'

'I'll speak to Sylvia and call you back. More likely be tomorrow. Thanks, Aaron.'

'Oh, boss?'

'Yes?'

'That butcher guy called in for you earlier. What's his name… James Cowley. He wanted to know if you'd like to go for a complimentary burger tonight at Holy Cow.'

Harry frowned. 'Can you leave a note on my desk? I'll deal with it later.'

'I'll go if you don't want to – their burgers are supposed to be awesome!'

'There's no such thing as a free lunch, Aaron.'

Nell hovered by the doorway as the delivery men streamed past her, humping one item of furniture after another, each wrapped up in thick cellophane. She had a fluttering feeling in her stomach as she watched the final pieces being unwrapped, as if a masterpiece she herself had painted was being unveiled to the public for the first time. Nell could only hope it was all up to scratch, even if Dawn had made the final decisions herself.

'Here and here, please, miss,' said a short, squat man, thrusting a clipboard under her nose.

'Let me just check that everything is there,' said Nell, disregarding the agitated look on his face and entering the office with a newfound sense of importance. She inhaled the smell of paint deeply as she ticked off each item on her checklist. The men stood waiting, hands on hips, as she cross-checked each item with the order form. The carpet felt springy beneath her feet when she crossed the room, and the new spot lighting seemed to throw out a light purer than she had ever seen before. A man struggled past her with a tall yucca plant in a stone-effect pot, placing it carefully in the corner where Nell had specified. It was the icing on the cake.

'Proper job,' said one of them.

She had to admit, it did look impressive. Even the crushed velvet chaise-longue she had harboured severe reservations about, looked quite at home here. Dawn really did have an eye for interiors.

When the men had gone Nell wandered back into the refurbished office and stood admiring her work. She stroked the leather-topped oak desk before studying the huge canvas on the wall. It was a small green square on a large red square. She had been baffled when Dawn had selected it, particularly by the £700 price tag. Now Nell fancied she could appreciate its appeal, the way it subtly challenged the viewer's perspective. It was starting to speak to her. Dawn clearly had vision.

A moment later Nell found herself hovering next to the lime green chaise-longue. After barely a moment's hesitation she sank down onto it, closing her eyes before kicking off her shoes and swinging her legs up. She surveyed the office, imagining the two Persian grey swivel chairs occupied by people of great importance as she outlined her plans to them. Suddenly it was Harry she saw sitting there, drinking in her every word, his long legs stretched in front of him, deferring to her, listening intently as she held court.

The sound of voices made her jump. She quickly rammed her swollen feet painfully into her stiletto shoes, wishing she had never taken them off. She stood up, adjusting her hair and waiting for Dawn and Janice to appear.

'Well,' said Dawn, who seemed not at all non-plussed to find a spotlit Nell standing in the middle of her office. She dropped her large bag on to the floor and gazed around. Janice came to stand next to her.

'Oh, it's wonderful, Dawn. It's lovely! You have such good taste.'

'It's not just me, Jan. I have Nell to thank for the way it's all come together.'

She froze as Dawn stepped towards her, embracing her in a warm hug. Her sharp edges seemed much less in evidence today, her breath oddly sweet. 'It's a triumph. And long overdue. Well done, Nell, you've done a fine job.'

Nell nodded and laughed, glancing over at Janice. 'I'm relieved you like it. It was quite a responsibility, you know.'

'I knew you were up to the job – no doubts at all about that.'

'It suits you, Dawn,' said Janice. 'Sit in your chair, let's see you.'

She sank into her office chair, her prominent figure at once looking majestic and authoritative behind the stately desk. She peered at them over her glasses. 'Well, does it become me, ladies?'

'Oh, yes,' said Jan and Nell in unison.

'Good. Now, Nell, would you mind organising some coffee? Jan, shall we go through my diary for next month?'

The two support staff left and Dawn reached down into the cardboard box of personal effects the decorators had carefully packed. She pulled out the photo of her father. She looked at his face for a moment before placing the frame carefully on the corner of her desk, angled towards her.

'I wish you could see me now, Pops.'

Nell stuck her head around the half-open door. 'Sorry, Dawn – decaf?'

'Not today, Nell,' she said, agitation creeping into her voice. 'Caffeine is my poison.'

'Of course,' said Nell, retreating past Janice's desk and down the corridor towards the kitchen.

'She doesn't usually drink at lunchtime,' said Janice in her ear, as if reading her thoughts. She squeezed Nell's arm in passing. 'Just a one off, in case you were wondering.'

'I hadn't even noticed,' lied Nell.

'We all need an occasional treat.'

Jan whisked the cafetière away and bustled down the corridor, whistling off key.

⟡

Nell was buoyed by the successful completion of her first project. She stood in the stark light of the bus stop, hopping from foot to foot, her scarf pulled almost around her ears, a handful of students loitering behind her, headphones in, eyes trained on their mobile screens. It was busier than in recent weeks.

She pictured again the chaise-longue against the far wall of the office, the grandiose desk, the statement Anglepoise lamp throwing light across the room. Dawn had certainly seemed more relaxed than she had been in recent weeks, and she was visibly pleased with Nell's management of the project. She finally felt like she was finding her feet at the university, serving a purpose.

A pungent, herby smell drifted under Nell's nostrils.

Instinctively she looked to her left to see a guy staring straight at her, his eyes trance-like, a joint in his hand. Nell had never tried dope, or knowingly smelled it, but it wasn't a cigarette he was smoking and the smell was not tobacco. Hesitantly she sniffed again, finding it curiously comforting.

When the welcome lights of the bus swung round the corner, Nell waited for the students to get on but the smoker held back, gesturing lazily with his joint for her to go in front. She smiled in thanks and watched out of the window as he took a last desperate drag before stubbing out the roll-up. The smell lingered about him like a cloud. Nell closed her eyes and inhaled what remnants of it she could.

She got off at the top of Tremaine Road, a handful of students also alighting at the stop. As she walked past number fourteen she spotted that the lights were on. Since there were no window coverings she could see a group of young people gathered in the sparsely decorated front room, which was lit starkly by a bare bulb. A surfboard was propped in the corner of the room, like an exhibit. The house had been for sale until a week or so ago, when the agent's board had briefly read 'Sold' before disappearing altogether. She glanced back, a wave of noise washing through the open front door as the group from the bus entered the property.

Nell felt a sudden weariness as she reached her own front path, the automatic light flicking on in the porch to welcome her home. She closed the door on the evening and called her cat, who pranced down the hallway towards her. She bent to tickle its neck.

'Oh, I'm whacked, Rambo. Whacked. How has your day been, eh? Eh?'

He butted his head into her legs, arching his back and purring with pleasure.

That night, Nell slipped into a deep sleep but was woken

just after two o'clock by what sounded like a crowd of people outside. She pulled the covers more tightly around her while she adjusted to the sensation of wakefulness. Voices were shouting and music was playing, then the sound of shattering glass prompted a cheer.

Nell went gingerly to the window and peered out. She could see maybe thirty or forty people on the front garden of number fourteen. Some of them danced to the music that spilled from the open windows; some sat huddled in twosomes on the kerb; others were entwined in front of the house, their indistinct forms picked out by the ambient streetlight. One girl staggered down the middle of the street, bottle in hand, while her friend, lying prostrate on the lawn, called out to her ineffectually.

Nell watched for a moment, stunned by the sight, before a light flicked on in Geoff Runcey's porch opposite and he swung open the front door, his burly form silhouetted against the hall light. He strode out, across his perfectly manicured lawn and down the road towards the student house. Nell held her breath.

She could see Mary Runcey lingering uncertainly in the hallway, her dressing gown clutched around her as she softly but urgently called her husband's name.

Nell couldn't make out Geoff's words, hearing only the deep reverberation of his vocal cords, but she saw a certain sobriety steal quickly over the group of revellers as they stood up unsteadily, falling largely silent, although the bass thrummed on, seeming to shake the foundations of the house.

'Sorry, mate, really sorry,' called one girl as Geoff retreated. Nell made out what sounded like other contrite murmurs before the music came to an abrupt end and a low murmur of voices, punctuated by one hyena-like howl, continued for a minute or two more before the front door closed. Nell watched Geoff slam his front door shut before she drew her curtains and returned to her bed.

She lay awake for some time listening to the low hum of music down the street. It was gone four o'clock before she finally drifted off, hoping that it was just an over enthusiastic housewarming party; a one-off event.

Chapter 16

Even Harry hadn't anticipated quite how excited Jo would be about his agreement to take on the penthouse. She had turned up at his office straight from school, bustling in, cheeks aflame and, once Aaron had made himself scarce, slathering kisses over him and telling him what a wonderful man he was. She had smelled vaguely, as she sometimes did, of Play Doh, a nostalgic smell that momentarily transported Harry back to his childhood. It had at first pleased him to see her so animated, so clearly thrilled, yet he couldn't ignore a simultaneous feeling of free falling.

'We'll do it for six months, see how it works out, OK?'

'It's a six-month lease, that's why it's a bit cheaper,' said Jo earnestly.

Harry nodded. 'Slightly irregular but… let's hope we can put up with each other for that long at least.'

'It will work out. Just wait and see.'

'Have you spoken to Susie?'

'Of course! She called her landlord straight away and she's emailing me his details so we can get in touch tonight to confirm. And guess what?'

Harry held her away from him by the wrists, amusement playing across his face. 'What?'

'Susie and Rob exchanged on their house today – they're are due to complete next Wednesday. Which means we can move in – ' Jo leaned over to consult Harry's desk calendar ' – a week tomorrow!'

'Hold fire. Have you contacted your landlord?'

'Of course! I actually sounded him out a couple of weeks ago.'

'Jo, we hadn't even—'

'I know, I know, but I did and it's fine and he has a waiting list for the flats so we can move in as Susie and Rob move out. What do you say?'

She planted another kiss on his cheek and stamped her feet in a fit of excitement.

'You'd better get packing then.'

'And you, mister.'

'Well, I haven't got much to move.'

'You have – just not from my place. You need to pay a visit to the ex and pick everything up.'

Harry murmured his agreement.

At that moment Aaron returned, wavering between them. Harry raised his eyebrows at him.

'Erm, that valuation, any news?' said Aaron. 'It's just that I've got another lady hoping I can do one in the morning, and you said—'

'I'll make a call and let you know.'

'Right.'

Aaron scuttled to the back of the office and picked up the phone.

'I've got to finish up here,' said Harry, noticing Jo's lips as if for the first time. He felt a sudden stirring of excitement. 'See you at home?'

'You will, Harry Manchester. And I am going to spoil you rotten.'

She gave him a lingering kiss then flounced out, her red coat flying behind her.

Harry ran his hand through his hair, exhaling noisily. He pulled out his mobile and wandered towards the window, staring out at the shoppers hurrying past under the streetlights, bundled up against the icy wind, hurrying to get home.

'Sylve? It's me.'

'I know it's you. It's always you when it says Harry on the screen.'

He closed his eyes momentarily.

'So, any news on the house?' she continued.

'Are you around tomorrow morning? Aaron can come and do the valuation then.'

Harry thought he heard Sylvia sigh. 'Or tomorrow afternoon, if it suits you better?'

'No. Tomorrow morning is fine. But I thought *you'd* do the valuation? I mean, who knows it better than you? And it's your job after all.'

'It's best to get another pair of eyes on it, someone who'll see it fresh. I've got a figure in mind but I'm keen to see if Aaron is in the same ballpark – he's pretty experienced at valuations now.'

'If you're sure.'

Harry watched an old man shuffle very slowly across the town square, pausing every few steps for breath. It's you who seems so sure, he thought to himself. 'Yep, no problem. So, what, ten o'clock?'

'Yes, ten. Thanks, Harry.'

'See you.'

He watched her name disappear from the screen before it went black. 'Who wants to wait forever?' he said quietly, continuing to watch the old man's glacial progress in the half light.

'I'm off, boss,' Aaron's voice interrupted his reverie.

'Before you go, ten o'clock tomorrow, The Oaks. Sylvia is expecting you – can you pop it in the diary?'

'No worries. Anything I should know before I go?'

Harry looked at him blankly.

'You know, hidden cellars, locked attics, false bookshelves – all the usual stuff we ask our clients when we do a valuation.'

'Oh, I see.' Harry rocked back and forth on his heels, his hands thrust into his pockets. The old man had disappeared from view now. 'I don't think so. Sylvia will be there and she knows everything there is to know – feel free to ask any questions that come to mind.'

'Have a good evening.' Aaron seemed to bounce out of the door and was quickly away up the road and into the night.

'And you,' said Harry, his words lost behind the bang and the jingle of the closing door. He flicked the sign over to Closed and pulled on his trench coat.

Almost as an afterthought he took four deliberate paces back to his desk and picked up the scrap of paper tucked under the pen pot, the name 'James' written untidily on it in black pen. He looked at it again before balling it in his fist and throwing it at the bin two or three metres away. It hit the wall, skirted the rim and fell silently in. Harry flicked the lights off and locked up, setting off in the opposite direction from his car.

৵

Something made Harry pause before crossing the street to enter Holy Cow. The burger joint was lit up as usual, its warm glow and luxurious red booths inviting people in from the dense evening fog. The unoccupied steel bar gleamed and the bench seats sat empty. No staff loitered, polishing the taps or chalking up the specials. The place seemed deserted.

Harry pushed open the door tentatively, poking his head in. The sound of Black Sabbath filled the room yet no one stirred. He stepped inside, closing the door firmly behind him, noting the Closed sign.

'Harry Manchester, I wasn't sure you'd come.'

Harry heard James Cowley's voice before he saw him. James stood up from behind the counter, wiping his hands on his apron.

'I didn't realise you actually did a shift in here – thought you just did the bossing, sampled the burgers.' Harry sauntered over to the bar.

James untied his apron from his ample girth. 'A successful businessman is always hands on, Harry, as I'm sure you know.' He tossed his apron at a modish youth who had appeared from the kitchen. James held out his hand to Harry over the counter and they shook silently.

'Take a seat. Beer?'

'Thanks.'

Harry hesitated at the long central table, glancing around him before taking off his jacket and sitting down, unbuttoning his cuffs and rolling his shirt sleeves back slightly. He was, as ever, cheered by the sight of his Rolex. He twisted it slightly on his wrist, feeling its pleasing weight. He didn't fancy being huddled in a booth with James. This table would do just fine for this short and sweet visit.

'Black Sabbath. A throwback to our youth,' called Harry, his leg now jigging to the beat.

James didn't appear to hear him. Moments later he appeared with two bottled beers and sat down opposite Harry, his pale belly protruding from between two straining button holes.

'You still making a row on those drums?'

Harry shook his head and they clinked bottles awkwardly. James rubbed his right ear lobe as he spoke, glancing repeatedly at the door.

Harry took a deep swig of cold lager, following James' gaze. 'Your Closed sign's up if you're wondering why it's so quiet.'

A smile played around James' lips. He seemed to be searching Harry's face for something hidden from sight. 'Private soiree this evening. Invite only.'

Harry shifted in his seat. 'I didn't realise.'

James thrust a menu at him. 'Here, you can get your order in before the others arrive.'

Harry took it from him, narrowing his eyes at the small fancy print. 'Classic burger sounds good.'

'You're nothing if not predictable, Harry. You like what you know and you know what you—'

Harry's phone began to vibrate in his pocket. He glanced at it. 'Sorry, James. Let me just take this… one moment.'

It was Jo. He didn't have to say anything as she repeated how much she loved him and how happy they would be, drinking sundowners while looking over the river in summer and sharing romantic baths in winter. She had it all planned out.

As he listened, waiting for a chance to speak, a blast of air whipped in through the open door and James stood up abruptly, rubbing his hands together. Harry looked round. A group of newcomers had appeared, led by Steve Kent, his black polo-neck now accessorised with a black leather jacket. Behind him were two local publicans and a host of Poltowan business owners. Harry knew most of them by face if not by name. He nodded at Nigel Ambrose, the studious-looking bookshop owner. Under his floppy fringe his eyes held a look of terror and he shuffled in as if being prodded from behind with the butt of a gun. Slowly he shut the door behind him.

'I'd better go, Jo. I'll be a bit late. Don't worry about dinner—'

Steve loitered by the table, sneering as he blew his beery breath over Harry, while James worked his way along the line of newcomers, shaking hands with each of them.

Harry slipped his phone into his pocket and took another mouthful of beer. He hoped he might see Diggory, sauntering in slightly later than the others and bringing some equilibrium to the gathering. He didn't materialise.

Steve continued to scowl, shoulders squared as he paced around the small space. The others formally greeted Harry, while Nigel smiled sheepishly before turning to admire the film posters on the walls.

James turned the key in the door and dropped the blind. 'So, ladies and gents, seems we have a bit of a party on our hands. Get your orders placed with Callum here and I'll bring over the beers.' James winked at Harry as he rounded the bar. 'Glad you came. There's a few things we could usefully discuss as we're all fellow business people together, with the best interests of Poltowan at heart.'

Harry found himself surrounded as the other traders took their seats next to him, while James pulled up a chair at the end of the table. Harry glanced at the key in the lock, the drawn blind. Steve sat down diagonally opposite him. He seemed to be the self-appointed ringleader, periodically cracking his knuckles, his gaze flicking around the table as if to reassure his followers, his thin lips pursed. Nigel sat down opposite, his eyes lowered as he moved the salt cellar around in circles, frowning at his own private thoughts.

James was clearly revelling in the idea of his own cleverness, his loud laughter overenthusiastic, his amiability turned up to high. He tapped a fork on his beer glass until the chatter stopped and only Black Sabbath remained. He gestured to Callum to turn the volume down. 'Thanks, everyone, for coming tonight. I thought it would be a nice idea to get some of my favourite fellow local traders together, treat you to the best burger you'll probably ever eat, and maybe chew the fat on the future of Poltowan and some of the current issues.' He paused to look at Harry, his eyes dancing in the light. 'It's not often we get the chance to express ourselves among like-minded people – I mean we're all in the same boat here. So let's enjoy ourselves and make the most of the opportunity.' He raised one eyebrow at Steve as he spoke.

There was a half-hearted murmur of agreement and Harry felt all eyes fix on him. He smoothed the rough wooden table with his hand, inadvertently catching Nigel's beer bottle, which fell sideways, its golden liquid pooling quickly over the menu and dripping onto one of the publican's shoes.

'Sorry, Nigel… sorry, mate. I'll get you another.'

'A generous offer when it's on the 'ouse,' said Steve, searching the gathering for support, his forced laughter sounding like a car struggling to start.

Harry stood up to get a napkin.

'Don't worry,' said James, gesturing for him to sit down. 'Accidents happen, particularly to those of a nervous disposition.' He called the young waiter who appeared promptly with a cloth.

Harry could hear Sylvia's words playing over in his head: *'You're simple. You're upfront. People trust you.'* He would not be cowed. 'So what's on the agenda? What are the topics people particularly want to discuss?' he said, irritated by the smugness starting to pervade the faces around the table.

There was a momentary silence before Steve spoke up. 'Don't arse around, 'arry. You know we're all against this Keep the Student Cap rubbish.'

'Did they choose you as their spokesperson because you're the most articulate or because you're the most charming?' said Harry.

Nigel laughed, briefly catching Steve's eye before silencing himself.

'Steve's right,' said James. 'It's important you understand just how much this means to people, Harry.'

He frowned, twisting his beer bottle round on its axis. 'Well, it's pretty damned important to me too given that I've put my neck on the line to defend it. It's not some idle whim.'

'But you've a vested interest,' said Lorraine, who ran the Able Seaman pub in Bosvenna Walk. 'You're in the property game. Once houses are let to students they're off the open market. It reduces the size of your stock. That's why you don't want more students.'

Harry steeled himself and went over his case yet another time, willing himself to keep calm, forcing himself to breathe in between sentences, daring himself to look into Steve's dead eyes. He continued talking over those who tried to interrupt or heckle, and those who made despairing noises, his voice carrying over the music.

Steve downed his drink and reached for another. 'There's no shortage of 'ouses, Lorraine. All this means 'arry's got one loverly house to put on the market that'll fetch a tidy sum.'

He grinned at Harry, exposing the gaps where his teeth had once been. 'Isn't that right? The Oaks is coming up for sale in the not too distant?' Steve didn't wait for an answer. 'He's found himself a younger model – a not too shabby one either – and he's moving onwards and upwards, aren't you, 'arry boy?'

There was a clatter as Nigel dropped his knife but no one moved to help him retrieve it.

'My private life has nothing to do with any of this, or with any of you for that matter.' He could feel his shirt sticking to his lower back.

'Harry's right about that,' said a face Harry knew with a name he couldn't recall. Harry knew he ran the newsagent's near one of the main student streets. 'But he's wrong about the rest. Your campaign will ruin my business, mate. Already people are going online in droves to read their news and whatnot – it's the students wanting their snacks, sweets and drinks that keeps a roof over my head. An increase in admissions will give me a bit of breathing space.'

Harry adjusted his glasses as a separate conversation broke out at the end of the table. 'He'll get a shock if he's the sole cause of our businesses going down the pan,' he heard one voice say. 'I won't be responsible for my actions.'

'I think the point is,' said Nigel, speaking in a low voice to Harry as if he had spent the last hour plucking up the courage, 'an increase in student numbers would be fine if there was accommodation for them all on the campus, but there isn't.'

'You bloody turncoat, Nigel,' said Steve, crashing his fifth beer bottle down on the table. 'They've said they'll supply the friggin' accommodation. Goldberg 'as said so.'

'They said that two years ago and nothing has happened,' said Harry. 'The plans are sitting gathering dust. The university is frittering away its money on other things.'

He turned his attention back to Nigel. 'And it's not just about accommodation. The students are tearing their hair out – they haven't enough resources, lecturers, places to study. It's not what they were promised.'

Steve sprang up, his chair screeching backwards. 'Codswallop, Manchester. You're telling me you care about the students' education now? Pull the other one.'

James passed Harry another beer. 'Business people have

to evolve. Any one of us in your shoes would have a well-established lettings arm by now.'

'For God's sake,' said Harry, raising his voice. He felt slightly light-headed now, his burger sitting largely untouched, six empty beer bottles on the table in front of him.

'How's yours taking shape, James?' said Steve, siting heavily back down in his chair.

'My what?'

'Your lettings business.' He took another greedy slug of his beer.

James looked at him. It was a while before Steve reacted. He put his hand over his mouth and his body began shaking with laughter, his bald head bowed.

James looked at Harry. 'Like I said, it's open season and any good businessman – or person should I say – will seize new opportunities and—'

'Is he serious? You're starting a lettings business?' said Harry.

James grinned, his own eyes looking slightly glazed now. He simulated a zip across his mouth. 'I cannot confirm or deny any rumours, Harry Manchester, all I can say is – watch this space.' He too began to laugh uproariously, Steve slapping him on the back as their stocky bodies heaved in unison

Harry worked the bottle top quickly between his fingers.

'I'm not sure there's room for another lettings agent,' said Nigel, contemplatively. 'That firm Graves seems to be increasingly busy around the town.'

'They're a competitor to Harry Manchester,' said a voice from the end of the table.

'They do sales *and* lettings,' said Harry. 'Another out-of-town outfit only interested in a quick buck.'

'Sounds like sour grapes to me,' said Steve.

'I'm not worried about them,' said Harry, his eyes resting on Steve for several seconds.

'So this younger model – where d'ya pick her up from?' said Steve.

Harry cleared his throat. 'What's selling well at the moment then, Nigel? I'm not a great reader but I do like a bit of crime stuff, serial killers, all that.'

Nigel's eyes lit up as he saw safe ground ahead of him for the first time all evening. He prepared to answer the question, closing his eyes for a moment as if willing his brain to catch up.

'More to the point, what didya do with the old one?' continued Steve. 'I mean she seemed alright, as older ones go. Bit mardy mayb— '

Harry stood up and rounded the table, the crowd's conversation falling quickly away, the rock music continuing to play.

'Come on, gents, take it easy,' said James, half-heartedly.

'Well, I'm only asking,' said Steve, his head bobbing around, eyes rolling. 'If the old wife is on the market again, along with the 'ouse, because if it's a kind of two for one offer to help shift the wife, then—'

Harry got hold of the collar of Steve's polo-neck and hauled him out of his chair, turning him round so they were face to face. Steve's head came up to Harry's shoulder and for a moment he looked genuinely frightened, before his eyes darkened again and he began to try and wriggle out of Harry's grasp.

'Getcha 'ands off me, you moron. Whatcha—'

Harry waited until Steve looked up and met his eye. His vacant, lazy-eyed look incensed Harry and he knew he was a split second away from landing a punch on the other man's wide, flat nose. 'If you ever speak of my wife like that again, I swear to God I will knock your block off.'

'You're a fuckin' lunatic.'

Harry shoved him away hard. Beer had severely compromised Steve's spatial awareness and played havoc with his balance. He fell backwards to the floor as if in slow motion, hands flailing, and seemed to slide for several metres before coming to a stop near the kitchen. He sat still, fists clenched, eyes glaring, his bald head an angry pink from the effort.

'They polished those floors today,' said James, twisting his fat neck to look around him. 'Did a good job.'

Harry leaned over and picked up his jacket. 'It's been a pleasure talking to you all but I must go. Thanks for the burger and for organising this little party, James. We should do it more often.'

James smiled dumbly at him through an alcoholic haze. 'See you, Harry.'

'You'd better drop that campaign, though, if you know what's good for you,' said a voice from somewhere near the end of the table.

Harry turned around, addressing the whole table, towering over everyone. 'For your information, I am going to push this campaign even harder, so that greedy, short-sighted business people like you don't end up ruining Poltowan for every resident and their family who deserve a home in the place where they grew up. I suggest you start looking at something other than your bottom lines.'

He grabbed the key in the door, willing it to unlock easily. He stepped out into the night, leaving near silence behind him. Instinctively he turned back towards his office, but two doors down ducked into an empty shop doorway. He removed his glasses and leaned his head against the icy window, closing his eyes. He was shaking with anger, his back soaked in sweat, his heart hammering. He let the window cool his forehead and cheeks as his breathing returned to normal.

When he stepped out into the main street minutes later, a swaying, shadowy figure appeared from his right. It was Nigel.

'Well. Quite a lively gathering,' he said, hiccupping slightly.

'More lively than I'd hoped.'

They walked together to the taxi rank before Nigel began to stagger off towards Helnoweth Alley.

'Can I just say—' said Nigel, his feet beginning to veer away as if independent of his body.

Harry turned sharply towards him.

'I think I agree with you. I mean, everything you said back there makes sense to me. There's far more than money at stake here. An increase in student numbers could prove to be really quite damaging, in many respects. I think you've just changed my mind.'

Harry lifted his hand warily in farewell. 'I'm glad someone has seen sense. Cheerio, Nigel.'

The bookshop owner veered away down an alleyway. 'Keep the Cap,' echoed backwards as he walked, interspersed with violent hiccups. 'Keep the Cap,' he repeated faintly, the words disappearing into the black night over Poltowan as Harry slammed the door of the taxi.

Chapter 17

Nell lay awake, listening to the music reverberating from number fourteen. Occasionally it would stop and she would feel her body begin to relax again, the silence a tonic to her ears. But each time it resumed even louder, the insistent beat bouncing off the walls and forcing its way out into the street.

High-pitched laughter rang out followed by the slamming of a door. Nell climbed out of bed and crept to the window, peeling back the curtain. All the lights in number fourteen were on and she could see people framed in each room, dancing, drinking, talking. It was like looking into a doll's house, seeing all the rooms simultaneously, each occupant unaware that you had a window into their private world.

She watched for a few minutes, wondering at their apparent ignorance of just how loud they were being at 2.48 in the morning. She recognised the curly-haired lad from the bus. He was currently leaning against the upstairs window, a beer bottle in one hand as he gesticulated with another. He had earlier offered to carry one of her bags back from the bus stop, having spotted that she was struggling with her handbag, shopping and a heavy file of paperwork on student housing requirements. She had declined, not having far to go, but was pleasantly surprised by the courteous gesture. Now she watched him through the window, wondering why he couldn't show some of the same generosity.

The lights were on in Geoff and Alice's bedroom too. She wondered if he would pay another visit to number fourteen.

Rambo rubbed his warm fur sleepily against her legs, clearly unsure about this strange interruption to their nocturnal routine.

'Oh, Rambo. What a pesky nuisance they are. It can't go on.'

She went downstairs, Rambo taking three steps at a time behind her, and put the kettle on, resigned to another sleepless night. The sound of raised voices drew her to the lounge window where she spied Geoff and Simon, a neighbour from the other end of the road, standing in the doorway of number fourteen, bathed in a shaft of light. They were talking – occasionally shouting – at two of the students, who lounged passively in the doorway as if immune to their words.

Nell retreated to the kitchen and the throbbing music quickly stopped. She sighed, stirring a spoonful of sugar into her tea. Upstairs she watched the now silent house from the window for a moment before climbing back into bed. She thought about Harry and how he had sat in her front room just a few days before. She liked the way he made the room look, made the house feel. She cocooned herself in the blankets and glanced mournfully at the empty space next to her.

There was no sign of life at number fourteen when Nell walked past the following morning, eyes shifting furtively right every few paces. The only pair of remaining curtains had been carelessly drawn, a yawning gap left between them. On the doorstep was a haphazard collection of bottles and cans; the open gate swung lazily to and fro in the breeze.

Nell enjoyed the unusual quiet of the 8.05 a.m. bus but her eyes felt puffy and heavy, her brain working as if submerged in treacle. When the alarm had sounded rudely in her ear, she'd felt as if she had been awake just minutes before. She had forced herself into the shower and eaten her breakfast mechanically.

Even Rambo seemed out of sorts, creeping around with a sly look in his eyes.

Dawn had asked Nell to be in earlier this morning. She had a *Guardian* journalist coming to interview her at ten o'clock and was insistent that everything in the office was shipshape. Nell had never read *The Guardian*. She was a dyed in the wool *Daily Mail* reader, although even she had started to take their headlines with a pinch of salt.

'She's writing a feature about strong female VCs,' Dawn had said, as if in answer to the question Nell hadn't yet asked. 'I contacted her a while ago, inviting her to come and have a chat. It's a great chance to make a splash on the national stage.'

Nell had known she was expected to show both interest and admiration, and had played her part until Janice appeared to take over the role.

This morning Nell was first in. She rolled up the blinds and switched on her computer before placing the daffodils she had bought the previous afternoon in a jar on her desk. She stood back and admired their instant brightening effect. She was sure Dawn would appreciate them on such an important day.

Nell had just sat down at her desk with a coffee when Dawn breezed in, muttering to herself as she did so.

'Good, good, bright and early. Coffee, please, and after that no interruptions until after nine-thirty. The Guardian will be here at ten o'clock.' It was as if she was expecting the entire editorial staff to turn up. 'Oh, and Janice will be along later – dentist.'

Dawn swept through the office, trailing Chanel No. 5 behind her. Seconds later her face reappeared, inches from Nell's. 'And watch those daffodils don't droop overnight – they'll set the entire damn' alarm system off.'

When Nell tentatively knocked on Dawn's door five minutes later, cafetière in hand, her boss was sitting facing the window in her swivel chair, stabbing away at her phone. Her terse thanks were muttered from behind a mane of hair.

'Not 'til nine-thirty, remember,' she called out more audibly as Nell closed the door. 'And please close the door firmly.'

Nell rolled her eyes before sitting back at her desk. She clasped her own lukewarm mug of coffee and eyed the file of student housing forms awaiting her attention. She had been tasked with trying to 'consolidate' – in Dawn's words – the existing accommodation, ensuring that they could prove that there was enough supply for a new influx of students.

She had reams of data on the number of beds on campus and in private housing locally, as well as the number of students who currently lived at home while studying, and therefore the percentage of new intake who were likely to do the same. It was a massive data crunching exercise with no small amount of conjecture thrown in. 'We need to use our imaginations too, Nell, be a bit creative,' Dawn had said pointedly when she handed over the first lot of paperwork. 'Numbers can only tell us so much.'

Dawn had then returned, directing her to the Cornwall Council website where five planning applications were underway to turn buildings in Poltowan into dedicated student housing. 'They'll all be passed eventually so don't forget to include those – there's nigh on a thousand beds there, always best to round it up.'

Nell had begun reading the first line of figures for a fourth time, the digits mischievously interlacing before her heavy eyes, when she was aware of someone standing in front of her. She leaped up, removing her reading glasses so as to make sense of the woman who had appeared by her desk. 'I'm so sorry, I didn't hear you come in.'

'No worries. I'm Beth, from The Guardian. I'm here to—'

'Of course, we're expecting you. Welcome to Poltowan University.'

Beth put her large bag on the chair and began to unbutton her long coat. Nell took it efficiently, smiling, and offered coffee.

'I'd kill for one, thanks. I know I'm early, I came down on the sleeper – what an experience that was.' Beth rolled her eyes at Nell.

'Long journey, was it?'

'Put it this way, whisky was my friend – if I hadn't indulged in a few before being shut up in my cell, I doubt very much I would have had even three hours' sleep.'

'I haven't done it,' said Nell, wondering if she had even had three hours' sleep herself. 'But I've heard it can be a bit – lively.'

'Lively? It's like being on a fairground ride all night, shut up like sardines – or is it pilchards down here?' Beth opened her eyes wide as if the exaggerated action would lock them open. 'But,' she held up a hand, 'on the plus side, I was woken by a very obliging lady who brought me a half-decent cup of coffee and informed me that my destination was approaching. After a few coffees I might be able to see that this place has a certain charm.'

Nell smiled sweetly through her sleep-deprived fog, hoping she had done enough by way of polite conversation.

'Anyway, I've got some emails to send so I'll just sit here and do that until Dawn's free. If that's OK?' asked Beth.

'Make yourself at home.'

It was all Nell could do to stay awake at her desk; the soporific tapping of Beth's fingers on her iPad were making her eyelids heavy, the numbers swimming before her, her head nodding closer to her desk.

Some minutes later Beth exhaled sharply, picking up her coffee cup and jolting Nell back to wakefulness. 'So have you been here long?'

'About a month, so no, not long,' said Nell, feeling chastised, straightening her posture and willing her brain to focus.

'What's it like, working here?'

Nell swallowed. 'I live not far away and they've just started a bus service from the end of my road to the campus. It's so convenient. A ten-minute run.'

Beth shifted in her seat. 'But working here, how do you find that? Is it a friendly place?'

'Oh, yes, very friendly. There's three of us in this building, Dawn, myself and Janice. She's at the dentist. But we all get along very well, and Dawn – well, she's quite a dynamo, always on the go, always doing—'

Nell looked down at the paperwork in front of her before glancing back at the reporter's expectant expression. 'I expect that's why you're here to speak to her. She has achieved so much since taking over, she's very well respected.'

The woman sat opposite nodding her encouragement, her head tilted slightly to one side. She showed no sign of responding.

'And, of course, it's a lovely place to work, with the gardens outside, the coast not far away,' Nell continued. 'Nice to have a bit of space to breathe.'

'The gardens are very attractive. I stare at a concrete building from my office window. And as for the sea – Regent's Canal is the closest I get to water in my lunch hour. I'm very envious.' She looked around her, taking in the paintings on the wall.

'Oh, and you'll love Dawn's office,' said Nell, realising the journalist was probably fighting to stay awake too. She felt a stab of solidarity. 'She's just had it all refurbished. In fact, I project managed it – she's far too busy to do it herself. She's got such vision and she's so particular about colours and materials – it all has to be just so, and of the highest quality. But it's come together beautifully. You'll see when you go in. There's even a chaise-longue!'

The journalist smiled before picking up her iPad and beginning to tap away again. 'And the campaign to increase student numbers – that sounds like it would be a fitting legacy for someone of Dawn's standing. It must be so important to have the support of all the staff here.' She spoke casually, barely glancing up, as if merely making polite conversation.

Nell hesitated, her eyes shifting towards Dawn's door. It stood bold and defiant in its oak veneer, as if challenging her to stray from the party line. 'Oh, yes, full support.' She picked at the nail varnish on her fingers.

Beth looked up at her, questioningly. 'And the Keep the Cap campaign – that's being run by a local resident?'

'Harry Manchester. He's a resident, and a local businessman, very well—' Terror struck Nell suddenly and she pushed away an image of Harry's blue eyes, looking quickly down at her desk.

'Very well?'

'He's very well, it seems.' Nell cleared her throat.

'And does he pose a real threat to Poltowan University's plans to raise the cap, do you think?'

She thought she heard Dawn's door handle turning.

'Oh, no,' said Nell quickly, her cheeks burning hot. 'He's only an estate agent. People say it is mostly self-interest that motivates him.'

'Not a credible threat then?'

'I shouldn't think so.'

It was past 9.30 a.m. when Nell hurriedly stood up. She excused herself and knocked quietly on Dawn's door. She could hear her boss talking inside and knocked a little louder. Still nothing.

She opened the door slightly. Dawn was standing at the window, talking as if addressing a crowd from the balcony at Buckingham Palace, her arms waving.

'… and it has always been a key goal of mine to make a difference, to make higher education available to more people but also to create a university experience that stands out, that really gives our young people an opportunity to express themselves outside the confines of an institution—'

'Erm, Dawn. So sorry to—'

'Half-past nine, I said,' bellowed Dawn, sitting down abruptly at her desk and slamming shut one drawer.

'It's gone half-past, Dawn. It's nearly twenty to ten and Beth is here, from The Guardian.'

Dawn stood to attention, tugging her azure blue suit jacket down over her hips and tossing her hair over one shoulder.

'Yes, of course. She's a little early but I can – I can manage that.'

'Shall I send her in?'

'I will see to it,' said Dawn, smoothing her eyebrows with her index finger before marching past Nell and entering the outer office.

'Beth, what a pleasure. So good to meet you. Do come this way. Please, follow me. How was your journey? Not too onerous, I hope. Now can we get you coffee, tea – what's your tipple at this time of day?' Dawn laughed, tossing her head and guiding the reporter into her office without waiting for a response, her words suddenly muffled behind the office door.

Nell returned her attention to the figures. Her posture slackened, her head finding its way into her hands before slipping on to the desk, followed by soft, contented snores.

❧

Dawn was pleasantly surprised by Beth's amenable attitude and her opening questions. Dawn couldn't have worded them better herself, giving her ample opportunity to talk about the employability record at Poltowan, the state-of-the-art facilities and the excellent staff-satisfaction survey, which had been carried out internally the year before. Beth seemed to be enjoying their chat, nodding enthusiastically and making occasional notes, the digital voice recorder sitting on the desk between them, a passive but all-knowing third party.

'It does sound like you feel you've earned your recent pay increase, which I know has caused some surprise in various quarters,' said Beth, her head bent towards her notepad as she finished the question.

This change of tack caught Dawn slightly off-guard. She had almost forgotten she was talking to a journalist rather than a malleable member of staff.

She closed her eyes for a moment, allowing a smile to spread across her face. 'Beth, as a journalist, you will know that figures relating to an individual's salary are invariably misrepresented. Any reporter worth their salt will do the due diligence to get the real picture before leaping on a sensationalist tack. Yet, sadly, that is what some have done as they desperately forage for a story.'

'I couldn't agree more, Dawn, my livelihood depends on it. So, an increase from two hundred and eighty K to three hundred and thirteen K a year is, by my reckoning, an increase of twelve per cent in twelve months. Please, enlighten me further about the numbers.'

Dawn inhaled rather more sharply than intended, sending her into a short coughing fit. 'Apologies, apologies. Firstly, any increase reflects our continued growth and success as a university, in the same way that any chief executive of an organisation would see their pay rise in accordance with how well their company is doing.'

Beth nodded quickly, starting to tire of being spoken to like a child.

'Student satisfaction and graduate employment have also risen,' said Dawn, now rising from her chair and turning to look at Michael out the window. He seemed slightly forlorn today, and still a little grubby, yet he remained strong in the face of gusting winds and a smattering of rain. He really was an inspiration.

She turned around and stood behind her chair, the bright white sky behind rendering her face all but invisible to her interviewer.

Beth shifted slightly to try and make out her interviewee's expression but Dawn's features remained shadowed.

'Understood. So I do have the correct figures but you would argue the rise requires greater context to be properly understood?'

'Precisely,' said Dawn, settling back into her seat. 'Did I ask if you wanted coffee?'

'I'm fine, thank you. Now, given that you currently have fewer than six thousand students here –'

'Though with an increase of over eight hundred from last year….'

'– and that the VC of Betchmouth earns two hundred and ninety-five K, for managing thirty thousand students plus the commensurate number of staff, does that seem right to you?'

'Once again, I draw your attention to the rate of growth we are seeing here, the change, the progress. It is one thing, Beth, to take the helm of a ship that is already steering a steady course in calm waters, and quite another to be made captain of a mildly seaworthy vessel in choppy seas, when the crew is an unknown quantity and the destination uncertain. The two are very different things.'

Beth raised her eyebrows, scribbling on her pad, and

couldn't help but nod in agreement with the powerful nautical metaphor.

'But the average salary increase for the majority of academic staff is one point five per cent. How does that sit with you, when the many highly skilled and well-respected lecturers who are delivering an education to your students receive a relatively paltry increase, despite the growth, the employability, the student satisfaction, you have spoken of?'

Dawn glanced at the photo of her father. When he had finally been promoted to factory manager two years before his death, the sense of achievement he'd felt at having clawed his way up from a sixteen-year-old production-line worker had blinded him to the burdensome legacy he had inherited. The factory was losing money and he was immediately tasked with making redundancies, something he was ill equipped to do.

She remembered him being called in late on a Monday night because many of the workers had occupied the factory, staging a sit-in to protest against the proposed cuts. It had been a baptism of fire for him. He had spent two weeks in negotiations with employees, unions and senior management, emerging tired and drawn, but triumphant. His inexperience in such matters had led him to tackle the problem face to face, talking to his old colleagues on the shop floor, addressing them as equals, drawing on the issues he knew mattered most to them, a far cry from the heavy-handed approach taken by many managers before him, who saw the protest purely as an inconvenience. Instead, he saw it as a problem that needed to be solved in a way that appeased everyone.

His approach sorted the diligent but disgruntled workers from those who were continually seeking opportunities to gain more ground in return for minimal effort. Redundancies were made, sorting the wheat from the chaff, and those prepared to compromise and dig in were rewarded, with productivity and loyalty rising as a result. The incident effectively reversed the fortunes of the company, and despite his keeping more people on than initially planned, the restructuring paid off.

It was the making of him, and Dawn saw him change as a result. He took on a steelier edge, an almost palpable air of confidence that he had often successfully feigned before but that now was part of him. He was a naturally reserved man yet he started to address others with quiet authority. They began to listen to him and do as he asked.

If only she could be rewarded with the same loyalty at Poltowan. Her efforts to drive and motivate people, to lead from the front, seemed largely to prompt belligerence and snide acts of defiance. Academic staff didn't like being told what to do. They clung on to their PhDs like life rafts in the swirling sea, wielding them in the face of economic reality. Well, Dawn had lived the real thing. She had won the coveted Young Engineer for Britain prize in 1979, leading the team that developed catalytic systems for car exhausts. She had a Master's in automotive engineering and had gone on to be a senior lecturer and head of department. She had the flimsy piece of paper as well as the life experience; that's why she was sitting behind the leather-topped oak desk, not them.

'Dawn?'

'Sorry, Beth. Would you remind repeating the question?'

'I was saying that the average salary increase for the majority of academic staff is one point five per cent. Surely that is unfairly meagre alongside your own very healthy increase?'

Dawn laughed. 'There will always be those who feel life isn't fair. People have to earn their due, put the time in, prove themselves, if they are to prosper and thrive. It's about survival of the fittest - a phrase, incidentally, coined by a certain Henry Spencer, not, as many think, by Charles Darwin.'

'But one point five versus twelve per cent? That's—'

'If things are going well here, which of course they are,

everyone wants a piece of the cake. And quite rightly, it is a team effort. But when things don't go so well those same people don't want any part of it – they will quickly look for another post or start tittle-tattling about the problems rather than putting in the hours to find a solution.'

'Are you saying you don't feel supported?'

Dawn narrowed her eyes at the journalist. 'I am speaking hypothetically, of course. My point is that I carry the can. I bear the responsibility, for good or ill. Only last month I was in Brussels taking part in high-level discussions about the impact of Brexit on the Higher Education sector.' She sighed, shaking her head. 'How we can make the best of this God-awful situation the country finds itself in. I lay awake at night, Beth, not just worrying about balancing the books and continually delivering the goods at Poltowan, but about the wider issues of influencing the outcome of Brexit and trying to secure the best deal that we as a sector can. No one else here does that, I bear full responsibility.' She pointed to herself with one well-manicured hand. 'And I'm paid accordingly.' She folded her hands in her lap and tilted her head in readiness for the next question.

'So it's fair, is what you're saying?'

'It's not for me to say what is fair, Beth. I am simply explaining the reality of the situation, which is what we need to focus on here. Never lose sight of the facts.'

Beth scratched her head with her pen, unsure whether Dawn's answer had been fair and accurate, or a dazzling display of obfuscation.

As she began to ask the next question a strange hum like a swarm of bees began outside. She raised her voice, Dawn frowning in an effort to hear, until the murmuring rose to a tumult, clearly punctuated by cries of, 'Keep the Cap!'

Dawn spun around in her chair. Swarming down the path

towards the grass quadrant was a mass of students, some holding placards, some pumping their arms in the air. Towards the front of the mob Dawn spotted Rockstr, although she couldn't now recall her name, recognising her blonde and red spiky hair, the surly expression on her pretty, pale face. Next to her stood a very tall youth with an unruly mass of hair who was laughing and shouting, apparently while giving out fliers to the rest of the crowd.

'I think you have a – situation,' said Beth, standing up to peer over Dawn's head in an effort to take in the scene. She was intrigued to see three of the students wearing wetsuits and goggles, complete with winter hoods.

Dawn gripped the arms of her chair. 'They are students,' she said, swivelling back to face Beth with a forced laugh before promptly rising to her feet. 'They are young, passionate, always enraged about something. It is good to see that fighting spirit!' She clenched her fist and waved it in the air. 'Now if you'll excuse me one moment...'

She abruptly released the Italian suede roller blind, which duly came crashing down onto the windowsill rather quicker than intended. 'You don't want to look at that rabble. I'll get you a coffee. Oh, and – ' she slid Beth's digital recorder across the table ' – you might want to pause that.'

'This is properly awesome,' shouted Rockstr at Ludo over the chanting, her banner down by her side now, her arms weary.

Ludo was only half listening. He was busy giving out the fliers he had hurriedly printed up the night before when he'd learned about the planned protest. He had leaped at the chance of capitalising on the students' energy and harnessing their growing disquiet.

'It's on Saturday,' he shouted to a group of lads frowning at the fliers as if unable to read the headline: 'Witness Rockstr and band's first open-air concert LIVE in support of Keep the Cap. FREE to all supporters. Saturday, February 18th. BYO'. The image underneath was a pop-art-style graphic of Rockstr's face, which Ludo had spent two hours editing digitally. At the bottom of the leaflet was a link to her Facebook page.

'You're fleeking!' he had said when they met up to join the protest, thrusting the posters in front of her.

She had acted nonplussed, appeared highly critical, but was secretly thrilled by the finished product and could already see it working well on the cover of her first vinyl release.

As they drew closer to the building, the chanting escalating, Ludo called Harry on Facetime, willing him to pick up. When he did, Ludo held the phone high above his head so that Harry was greeted with a bird's-eye view of the throng of students surging into the quadrant in front of Dawn's office. The statue now wore an alarming wetsuit hood, and on its arm hung a bag labelled 'Swag'. Ludo held the phone at full stretch for almost a minute before speaking. Students jostled for space all around, shouting, waving placards, giving no sign of winding up the protest.

'What the hell's happening?' said Harry.

Ludo laughed. 'It's mad, isn't it? The kids are all here. We're doing our thing, making our feelings known, our voices heard. It's an excellent and timely prelude to Saturday's gig, don't ya just think?'

'How many people are there?' Harry was incredulous at the scenes he had just witnessed on his compact mobile screen.

'About two hundred – maybe more.'

'Is she there? Is Dawn there?'

'Harry man, she's let her office blind down and kind of battened down the hatches so I'm guessing she's hiding like the coward she is. Apparently, she's got a journo from The Guardian there so it'll be great fodder for her.'

'Show me again.'

Harry pushed his glasses higher on his nose and frowned at the commotion in front of his eyes, captivated by the sight of the heaving mass of animated students, the tinny sounds of their chanting and yelling, the sheer energy of the unfolding scene.

~

The clamour continued to mount, cries of 'Keep the Cap!' now booming directly beneath the office window. Dawn pulled the door to her office firmly shut, leaving Beth sitting alone in the darkened room.

'Nell!' Dawn whispered loudly, banging on the desk as she spoke to her slumbering colleague. Nell appeared, wide-eyed, from under her greying bob of hair, wondering for a moment if she was dreaming. Dawn glared at her. 'We'll discuss the unscheduled cat naps another time but for now, get on the phone to Hornblower and tell him to sort that crowd of hooligans out – and fast.'

'Yes, of course,' said Nell, fumblingly dialling Andy Hornblower's extension, the rising din from outside suddenly registering with her. 'What's—'

'Bloody students!' hissed Dawn, glancing over her shoulder. 'They're revolting!'

Nell opened her mouth to respond but as she did so Andy picked up. She was in the midst of trying to explain the urgency of a situation she had no knowledge of when Dawn grabbed the handset from her.

'Andy, get out there and sort this rabble out. I have a *Guardian* journalist in my office at this very minute drinking in every impudent and idiotic word spilling from their greedy, over-entitled mouths.'

She slammed the phone back into its cradle and walked down the corridor to take in the protest from another angle.

'It's the Dawn of a new era!' shouted one lone voice. She swore under her breath. As she watched, unseen, she saw the weedy figure of Andy Hornblower ineffectually trying to push his way through the crowds, doubtless apologising as he went.

'Give me strength,' she said under her breath. 'Nell, another coffee for Beth, please. And one for me – make it strong.'

Andy's subsequent arrival in the office was characteristically hapless. He shambled in wearing an expression that suggested he was exhilarated by the furore he had witnessed. If he had been able to muster even an ounce of feigned indignation it would have helped to placate Dawn. Instead he seemed incredulous and impressed.

'It's quite a turn out,' he said, pulling at his ear lobe.

Dawn gripped his arm and guided him towards the kitchen. The door closed behind them. Nell could make out Dawn's raised voice but not the words. As she hovered nearby uncertainly, Beth materialised beside her once more. 'I suppose it's quite normal to have these – uprisings, for want of a better word?'

Nell's eyes were heavy-lidded and slightly aghast. 'I haven't been here long enough to know. I suppose it is. It's what students do, isn't it?'

Dawn and Andy appeared from the corridor, Dawn's face quickly transforming its expression of thunderous rage into one of stoic amusement. She introduced Andy to Beth and explained that they were just discussing the best way to ensure the situation didn't get out of hand.

'Andy and I are going to go out and address them,' said Dawn, doing up a button on her blouse and puffing out her chest like a winter robin. 'We like to engage in dialogue,' she said, trying to couple the final word with an encouraging smile in Beth's direction. 'And Andy's ex-police after all, he's used to such scenes.'

He nodded, looking unconvinced.

'You were in the police?' said Beth, her interest piqued.

'Oh, not as a policeman, you understand. I was Media Officer with Thames Valley Police.' He squared his shoulders, lifted his chin.

Beth raised her eyebrows encouragingly. 'And what exactly did that entail?'

'I would advise the Senior Investigating Officer on the media strategy to adopt and sometimes I'd be sent to incidents to liaise with press and try and ensure only the proven facts got out, all the while being mindful to—'

'And how do you usually handle *these* situations?' said Beth, surreptitiously flicking her voice recorder on again. She looked at Dawn now.

'Oh, they are few and far between," said Dawn. "We encourage free speech here. We urge students to find their passion and express themselves through it so, somewhat ironically, we have to expect these occasional shows of defiance – we'd be disappointed if they didn't have the chutzpah to rally against something. But, as you can see, it's peaceful, well-ordered, thoughtful—'

An explosive sound followed by a loud crack and the shattering of glass took them all by surprise. A brass piggy bank landed at their feet amid a glistening carpet of glass shards: the half-glazed internal door to the Vice Chancellor's office was shattered, a pig shaped hole in the corner. Dawn froze. All at once she was back in the Cortina Mk4, the windscreen splintering all around her, fragments of glass embedded in her hair, on her dress, sparkling like diamonds. She could smell the thick, acrid odour of engine oil. When she lifted her hand to her face, it was shaking so violently that Nell instinctively reached out to her and held it in hers. As she did so, she thought she heard Dawn mutter the word 'Pops'.

'Gold Digger – we know you're in there,' bellowed a voice as a scuffle was heard breaking out at the back of the building.

'Sit down a moment, Dawn.'

She allowed herself to be seated behind Nell's desk. 'Call the police. Nell, call the police,' said Dawn, her face ashen, voice just a whisper.

Shouts of 'Keep the Cap!' echoed around the office interspersed with plaintive cries of 'Stop Gold Digger squeezing the life out of Poltowan!', followed by hearty cheers. The crowds were closing in, encouraged by the bold action.

Andy bent to pick up the piggy bank, passing it from one hand to the other as he felt its not inconsiderable weight. 'Very odd,' he said, looking up at Dawn, then at Beth, his expression puzzled. A pair of ornate glasses had been carefully drawn around the pig's tiny eyes. They perched above its protruding nostrils.

Beth scribbled frantically on her notepad while Andy rocked slowly from heel to toe, the pig grasped between his hands like a chicken. 'I'll speak to them, Dawn. I'll go out and—'

She nodded at him, hands gripping the edges of the desk. 'Whatever you think, Andy.'

He waited, bracing himself for the barb that would doubtless follow, but nothing came. A strange stuttering murmur had started before Andy realised the sound was coming from him. He silenced himself.

'Police,' said Nell into the handset, breaking the weighty stillness that followed. 'Poltowan University. A – a riot... Yes, violent... Now.'

Nell replaced the handset and put her hand tentatively on Dawn's shoulder. 'I'll make you that strong coffee. It's a shame we haven't got any brandy to pop in it, take the edge off.'

'My filing cabinet. Far wall. Bottom drawer,' said Dawn. She seemed to have shrunk into herself, broad shoulders rounded, head bowed under her plentiful hair. She began to pick repeatedly at the hem of her jacket, her eyes fixed on the jagged hole in the door.

Nell hesitated before heading for Dawn's office while Beth scribbled on her notepad, following a pace behind. 'What was your full name, sorry?'

Nell turned sharply. 'Me? Nell – Nell Charles.'

Beth smiled and retreated back to the chaos of the reception area where Andy was still frowning meaningfully in the direction of the growing cacophony outside, straightening his tie as he did so.

'I'll go and see if I can't—' His voice tailed off as he approached the door with exaggerated steps.

Within seconds the police siren sounded outside and a flash of blue flickered fleetingly over the whitewashed walls. Andy turned around, one finger pressed thoughtfully to his lips. 'Perhaps I'll – no point in adding to the confusion.'

Ludo and Rockstr had not seen anyone hurl the piggy bank through the glazed door, but as Ludo looked up now he saw the commotion at the front of the crowd, the smashed glass, the faceless group of three covered head to toe in Neoprene, just their eyes visible in their darkened faces. They were chanting loudly as they threw green paint over the front of the building, egged on by the cheering group behind.

'Oh, no, man,' muttered Ludo. 'That wasn't in the plan.'

'What the hell?' said Rockstr, grabbing his arm and standing on tiptoe to try and see over the sea of heads. 'What the hell are those goons doing? Peaceful, it said.'

Within minutes they heard the urgent wail of a police siren growing louder and louder in the near vicinity and a squad car appeared from the other direction, its wheels skidding slightly on the gravel car park. There was a cheer from the group at the front.

'Is that police car at your end, Ludo?' Harry glanced out of his shop window, then back at the screen in his hand. 'Are the cops at the university?'

'Some crazy savages have only gone and smashed a window. Now they're redecorating The Goldburger's office in a questionable shade of lime green.'

Harry laughed. 'They could have saved her a fortune. Sounds like she's just blown the budget having her boudoir refitted to the highest spec.'

'Whatcha saying, Harry? I can't hear you? Listen, I'd best go. I'll catch you later.'

Harry drummed his fingers on his desk, smiling at his reflection in the screen as the riot footage disappeared into sudden blackness. At last his army had been mobilised. He was no longer a lone general striding towards certain oblivion. He sat up straighter at his desk, and for the first time decided to log into Facebook to get the latest news, gauge the mood.

He was greeted with several live video clips of the protest and watched as support and interest spiralled, comments appearing before his eyes, the reactions to each clip steadily mounting in numbers. Already it topped 480 people. Ludo had posted a digital poster for Rockstr's gig too and Harry marvelled at the design. It was gathering likes at almost the same rate as the live footage being posted from the campus. He felt a rush of optimism, of excitement even, flood through him. He, Harry Manchester, was right at the heart of things. Suddenly he felt invincible.

His phone bleeped, heralding the arrival of a text, and he picked it up hurriedly. *Got the keys!!!!* The words were followed by half a dozen emojis of smiling and laughing faces, each one adorned with hearts.

He stood up, stretching his arms high to the ceiling. He had lost two more prospective sellers to Graves that morning and he knew he needed to up his game on the professional front, do something to compete with their cut-price commission, do something to match their long waiting list of eager landlords.

He hadn't dared to look at his accounts for the month yet. It was unusual for him. He was usually all over it, his finger firmly on the pattern of incomings and outgoings. But his mind had been elsewhere, his time taken up with other pressing matters, and business had been quiet. It would pick up again, it always did.

His phone pinged. *Can't wait to see you! Meet you at the penthouse – OUR penthouse – at 5 p.m???xxx*

Harry was about to tap a short reply when Aaron appeared, lumbering rather sheepishly up to his desk. He placed two sheets of paper in front of Harry. 'There you go, boss. The Oaks. All written up and ready to go – when you've given it the once over, of course.'

He hovered, hands in his pockets, waiting for Harry to respond. 'Mrs Manchester seemed keen to press on and get it on the market so I took some photos yesterday lunchtime and popped back to snap a few more on my way in this morning. I made it a priority.'

Harry continued to stare at the glossy colour photo of The Oaks in front of him, the pale blue sky framing its Mock Tudor frontage beautifully, the driveway leading the eye enticingly into the shot, a low winter sun glinting off the handsome leaded windows. Sea glimpses, read the subhead.

'Well, I'll leave it with you, boss. Just shout when you've had a chance to check it through.' Aaron walked slowly back to his desk, still watching Harry.

'Yes,' he said finally. 'Yes. Thank you, Aaron.' He leaned his head in his hands and began to read through the particulars, eyes shielded from Aaron's sight.

Aaron sat waiting, his hands growing sweaty, his mouth dry. He flicked his laptop onto Facebook and began to watch the protest at the university, the sound turned off.

He exclaimed involuntarily. 'Boss, have you seen this?'

Harry eventually looked up.

'The university – there's been a massive riot against the student increase! It's gold for your campaign, gold!'

Harry smiled, sitting up. 'For our campaign, Aaron. I like to think you are part of it too. It's the Harry Manchester ethos, looking after our community, safeguarding its future.'

Aaron swallowed hard and edged slowly back towards Harry's desk. 'Actually, boss, I've got something to tell you.' He jangled the loose change in his pocket. 'I'm handing in my notice.'

Harry searched his young associate's face for signs of humour but could find none. Aaron's mouth was set in a tight line.

'When did this happen?'

Harry had always been impressed by Aaron's dynamism, his willingness to learn, the speed with which he picked things up. He seemed to enjoy the work, and Harry had genuinely thought he was a manager in the making, maybe even a partner further down the line.

'I just – I appreciate everything you've done for me, Harry, I really do. I've learned tonnes… loved it here. But I need to try new things, experience new ways of working, while I'm young.'

Harry nodded, adjusting his glasses. He supposed he should have seen this coming. 'So it's not the money or the work – just the need to expand your horizons?'

'I love the work.' The young man dug his hands deeper into his pockets. 'But the business landscape is changing. I think it's important to get a perspective on different areas of the estate agency business, set me up for the future.'

These didn't sound like Aaron's words. Harry sat back in his chair, folding his arms across his chest. 'I assume you've got another job already lined up?'

Aaron stared at the floor, his hands working vigorously inside the linings of his pockets. 'I'm off to Graves, boss. They've offered me a senior agent post, managing the sales and learning the ropes of the lettings.'

Harry rocked back on his chair, taking in his employee's carefully styled hair, the close-shaved sides and the gelled wave on top. He had his whole life ahead of him. 'Good for you, son,' said Harry eventually. 'Good for you.'

Harry stood for some moments in the draughty lobby of the apartments, gathering his thoughts. He had packed up his scant belongings from Jo's flat the day before and she and a friend had moved them earlier in the day. This was his home now yet he had never felt more lost, less grounded. He flipped his car key over and over in his fingers, trying to ready himself for Jo's tsunami of enthusiasm; trying to focus on the cold beer he would soon have in his hand. He bypassed the lift and climbed the stairs slowly, taking in his new surroundings, inhaling the unfamiliar smells. He paused, studying the ornate gold numeral six on the door, before ringing the bell.

A giggling Jo embraced him excitedly and squeezed him tight, almost knocking off his glasses in the process. He should have brought flowers or Champagne. Music played softly, the lights threw a warm hue across the cream carpets and he detected an aromatic scent coming from the kitchen.

'So, how is it so far?' he said eventually, holding Jo out in front of him. Her cheeks were flushed, her eyes danced. She wore a low-cut red top that framed her generous cleavage, teamed with tight black trousers and low heels.

'Did you move house dressed like that?'

She burrowed into his arms again, nuzzling his neck. 'I have changed to make sure I look nice for my lovely man when he comes home from a hard day at the office. Oh, isn't it wonderful!' she said, more as a statement of fact than a question. She finally released her grip. 'And it's ours, Harry Manchester! Come into your new home.'

There were still some boxes piled in various corners, but Jo's distinctive furniture was in situ. Harry scrutinised one of the Sonos speakers in the hallway. 'Good kit this,' he said, tapping it.

'Oh, Harry, is that all you can say? Come on.'

'It's beautiful, Jo, really. It already looks like a home.'

'Our home.' She took his hand and led him through to the kitchen. 'Champagne?'

He had his heart set on a cold beer. 'Of course. Shall I?'

Harry took his jacket off and threw it over a chair, turning his sleeves up before uncorking the Champagne that stood expectantly – symbolically, he thought – on the marble work surface. 'This is a treat.'

'Well, I knew you wouldn't have time so I thought I'd indulge us. It is a special occasion after all. And there are candles in the bathroom so we can have a long soak too.' She ran her finger slowly down his chest and they clinked glasses. 'To our new home.'

Harry raised his glass silently to her and smiled.

Later, ensconced in the sunken bath, Jo delicately traced the outline of the pink scar on the bridge of his nose before losing herself once more in his blue eyes, the sparkle starting to return to them. She loved to study him without his glasses on. It was like seeing him anew. 'You're my hero.'

He frowned. 'I don't think being mugged in Plymouth makes me a worthy candidate for that.'

'No, you fool. For doing all you do, for putting others first, for trying to save Poltowan from the hands of that—' Jo was slurring her words slightly now, and the term she was looking for eluded her. 'And thank you,' she added.

Harry raised his eyebrows.

'For making this commitment to me, to us. I know I was pretty persistent, or insistent, or perhaps both.' She giggled. 'But it means a lot. You mean a lot. And I know you and Sylvia still have to, you know, sort—'

Harry leaned towards her and kissed her lips lingeringly. It was the only thing he could think of to do.

Chapter 18

Sylvia watched from the upstairs window as Harry banged in the For Sale sign at the end of the drive. He hammered it quickly and hard, throwing his considerable muscle behind the lump hammer to drive it into the earth. He finished with an almost frenzied display of battering that took her by surprise.

He stood back for a moment to look at it, kicking halfheartedly at the bottom of the post after raining down the final blow. It stood fast. He stared at it for a moment before starting back towards the house.

Sylvia turned away. Out at the back, just over the hedge, a flurry of activity had started as people unloaded three transit vans packed with large black boxes and generators. They ambled slowly to and from the marquee, which seemed to have sprung up out of nowhere the day before.

The weather looked promising. It was a bright February day and there was a hint of warmth in the mid-morning sunshine that flooded through the bedroom window. Sylvia closed her eyes, letting it bathe her face.

She could hear Harry in the kitchen downstairs, opening and closing drawers and cupboards and talking in the gruff voice he reserved solely for Sting. She listened.

'Sylvia?' His voice floated up the stairs, as she knew it would.

'Sylvia?' She heard his heavy tread, his voice growing clearer.

She placed both hands on the windowsill, examining her thin fingers, the age spots starting to take hold on her skin.

His feet retreated back down the stairs and she imagined him standing ponderously in the hallway, Sting purring affectionately alongside.

Slowly she roused herself, opening her eyes once more to the bright light and rejoining the present. 'I'm coming,' she called with some effort, but her voice cracked as she did so, fading to nothing.

Harry's voice rose from the back garden and she looked out to see him striding purposefully towards the field alongside a young guy who stood even taller than him. The younger man's arm was thrown loosely around Harry's shoulders, almost protectively. They appeared to be sharing a joke as they disappeared through the gate in the hedge.

She lingered by the bedroom window and watched the activity unfold before her. The cars coming and going, unloading more gear; young people chatting and laughing, embracing, Harry directing things from the middle of the field, stopping to talk to people as he went. She had always admired that about him; his social ease, his ability quickly to find common ground with people, and the way they seemed to gravitate towards him, to find some sort of comfort in his presence.

Sylvia had never been at ease among people. She had always experienced anxiety in social situations, trying too hard or too little, and almost always resorting to silence, choosing shut-down mode as the safest way to navigate gatherings. Since she'd been with Harry, she'd gained confidence. She could play second fiddle while he took the lead, and she felt it suited her, allowing her to find her groove without having to endure the spotlight. There were far fewer expectations of her when she was with Harry. People expected him to perform, to hold court, to lead the way. It meant the demands on her were few.

She watched him walking back to the house alone now, before the familiar sound of 'Bohemian Rhapsody' stopped him in his tracks. He pulled his mobile from his pocket and paused, bending to replace a divot as he spoke.

It was probably *her*, thought Sylvia, shoulders sagging. Harry turned his back on the house, his free hand in his pocket, toeing the grass while he spoke. Sylvia had heard from Nell that they'd moved into an apartment on the river. She had seen it on Facebook and agonised over telling Sylvia, eventually letting it slip while they were walking one day. Sylvia had given little away. In truth, it had simply failed to penetrate her numb state and she had placed the information as if in a mental pending drawer, to address when she felt able. She had not yet felt able.

When Harry finished the call, continuing his walk towards the house, he caught sight of Sylvia standing at the window. He didn't break stride or raise his hand but returned his gaze to the path in front of him and kept on walking.

The back door banged shut and she heard him stamping his boots. 'Sylvia.'

She began to descend the stairs. Harry was standing at the bottom.

'OK if I bring a couple of the guys in for a coffee in the kitchen? Not the whole crowd, just Ludo and Rockstr probably.'

Sylvia nodded, one hand resting on the banister rail, her foot still on the bottom stair, as if she was unsure whether to descend fully. 'There might still be biscuits in the tin.'

He looked at her expressionless face: eyes almost unseeing, mouth set. 'Will you join us?'

She shook her head, still hesitating on the stair.

'Come on. It'll do you good.'

The back door banged again and the sound of exuberant voices filled the room beyond. Sylvia turned away to climb the stairs again but Harry took hold of her hand. She turned to face him, surprised.

'Come on, have a coffee with us. I'll introduce you.'

'No, Harry, really. I've things to do.'

'Like what?'

She stared at him, trying to wrench her hand away but Harry held it firmly.

'Harry. Let me go.'

He let her hand fall and tried unsuccessfully to swallow the words before they came. 'If you'd just try...'

Sylvia looked up towards the top of the stairs as if at the summit of a mountain. 'This is me trying, Harry,' she said softly.

He stood motionless until the creak of the final stair sounded and Sylvia disappeared from sight, the bedroom door closing gently behind her. He took his glasses off and rubbed at his eyes. She curled up on the bed. She could hear a chorus of people below and the squeak of the larder door, the rattle of the biscuit tin. It wasn't long before Harry's deep voice began to resonate through the ceiling once more.

With a trembling hand he filled the large cafetière.

'I bet good old Harry's even got Jammy Dodgers,' said Ludo, fishing hopefully in the biscuit tin.

'Custard creams! These are the dog's,' said Rockstr, dipping her hand in at the same time.

'Harry, have you met Josh, like, properly? Harry – Josh. He's our support tonight, if you remember, fronting the mighty Drones.' Ludo made a flamboyant sweeping gesture with his arm and Harry turned briefly to shake hands with the visitor. 'And son of Darren Toddington,' added Ludo, causing Josh to roll his eyes.

'Ah, yes,' said Harry, straining to focus. 'How is your dad? We did meet some time ago. He wouldn't remember, I expect.'

'He's pretty stressed out – as usual,' said Josh. 'They say living in Cornwall is all about a work–life balance but he is positively unbalanced.' He sniggered, taking a biscuit from the tin. 'Ludo was saying you used to play in a band?' He crunched a slightly stale ginger nut as he spoke.

'Many moons ago,' said Harry. 'Drums. Wasn't up to much – nothing like your act.'

Josh flicked his mane of red hair away from his eyes. 'Well, see what you think later. It's good to know you're on stand-by if our stick man has a bad day.'

'We should try and get you up there, have a bash and show them what you're made of,' said Ludo, his long body lounging across the work surface. 'It's being filmed by some of the top talent on my course – it could be video gold! And it all helps to show that you're no one trick pony – Harry Manchester: businessman, property magnate, campaigner, social rights champion, lothario, drum—'

'Alright, Ludo,' said Harry curtly, turning his back on him to plunge the coffee with more zeal than was required. Ludo exchanged a puzzled look with Rockstr who froze, eyes widening, custard cream in hand.

'Sorry, man. Too much. Sometimes I'm just too much.'

Harry placed the coffees clumsily on the island, watching as the liquid swooshed side to side, teasing the edges of the mugs. 'Sometimes it's all just too much,' he muttered.

❧

'It sounds promising,' said Nell, her hand shielding the glare of the bedroom light from her eyes as she squinted through the near darkness into the back field. 'I like her voice… Rockstr's. A bit Stevie Nicks, don't you think?'

'Turn the light off, you'll see better.' Sylvia was sitting on the small sofa in the bedroom, watching Nell. '"*Go Your Own Way*",' she said, as if to herself.

'Come on, Sylve, we can enjoy ourselves tonight. We've got VIP seats, a bottle of fizz in the fridge. It'll be fun.'

'Fleetwood Mac. 1977.'

Nell pressed her nose close to the glass. 'I can't see Harry but I can hear him. He's in his element. I bet he wishes he was up there playing. I remember him in that band with Paul whatshisface and James Cowley.'

'It's an important night for him,' said Sylvia, rousing herself to get up and wander over to the window, clicking the light off on the way.

'It'll be fine,' said Nell. 'Looks – and sounds – very professional. Not sure what that warm up band will sound like but from the little I just heard of Rockstr, she's a star in the making, I reckon.'

Sylvia stared at her own reflection in the window. 'That warm up singer is the son of the deputy leader of Cornwall Council. Toddington, I think he's called. Harry's hoping the father will come along tonight.'

'Well, so long as word doesn't get back to Dawn Goldberg that I'm here, in any capacity at all, I'll be happy. She won't stand for any disloyalty.'

Sylvia puzzled over the dark shadows being cast on her cheeks. 'It's hardly disloyal to attend a concert, Nell. You've worked part-time for her for... what, four or five weeks? You have a right to your own opinions, and what you do in your own time is your business.'

'Oh, you don't know Dawn,' said Nell, forcing a laugh. 'She is ruthless. Two lecturers have left since I started there – out of the blue, gone.'

Sylvia squinted through the glass, the rapidly deepening dusk gaining a proper stronghold now, the lights in the marquee and around the perimeter of the field shining boldly, the neglected space suddenly transforming into a grassy arena.

'No one seems to want to speak about it but from what I can gather she considered them disloyal,' continued Nell. 'They made some comment on Facebook or liked the wrong post or something and that was that – curtains.'

'Facebook seems to embody all of the modern horrors of our society. If they were foolish enough to spout off on Facebook, maybe they deserved it.'

Nell lowered her voice. 'Between you and me, she seems to be rather fond of the old… you know.'

Sylvia turned to look at her. 'The old what, Nell?'

'You know,' said Nell, miming drinking from an imaginary glass.

'Oh, a drink,' said Sylvia. 'Well, it's a high-pressure job, I suppose.'

'Yes, but drinking on the job – in the mornings sometimes. And she keeps brandy in her filing cabinet.'

Sylvia fell silent, her gaze returning to the darkness beyond the window. 'Everyone has their own vice, I suppose,' she said eventually.

Nell shook her head. 'Talking of which, is it nearly time for that fizz, Sylve? The revellers will be arriving soon.'

The kitchen door slammed again downstairs and Harry's voice carried up to them. 'Sylve? Sylvia?'

She rolled her eyes at Nell and moved slowly through the gloom towards the door. 'Yes, Harry?'

'You coming over for the soundcheck? They're just about to run through a couple of songs, make sure everything's OK. You and Nell want to come and watch?'

'We're coming, Harry,' called Nell, standing up. She took Sylvia's arm and manhandled her out onto the landing.

Chapter 19

A little before seven o'clock people started trickling into the field, collecting in groups and pulling beers out of carrier bags, their laughter carrying across the neighbouring fields. By 7.30 p.m. crowds were swarming in and some semblance of a queue had started to form at the five-bar gate. Harry had asked an old acquaintance of his, a bouncer, and a group of his mates to provide security for the night, and they stood nodding to people as they filed past, their imposing, bulky outlines looking incongruous in the bucolic setting.

Harry surveyed the scene from inside the marquee, hands thrust into the pockets of his black jeans, which seemed to fit a little more easily than when he'd last worn them. Relief started to flood through him as the shadowy throng emerged from the darkness into the harsh floodlights. They had hoped to attract a three hundred strong audience, and Harry would have settled for two hundred, but the field was now a sea of bodies, and a convivial and expectant buzz pervaded the air.

Finally, just before eight o'clock, it was only stragglers arriving and the audience was becoming restless. Some called out for Harry, others for Rockstr, while some began chanting 'Keep the Cap', gathering both momentum and volume.

Dennis Flintoff strolled in at the gate just as the spotlights lit up the stage. He was barely recognisable tonight in a flat cap and padded black jacket. He wore an expression of wry amusement on his face as he wandered along the back of the perimeter fence, taking in the atmosphere.

Alongside him was his junior reporter, Keith, whose face was positively animated, eyes darting left and right, fingers twitching to start scribbling in the dog-eared notebook in his pocket. He shouted that Dennis' estimate of one hundred people, "if they're lucky", looked way off.

Dennis nodded, eyebrows raised in agreement. 'More like four hundred and rising. And it's not even free beer.'

The call he received a few seconds later came as little surprise to him. Dawn's vowels were elongated; she had doubtless already sunk a few gins. 'So has anybody turned up to the gypsy party or is it just you, Harry and his mobile phone?' Laughter reverberated down the phone, but it sounded unusually forced.

'You might be surprised. I would guess there are nigh on four hundred people here. It should be starting any minute. You should have come.'

Dawn muttered some expletives under her breath. 'Four hundred? Well, if that's accurate it says more for the singer than it does for the cause – or that meddling estate agent. Students will go anywhere for a freebie.'

'All the same, they're here.'

Dennis waited for her to speak again but met with silence.

'Are you OK, Dawn?'

'Has he spoken yet? Has he rallied his troops and told them he has a dream—' She started to laugh again then took a long slurp of her drink. 'He has a dream that one day this town will rise up—'

'I'll be sure to report back, don't worry.'

'Call in on your way home, Dennis. It's just me and a bottle of gin.'

He swallowed hard. 'It's not quite on my way home, Dawn.' He was moved by the resulting silence. 'But I'll see. Go easy on the gin.'

'I'd like to see you, Dennis.' Her voice wavered.

'Are you OK?'

'Absolutely fine,' she said, a little too quickly. 'I'll have a drink waiting for you.'

Dennis slipped his phone back into his inside pocket and flexed his pecs, fatigued from his morning gym session. He drew in his abs, enjoying his new shape. His pulse had quickened. He found himself being carried along by the crowd, propelled towards the middle of the throng, noise rising around him, the chanting rousing, bold. He thought of Dawn's painted fingernails, her long eyelashes, her becoming scent. She would be lying on her large sofa, probably in her silk dressing gown, glass of gin in hand. She would be there now, alone.

Keith interrupted his reverie, digging a sharp elbow into his side as the two of them were thrown together.

'Sorry, boss, bit lively here. Got some great shots and a few brilliant quotes already. Harry Manchester – he seems like a top bloke.' Dennis raised an eyebrow at him from under his cap, but Keith's enthusiasm blinded him to his editor's reaction. 'Anyway, turns out people do feel pretty strongly about this cause – it's not just the free music. There's a definite mood: a revolution is afoot.'

Dennis could feel it. There was a palpable energy, a restiveness. Scenes of a possible student uprising vied with images of Dawn Goldberg, reclining semi-clothed and half sozzled.

❧

'Ready, mate?' said Harry to Ludo as they stood in the wings, the young man jigging restlessly from one rangy leg to the other, slapping his thighs in time to the beat.

'You bet I am,' he replied, grabbing a can of beer from on top of a speaker and having a last swig. Adrenaline coursed through his body. Ludo was born for moments like this. Harry smiled, seeing the fire in his eyes. He clapped Ludo on the back. 'Go on then. Let's get this party started.'

The pair of them clasped hands briefly before Ludo gave the sound man the nod and danced onto the stage, to uproarious and enthusiastic cheers of the crowd.

'Good evening, Poltowan!' He waited for the obligatory cheer. 'We all know why we're here, in a field in Cornwall, in February, perched nearly on the edge of the world!' The crowd cheered loudly again, 'Keep the Cap' once again ringing out in the night air. He waited while they chanted it several times. 'And it's not to listen to me!' They booed and laughed in equal measure. 'Poltowan University needs saving, Poltowan needs saving, us students need a better deal, and the good people of this town deserve much more than they're currently getting.' There was a huge roar of agreement. 'Keeping the cap is instrumental to all of those things, and it's essential if we are all to thrive and live happily alongside each other in this beautiful place.'

Ludo began to walk the stage, flicking the microphone cord flamboyantly up and down as he did so, enjoying himself now.

'Give us a shout out if you're a student!' His words were greeted by a huge cheer. 'Give us a shout out if you're a resident!' Another loud noise rose up. 'Together we are one!' The crowd cheered again, interspersed with several piercing whistles.

'Get off!' someone shouted.

Ludo laughed, taking a moment to drink in the sight of the sea of people before him.

'The legendary Harry Manchester will be saying a few words after our first act, shortly before Rockstr – you saw her here first – takes to the stage.' The crowd's murmuring grew louder and bodies began jostling each other, waves of excitement rippling through the mass of people. 'But, without any further messing, ladies and gents… here are… The Drones!'

Cheering and clapping ensued as Josh Toddington appeared, clad in skin-tight black jeans, high-fiving Ludo as he adjusted the microphone, his band filing on behind him.

As the drummer smashed the hi-hat to kick off the first song, Harry felt a rush of pleasure surge through him. He allowed himself to imagine, just for a moment, that he was the rock star he had always dreamed of being, that the roaring, hungry horde was there for him, awaiting his musical majesty. It must be something like Freddie himself had experienced, that visceral thrill, that inimitable rush. He forced himself out of his fanciful world and stepped out of the wings, joining the crowd.

He was following The Drones' second song intently, marvelling at the dexterity of the drummer, when a man pushed past him, causing a swell of beer to rise up from Harry's bottle. He turned instinctively as he steadied it.

'Hey,' said Harry, touching the guy's arm. He half turned, as if intending to continue on his path, but his expression changed quickly when he saw Harry.

'Ah, sorry, Harry.'

'Darren Toddington, I believe. We did meet once, a few years ago.'

Darren chewed vigorously on a piece of gum, his eyes flitting across Harry's face. He belatedly registered Harry's outstretched hand and snatched it firmly in his.

'So glad you could make it, Darren. I believe that's your progeny on stage? It's quite a talent he's got.'

'Good to see you, good to see you. It is, yes, that's the one.' Toddington's words seemed to pile on top of each other as they tumbled out of his mouth.

'Seriously – they're good,' said Harry. 'They've got something.'

Darren had turned away from the stage, his attention fixed elsewhere as he shifted from one foot to the other.

'Can I get you a drink or something? We've got some beers backstage.'

Darren gripped Harry's arm. 'That would be good. I've got to just…' he turned away as he spoke, his next words lost to the night sky '… and then I'll be back. Yes, great. Back in two.'

'See you backstage then,' called Harry, Darren already pushing his way through the sea of bodies.

When Darren appeared backstage five minutes later it was as if he had shed his agitation like a cloak. He walked more confidently, swaggering almost, a beatific smile on his face.

'Impressive turn out,' he said, raising his voice to counter the volume of the band.

Harry handed him a beer, studying him before he spoke. 'I'm pleased. I was unsure, if I'm honest, how many would come. I knew there was strong feeling about the proposed expansion but it's still hard to second guess people, to know if they'll actually stand up and be counted.'

Darren nodded. 'It's a smart idea. Music is emotive, brings people together. I think you hit the spot.'

The next song ended and Harry steered Darren to a quieter area, handing him another beer. The two men shared a toast, Darren drinking down half of his bottle with a few thirsty swigs, still chewing gum in between. Harry stole another glance at him, noticing this time that Darren's pupils were weirdly dilated, lending him an almost demonic look.

≪

Outside, James Cowley watched Harry and Darren intently through a narrow gap in the marquee side, his corpulent frame casting a ghostly silhouette in the weak pool of light. His lips contorted into a smile as he recalled Harry's long-held dreams of becoming a professional musician: a large tent on a field in Cornwall was a far cry from Madison Square Garden. James snorted at the thought, fingers working at the tiny piece of warm foil in his pocket.

A break in the music gave him a chance to eavesdrop on the two men's conversation. James stooped to hear better, eyes trained on them through his canvas spy hole.

'I'm keen to know though, Harry… how do you reconcile the lettings side of your business with arguing against so many houses being let to students?'

Harry drew himself up to his full height, standing almost a head taller than his acquaintance. 'We just focus on sales, Darren. Letting is firmly off my agenda.'

Darren was rocking from heel to toe, picking at the label on his beer bottle. 'I hadn't realised. I just assumed all agents did both, particularly in university towns.'

'We're sales experts, we don't need lettings to make ends meet. It's all word of mouth round here.'

Even from his narrowed vantage point James could see that familiar twinkle in Harry's blue eyes as he spoke. He squeezed the foil-covered tablet firmly between his thumb and forefinger, his eyes never leaving the scene.

'So you've never been tempted – to diversify?'

'I'd rather close the business. I want to help get local people on the property ladder.'

Darren emitted a murmur of approval. 'I admire what you've put into this, Harry. I admire your passion. It would have been easy for you to cash in on this like lots of people, just go where the money is.'

James angled his head to hear the reply as Harry's voice dropped. 'I have to be honest, at times I've wondered what I've taken on. There's no shortage of people in favour of having more students in the town. And Dawn Goldberg – well, she's quite a formidable character.'

Darren's dark eyes looked towards the stage and over the bustling crowd. 'She is certainly not easily cowed.'

'But I don't want to get bogged down in any personal battles. It's so much bigger, so much more important than that. I'm Poltowan born and bred. I won't stand by and watch it go to the dogs – not without a fight.'

The music struck up again, a rousing drum solo leading in a quick-fingered electric guitar riff and the opening lyric. James lunged backwards into the shadows once more as Harry turned to say something he couldn't catch, placing his beer bottle down on the trestle table and exiting towards the stage. Darren followed a few paces behind.

For a large man, James was fast on his feet. He ripped the foil quickly between finger and thumb before slipping into the marquee and dropping the tablet decisively into Harry's beer bottle. Moments later his was just one of many bodies in the swaying crowd, lost in music under the Cornish sky, brimming with expectation.

Harry and Darren returned backstage, Harry instinctively retrieving his beer, one ear cocked towards the band. He had managed to engage Darren in a brief conversation about music, though he clearly had other things on his mind.

'The hardest thing about my job is separating personal feelings from professional ones,' said Darren, looking earnestly at Harry. 'I have to see things from a strategic point of view, for the good of Cornwall as a whole, it's my job.' He sniffed loudly.

'But sometimes it's tough to make the right decisions, and often the more you know, the harder it becomes to see what's right. None of us can look into a crystal ball.'

Harry recognised the opening bars of the next song, his foot tapping uncharacteristically out of time. It felt clumsy, heavy suddenly. Darren began to talk about why he'd joined the County Council, how he'd harboured naive aspirations to make a difference, and how he had grown disillusioned with bureaucracy, wasted resources, too many people with hidden agendas. Outside, the crowd began to sing along to a cover version of 'Castle on the Hill'.

'You have it beaten out of you, Harry, slowly but surely. They suck the fight out of you, drain you, until you're one of them.'

Harry nodded, unsure quite what Darren was driving at. 'Local politics. I've heard it's rife with bureaucracy,' he said, to be supportive. His tongue suddenly felt thick and unwieldy.

'It's not just the Council, Harry. It's the public too. We've got countless law suits underway – with our own people, Cornwall residents – suing us for a perceived failure in our duty of care. One guy, driving too fast early one icy morning – he's suing us for not looking after the roads properly. A woman tripped over a pothole – our fault.' His eyes widened. 'A kid last summer broke his leg slipping by the swimming pool during a lesson – the family want significant damages from the school. It just goes on and on.'

Darren came closer to Harry, shaking his head, breath fragrant with fruity hops, jaw working. For the first time Harry noticed how tired he looked, dark hollows under his eyes, his face lined with tension. The music, slightly muffled by the marquee, still pounded around them. A wave of nausea took Harry by surprise.

'Two million pounds we paid out last year just in compensation,' said Darren, one eye twitching as he spoke.

Harry shook his head, wondering how he could extricate himself from this conversation. He felt a sudden need to be alone. 'That's a hell of a lot of money.' His mind was beginning to wander, eyelids growing heavy.

Darren ran his hand through his greying curly hair. 'Sometimes I wonder how much more I can take. It's like swimming against the tide every day. And whatever you do, it's not enough; whatever you do, someone blames you.'

Harry looked around. 'Shall we listen to the end of Josh's set?' He glanced at his Rolex, struggling to focus on the tiny hands. 'This is probably his last song.'

'And then I think, how do I walk away? I mean, isn't that cowardly, defeatist, when if I stay, I can have the privilege of being able to effect some positive change, however small? I mean, how many people can say that? How many people can go to bed at night knowing they have really helped to make the world a better place?'

The Drones had launched into a cover version of '*I Want to Break Free*'. Harry looked hopefully towards the stage, yet simultaneously fought a sudden urge to lie down and close his eyes.

'I almost didn't come tonight,' continued Darren. 'Things like this – I know people are watching me. They know me, they know I've had to make decisions that affect their lives. They blame me, I know they do. Sometimes I even feel, you know, threatened. I feel physically threatened.'

His face was contorted now, eyes fixed on Harry as if demanding an answer. 'People are actually out to get me.' He whispered the final words close to Harry's ear.

Harry nodded, shuffling backwards. He went to place his half-finished beer on the table, catching the edge and watching helplessly as the bottle dropped to the ground, a swell of bubbles escaping over the soil. He waved his hand dismissively but Darren barely seemed to notice.

'Has it affected your business at all, Harry, this campaign, your stance?'

Harry leaned back against the table. 'I have seen some impact.' He formed his words with exaggerated mouth movements, working hard to shape each sound. 'Just recently… being undercut by Graves who want to sell residential homes to landlords. But I must – see out the storm.' Articulating the last sentence required huge concentration. He glanced once more towards the stage entrance.

Darren seemed to look at him curiously. 'That's why I admire you. You're bravely pitting yourself against a lot of people – and one in particular – knowing full well they'll push back, point the finger, make accusations. It could change public perception of you, jeopardise your business, damage long-term friendships, but you carry on anyway. I really – I really think it's admirable.'

Harry noticed beads of sweat on Darren's forehead, despite the cool night. For a desperate moment he thought the Councillor was about to cry. With a great effort Harry clapped him across the shoulders, his hand colliding with him rather harder than intended. 'You probably make far more difference than you know.'

Harry urged him out into the throng just as the final impassioned line of the song rang out.

Josh slid on his knees across the stage, the drummer flicking his sticks in the air and catching one while the other rolled under the amp. He smashed the cymbal single-handed and defiantly as the crowd roared their appreciation.

'Will you excuse me?' shouted Harry with some difficulty.

'Of course. And listen, sorry for bending your ear. It's been a hard week. A hard few months actually. It's nice to meet someone like-minded.'

Harry took a deep breath and climbed slowly on to the stage, his knees weakening further with each step. As he reached the wings, Rockstr was adjusting her nose stud while staring into a compact mirror and Ludo was hovering behind her, his gangly frame in perpetual motion. The band members occupied themselves by twanging guitars and uncurling leads.

'Hey, man,' said Ludo spinning around. 'The Drones finished with a little number especially for you, what did you—hey, are you OK, Harry?'

He steadied himself against a sturdy pole, his head momentarily bowed. 'Yes, of course.'

'I saw you talking to Mr Toddington. Did you manage to charm and persuade, use your influence to the max?'

Harry lurched suddenly towards his young friend. 'Toddy – seems a little unbalanced.'

Ludo placed his hand on Harry's arm, steadying him. 'Harry mate, have you had a few too many yourself? You're due onstage any second, man. Come on.' He took Harry by the shoulders and looked him in the eye. 'Get a grip, you're sounding blattered.'

'Unbalanced as in… unhinged, unstable. Todd… ington.'

'Harry. Listen to me.' Ludo's eyes bored into Harry's. 'This is your big moment, don't blow it.'

He straightened himself and shook his head slowly from side to side. 'I'm fine, Ludo. Fine.'

'I'm not so sure.'

'I've had two bottles, three at most.'

A lone voice began shouting: 'Keep the Cap!' Soon most of the crowd were repeating it at the top of their voices.

Harry attempted to straighten the collar of his shirt under his jumper, grabbing clumsily at his suit jacket.

Ludo watched him as he walked unsteadily towards the edge of the stage.

Rockstr glanced at him in her mirror as he passed, looking him up and down. 'One hundred per cent, Harry.'

Chapter 20

The field full of people undulated in front of Harry's wavering vision. He homed in on a face at the front, a guy he thought he recognised, though he couldn't think from where. He stared, waiting for everything to stop shifting, nausea still coiling in the pit of his stomach.

Pockets of residents stood side by side with the students, incongruously but harmoniously. There were so many faces he knew, smiling up at him, grateful for this unifying event. He was giving them hope, he thought vaguely, clinging onto the microphone stand. Somewhere beyond the dark perimeter hedge, where the lights of The Oaks shone intermittently through the bare network of waving tree branches, he knew Sylvia was probably listening too.

'We have before us living proof of how residents and locals can live companionably together.' Here he paused, awaiting the cheer that would follow. It did. He staggered sideways, righting himself swiftly.

'But we need to strike that all-important balance. And that... means we need to—' He paused dramatically, holding one arm aloft, his body swaying. 'Keep the Cap!' The ensuing roar of approval was louder than it had been all evening, with the whole audience appearing to chant, their breath visible in the cold air, voices drifting up and away over the inky black fields.

As Harry summoned all his concentration to focus on the

crowd, a husky voice he recognised hollered from near the stage.

'Is this the anti-progress rally?'

James Cowley and Steve Kent stood smugly together, Steve's black woollen hat and leather jacket alongside James' dark green Puffa jacket, both at odds with the rainbow of colours being paraded by the students, who also managed to show an alarming amount of flesh given the chill February evening. The two men stood as if poised for a fight, their legs astride and thick necks rigid, their presence somehow at odds with the occasion.

A momentary silence fell. The mood shifted suddenly in response to the hostility in Steve's tone. The anticipative buzz became an edgy murmur.

The words that had been on the tip of Harry's tongue evaporated into the night sky. He adjusted his glasses as he made out the two surly faces in the crowd. His shoelace was snaking out in front of him and he thought briefly about bending down to do it up. He had been planning to say something about how important it was to get the community together and have their voices heard, and how the turnout was a bold statement about the strength of feeling among both students and locals.

'Don't let him 'oodwink you into thinking change is bad,' continued Steve, turning now to address the crowd, voice straining without a mic to help him. 'At best it's a total lack of vision, a complete failure to understand today's world. As worst it's Nimbyism and self-interest.'

Harry noticed now that several of the other traders were standing behind Steve and James. He frowned as he tried to make out each face. Nigel was conspicuous by his absence. He had clearly stood by his inebriated declaration of the other night.

There was some movement as people began shuffling to see where the confrontational voices were coming from. Muttering started among the crowd, a wave of unrest rippling through the spotlit audience. 'And *you're* not in it for reasons of self-interest? Pull the other one.'

The eyes of the crowd were mostly turned towards Harry, in expectation of a trenchant response, while others glowered at the hecklers, some people responding to them with their own volley of abuse. Harry took a deep breath, gripping the microphone in his left hand, but his voice wouldn't come.

'More students means a bigger, stronger university, and a bigger market for local businesses,' came Steve's voice again. 'Better business means job creation – and more opportunities for Poltowan's graduates. It's one big 'appy circle.'

'Another one who's swallowed the PR guff whole and asked for seconds.' It was Dave White speaking, standing in the middle of a crowd of students, his balding head visible thanks in part to his height. 'Spend a day behind the scenes at the university and you'll soon change your mind, mate. Lifting the cap isn't about community and economy. It's about one thing only – the advancement of Dawn Goldberg.'

'We've lived here all our lives – we've seen Poltowan change, and not for the better,' called another voice.

Harry's head was starting to spin as he struggled to follow this exchange, aware that he should be taking control, directing proceedings. This was his moment, after all. But his tongue seemed suddenly paralysed.

'The uni is already overcrowded,' called another voice. 'They're quick to build shiny new offices and wanky new research buildings, but we haven't anywhere to live.'

'It's a fucking joke! Go and line your pockets somewhere else, Burger Boy,' shouted someone else, in close proximity to Steve and James.

'Bring on Rockstr!' called another plaintive voice from the back, followed by a cheer and several inaudible comments.

As Harry concentrated all his will on moving to the front of the stage, his knees gave way, his large frame concertinaing heavily to the floor. He looked up, trying to make sense of the mass swarming in front of him. Everything was on its side, people's faces fusing into one.

''Ave another drink, 'arry!' called a familiar voice. A cheer quickly faded to an uncertain murmur of concern.

'Keeeep the Cap,' came a deep roar-throated roar from the back of the crowd, followed by a spontaneous and deafening round of applause.

The next thing Harry knew Ludo was sitting him up, whispering urgently into his ear, his Irish accent somehow more pronounced. 'For fuck's sake, man, come on. Come on!'

Harry was vaguely disconcerted by Ludo's unusually severe tone. He was unsure what happened next but had a hazy sense of being manhandled along the stage by many unfamiliar hands. When he finally came to he was sitting on the hard floor propped up against a cold metal pole, Ludo staring earnestly into his eyes.

'What happened, man? What the… what are you playing at?'

Before Harry could answer, Ludo had dashed back onstage and Harry heard the ugly buzz of feedback briefly before Ludo announced: 'Good people of Poltowan, I give you, R-R-Rockstr!'

The lighting changed suddenly, a multi-coloured strobe effect flickering over Harry's face. He closed his eyes.

A muted trumpet cut mournfully through the air. Silence fell over the ancient Cornish landscape, expectant under the perfect black sky. The audience watched, transfixed for a moment, before the lights flashed on, bringing the stage into sharp relief against the night canvas.

A guitar joined the melody, and then another, and the drums kicked in as Rockstr threw her arms in the air, launching into her opening line, her sugar-sweet voice quickening the tempo. The student contingent roared while residents began to nod their heads and move their bodies in growing appreciation of the unfamiliar sound.

At the back of the field, Steve, James and their associates slipped away into the night.

❦

Through the trees, in the darkened bedroom window of The Oaks, Sylvia and Nell stood together, half-full glasses of fizz in hand.

'That's one thing I'll say for Harry: he keeps calm in a crisis.'

Sylvia looked witheringly at her friend. 'What crisis?'

'Those blokes heckling. I didn't hear Harry ranting back.'

'We couldn't really hear what they were saying or see what was going on.'

'Well, it wasn't supportive, I know that much. Yet Harry, he takes it all in his stride.'

Sylvia smiled to herself. This seemed to be the prevailing view of Harry, that he was the embodiment of clear thinking regardless of the situation, yet he frequently revealed his patience to be tested by the smallest things. He had broken numerous items when trying to apply his minimal DIY skills, quickly erupting into pure rage when flat-pack furniture failed to materialise with the ease promised by the manufacturer. It was Sylvia who always had to step in, poring painstakingly over the unopened instructions to rectify the damage so often wreaked by him.

'Sorry, Sylve,' said Nell, glancing sideways at her friend's profile, lit eerily by the faintest wash of the floodlight in the field. 'Am I going on a bit? He's not who you want to talk about, is he?'

Sylvia drained her glass. 'I just hope Jo is good at constructing flat-pack furniture.'

'I'm not sure she's that type,' said Nell, regretting her words as soon as they left her mouth. She reached behind for the bottle and topped up their glasses.

'Too glamorous to be hands on, I suppose,' said Sylvia. 'Blind leading the blind.'

'What will you do, Sylve, when you sell this place?'

She was silent for a long time, her eyes looking far beyond the teeming field, the distant music. 'John Lennon said life is what happens when you're busy making other plans, but even when you stop making plans, and draw breath, life still happens. If it doesn't happen directly to you, it is happening to the people around you. You can't escape it, ever.'

Nell shivered involuntarily and clutched her glass to her bosom. 'What is it you want? What do you want to do?'

Sylvia laughed. 'It's the million-dollar question, isn't it? What do any of us really want to do with our lives? It seems to me it takes most of our time here to work out what exactly it is we want and, perhaps more importantly, how to go about it, but by then the sands of time are running down, doors start closing rather than opening, you start looking backwards not forwards... It just gets harder and harder to—'

She looked away in the direction of the music, her shoulders rounded. Rockstr was playing a jazzy number now, her velvet voice floating through the night and drifting through the slightly open window.

'You're a fool to let him go, Sylvia. While you've got a chance to get him back, take it.' Nell felt her cheeks growing warm as she spoke but she couldn't contain herself.

'You told me they'd moved into a penthouse, Nell. Our time has gone. It's ridiculous to pretend otherwise.'

The two women sat in silence as strains of music teased them. Long-suppressed anger mixed with frustration gripped Nell.

'She is better for him, much better,' said Sylvia in a low voice.

'Oh, rubbish. You know how he feels. You pushed him out, made him go. Admit it, Sylvia, he had no choice.'

'There is always a choice. And he made his.'

'Was it a test then – some stupid trial of faith? How exactly did you expect him to prove his love for you, to prove that he loved you enough for you actually to let him?' To her surprise, Nell found that she was close to tears now, the anger having morphed quickly into an overwhelming sadness.

Sylvia narrowed her eyes in the darkness. 'Of course it wasn't a test. We just stopped working. It happens. Two people can still love and care about each other, even if they can't be together anymore.'

Nell emptied the barely visible dregs of the bottle into her own glass and drank them down, emitting a small hiccup afterwards. 'I find it all absolutely baffling.'

'Because you've never been in a relationship. At least not a—'

'I can see when two people need their heads banging together.' She stood up rather too quickly, putting her hand out to the windowsill to steady herself. She felt suddenly lightheaded and slightly dizzy. 'I am quite happy to be single, thank you very much, since it seems it has saved me a lot of unnecessary grief.'

'We should have swapped,' said Sylvia, looking into her glass.

'Swapped?'

'Swapped lives. Me on my own with a cat. You with Harry.'

She turned to look up at Nell now, examining her face in the half-light. 'You could have made him happy. He always liked you.'

Nell sat back heavily on the bed, her head still spinning slightly. 'It nearly was me. If I hadn't sprained my blinking ankle, it very nearly was me.'

Without replying, Sylvia watched through the black trees as the crowd began to jump in the air in unison, the tempo quickening as the concert drew to a close.

Chapter 21

Harry sat on a plastic chair in the wings where he gulped down cupfuls of water to sate a savage thirst. His head was growing clearer now, but his body remained heavy and lethargic.

'Please, please, continue to make your voices heard.'

He listened as Ludo's words rang out into the night. 'Lobby Poltowan Council, lobby Cornwall Council, and spread the word about how important this is. Time is not on our side. A decision will be made on Thursday, March the second – just a couple of weeks away. Keep up the good work, people.'

He left the stage to deafening chants of 'Keep the Cap', and reappeared in the wings, looming over Harry.

'Good job, Ludo. I'm sorry. I really don't know what happened.'

'Beer. Beer is what happened. Your big moment and you go and get steamin'. I thought you'd know better than that.'

Harry watched as Ludo hopped down the steps and into the dark. He eased himself up, standing still for a moment as he waited for his head to clear.

'Can I get you something, Harry? A coffee or—'

Rockstr stood with one hand gently touching his arm.

'No. I'm fine now, thank you. I know Ludo thinks it was the beer but I only had two bottles, spilled another – I can hold my drink.'

'You think someone spiked it?'

Harry looked at her, noticing the horrified expression in her wide brown eyes.

It was not something he'd considered until now. He began to nod his head. 'Yes. I think that's exactly what happened.'

'But who did it?'

Ludo reappeared quickly beside them. 'He sobered up yet?'

'He thinks his drink was spiked.'

'Don't try that one, Harry Manchester, at least be honest about—'

'Seriously, Ludo. I had two beers. And even if I'd had four, five, six – I've never felt like that before.'

Ludo studied his face. 'You think it was those goons, James Cowley and his neckless sidekick? You think they gotcha?'

New possibilities were opening up to Harry all the time. He scratched his head.

'That Toddington seemed a bit edgy,' said Ludo. 'In fact, you said he was unbalanced.'

Harry nodded. 'But what's in it for him to see me make a fool of myself, to try and scupper our cause? He actually seemed sympathetic.'

The three of them stood in the half-light backstage, looking at each other, the noise of the crowd having largely subsided. There was just the clatter of the band packing up their instruments.

'It doesn't matter now,' said Harry, suddenly overcome by a sweeping tiredness. 'We can't prove anything. I don't think even Cowley would stoop that low.' He looked around at the detritus from the crowd, the plastic chairs and trestle tables in the wings, the mess of wires leading to lights and speakers.

'You go, Harry. You've done enough. I'll make sure it's all sorted out here,' said Ludo. 'They're picking up the marquee tomorrow. Rockstr and the band will give us a hand. Leave it with me, fella.' He steered Harry down the steps. 'Sorry for doubting you, I just couldn't believe you'd blow your moment, you know? Not when it meant so much.'

'It still does, Ludo. And me falling on my arse onstage won't make much difference – you were both fantastic.'

'You gonna be OK getting back to the house?'

The men shook hands and Rockstr followed, reaching up to embrace Harry. She and Ludo stood and watched as he lumbered away through the semi-darkness, easing himself through the gap in the hedge towards the lights of The Oaks.

∽

Harry took out his phone. He had four missed calls from Jo. He dialled her number as he made his way towards the house, pausing as she answered.

'How did it go?' she said eagerly. 'I've been trying to reach you.'

'How did you expect me to hear the phone when there's live music blaring? Plus I've been trying to talk to the right people, introduce the acts – it's been chaos here.'

Jo was taken aback by his tone. Something tugged sadly at her heart. 'I just wanted to make sure it was going well, I've been worrying about you.'

'About four hundred people came, we reckon. So, yes, it went well.'

'Are you OK? You sound—'

'Why does everyone keep asking me that?'

'Have you called a taxi? I can pick you up, it's not too late and I'm—'

'Give me a chance.' He stumbled slightly, jarring his knee. 'I'm not even back home yet.'

Jo fell silent for a moment.

'Hello? Are you there?' said Harry, continuing his stuttering progress back to the house.

'This is your home, Harry.'

'Oh, you know what I mean. I still own half of this damn' place, don't I?'

'Not for much longer.'

'Give me a break, Jo. I'll see you in a bit. And don't worry, I'll call a taxi. You get off to bed.'

Jo looked out of the window at the sparkling lights of Poltowan. She could hear the river's gentle burble not far away. She hugged her arms tightly around her and watched for a moment as a car's headlights climbed slowly up the main road out of Poltowan and disappeared into the night, its progress slow and faltering.

She turned the lamps off one by one and blew out her scented candle before tipping away the dregs of her cup of tea in the sparkling kitchen sink and replacing the mug she had put out for Harry.

Her friends had warned her about this, the as yet unbroken ties to his former life, his unwillingness to discuss Sylvia or commit to starting divorce proceedings. But she felt she knew Harry's heart. She had seen the earnestness in those blue eyes. And she had never felt more alive than when she was with him; never felt more optimistic about all that life could bring than when he looked at her; never felt safer than when she was wrapped in his arms. She clung to the belief that she simply needed to give him space to adjust, even if it defied her almost overwhelming impulse to rush headlong into this newfound and precious thing, clutching it as if her very life depended on it.

She lay in bed, her eyes wide open as the room slowly came to life in the darkness, the still unfamiliar shapes starting to emerge like ghostly friends. As sleep began to take her, the sound of the river became a low, persistent whisper in her ear.

✍

Harry leaned heavily on the counter in his former kitchen, his head bowed. He was pleased to find the place empty. He closed his eyes.

'Ah, here he is!' Nell emerged from the hallway, placing her hand lightly on his back, her voice slightly higher than normal. 'Are you OK, Harry?'

He muttered under his breath, straightening himself up slowly and bending his leg.

'You've got dust or something all down your arm. I daren't ask what you've been doing out there, Harry Manchester, under cover of darkness with all those young things…' Nell winked at him.

He brushed half-heartedly at his tender right arm. 'Where's Sylvia?'

'Oh, she's about somewhere, she'll be down in a minute. Can I get you a glass of something? You look like a drink would—'

He raised his hand to silence her. 'I'm fine, Nell. Thank you, I'm fine.' He stood still rubbing his temples thoughtfully. 'I'd better get off.'

'It sounded fantastic, and what a great turn out.'

'It seemed to go pretty well.'

'But what happened towards the end? We couldn't quite hear your speech but it sounded like the crowd were a bit lively—'

'Just some heckling, Nell, to be expected.'

Sylvia ghosted into the room.

'They had the cheek to heckle him,' said Nell.

Harry winced. 'It was quickly sorted out – it's no big deal.'

Sylvia moved closer to him, frowning at the marks on his sleeve. 'It's a shame there are always troublemakers.'

Harry gave her a weary look. 'I would have been surprised if there hadn't been. The concert was in support of what appears to be a highly contentious issue.'

Sylvia raised her eyebrows at him. His blue eyes had taken on a grey cast, the way they did when he was tired or irritable. 'Are you in pain?'

He took his glasses off and placed them on the work surface, leaning both hands once more on the edge of it. 'I slipped over, banged my hip and my arm. It's just bruising.'

'You shouldn't drink so much,' said Sylvia, going to the cupboard and taking out a packet of paracetamol. She popped one carefully from the foil and repeated the action. Then she took a glass and filled it with water. She crossed the kitchen and handed them to him.

'It's not drink,' he said, taking what was offered without complaint. 'I only had a couple of beers.' He swallowed the pills down with an audible gulp before wiping his hand across his mouth. He looked at the two women watching him, suddenly relaxing slightly.

'You look tired,' he said to Nell, putting his glass down on the work surface with a thud.

'Oh! Those blinking students opposite – and now some more are moving in down the road. I thought the first couple of times were housewarming parties – I was prepared to give them the benefit of the doubt. After all, they seem nice enough, but these get togethers appear to be a regular thing. I've started taking that dopey cough mixture—'

'Drowsy,' said Sylvia, catching Harry's eye. He smiled.

'… well, whatever it is, it gets me off. Not that it stops me waking up at three when they really get going.'

Harry shook his head. 'This is exactly what I mean. And with that bus stop at the end of your road, this is only the tip of the iceberg if the cap's lifted. All this,' he swept his arm dramatically in the direction of the back garden, 'is to ensure people like you get a good night's sleep, Nell.'

She gazed at him through her slightly fuddled haze, noting the long eyelashes usually hidden by his glasses, his firm lips, the virility implied by his six o'clock shadow. She stood for a moment, wondering if she really could have made him happy, and fleetingly considering whether her time was still to come.

'Nell?' Sylvia repeated her name.

'Sorry, Sylve, I was miles away. Must be the bubbles.'

Sylvia took two cups out the cupboard. 'Are you joining us?' she said over her shoulder towards Harry, her hand hovering over the shelf.

Apathy had overcome him. Suddenly he wanted just to stay in his own home – because that was what it still felt like – and to sleep in his own bed, and to wake to a simpler world, the world that seemed to have deserted him when he wasn't looking. He thought of Jo, in all probability waiting for him with a hundred questions, anticipating his return like an excited Labrador. He tried to suppress an inconvenient pang of guilt, habitually adjusting his Rolex as he did so.

'I'll have a quick one, then I'll call a taxi.' He watched as the second hand completed a thoughtful lap of the large kitchen clock, prompting the hour hand to jolt sharply into midnight. 'Actually, have we still got that brandy?'

❧

While Sylvia's prosaic and unadorned perspective had often infuriated him, Harry realised now, as he sank back in his old recliner, in his old lounge, that he had come to rely on it. He was starting to see that the romantic world Jo lived in was actually more wearing and difficult to navigate than the cold hard truth. He was continually protecting her, unwilling to shatter her idealistic and sunny outlook, while all the time shouldering more and more of the burden himself.

After Nell had gone to bed, and as he savoured his third 'and last' brandy, Harry found himself telling Sylvia all about the loss of business to Graves, Aaron's resignation, the evening with James Cowley, and his conversation with Darren Toddington. Everything came spilling out as if a previously stoppered hole had been suddenly unplugged.

When he finished his monologue, Sylvia rose slowly to stoke the fire. Only when she had folded her thin body back into her chair and taken a sip of her coffee did she show any sign that she had heard a word he'd said.

'I did tell you it was a dangerous game. There might be many residents who support you but local businesses stand to lose out – and they'll not go down without a fight. You're effectively waging a one-man campaign against a whole community.'

'But it was you who said before that I was all they had – all the residents, and the students had – to save Poltowan.'

'You are.'

'But it's not a one-man campaign, Sylve. I've got Ludo and I've got all the people who turned up tonight – and in good voice too. You must have heard?'

She glanced at him from the corner of her eye as Sting leaped onto her lap. 'And you think they'll carry on the fight, write to the powers that be, spread the word, do all the things that involve making a bit of an effort?'

For a moment Harry looked lost. 'I don't see why not. They were here tonight, weren't they?'

'Yes, for a free concert by someone who, by all accounts, might one day be a big name.'

Harry fell silent.

'As for your downturn in business…'

'It's not a downturn, Sylve, just—'

'It's a worrying trend, Harry. Don't bury your head in the sand. You've lost, what, five sales to Graves in the last three weeks?'

He nodded.

'Putting principle over profit is all very admirable but you may find that even with your reputation, refusing to sell to landlords will harm you. There is only so much business to go around.'

'There're over twenty-five thousand people in Poltowan. That's a lot of houses.'

Sylvia pursed her lips. 'But this trend will only continue. Look at Nell's road. And now Graves have pinched Aaron as well.'

Harry ran his hand over his jaw. He had been wondering why Sylvia had become pleasantly soft focus. Now he realised he had left his glasses in the kitchen. He slid further down into his seat, the brandy warming his insides.

'It's only a short while until the decision. If it doesn't go your way, what then? Things will get even harder.' Sylvia watched Harry closely. 'And no doubt you're having to pay a fortune for your new home.'

'Oh. You know about that.'

'This is Poltowan. Of course I know. And it's nothing to do with me. I'm just saying, if business is faltering and you've increased your outgoings… Well, you need to be careful. You're still paying for half of this place too – and God knows, I can't afford to keep paying the mortgage on my own. I would if I could. The sooner we sell it the more—'

'I don't want you to pay it on your own. I don't even want to sell up. But I'll keep paying until we do, no question.'

'And there's the roof. We'll have to—'

'What do you mean – the roof?'

'Didn't Aaron tell you? He went up in the loft and got that surveyor you know to have a quick look too. He thinks we might need part of the roof replacing. There are signs of damp as well.'

Harry finished his brandy and closed his eyes. 'No. He didn't tell me. And you didn't tell me.' He let the brandy take him, welcoming its capacity to insulate him from reality, just for a moment. 'Nobody told me.'

'You should go,' she said eventually, her voice softer than he had heard for some time. Perhaps it was the brandy.

'I think someone spiked my drink tonight.'

Her look suggested he would have to do better if he expected any degree of sympathy from her.

'I felt very strange suddenly: nauseous, tongue-tied, weak-kneed. I fell over onstage.'

Sylvia was silent for a moment 'And everyone saw you?'

Harry nodded. 'I was trying to make my key points, get the message across. There was some heckling – James Cowley and Steve Kent, I think. And then, I just collapsed.'

Sylvia blew sharply through her lips. 'Do you not think it would be wise to see a doctor rather than go and drink three brandies?'

'I'm OK now, Sylve. Really. It wore off quite quickly. But it was very strange.'

'Maybe it was just the stress of the occasion. You got yourself worked up.'

Harry nodded again. Perhaps she was right. Perhaps there was no culprit. He was being paranoid. Even James Cowley wouldn't be that underhand.

'You should go.'

He shifted his body to one side, pulling his phone out of his pocket and calling a taxi. 'One round the corner as luck would have it,' he said to her.

He eased himself up, massaging his hip, glancing at Sylvia as he did so. She had already turned away. In truth, she was beginning to feel the uncomfortable stirrings of anxiety, heightened when Harry pulled on his suit jacket in the hallway, his imminent departure looming like a darkening sky between them.

'Nice for you to have Nell here tonight,' he said. He knotted his woollen scarf with several pronounced movements around his neck, a knot that Jo had shown him some days before. Sylvia handed him his glasses. He looked different tonight.

'I don't need company, Harry. I'm perfectly fine here on my own. I like the peace and quiet.' Sting rubbed first against Harry's shins then made a figure of eight through Sylvia's legs, as if herding the two of them together. They both watched silently as he repeated the move.

A car's brakes squeaked in the drive and Harry cocked his head to one side. 'That's the thing with these hybrid taxis – you never hear their engines anymore. Give me diesel any day.'

'Diesel is highly polluting. The latest research proves it. Hybrids are better all round.'

'It's not what they used to say.'

The taxi's horn sounded briefly.

'Times change.'

He bent to kiss her cheek before unlatching the door into the cold, clear night. 'Thanks for letting me offload.'

Sylvia laid her hand very lightly on his arm. 'Be careful, Harry. You'll lose everything you've worked for.'

∽

Andy Hornblower pulled repeatedly at his ear lobe as he stared at the screen in front of him, its harsh light throwing ghostly green shadows around the dark room. His brow was furrowed with deep lines, mouth hanging open with the effort of concentration. He tapped a few more buttons, uncertainly navigating his way around the screen, his eyebrows rising in surprise every time his action brought about the desired result. He wasn't a regular user of Facebook, only occasionally choosing to share photos of his lengthy weekend cycling trips, usually depicting views of the trying hills around Zennor or the windblown environs of the Lizard.

He was surprised that Rockstr didn't have tighter privacy settings. Her profile gave him access to all her information and photographs, and the more he looked, the more he felt he knew her face, those wide, challenging eyes, the punky hair, the striking bone structure.

Ludo, Andy had discovered, had locked his profile, giving access only to approved friends, something that impressed Andy. Yet Rockstr's life was laid bare for all to see. He trawled her conversations and messages, watched some videos of her singing for longer than he'd intended, and finally, when scanning a historic conversation between herself and a friend called Jonny Gowers, he found what he was looking for.

You haven't changed Moira Highgate :)

Moira Highgate. It came flooding back to him. Andy went straight to Google and tapped in her name, already beginning to recall why he knew her from his time at the Thames Valley Constabulary. The local news report from three years before completed the picture. He sat back, rocking in his chair, his hands behind his head. Finally, he thought, a rare quiver of excitement travelling up his spine. Finally.

Chapter 22

Dennis drove too quickly along the dark lanes leading to Dawn's house, finally inching up the winding drive. It was in darkness but for a soft glow in the lounge window. He was already rehearsing excuses in his head for making a quick exit, vowing not to stop for a drink, intending only to hover in the hallway. He cleared his throat as he rang the doorbell, the porch light suddenly blinding him. He shielded his eyes as he waited.

He didn't know whether to be relieved or disappointed when Dawn answered the door fully clothed in a slightly frumpy leopardskin onesie, albeit one with a plunging neckline.

She stepped back to let him in. 'I didn't expect you.'

He lingered in the hallway, the unfamiliar scent of someone else's home assailing his nostrils as he tried to adjust his eyes to the dim light within.

'You said to—'

'Drink? I've got red wine open. I progressed from the gin. I'll get you a glass.'

He followed her into the kitchen.

'Well, make yourself at home, Dennis. Take your jacket off, kick off your shoes or whatever it is you do when you're at home. Does Mrs Flintoff usually relieve you of those items as you enter?'

Dennis took his coat off and unlaced his shoes, placing them by the bar stool. He had only visited a couple of times before but the grandeur of the kitchen still impressed him with its raised ceiling and state-of-the-art appliances, its vast marble island sitting proudly in the centre.

'Here.' She handed him a goblet of wine. 'Come through.'

Next to one of the sofas was a huge pile of papers while a laptop lay open on the floor, a pair of glasses perched studiously on the keyboard. Frenzied jazz music played at low volume in the background.

'Working?' he said. 'On a Saturday night?'

Dawn slopped wine from her glass on to the table as she sat down. 'Firefighting is a more accurate term.'

He sat next to her, crossing his legs and relaxing his shoulders, smoothing his hand over his firm thigh.

'So?' she said.

'So it went reasonably well. I mean, I didn't hang around after the warm up act, but it was a good turnout. Toddington was there.'

'Darren Toddington?'

'His son's in the support band. I doubt it was any more than that.'

Dawn took a deep draught of her wine. Her heavy eye make-up was smeared, making comedic dark shapes under her eyes. Her hair looked unusually unkempt.

'And Manchester? He did his Martin Luther King, I suppose?'

'He was just starting to speak when I left. I've heard it all before. Are you OK, Dawn? You seem a little—'

'Drunk? Is that what you were going to say, Dennis? Well, maybe I am, just a little. And maybe it's better that way.'

'What's wrong?'

She laughed, smoothing her hands along her leopardskin legs before tucking them underneath her and shuffling closer to him. He could smell the heady cocktail of alcohol on her breath.

She took his hand in hers, lacing her fingers loosely in his. She was unused to people asking her how she was in such an earnest way, as if he might even care.

He began to run his thumb over her warm hand. It was a gesture of such casual tenderness that Dawn began to cry without warning. It was as much a shock to her as it was to him when her tears fell on his fingers, followed by a low primal wail that sounded as if it had been a long time coming.

Dennis snatched his handkerchief from his pocket and handed it to her before placing one arm awkwardly around her shoulders.

'What is it?'

The mournful moan continued, emanating from a mass of hair, her face hidden now. He waited, patting her shoulder in a way he hoped was comforting. It was a while before she spoke, and when she did he could only make out certain words. "Guardian" seemed to be a recurring one, followed by "protest" and "glass".

'Slow down, Dawn. Blow your nose.' He reached for her wine. 'Have a drink.'

She pulled away from him, wiping her nose unceremoniously on his handkerchief and eyeballing him, her eyes sitting now in pools of black, yet even in their smeared state Dennis admired their distinctive almond shape and fought a sudden urge to run his finger along her fine cheekbones.

Dawn recovered herself quickly, the surprise tears sobering her. She'd had no intention of telling Dennis about *The Guardian* journalist or the student protest, and she certainly didn't want to go into her father's death, but one thing led to another, his patience and warmth so disarming that Dawn spilled the contents of her head and her heart with ease as Dennis stroked her hand and nodded silently.

He decided she had never looked more beautiful to him than curled up on the sofa in her onesie, her hair carelessly about her shoulders, her eyes bright with tears.

'I know about the protest, Dawn.' Indeed, he had been puzzling over how much space to give it in the following week's paper, particularly with the concert taking place too. He had hoped a more pressing front-page story would break in the meantime, allowing him to relegate both events to the community pages. 'But I had no idea about your father.'

'Why would you?' she sniffed. 'I've never spoken about it. My mother won't talk about it. She blames me.'

'I'm sure she doesn't. How could—'

'"Your lofty ambitions", she said to me once. "" If it weren't for your lofty ambitions".'

Dennis shrugged. 'She wouldn't have meant it.'

'Oh, you don't know my mother.' Dawn raised her hand to her mouth to stop wine from cascading down the open zip of her onesie. 'If there was someone else to blame, she would find them.'

Dawn blinked. '"If it weren't for your lofty ambitions my husband would still be here now." That was what she actually said to me. No mention of him also being my father.'

'And you witnessed the crash? That must have been traumatic to say the least,' said Dennis, shuffling closer to her.

'In her self-absorbed world he was simply her husband, and it was her loss, her life that was turned upside down.'

Dennis hesitated only momentarily before pulling Dawn to him, his arms wrapped tightly around her, her potent red-wine breath at first on his cheek, then on his lips, their tongues meeting – before she hiccupped noisily, bringing the ill-conceived kiss to an end. Just as she did so, her mobile started to ring, vibrating its way across the carpet like a small and needy pet.

She sniffed loudly. 'Who on earth is that?'

Dawn was characteristically curt with Andy Hornblower, in spite of her highly charged emotional state. She sat up suddenly as his story began to unwind before bringing herself to her feet and swaying precariously towards the television set.

'Oh, you are brilliant, Hornblower. Brilliant! I'll tell Dennis now – I mean, I'll call him obviously – and see if we can't expose that… that schh-arade for what it really is.' Dawn signed off with an exaggerated 'mwah', leaving Andy continuing to stare at the phone, wondering if he had dialled the right number.

She landed heavily on the sofa next to Dennis, unwittingly forcing his little finger in a direction God had not intended. He winced, easing it out from under her rear to examine the damage.

'You will never guess what, Dennis!' She clapped her hands together excitedly before reaching for her wine glass. 'I have just got you your front-page lead for Wednesday! It's a scoop bigger than you'd have had on any of the nationals you never worked on!'

Dennis' finger throbbed hard, his cheeks flushed pink with pain and reproachfulness. 'I chose not to move to London, Dawn. I *chose* to come back here and have a family.'

'Your sales will go through the roof!'

'You chose your career instead of a family.'

'It turns out that the artist formerly known as Rockstr, or whatever it is she calls herself, who Harry Manchester has been proudly pushing as the face of his so-called campaign, is fresh out of Her Majesty's Prison, having done time for selling cannabis!'

Dennis twisted the stem of his glass in his hand. 'And who is your source?'

'Andy Hornblower. My comms director. Useless most of

the time but he once worked for Thames Valley Police. He recognised her face and did some digging. Bingo!'

'And Harry was unaware of this?'

'I don't think even he would have been stupid enough knowingly to make a song and dance about having a convicted drug dealer fronting his cause, do you?'

Dawn cackled with laughter before taking a circuitous route to the kitchen to top up her wine. When she returned, Dennis was putting on his shoes in the dimly lit hallway.

'Barbara will be wondering where I am. And I can't have another drink anyway, I'm driving.'

She watched him tie his other lace as she processed his imminent departure. 'So dull, Dennis. Why are all men so dull?'

He looked at her for a moment before leaning closer to kiss her on the cheek, lingering as he inhaled the scent of coconut from her hair.

'Call me tomorrow,' she said. 'I'll get the other details on the drug queen for you, put you in touch with Andy Blowhorner.' She kissed him wholeheartedly on the lips as he opened the front door and stepped out into the night. 'And we'll do this again – properly next time,' she called.

'I'll have to get both sides of the story,' Dennis said, almost to himself, the words melting away into the mist like the bright white of his disappearing tail lights.

꿍

Sylvia's words were still playing over and over in Harry's head when he climbed into bed next to Jo's silent body. He knew she was awake. She was somehow too still, her form too alert. But he was relieved that she chose to feign sleep. He turned onto his side, staring into the darkness. He could hear the river below. Its lazy babbling began to form words in his ear, at first indistinct and then clearer.

Sylvia's words mingled with Darren Toddington's until the two voices became a warning chorus: 'It'll jeopardise your business, damage long-term friendships; you could lose everything you've worked so hard for.' He pulled the pillow over his head, squashing it down over his ears, trying to block out the goading river but it continued, seemingly interminably, until he heard the persistent three-note phrase of a song thrush and noticed the cool morning light leaking around the edges of the blind.

Chapter 23

Harry had struggled to sleep for a week following the concert. Anxiety about his financial situation had induced a galloping heart, while perplexity over Jo had continually tugged at his emotions. A painful and persistent melancholy inextricably associated with Sylvia plagued his entire being, while his midnight-mind ran wild with every possible permutation of the outcome of the vote. He had also awoken several times believing he was on stage naked, trying in vain to address the people of Poltowan, yet unable to form any words. He had spent the previous two nights at Diggory's, on the pretence of helping his friend with his business planning. In truth, he had simply craved some space.

He walked slowly through the Poltowan streets, cloaked in the quiet stillness of Sunday morning, a suggestion of mist floating off the sea and dampening the birdsong, muffling the distant thrum of a car engine. It was like the soft sound beater on his bass drum, he thought idly to himself, subduing the volume, layering it with a welcome mellowness. He thought again of the gig, a spark of excitement zipping briefly through his solar plexus as he recalled the roaring crowd, the buzz of being onstage again, seeing everyone in thrall to Rockstr, their animated faces lit by the floodlights, their collective breath clouding the February air.

The church clock struck eight o'clock as he rounded the corner to his office, its bells sounding oddly poignant as they reverberated off the shuttered doorways and curtained windows, their cry going unanswered but for Harry's heavy tread.

There had been a time when a steady stream of locals walked the streets to attend Sunday morning services but numbers had dwindled as residents moved out of the town and students moved in, a sort of social osmosis. Harry looked around him, hoping he would see a group of elderly worshippers maintaining the proper order of things. No one came.

He paused to look up at the sign above his door: *Harry Manchester.* He noticed that the M was slightly cracked at the bottom, while the bold red letters had lost their lustre, dulled by time. He frowned up at them. Maybe it was an illusion created by the mist. He unlocked the door and banged it shut behind him.

He half-hoped that the bank statement he had received the morning before would have magically disappeared. Instead it sat propped up against his phone, patiently awaiting his attention. He threw his bunch of keys on the desk. Harry picked up the envelope and ripped it open with his thumb. As he did so, his mobile bleeped with the arrival of a text. He paused, fumbling in his pocket to retrieve it, noticing the answerphone light on his desk also winking at him.

The text was from Ludo, typically upbeat and oozing enthusiasm, with little purpose. Envelope still in hand, Harry pushed the answerphone button. It was Mrs Garrick, whose house he had been marketing for the last month. It was a convoluted and apologetic message and Harry impatiently fast forwarded the middle of it to reach her inevitable final words: '… I hope you'll understand but I do need a quick sale and, well, Graves have someone ready to buy.'

He pushed delete. Mrs Garrick's house was in Sylverton Place, two streets away from Nell's. It was the third house on that road they had got their hands on in the last month. He paused, his mind wavering. He would call her in the morning, see if he could pop round and see her, persuade her to stick with him a little longer, to have faith.

His thoughts were still on Sylverton Place as he stared at his bank statement. He felt his skin prickle with heat as he digested the numbers. It was unlike him not to keep a weekly, sometimes daily, check on his work balance, but he had been delaying it, quietly sure of an upturn, confident that things would change. It was worse than he'd thought. He had lost numerous potential sales over the last six weeks, undercut by Graves and their list of investors, and he still had two members of staff to pay, at least for another month.

He sat down heavily on his chair, reading through the figures again, trying to calm himself, make sense of them. The fall in income was sharp, unprecedented. He would struggle to weather another month like this; another quarter would finish him.

He dropped the statement on his desk and ran his hand quickly over his prickly stubble, which was darker, more plentiful than usual, his jaw slightly leaner. The streets outside were still empty, the shops shut up, as if they too had run out of ideas; they stared back at him blankly.

Harry made himself a strong coffee and began to trawl through his database, making a note of current vendors, potential vendors and would-be buyers, printing out a map and highlighting streets affected by student lets, checking the prices of recent house sales and totting up figures on his calculator. His phone bleeped but he quickly forgot about it, lost in comparisons with the previous year, absorbed in figures relating to declining resident numbers, rising student numbers, the growing number of multi-occupancy homes. It painted a gloomy picture.

Just after ten o'clock his phone sounded again. He checked it, picking up the text from Jo, sent almost an hour before. He felt a stab of guilt. He had meant to text her. She didn't sound angry, more distressed. The second text was from Dennis Flintoff asking him to call.

Harry picked up his phone, rising to his feet as the ringtone sounded.

Jo answered quickly. 'Where are you?'

'Sorry. I meant to text. I'm at the office.'

'It's Sunday.'

'I've got some stuff to catch up on.'

'But you worked yesterday, you were at Diggory's last night and —. I've hardly seen you this week Harry. I miss you.'

He watched two seagulls tussling over an unknown morsel some distance from his window, their shrill squawks cutting straight through him.

'We need to spend some time together,' she continued, her voice sounding younger than he remembered. 'I feel like since we moved in, we haven't really—'

'Jo, can this wait? I've got lots to do. The student cap decision is being made in four days, I'm losing business hand over fist, I've got a house to sell and my best member of staff has just resigned.' He lowered his voice and tried to slow his delivery. 'I just need some time.'

'I do understand.' She tried to steady her breathing. 'But I want to help. I can come in and lend a hand. There must be something I can do.' Her voice had taken on a pleading tone.

'What do you know about estate agency? About campaigns? About anything?' He stood up, massaging his left temple. Something inside appealed to him to stop talking, to stop giving voice to the unkind thoughts that had begun to stream through his mind, forming words that couldn't be unsaid. But he couldn't stop, not now, his voice breathless with urgency. 'And, yes, you could have helped... by not insisting we move to a penthouse flat that we can't afford just so we can hear the bloody river at night! You live in another world, Jo. I'm not made of money. I'm not the business tycoon you seem to think I am. I can't fund this – this lavish lifestyle. I am not that man.'

'It was never about that, Harry.' Her voice was wavering now, threatening tears.

He knew he had hurt her, but the dam was in full flow. It was as if he wanted to punish himself too. 'You can't have it all your own way, demanding I divorce my wife and sell my marital home when I haven't even had a chance to consider it properly. I'm being carried along on the crest of a wave, your wave, pushed and cajoled and bullied by you, and I'm sick of it. I can't live like this. So, no, you can't help Jo. No one can.'

He ended the call and rested his head in his hands, unable to make sense now of the peculiar mix of emotions rushing through his body. There was anger, frustration, panic, guilt, and yet a certain pleasure at being able to inflict pain, a shameful but delicious sense of power that seemed to override everything else. He felt dizzy with it.

The office seemed to be slowly closing in on him, his name looking back at him from almost every surface, every piece of paper, taunting and teasing him. He could feel the unexpected hot pressure of something approaching tears behind his eyes, a contracting at the back of his throat. He stood up, coughing loudly, and stuffed his bank statement into his inside pocket. 'Come on, Harry!' he shouted.

He grabbed his phone and plugged it into the mini speaker on his desk, searching clumsily for his Queen playlist and pressing 'shuffle'. The unmistakable beat of '*Another One Bites the Dust*' began to play and he flicked it onward quickly. It was immediately followed by the familiar bass guitar hook of '*Under Pressure*'. He looked heavenwards for a moment, wondering if God was in charge of shuffling his songs today. After a momentary silence Freddie's sultry voice launched into

'*Don't Stop Me Now*' and Harry inhaled deeply, turning the volume up. 'That'll do,' he said to himself as he settled back into his chair and forced his eyes closed, losing himself in the music.

Harry was still sitting, eyes closed, at his desk fifteen minutes later as '*I'm Going Slightly Mad*' blasted from his speakers. He rocked slightly, trying to summon calm, to immerse himself in the beat, his version of mindfulness. He sat back, starting to feel it clear his head of its current burdens, when an uneasy feeling of being watched crept over him. He opened one eye to see James Cowley looking through the window, one hand shielding his eyes, a smug smile on his unfortunate face.

Harry jolted upright and switched the music off before gathering himself and strolling towards the door, drawing on any calmness he could salvage. He yanked it open.

'So this is where you escape to for a bit of peace and quiet from the mistress, Harry,' said James, lips twisting into an unpleasant smile. 'She wearing you out, is she? I suppose that's the trouble with a young—'

'You seem a bit lost, wandering the streets on a Sunday morning, peering into other people's windows. Are you looking for a life of your own?'

James cleared his throat, moving closer. 'I was hoping for a quiet word actually. I've got a proposition you might be interested in.'

Harry stood his ground as James edged closer, eyes flitting behind Harry to his shop doorway, as if willing himself to be invited in, out of the cold morning air.

'Nothing you say is of the slightest interest to me,' said Harry.

He made as if to retreat back inside but James laid a hand on his arm. 'Let me come in for two minutes Harry. I think you might just want to hear this. I know times are a bit tight, with Graves and—'

'Times are not tight.' Harry shook his arm free.

'Listen,' said James, his eyes just inches from Harry's, an earnestness in them that he remembered of old, 'my new business is getting off the ground.'

'Let me get this straight. You turn up at the concert last weekend trying to undermine the whole spirit of the thing – and frankly only succeeding in making yourself look like a dim-witted loser – and now you think I might want to help you?'

James held up his hand. 'That's the beauty of it, Harry. That's what people saw – me against you, completely at odds. Listen, my new venture is sales, lettings and management, specialising in the student market – sweeping up the bits of business you've made it quite clear you don't want.' He squared his shoulders. 'Quick sales, attractive rental yields, reliable tenancies, high occupancy rates—'

'Why is this of any interest to me, Cowley?'

'Well, you know what it's like,' he continued, adopting an ingratiating tone. 'Trying to raise your profile, get your name out there, particularly without a smart shop front like yours – it's not easy. We've had our differences, I know—'

Harry shook his head, any calm he had summoned dissipating quickly into the morning mist. He pushed at the door again, but James Cowley's large shoe kept it wedged open.

'Harry. Look, I know you're a man of principle but I also know you're a man of business. You turn people down every week – hell, every day – who don't realise you aren't in the lettings game, who don't realise you won't get involved in selling to landlords. But they come to you first because you're Harry Manchester, Poltowan born and bred – you're the go-to estate agent. You're trusted. They want a quick sale to a ready and waiting landlord; they want to let their place to a ripe and ready student market – but you can't help them. I am looking for exactly these people – potential buyers and investors.'

Harry had stepped inside and was still trying to push the door closed, now resisted by James' hand. 'Just listen, Harry. If you pass these people on to me – that's all, just give them my number, it doesn't make you complicit – I will pay you a handsome commission for each lead that converts. They don't know how I got their details, you keep your nose clean. That way, you're helping people but you're not going against your precious principles. You stick to what you're good at, I do the rest.'

Harry abruptly swung the door open so he could announce: 'I can't believe you're stupid enough to think I would even consider your proposal. You're dafter than I thought.'

He slammed the door shut and turned the key. Outside James had both meaty palms pressed to the window, his voice muffled now. 'If you change your mind, the offer's there. Two hundred and fifty a lead, Harry. It's business, good business. Just between you and me.' He tapped his nose and that grotesque smile crept back on to his face. 'Think of the money – a wad of cash in a little brown envelope every week, no questions.'

Harry sat back at his desk and waited for James to disappear. As he shuffled his papers he noticed a bright pink post-it note on the floor, covered in Aaron's loopy writing. *Surveyor got quote for roof repair on Oaks – reckons circa £15k as listed building.* Harry screwed it up and hurled it across the room.

When Jo's curt text came through later that afternoon, Harry was sitting sipping a G&T with Diggory in the Wild Grape. He had been back to the penthouse to see her but she was nowhere to be found. He had lingered a while, testing the Sonos sound system while he awaited her return, but he couldn't settle. It was as if he was a guest in someone else's home, unfamiliarity challenging him at every turn. It took him some time even to find the light switch, which was encased in a barely visible panel on the wall. He had soon given up, eventually finding himself back at Diggory's.

He had always considered Diggory a good sounding board – he would listen and nod, never inclined to interrupt and certainly not given to displays of emotion, whatever worries Harry was sharing. His mellow demeanour invariably allowed Harry to unburden himself.

But today Diggory's blithe spirit needled him. He wanted a reaction, some expression of outrage that demonstrated Diggory could feel his pain, that he took his friend's concerns seriously. In fact, Diggory's casual air was disguising a growing concern for his friend. He could never recall seeing Harry so down, so intense, so uptight. There was little hint of the gaiety that was usually one of his trademarks and all Diggory's attempts at humour fell flat, Harry's knuckles whitening around his beer bottle with each flippant comment.

'So,' said Diggory, shifting in his seat and trying to maintain a serious expression, 'that text from Jo – I mean, how much are we talking?'

Jo's text had been poorly but innocently timed. She had forgotten to tell Harry that the management fee on the penthouse flat was due and that the entire sum had to be paid six months in advance. The text imparted the bare facts, such was her state of hurt and agitation. He had only just paid the first month's rent and a hefty deposit, while the mortgage on The Oaks had left his account two days before.

Harry picked at the coaster. 'Pretty big. Things have never been this bad financially. The future looks bleak.' He peered earnestly through his glasses but Diggory was distracted by the blue bar lights which danced jauntily, reflected in Harry's lenses, lending him a slightly wacky appearance. Diggory tried to hide an ill-judged smile and failed.

Harry sat back, shaking his head. 'Can't you just be serious for one moment?'

Diggory thought better of trying to explain the source of his amusement. 'Do you want to patch it up with Jo?'

Harry lowered his head, twisting his glass slowly in his hand. 'I can't stop thinking about Sylvia. I mean, I think Jo's great and she's, you know, an attractive girl.'

'She's smitten by you.'

'That's just it: I can't seem to be what she wants me to be. She has this image of me, of us, and it's – I don't recognise it.'

'She wants to change you?'

'She thinks I'm someone else – a high-flying businessman who's a social animal and has this great lust for life.' He threw up his arms, exasperated.

Diggory did allow himself to laugh out loud this time. 'Mate. You just described yourself perfectly. That *is* you – or at least it was until about six months ago when you – when things started to change.'

Harry considered his friend's words as Diggory finished his beer. 'You've not been happy for a while, mate,' he added. 'And this campaign – it's killing you.'

'It could be the making of me.'

'Well, either way, the two possible outcomes are pretty extreme.' Diggory stood up. 'Same again?'

Harry watched him saunter to the bar. He felt subconsciously for his Rolex and adjusted it on his wrist, running his thumb over the smooth face, listening for its reliable ticking.

Diggory placed the drinks on the table. 'I'd offer to lend you some money, mate, but I wouldn't have the sort of sum you need.'

Harry half smiled. 'I would never ask you, Dig. It's not about now anyway. I've got savings, but they're ours – mine and Sylvia's. It's about how the business keeps going in future with all this change, particularly if they lift the student cap. I can't see how it will resolve itself.' He leaned forward. 'People want to move because of the growing number of students, yet it's only investors who are prepared to buy for that same reason, so residents end up selling to investors and it's a vicious circle. Self-feeding.'

'There's money to be made, that's the crux of it. Not everyone is as principled as you.'

Harry drew a line slowly through the water droplets on the outside of his glass and thought of James Cowley's face pressed against his window that morning. Eventually he told Diggory about the offer James had made.

Diggory whistled. 'Well... I know I wouldn't be able to put ethics above easy money like that. Particularly when things are tight.' He mulled it over. 'I mean, you get calls all the time from people thinking you do lettings – I know it gets your goat.'

'It certainly does.'

'So, it would be jobs for the boys. Passing on a few leads – you could make a grand a week the way things are going.'

'If I have anything to do with it, that is not the way things are going. That's the point. And I couldn't do it. I couldn't do it on many counts, not least effectively working for James Cowley, that smug, self-satisfied bastard.'

'And to think you used to be mates.'

'Mates is a bit strong. We played in a band together. He was alright then. A bit of an arse, but alright. Since he built his meat empire he's unbearable. An absolute tosser.'

'I admire him for having the balls to ask you.' Diggory began to chuckle, shaking his head as he imagined Harry's gruff response. 'But why not keep it in your back pocket, just in case – 'til you get your finances sorted. You never know.'

Harry shook his head. 'He got pretty short shrift, I can tell you.'

The two men left the bar as dusk fell, climbing the stairs into the brisk grey evening.

'Good luck on Thursday, mate.' Diggory held out his hand. 'I hope it goes your way. I really do.'

'I thought you were on the side of commerce and so-called progress.'

'You know me. I just want everyone to rub along together. And you're my mate, always have been, so I hope they keep the cap and be done with it. Then everything else will fall into place – just wait and see. You'll soon have that smile back on your face again.'

Harry felt a surge of tenderness rising like heat within him. He shook Diggory's hand firmly. 'I'll keep you posted.'

They were only a few paces apart when Diggory turned to him again. 'You can stay at ours again tonight, you know, if you want more time. Chloe won't mind.'

Harry scratched his head. 'I might do that. Thanks, Dig.' It was a small but notable relief not to have to go back to the penthouse just yet. He had been fighting a sense of discomfort since his row with Jo earlier, unable to reconcile himself with the words he had said yet knowing that he was highly likely to voice more injurious sentiments with very little encouragement. Jo didn't deserve it, he knew that.

Dennis stared out of the window of his office, watching as a a group of pint-sized schoolchildren, all clad in matching fluorescent bibs, snaked along the road in the direction of the beach. An exasperated teacher called out to them that it was now Monday and they mustn't dawdle as if it was still the weekend.

They continued to toddle noisily onwards, unconcerned. Dennis watched their stuttering progress.

He was inclined to hope that Harry wouldn't return his message. He had spoken to Andy first thing, and Keith had started researching Rockstr's background, firming up the facts and securing quotes from someone who claimed to be a family friend. A message had been sent to Rockstr via her Facebook page, asking her to get in touch with Keith, but she was still fast asleep in Ludo's arms, her phone switched off, after celebrating the success of Saturday's gig for most of Sunday night.

In his youthful enthusiasm – coloured by a nascent sense of professional ethics – Keith had been ready to go and find Rockstr's student digs, knock on the door and get her take on the revelations, but Dennis had dissuaded him.

'We've plenty of time for that. We've reached out and she hasn't responded. We've legitimised the story and checked the sources. We'll start laying it out today and go to press tomorrow. It'll hit the news stands Wednesday. Then we'll run a follow up story with her side of things, once she knows she can't stop us from publishing it.'

Keith nodded. 'What about Harry Manchester? Shall I call round at The Oaks, get a few words from him?'

Dennis had rounded his desk slowly, hands in his pockets, head down in concentration. 'Again, I've reached out but no response.' He tightened his biceps reflexively. 'You'll learn, Keith, that sometimes you can overcook stories. We've got the bones of it. Let's put it out there. We can worry about adding more meat later, give it a bit more colour online. Time is of the essence with the final planning decision on Thursday. It's a great scoop.'

Keith had wandered back to his desk, unsure of the wisdom – or the principle – of not talking to the other parties chiefly involved in the story. The one-sided nature of the piece sat uncomfortably with him. He had been trying to wrestle his way out of a Portaloo when Harry had collapsed onstage, returning instead to the mesmerising sight of Rockstr ending her first song and remaining ignorant of Harry's embarrassing incident.

By the time Rockstr emerged from Ludo's bed and found her phone under a pile of clothes on the floor of his houseboat, it was just after three o'clock on Monday afternoon and she was tired. On picking up the Facebook message from the *Poltowan Post* she decided the call could wait until the next day; she had an essay to finish, and she hadn't yet put in her daily hour of guitar practice.

Chapter 24

The revolution underway at UK universities. Dawn stared at the bold, shouty headline in front of her and blinked before reading on.

> *'Beth Goddard pays a visit to Cornwall's Poltowan University, where its handsomely paid Vice Chancellor is pushing for an increase in student numbers of 3,000, and existing students are angrily voicing their opposition, claiming overcrowding and mis-selling.'*

Dawn's eyes grew wider as she read on, chin dropping slightly, neck shrinking into her shoulders. She glanced at the empty chair opposite her. To think she had invited that woman into her office, made her welcome, given up her time, all on the premise of talking about successful Vice Chancellors and the huge progress that Poltowan was making. This story had taken a decidedly different tack. Surely Beth Goddard hadn't been taken in by that lame side show? Dawn stood up and turned towards the light of the window, holding the newspaper out in front of her.

> *'The dissatisfaction of Poltowan's students was plain to see as they stormed into the quadrangle outside Dawn Goldberg's office, waving placards and chanting 'Keep the Cap'.*
>
> *It is hard not to sympathise with them when Goldberg is paid £313,000 a year following a controversial 12% pay*

rise, and her office has recently undergone a stunning refit, complete with chaise-longue and beautifully framed art by renowned Cornish artist Alasdair Lindsay. Yet I found students living three to a room, and in one case nine to a two-bedroomed house, due to lack of accommodation in Poltowan itself, while lecture theatres were crammed and students sat in corridors working on their laptops due to a shortage of study space. The arrival of 3,000 more students is unlikely to improve the experience at an academic institution described on its website as 'boutique' and 'offering unprecedented access to highly regarded lecturers'.

Dawn threw the newspaper on her desk and looked out of the window at Michael. He had taken on an irritating similarity to Andy Hornblower today, his eyes not quite meeting hers, his shoulders drooping a little. Even his manhood looked a little shrivelled. 'Not you as well!' she shouted, turning away and hurling herself into her swivel chair, which groaned in response. Her eyes sought her father's in the photograph. He seemed to challenge rather than applaud her, his expression hovering somewhere between reproach and disappointment.

She took the small bottle of vodka from her desk drawer and helped herself to a swift capful before straightening the newspaper noisily on her desk and continuing to read.

Beth Goddard had said some complimentary things about Dawn in the article, referencing her *steely and determined nature* and saying she *clearly possessed the ruthlessness and single-mindedness necessary to be successful in such a post.* She had even flippantly noted that, *If out and out Remainer Dawn Goldberg had been leading the campaign to stay in the EU, Britain might be in a very different place today,* words that had prompted a strange fluttering in Dawn's navel and caused her father to smile almost approvingly.

Yet the thrust of the piece was the protest and the alleged sense of unrest among staff and students. Beth had also managed to locate Dave White, who had readily regurgitated his insightful comments about the *culture of fear* among lecturers, the obscene pay rise received by Dawn, and the recent departure of his esteemed colleague, Phil Pullen, who had disappeared like so many before him, overnight.

Dawn's spirits lifted slightly when, towards the end of the article, member of staff, Nell Charles was quoted as saying that university employees vehemently supported the campaign to increase student numbers, and that the threat posed by Harry Manchester's opposition was, perhaps regretfully, not credible: *He is only an estate agent. People say it is just self-interest.*

Dawn took heart from the words and allowed herself to raise an eyebrow before reading on. The piece acknowledged the achievements of Poltowan University when it came to employability and nationwide ranking, but this small nod to her success was quickly negated in the final sentence: *My visit to Poltowan University showed that such box-ticking simply serves to mask the worrying state of some of our higher-education establishments, which all too often exist to serve the career ambitions of Vice Chancellors and not those of its fee-paying students.*

She flipped the page over and scrutinised the large colour photograph of herself. That at least showed her in her best light. It had been taken in a London studio a year or so before, the lights lifting the highlights in her hair, her smile wide but still sincere. She looked strong and capable, yet approachable.

There was a knock at the door and Janice poked her head around. 'Coffee?'

'And doughnuts, I think.' Dawn held the paper in the air. 'Read this, Jan.'

She tiptoed into the room. 'I have actually, I just looked

online. It does say some rather good things about you, Dawn, although I know the overall piece is a little… downbeat.'

'Downbeat? She came here with an agenda and that bloody protest played right into her hands. I bet she couldn't believe her luck. She'd obviously done a fair bit of sniffing around, digging up the usual names and scribbling down tired old quotes from the likes of White and Pullen. Hardly a balanced view. Did she ask you? Did she ask you for a quote?'

Janice shook her head. 'I missed the whole thing, Dawn, remember? I was at the dentist. If I'd been here,' she nodded her head in the direction of reception, 'I'd have made sure she had her story straight, don't worry. I'd have put her right.'

'Of course, of course, you weren't here. It's a bit of a blur.' Dawn fell silent, trying to piece together the events of that day but finding herself unable to think beyond Beth sitting in her office admiring her chaise-longue.

'Today of all days,' said Dawn, sighing. 'Do you think it could influence the vote tomorrow?'

Janice placed her hands on her hips, head tilted to one side. 'If one article sways the vote I'll… I'll be gobsmacked. That planning committee has done its due diligence – they rely on facts and figures and their own eyes and ears, not the opinions of someone who has stepped over the threshold of Poltowan a grand total of once.'

Dawn's features softened slightly.

'Anyway, I'll get those doughnuts – give us some sustenance for the long day ahead. I'll pick up a *Poltowan Post* too. Back in a jiffy.'

❧

Sylvia couldn't sleep. She had got up at dawn, the bruised sky beginning to lighten reluctantly as she left The Oaks and walked down the road towards the beach. She walked slowly, deliberately, each step requiring great effort.

The knot in her stomach had been twisting and tightening through the small hours, the tension in her muscles growing, the pressure behind her eyes intensifying. She'd been overcome by an overwhelming urge to escape the four walls of her home, to stride out calmly into the wide-open arms of the sea. She paused as her shoes sank into the soft sand of Poltowan Beach, closing her eyes, relishing the breeze that peppered her face with tiny suggestions of rain, the waves calling softly to her.

She couldn't shift the next night's planning meeting from her mind. She had tried not to dwell on or invest any hope in it, yet it had been all she could think about since the concert. The image of Harry leaning against the kitchen island, marks all down his sleeve and his earnest blue eyes looking imploringly at her, kept stubbornly returning to her. It prompted an unfamiliar wrench somewhere deep in her chest, like a thirst that could not be quenched.

She stood watching the waves break, the tide rolling softly to and fro, its constancy reassuring, mesmerising. All the while she imagined giving herself to the vast ocean – pictured the act of walking, fully clothed, into the ice-cold water. It would quickly be over.

Returning along the coast path at 8.30 a.m., Sylvia moved slowly across the patchwork landscape, her mind slipping momentarily from thoughts of Harry as she pondered the imminent arrival of lambs and calves in these sea-blown fields. Something like sorrow pulled unexpectedly at her heart.

As she emerged back onto the road she took a right, away from The Oaks, and habit led her towards the newsagent's. The vague sense of dread that had been threatening through the night returned like a sickening punch to her stomach as the full force of the *Poltowan Post* headline hit her: 'Keep the Cap

Campaign Fronted by Former Drug Dealer'. There was a photo of Rockstr on stage, in the full throes of a vocal.

Sylvia flipped the paper over and paid, leaving the shop without her change, the cashier calling after her in vain. She returned to The Oaks with her head bowed, willing herself back to the privacy of her own home. In the kitchen she spread the paper out on the island and, hands pressed to her hot cheeks, read the whole article, gradually slumping on the stool as she neared the final paragraph.

When she had finished the piece, she skimmed it again. The facts appeared to be undeniable but there was scant detail, other than that Rockstr had spent eighteen months in prison for selling cannabis, being released the year before when she'd gained a place at Poltowan University. There were quotes from the University's Head of Communications, Andy Hornblower, who spoke in a verbose and non-committal way about Rockstr being *a somewhat surprising choice to front a campaign purporting to be for the future of Poltowan, a campaign which has undoubtedly been irreparably damaged by this student's unfortunate past mistakes.*

Sylvia tutted out loud in an uncharacteristic demonstration of feeling. Andy Hornblower went on to talk about *Harry Manchester's blatant misjudgement, yet another sign that he is out of touch with what is really going on*, before singing the praises of Poltowan University as *a place that opens its arms to any well-motivated student, no matter what their past misdemeanours.*

Sylvia smoothed the page and shook her head. After a moment she reached for her phone and dialled Harry, steadying one hand with the other.

He was gruff when he answered and, Sylvia knew, tired. She had no choice but to impart the news. No, he had not seen the *Poltowan Post* yet, and no, he had not heard about any scandal surrounding Rockstr. Sylvia filled him in. There was a stunned silence at the other end of the line, eventually punctuated by a heavy sigh and a blasphemous outburst.

'What does it say? Exactly?'

Sylvia read the whole piece out to him, raising her voice occasionally over his protestations and exclamations of disbelief.

'I need to get straight on to Ludo,' said Harry.

'Did he know?'

'He's a bloody fool if he did. I just can't believe it! All that work.'

'It doesn't undermine the message of your campaign, your manifesto behind keeping the cap, Harry. It's just an unfortunate association.'

'Unfortunate doesn't begin to cover it.' He breathed heavily, an image of Dennis Flintoff and Dawn Goldberg together flashing to mind. 'Nothing about the concert? Or about me collapsing on stage?'

Sylvia flicked through the paper. 'I think this story has eclipsed the concert, Harry.'

Dawn re-read the *Poltowan Post* for a fourth time as she finished her doughnut. The paper had been gleefully presented to her by Janice moments before. 'Every cloud,' said Dawn, without looking up. 'Every cloud.'

She wiped her fingers on a napkin and called Dennis, swivelling around to study Michael as she did so. Thankfully he had recovered himself, his back a little straighter, his chin held high. Pride, thought Dawn to herself: a man must have his pride.

Dennis contrived to answer in his deepest voice, a smile

already playing across his lips as he received the call he had been waiting for all morning.

'Good work, Dennis. Very good work.'

'Why, thank you, Ms Goldberg.'

Dawn licked some remaining sugar from her fingers. 'Do you think it's enough?'

Dennis smoothed his hair in the mirror, flexing his pecs. 'Put it this way, Dawn, I am pretty damn' confident that story will not help Harry Manchester's cause.'

Half an hour later Nell rang Sylvia, her words quick and muddled. Sylvia had to ask her to repeat her story twice before she understood that Nell was apologising for her quote in a piece in *The Guardian* that day.

'I didn't say it, Sylve. Please tell Harry I didn't say it – or, at least, I might have said it… but I was under pressure to be supportive if I wanted to keep my job. And I was so tired! I didn't know Beth would use it. I thought she was just, you know, making conversation. Dawn was approaching and I panicked.'

Sylvia pressed some old tea bags firmly into the food compost bin as she listened. 'What exactly did you say?'

'I had no idea I was on record… she wasn't interviewing me. She didn't even have her notepad out at that point. I feel awful…'

'What did you say, Nell?'

'Well, it says in the piece that I said Harry was only an estate agent and that his campaign was purely motivated by self-interest, but you must believe, I would never, ever mean to say such a thing—'

There was a moment's silence before Sylvia spoke. 'You mean, you were misquoted?'

'Not as such, Sylve. I did say something like that but it was only—'

'Whatever you said or didn't say, it's done now.' Sylvia turned her laptop on and headed straight to *The Guardian* website, her fingers tapping capably at the keys. 'I've got to go.'

She read the piece quickly, scrolling down the page. At first she was buoyed by the tone, believing it to be a timely counterweight to the *Poltowan Post* article, but as Sylvia reached Nell's quote it felt as if someone had sucked the breath right out of her.

Chapter 25

Rockstr stared at the stark porcelain beneath her. Without warning she retched again, tears streaming down her face, stomach straining, face burning. When the urge to throw up finally subsided, she sat down on the toilet lid, her head in her hands, listening to banal snatches of conversation as people came and went outside. Finally, she was alone. Only the persistent dripping in the water tank was audible as she stared at her mobile again, the *Poltowan Post* headline screaming at her accusingly.

An unknown person had tagged her on Facebook, sharing the article, and so far it had generated over a hundred comments. She blew her nose loudly and began to scroll through them. Her red-rimmed eyes stared vacantly as the words swam in front of her. Aside from a handful of nasty, gleeful comments, the majority were supportive, extolling her musical talents and applauding her spirit and apparent contrition for her crime. Some had posted links to her videos; others had seen her set the previous Saturday night and offered messages of support, vowing to boycott the *Poltowan Post*.

She looked up at the ceiling, resting the back of her head against the cold pipe, trying to gather herself as she focused on an unsightly speckled damp patch that was spreading across the room, almost before her eyes, its spores multiplying by the second. Her phone bleeped several times in quick succession as more comments poured in.

Dennis Flintoff, be very ashamed, read one of them. *Your paper's desperation to shift a few more copies has resulted in irresponsible, one-eyed reporting that is not in readers' interests. Are you in support of lifting the student cap, by any chance?*

Others followed suit, condemning the choice of front-page story and questioning the absence of Rockstr's right to reply. *Where's the balance? Lazy, half-arsed and downright unaccountable reporting.*

It was a strange kind of relief that washed over Rockstr then. She had been bracing herself for this moment since her arrest. She had known it would come back and haunt her – just not when or where. These things never went away completely.

She would always remember the chilling moment she was caught, when the sheer stupidity of her own actions rebounded on her, taking with them her dreams of a place at the Royal College of Music. And nothing, after all, could ever be more harrowing or more heartbreaking than the faces of her parents when she told them. She had carried that image in her scarred heart ever since; it was what drove her on.

Now she risked inflicting the same pain on Ludo: trusting Ludo with his unbridled enthusiasm and honesty. She grabbed her bag and headed towards the river, ignoring someone calling her name along the way. A sickening and familiar feeling of panic began to gnaw at her. For the first time she thought of Harry too, his generous smile, his warm blue eyes. She broke into a run, unable to stem her tears.

When Harry arrived at Ludo's houseboat he was met by the sight of his friend's backside sticking up in the air as he cleared away debris from a gathering, his trademark boxer shorts sitting high about the waistline of his low-slung jeans. For the first time Harry thought how slipshod it looked, how pretentious.

Ludo heard his footsteps and turned, an empty of bottle of cheap Prosecco in his hand.

'Ah, morning, fella.' He squinted against the daylight, face lighting up at the sight of his visitor. 'And how is Mr Harry Manchester, lobbyist *extraordinaire*, on this beautiful—'

Harry handed him a tightly folded copy of the *Poltowan Post*. Ludo fell silent at the realisation that something was seriously wrong. He placed the bottle carefully on the deck as he read, running his hand through his hair.

Harry glowered up at the lanky figure before him, thinking he looked younger today, childlike almost. Why had he been foolish enough to let youth lead experience? The anger that had taken hold of Harry since Sylvia's phone call heightened. When the words left his mouth, they gathered vitriol at an alarming rate as Harry finally let the fear and frustration that had been building for some months, overwhelm him.

Ludo looked down on him from the boat. He absorbed every word, eyes fixed on Harry's, their familiar deep blue now a bleak shade of grey. When the tirade subsided, Ludo lowered his gaze, reading from the top of the story to the end, re-reading, trying to make sense of it.

'I'm not thrilled by the news either, Harry,' he said, his hands shaking slightly.

Harry began speaking again, his voice a low growl. 'This might be just a joke to you, just a project.' He steadied himself. 'But, Ludo, this is my town, my life.'

He shook his head. 'I'm sorry, Harry. I just don't get this, man. It doesn't make sense.'

Harry turned and walked away, his tall, broad figure listing very slightly, his jacket flapping in the breeze.

'I had no feckin' idea,' said Ludo, looking up to see Harry slowly retreating. 'No feckin' idea at all,' he repeated under his breath, gripping the handrail tight.

&

Ludo was still standing in the same position when Rockstr came running across the stretch of grass towards him. He didn't see her at first, too busy staring at the newspaper, wading through the revelations, trying to unpick his conversations with her, identify any signs, but he was struggling to think straight, his mind jumping wildly from one exchange to another, Harry's words delivering a hammer blow at every recollection.

He had quickly understood that Rockstr was a private person, guarded about herself and her past, carefully drip feeding him details to add to his picture of her, and he was equally aware that his own inherent guilelessness sat at the other end of the spectrum, accepting that it would take time to get to know her properly. To his surprise, he had also realised that it was time he was prepared to give. She had a depth, a shrewdness, that appealed to him. He wanted to know more.

Ludo looked up, suddenly aware of rapid footsteps, the sound of panting. She stopped just in front of him, her look hovering uncertainly between sadness and defiance. 'You know,' she said breathlessly, glancing down at the paper in his hands.

He peered intently at her. She looked different; she had a hardness about her, an impenetrability, yet something in her seemed to cry out to him. For several moments he stood staring at her, and she back at him, before the clouds of confusion began slowly to part. Now her reticence made sense. It was not her feelings for him she was unsure about, but this huge, wearying secret consuming her from within.

Ludo threw the newspaper onto the riverbank between them. She watched as its pages lifted noisily in the wind, the front page flipping decisively over to another story. He looked at her size four feet in their dirty Converse boots, her narrow frame, bent against the wind, one hand awkwardly clutching her bag. She made as if to turn around, but he couldn't bear it.

He held his hand out and finally she took it, stepping up onto the boat before letting herself be held.

The couple eventually retreated inside the compact cabin, not emerging until the following morning.

A mile or so away, Harry eased himself once more onto the ageing mattress in Diggory's spare room, and watched as the room's boxy shapes receded into darkness.

Chapter 26

Harry was sitting in his car by the river. Sylvia had told him about the piece in *The Guardian* the day before, but it had come so quickly after her news about the *Poltowan Post*'s front page that he had been unable to take it in. He began to scroll through the article on his phone, the tiny print testing his patience. As he read, some of Sylvia's words began to return to him. She had said it gave a pretty damning report of the university's set up, and that the journalist wasn't especially complimentary about Dawn. She had also mentioned Nell's comment but in a dismissive way.

He read Nell's words and reread them, pulling his handkerchief out and blowing his nose noisily. Then he read the article again. He looked out of the window, down the river towards the sea – just out of sight, but there all the same; vast, timeless. He felt as if he had been waiting months, not weeks, for this day of reckoning.

Harry had been sitting there for a good hour before 'Bohemian Rhapsody' began to play from his pocket. For the first time he could remember, the startling sounds irritated him, needling at his brain. He grappled for his phone, trying to silence the song. Somehow he had missed three calls.

The first voicemail was from Jo. She sounded subdued, yet her words were laced with concern. She was calling about the *Poltowan Post* article, which she had just seen in the staff room, while someone else had said there was a piece in the previous day's *Guardian* too. She finished with a resigned appeal for him to call her.

Next was a garbled message from Aaron, warning Harry that a number of residents had called in to see him, keen to gain clarity on the *Poltowan Post*'s cover story. Aaron had been both unprepared and uninformed so was unable even to spin the truth. 'I managed to get rid of them in the end, boss, but I have a feeling they'll be back after the vote. I think they wanted to show their support but it's difficult to tell.'

Harry clicked forcibly on the third message. It was the management company warning him that if he didn't pay the management fee and up front rent due on the penthouse flat, they regretted that they would have no option but to take further action. He paused, looking skywards for a moment, watching as heavy clouds scudded low overhead.

He dialled James Cowley, closing his eyes as he spoke the words James wanted to hear. The matter was swiftly settled, and Harry gave him three leads straightaway, James barely concealing his smugness. Harry hung up, feeling as if a light had gone out inside of him.

Darren Toddington snorted the last of his cocaine off the cistern in the disabled toilets at Poltowan Town Hall. The rush was instant, and he flushed the toilet and threw open the door with a bang, straightening his tie in the mirror and smoothing his hair, pausing to check his nostrils as an afterthought. He would be voting on principle today, and he would not be daunted by the threats – veiled or otherwise – of others. He swaggered into the lobby and greeted a couple of fellow committee members with a hearty welcome, before strolling into the stately oak-panelled meeting room.

'Ah, Jason. Thought you'd be here bright and early.' He shook

Jason Redthorne's hand, feeling his colleague's knuckles crunch slightly within his vice-like grip. Darren's dark eyes glinted oddly under the powerful spotlights, lending him a maniacal look.

Jason studied him for a moment before drawing his own conclusions. Darren's recent moods had oscillated between gloomy listlessness and skittish irritability, with very little in between. He had seemed incapable of making even the smallest decisions and appeared largely preoccupied. Jason was still unsure which way Darren planned to vote, he had been so mercurial.

'Ready for the big one?' said Darren, rubbing his hands together. 'It's pivotal, today's decision, historic even. The future of Poltowan is firmly in our hands and we must use our power wisely.' He raised his voice as he spoke the final few words, the increasing number of people filling the room turning to look at him as he threw his arms wide to emphasise his point.

Jason nodded at him, managing a thin smile. 'You'll be supporting the lifting of the cap then, using your power to ensure Cornwall's future?'

Darren narrowed his eyes. 'I think the evidence is pretty clear. Maintaining the cap is in the best interests of students, staff and residents. If you'd been at the concert on Saturday night, it offered a very good barometer of public feeling – a perfect snapshot of how life in Poltowan should be.' His hollow-eyed face loomed closer. 'This isn't a case of town versus gown – most of the community want the same thing.'

'It remains to be seen how the story in the *Post* will have changed minds.' Jason left the sentence dangling like fish bait, watching as Darren suddenly emitted a forced but scornful laugh.

'It's a non-story. Selling weed! I'm all for relaxing cannabis legislation – we're supposed to be a liberal-minded society, for God's sake.'

'The evidence is there – it's a gateway drug.'

Darren leaned his face closer to Jason's. 'It's not the drug that causes problems, it's the people who use it. People need to take responsibility for their own actions. Everything in moderation and all that.'

Jason studied him intently.

'Anyway,' continued Darren, 'that lass paid the price and now she's busy reinventing herself, so good for her. And I'll tell you what – she's bloody talented! Fantastic voice. My son would do well to hang on to her coat tails.'

'Then I hope, for her sake, she hasn't blown her future for the sake of Harry Manchester's campaign.' Jason raised an eyebrow before excusing himself. As he left he saw Dawn Goldberg in the doorway, standing back to let her through.

'Ever the gentleman, Jason. Thank you.' She stepped closer and kissed him on both cheeks. He stood rigid as her Chanel No. 5 assailed him and her mane of hair tickled his cheek.

'This,' said Dawn turning to her companion Janice, 'is Jason Redthorne. Not only is he deputy on the Strategic Planning Committee, but his is the voluptuous and very comely beast parked outside – the Bentley GT V8 S no less.'

Janice smiled politely at Jason, raising her eyebrows in admiration, despite her unfamiliarity with the GT V8 S model. 'It certainly sounds very smart,' she said, hopefully.

Jason began to excuse himself with a barely perceptible nod of the head, but Dawn caught his arm, putting her lips close to his ear. 'I suppose you saw the *Poltowan Post* yesterday? Not a good look for the Keep the Cap campaign, I fear – a very clumsy oversight.'

Jason turned to look at her. 'But an equally damning piece in The Guardian, I would say? It was certainly food for thought.'

Dawn forced a smile before sweeping into the room, her heavy make-up doing its best to disguise a sleepless night peppered with recurring memories of the car crash. These had plagued her ever since the student protest. Two double-strength Irish coffees had also helped to pep her up an hour before – she now felt ready graciously to accept, and to bathe in, her victory.

∽

The public gallery was almost full, despite there being a good forty-five minutes until the meeting opened. A number of business owners loitered in the centre, chatting in low voices, while numerous residents took their seats, steeling themselves nervously for the showdown. Steve Kent and James Cowley propped each other up in a corner, their smiles smug as they danced impatiently from foot to foot. James had received Harry's earlier call with glee, and now radiated an even greater air of self-importance.

Some press had already gathered in the cosy mezzanine area at the back, including Dennis Flintoff who stood leaning on the balcony ledge with one elbow, his bicep tensed to best effect as he watched Dawn's arrival with more than a passing interest.

At the back of the room stood Ludo and Rockstr, Ludo's hands dug deep into his pockets, his eyes nervously searching over people's heads for Harry's distinctive form. Rockstr had her arms wrapped around herself as if to keep out the cold.

Nell hovered at the side of the room, having crept in early in the hope of seeing Harry face to face. She had lain awake all night, accompanied by the loud drum and bass beat coming from number fourteen and cars coming and going a few doors along, torturing herself with her own foolish words to *The Guardian* journalist. At five o'clock she had made a cup of tea, fighting the gnawing ache inside every time she thought of that article, or recalled Sylvia's cool tone, or pictured Harry in her front room. She had vowed to try and make amends. Harry and

Sylvia were, after all, her oldest friends.

There was a growing buzz of anticipation fused with nervous energy as the for and against camps instinctively ordered themselves into two distinct factions, while committee members hovered quietly in between. Outside, dusk became darkness as the town clock silently passed 6.30, the last light fading on Poltowan's uncertain future.

၁

Harry had not moved from his car in almost three hours. As the meeting time approached, fury began to give way to anxiety. He decided to walk the short distance to the Town Hall, taking the tow path, with a view to arriving at the meeting fifteen minutes before proceedings began. He hoped to clear his head and regain some calm before doubtless being subjected to intense public scrutiny.

He left just before dusk, welcoming the cover of twilight. He threw a wistful look in the direction of the apartments, hidden behind a stand of trees further along the river but still radiating a palpable presence, their lights starting to twinkle. He had put off doing any more than sending a placatory text in response to Jo's earlier voicemail – albeit one that had taken him fifteen minutes to compose – so unsure was he of what to do next. Guilt gnawed silently at him.

As he walked along the gloomy riverside path, Harry's pace slowed. The pressure in his head continued to mount. He pictured the officious letter from the management company that he had energetically speared on the paper spike on his desk, along with the quote for the new roof at The Oaks, and two more letters from vendors apologetically advising of their decision to switch estate agents. Then he imagined a steady stream of brown envelopes stuffed with wads of notes appearing on his office doormat overnight.

He was trying to focus on the imminent decision, to prepare himself for the inevitable questions from marauding journalists, but it was as if his mind refused to allow him to switch tack. James Cowley's smiling face loomed large in his mind, and still his heart raced, his mouth felt dry. He mentally ran through a slideshow of all the local people who were relying on him to pull this off, the six people who had stopped him in the street that morning, shaking his hand and wishing him luck; the four phone messages; the heads appearing around his door the previous week – all the faces drawn with anxiety and tiredness.

Then he thought of Ludo. Harry shook his head in shame as his own words flooded back to haunt him, Ludo's stunned expression seemingly accepting of the onslaught. Not once had he retaliated.

He pulled his phone from his pocket and began to compose a text to Ludo as he walked. He grappled to find the right words to express his remorse, composing a clumsily apologetic text that concluded, *'On towpath, will be with you in...'* As he narrowed his eyes to find the numbers on the keyboard, Harry's foot slipped abruptly sideways, his bad knee giving way with the sudden shock. He found himself sliding sideways, unable to gain any traction. He reached out to the damp bank to steady himself but he was already in the river, the water around his knees, his feet sinking into the deep silt. His phone slipped from his grasp into the darkness.

He called out breathlessly, his hands sliding rapidly down the bank, his nails clawing uselessly at the mud, the icy water rising quickly around him. He inhaled sharply. He seemed to come to a halt but as he tried to lift his feet, powerful suction pulled at him, each effort drawing him further in.

He shouted again, his voice dying in the night sky. The glacial temperatures quickly penetrated his bones and shortened his breath. His heart physically ached as it hammered inside his chest. He stopped sinking but each time he tried to prise his foot out of the cold mud he became further enmeshed, stuck fast. His breaths came short and shallow, his whole body numb with cold.

He moved his hands continually in a slow breast-stroke motion, trying to counter the continued suction from beneath, trying to still his now wildly chattering teeth, to control his wretched gasping. He focused on the apartments, wondering if the lights he could see high up were the penthouse. Dusk had become night without him noticing.

He called again, shouting Jo's name this time. Summoning all his courage, his next shout was deeper, more resonant, but it seemed to dissolve into the blackness almost as soon as the words left his mouth. He was sure he was still sinking, the water rising steadily around his chest

He imagined Sylvia's voice, asking how he had managed to end up in the river, questioning why he had chosen to walk that way in the darkness. He called her name, his thoughts growing looser, more fragmented, his arms losing their power as cold deadened them. He loved his wife, he thought despairingly, had never stopped loving her. He had just forgotten how. He tried once more to lift a foot, galvanised by the realisation, but began to rock backwards slightly before righting himself, the water now lapping at his collarbones.

He called Sylvia's name again, convulsing between each syllable. She had always supported him, in her way. She would be willing him on tonight, watching the webcast of the meeting, inwardly incensed by Dawn Goldberg's shameless front. If his campaign were successful she would be quietly approving, yet still questioning, challenging, urging him onwards. Perhaps she would come looking for him when she discovered he wasn't at the meeting. Yes, she would be here any second, he thought; she would know the danger he was in.

He watched the lights of the apartments further along the river, their ethereal glow blurring before him. Life there seemed to be another world away, as if he was looking through a thick window. His arms slowed and stopped. He tried to urge them back into action but it was like activating someone else's limbs. They floated heavily in the water like a dead man's.

Jo's smiling face swam into his mind. She would be waiting for any news of the decision, checking her Facebook account, texting her friends to see if they had heard. She loved him. He sighed in between laboured breaths. He supposed he loved her in his way, but it was all wrong. He resented her for not being Sylvia, for so readily expressing the love that Sylvia couldn't show him. Jo so desperately wanted to love him and, most of all, to be loved. But he failed on the last count. He failed because his love still lay elsewhere.

The water was ice-cold on his neck now. It sloshed around his chin. An immense tiredness washed over him. He closed his eyes, quickly willing them back open. He felt as if he hadn't slept for weeks.

The meeting would be well underway. Or would it be finished? He was unsure how many hours he had been there. He called out again, but this time it was a spiritless cry. If this is how it ends, he thought resignedly, starting to surrender to the heavy wooziness that flooded his mind and body, eliminating the anxiety and pressure, I hope Ludo will carry on my work. Ludo's tall rangy frame came to mind then, almost as if he was looking down at Harry, his eyes wide, his face animated, his voice insistent. Harry felt as if he was being tugged and pulled, yet his body wouldn't shift.

Come on, fella. Keep your eyes open. Harry heard the words from somewhere far away. *Keep them open, stay awake, fella.* He smiled, remembering Ludo's perpetually sunny nature. Harry twisted and lurched slightly, the mud pulling him back down.

He coughed and choked in the silty water, the taste of it dirty, bitter, as he tried to fight off a torrent of fat brown envelopes, relentlessly pushing at him, starting to carry him away.

So many people who believed in him, who trusted him. Perhaps this was the best way. He was unsure if he said Sylvia's name out loud or if he thought it, but his numb lips didn't seem to belong to him anymore. He wanted to say he was sorry. He wanted to say he had been a fool. He wanted to say he loved her and that he should never have listened to her; he should never have left. But the brown envelopes were starting to weigh him down, his chin beginning to dip below the surface. Perhaps it would be easier to let go.

There was a loud splash, somewhere nearby yet far off too. Harry fought to open his eyes, willed himself to prise open his leaden lids. He thought he could see Ludo's face. There were arms wrenching him, hands under his armpits, fingers grasping at his thighs. 'It's Harry – Harry Manchester. Harry mate, stay with us! Harry...'

It was the last thing he remembered.

Chapter 27

Sylvia sat at the island in her kitchen, the corner light no longer enough to counter the unrelenting blackness of evening, enshrouding her as she sat, pen in hand, blank sheet of paper before her. She cut a ghostly figure, her hunched, thin form insubstantial and vague in the gloom, her hand poised but inert. A last she scratched her husband's name at the top of the paper, as if the sudden burst of alacrity would invite her other thoughts to flow. But they didn't, and she sat paralysed once more.

She glanced at the pills sitting inoffensively in the small jar on the counter top. Next to them was a bottle of Pinot Noir. Her own fate was in her hands. They would assist her, certainly, but not until she had written the words Harry deserved to hear.

It would be a blessing for him, a release. He was too good a man to free himself – not properly, not emotionally. But she could do it, swiftly and cleanly, like snipping a piece of twine.

She thought suddenly of Nell, and of how she had changed. Even poor Nell had carelessly damaged any hope that Harry would one day wake to the possibility of the two of them as a couple. Her shoulders rounded a little further. It was a story that would never be written, even in Sylvia's absence.

She turned her attention back to the sheet of paper, her pen hovering. She shaped the first sentence, a basic irrefutable truth made concrete by the black ink. The next line came to her with such searing clarity, it was almost as if a persistent fog had suddenly lifted from before her eyes. I just stopped loving myself, she thought.

But before she could commit the revelation to paper a loud rap on the front door made her jump. She hesitated, inclined to let the summons go unanswered. Seconds passed. She laid her pen down and began to stand up but froze. All was quiet again. Part of her surrendered, relinquishing herself instead to the ending she was about to write.

∽

This time the bell rang loudly and the knocking on the door resumed almost simultaneously. She walked quickly into the hallway, turning the key in the door and flicking on the porch light.

'Sorry to disturb you.' Ludo sounded slightly breathless and appeared agitated, his long limbs twitching as if desperate to be back in motion.

She noticed his bicycle abandoned next to him on the drive, the wheels still turning. There was no light on the front of it. He really should have a light.

'It's Harry,' he said.

'Did they vote to keep the cap?'

'He's had an accident, nearly drowned – but he's fine, he's fine… well, he's in hospital, but they think he's gonna be OK. I just thought you might want to – I mean, I think he'd like to see you and I don't know… anyone else to contact.'

Sylvia stared at him. 'Drowned? Where?'

'He didn't drown, I shouldn't have said that word. He fell in the river.'

'Where is he?'

'In the hospital, the ambulance just picked him up.'

'I'll come.' She glanced down at her oversized jumper, her slippers. Then she looked back at Ludo. 'Come with me. I'll drive us.'

'That'd be grand. And, yes, he won, Sylvia – they voted to keep the cap. It's awesome but he doesn't yet know, by all accounts. He didn't make it to the meeting—'

Sylvia pushed the door half closed while she changed her shoes and pulled her coat on. She vaguely registered that it was her gardening coat, not her public one, as she pushed her arms into the loose sleeves before pulling a dog-eared seed packet absentmindedly out of the pocket. She retrieved her keys from the dish by the door and, as she did, Sting shot in from the darkness, rubbing against her legs, meowing softly. She had already bidden him farewell that afternoon, although he didn't know it. She ran her hand swiftly over his back before stepping out into the bracing night air.

Ludo found himself staring at her, watching her movements with fascination. 'Sorry to have disturbed you, it's just that I—' His voice tailed off. He was admiring her thin but elegant frame, the strong bone structure and wide eyes, almost lost under her unruly grey hair, which was clumsily pinned up like an afterthought. He realised he was shaking. There was an air of unreality about the whole evening; the light, the smell of the air, both of them felt unfamiliar.

Sylvia sat upright at the wheel while Ludo folded his lanky form into the small passenger seat, his hands fumbling for the seatbelt. He talked incessantly, filling her in on the details of the meeting, the heated discussions, the personal tensions, only falling silent when they pulled into the hospital car park.

Sylvia turned a little too sharply into a space and quickly cut the engine. 'Thank you for telling me.' These were the only words she had spoken since they'd left The Oaks.

Ludo flung open the passenger door, slamming it a little too hard behind him, hunching his shoulders for warmth. 'They're going to review the cap in eighteen months,' he said as Sylvia fiddled with her central locking fob. 'But Harry's got a lot to be proud of. He's almost singlehandedly saved this town.'

'For now, at least,' said Sylvia, rounding the front of the car and, for the first time, taking in Ludo's sodden trousers and shuddering shoulders.

∽

The white lights were blinding and it took Harry several attempts to open his eyes. Everything was soft-edged. A new lightness pervaded his mind and body. He wondered momentarily if he was dead, and decided that if that was the case, he must find a way to locate Freddie Mercury. His eyes closed again.

A warm hand pressed his. He prised open his heavy eyelids to find Sylvia's face close to his, her eyes peering at him questioningly. He squeezed her hand and tried to speak but was quickly seized by a violent coughing fit. Somebody else rubbed his back. He tried to look but his neck didn't want to turn. Everything seemed to be too much of an effort.

When he did start to come to thirty minutes later he looked at Sylvia and instinctively asked for his glasses. She shook her head. 'They appear to have been jettisoned along with your phone.'

'What happened?' He looked around at the clinical white room, a vague chemical odour beginning to creep into his nostrils.

'You went for a swim, fella, in the dark, when you were due at a very important meeting. Your attention-seeking seems to know no bounds,' said a familiar voice.

Harry turned his head to look towards the other side of the bed where Ludo sat, his lean frame awkwardly perched on the edge of a hospital chair, a grey blanket wrapped around his shoulders. He took Harry's hand and gave it a brief squeeze.

'I'm so sorry, Ludo,' he murmured.

His friend smiled back at him. 'Hey, you'd had a shock, we both had. Really, it's fine.'

Harry looked back at Sylvia, to check she hadn't slipped away. She was there, her head bowed as she studied the machine stitching on the blanket, all the while silently thanking God. He gripped her bony hand.

'Ludo rescued you. You were nearly unconscious in the water.' She looked down at her hand in his, releasing it to stroke the long fingers that were so familiar, as if revealing themselves after an interminably long absence.

It was if she had been violently shaken into sensibility since Ludo had knocked at her door, her dormant emotions activated. She felt suddenly exposed. 'Do you remember anything?'

Harry looked at Ludo, frowning. 'You saved me?'

'Hey, it wasn't just me – it took six of us and a fortuitous plank of wood to get you out of the mud, Harry, thanks to your hefty size. And you fair stank! No offence.'

Harry stared at Ludo, noting his chattering teeth. Gradually it came back to him: the sensation of freezing water all around him, the inability to move his feet, his heavy legs, the enveloping darkness, the gradual resignation to his watery end.

'Anyway, the docs say you're fine but not to shock you.'

Harry heard Sylvia laugh softly, a sound that triggered a memory from long ago. He turned his head once more so that he could see her eyes.

Ludo dropped his voice. 'But I think we should tell you anyway.' He looked at Sylvia and smiled, his fingers gripping the bed frame.

Sylvia leaned towards her husband and he closed his eyes for a moment, inhaling her familiar smell. 'The Council voted to keep the cap, Harry.'

'You won, fella,' said Ludo in an exaggerated whisper. He placed his hand on Harry's solid shoulder. 'You only went and bloody won it for us!'

Harry stared at the ceiling, trying to process the news. Perhaps he was dead after all.

'They'll review it in eighteen months' time, so we have a period of grace anyway,' said Sylvia.

'Hey, don't spoil it,' said Ludo. 'Eighteen months is a lifetime. It won't even be an issue when review time rolls around. We have plenty of time to strengthen our case. It will be a no-brainer by then.'

Harry lifted his hand to his face, searching for his glasses. Sylvia took his fingers gently and guided them back to his chest. 'I'll get your other glasses from home. I think you might still have a pair in the office.' She pictured the tortoiseshell-framed glasses on the bookcase next to the speaker, arms folded as if they too were awaiting Harry's return.

Ludo stood up, his chair shrieking as its plastic feet scraped across the lino. 'I'd best go and tell everyone you're going to live after all. Everyone's asking, man, and Facebook's gone crazy.' He folded the blanket loosely over the chair back and touched Harry's arm. 'I'll visit ya when you're home. And well done, you're a proper legend.'

Harry caught Ludo's sleeve as he turned to go. 'Did you really rescue me? I thought I was dreaming. I remember something but—'

'We hauled you out of the water. I thought it was mighty odd that you hadn't turned up for your crowning moment. As the meeting drew to a close I was struck with horror that you— your last text said you were on the towpath and then just kind of, petered out. A group of us hurried back from the meeting along the riverside and suddenly there you were, sort of murmuring to yourself, paddling your arms around.'

Harry's body felt heavy all of a sudden. He remembered the tiredness, the overwhelming fatigue.

'That stuff I said about Rockstr,' he said, shaking his head slowly. 'I didn't mean any of it.'

Ludo could see the anguish in his friend's eyes. 'No sweat, Harry Manchester. Anyway, I didn't tell her the half of it, you foul-mouthed swine. Things will work out, really they will.'

Ludo closed the door softly behind him. Outside he paused for a moment, arms wrapped tightly around his shaking torso. He closed his eyes for a second before making his way back down the corridor.

∽

Harry and Sylvia stared at each other. Sylvia lowered her head, her hand still gripping his. When she lifted it again her eyes were wet and shining, the stark hospital lights reflected as tiny dots in the hazel pools. She tried to speak but no words came out. She tried again. 'Did you want everything to just end—'

Harry frowned, struggling to lift his heavy head off the pillow, suddenly understanding her meaning. 'I would never leave like that, Sylve. It's a fool's way out, a coward's way.' He rested his head back and looked up at the ceiling. 'I was just trying to text Ludo on my way to the meeting—'

'Why didn't you drive?'

'I needed some time to try and gather my thoughts, clear my head. Everything was getting on top of me.' He shook his head again, recalling the relief he had felt as he had let the water take him, the lightness of being.

Now, as he lay there, he felt his body grow taut again as it remembered the burden of living. He thought of Jo.

'What time is it?'

'Eleven o'clock.'

'At night?'

Sylvia nodded. 'But you can go home shortly. They're happy that your confusion was a temporary state brought on by hypothermia. Apparently, it's passed.' She smiled sardonically at him.

'So the meeting – what actually happened?'

'The planning committee voted eight to four to keep the cap,' said Sylvia, her words deliberate, her voice soothing. 'It was passed with a proviso that it would be reviewed in eighteen months' time. There were some quite strong views expressed, according to Ludo. Jason Redthorne is certainly of the opinion that Dawn Goldberg should stand down as VC, chiefly in light of her ridiculous pay rise. He was quite outspoken apparently, and there was a great deal of support, not helped by that Guardian article I shouldn't wonder.'

Harry studied Sylvia's face as she spoke, drinking in every word, every familiar intonation. She looked at him, unsure if he was listening. 'It's all over the local and county news, and even Radio 4 has been trying to get hold of you, so Ludo said. He seems to be managing your media requests, insisting you are allowed to recover fully without being badgered.'

Harry eased himself up to a semi-seated position and smiled, his shoulders groaning with the effort. 'He'll be in his element.'

Sylvia rummaged in her handbag and handed him her mobile phone before standing up abruptly to leave. He stared at her.

'You'll want to call Jo, to pick you up.'

Harry looked at the mobile phone as if he had never seen one before. 'I don't know her number.'

Sylvia rolled her eyes.

'I only know yours. In the river, I remember thinking, I only know your number.' He reeled it off. 'Everyone else – they're just names. I push a button and their number appears. I only know yours.'

'Will Ludo have it?'

Harry looked down at his wrist. 'My Rolex…'

Sylvia reached across to the small bedside table and retrieved it. He took it, running his thumb over the inscription on the back and then over the face. He held out his wrist to Sylvia and she slipped the watch over his hand, clipping the links gently into place.

'Never had a chance to test its waterproof claims before,' he muttered approvingly. He kept his hand held out to her and, after some consideration, Sylvia took it in hers. 'Can I come home?'

Something inside her fluttered joyfully.

Chapter 28

Jo stood motionless in the shadows as the doorbell chimed somewhere deep within the walls of The Oaks. Light leaked from a downstairs window, a faint suggestion of a presence within. She clasped her bag in front of her and cleared her throat, trying to slow her hammering heart.

A local news feed on Facebook had reported Harry's victory live, the result popping up before her eyes as comments began to fly. The next update, seconds later, made much of his absence from the meeting. It had given rise to some unkind speculation, quickly countered by an army of local people offering robust support and thanks for his campaign.

Jo had stared at the words in disbelief, her emotions plummeting from their sudden, soaring high; there would be no possible reason why Harry wouldn't attend tonight's meeting. It was pivotal, the culmination of all his hard work. She had felt suddenly dizzy, weak with an overwhelming sense of dread, when another update appeared with unconfirmed reports that he had been found in the river.

She could not read on, instead dialling Harry's number once more while grabbing her keys and running down the stairs to her car, too anxious to wait for the lift. The ringtone finally ceased when she started the engine, his answerphone message playing again, voice upbeat and warm in a way she had not heard for some time. She had arrived at The Oaks through a screen of tears, to be met by a silent house.

It was several moments before she realised that the front door was very slightly ajar, inviting her in. Her hand hovered over it before she pushed at it. It gave easily and she stepped inside the gloomy entrance hall. Her shaky call of greeting was met by her own voice echoing back at her. She didn't recognise Harry's connection to this place: the large painting in the hallway, the tall vase of listing grasses by the door, the slightly musty smell of a house starved of light. It was not what she had imagined, even in her wildest and frequent imaginings. Her feet tapped softly on the parquet. She despised parquet flooring.

She hesitated in the doorway of the kitchen, drawn by the light inside. She tried to imagine Harry sitting at the curving breakfast bar but the image wouldn't come; he didn't belong here. 'Oh, Harry,' she said aloud, her voice wavering. 'Where are you?'

A piece of paper on the work surface caught her eye, a pen lying discarded next to it, a single elegantly slanting black line of ink displayed unguarded for her to see. She stepped towards it, immediately recognising Harry's name at the top.

I never once stopped loving you. I—

The unfinished sentence hung there as if the words that might have followed were too much to bear. Jo stared, trying to make sense of it. Heat rose quickly through her body, the flames licking at her neck, her cheeks, her forehead.

She left the kitchen and climbed the stairs quickly, her hands blindly sweeping the wall to find a light switch, the final stair moaning under her weight. The room opposite the stairs was half illuminated and she entered, finding another switch as she went. Facing her was a wall of vinyl, each shelf packed full, while underneath sat an immaculate turntable. In one corner of the room was a large swivel chair, sitting empty but expectant. Behind it, on another shelf, sat a pair of Harry's glasses. They seemed to watch her as she stood there awkwardly, a stranger in this silent room. It was as if he had never left, this place so perfectly preserved, awaiting his inevitable return. She picked up his glasses and held them for a moment before returning them carefully to the shelf.

She swiped a tear away and turned the light off. Four other dark doorways beckoned to her, challenging her to enter and piece together more about the man she loved. She stopped and stared at each of them in turn before turning her back and descending the dark stairs at speed. As she reached the bottom she shrieked when something flew at her across the hallway, shooting past her and up the stairs. 'The cat,' she said, trying to steady her gasping breaths. 'Just the cat.'

She pulled the front door closed behind her, the black words on the white paper clearly emblazoned on her mind. *I have never once stopped loving you. I—* That incomplete sentence tormented her more than the words she had seen.

At that moment Harry was on his way back to The Oaks in Sylvia's car, wondering how he could get word to Jo that he was OK. That he was sorry. That he was going back home with his wife. He felt exhausted as he watched the familiar Poltowan coastline spiral away behind them, blanketed in darkness, the sea visible only when it sparkled in slivers of moonlight.

He didn't see Jo's blue Mini hurtle past in the blackness. They had passed just feet from each other, travelling in opposite directions.

The hospital staff were pleasant but unhelpful. They couldn't give Jo any information about whether Harry had been admitted unless she could prove her relationship to him. 'We live together,' she said, her voice breaking. 'We love each other.'

At that moment a nurse appeared, recognising Jo as the teacher of her children. She placed an arm around Jo's shoulders, exchanging a few words with her before striding purposefully back to the desk and checking the computer. Her colleague stood back, face etched with irritation.

'Right, he's in 4B, a private room. Come with me, Jo. I'll take you myself.'

The cold, hostile corridors seemed endless as Jo followed the nurse, twisting left and right, past hobbling patients and a prostrate body being wheeled by on a trolley. She tried to close off her senses to the smell of disinfectant and the thick, stale air.

The nurse slowed to a halt and stuck her head into a small room. The bed was empty, its bedclothes recently disturbed. To either side of it stood an empty chair, each one angled earnestly, lovingly, towards the absent patient.

'I'm sorry, Jo. He must have just been discharged.' The nurse looked at Jo's red-rimmed eyes and squeezed her arm. 'But that's good, isn't it? It means he's on the mend, he's gone home. He'll be there, I expect – you must have missed him by minutes.'

Sylvia's car turned inland and Harry pondered the jagged skyline and neat rows of houses climbing upwards, a townscape that was as familiar to him as his own face. He knew he would always remember this moment, as they rose slowly up Lannoweth Hill, crowning the top of the town, before winding their way back towards the coast, towards home.

When they pulled into the drive, Diggory was standing on the doorstep, hands thrust deep in his pockets. He looked up and smiled before bowing theatrically and wandering slowly over to the car. He shook hands with Harry as he eased himself out of the passenger seat, before clapping him gently on the back.

'I don't know whether to say congratulations or commiserations, mate. You don't half like to make life complicated.'

Harry smiled and ushered him inside. They were alone together for a few minutes while Sylvia retreated to the kitchen.

'Dig, before she comes back, I need to get word to Jo. My phone's gone. I haven't got her number. Can you contact her for me, let her know I'm sorry? Tell her I'm here.' Harry rubbed the bridge of his nose. 'At The Oaks.'

'And you're staying here, you mean?'

'That I'm here,' repeated Harry. 'I need to explain things to her but, for now, can you just let her know I'll go round tomorrow and we can talk then?'

Diggory raised his eyebrows in surprise. 'Thanks, mate. Any more of your dirty work you want me to do, just ask.'

Harry gave him the apartment number. As he was leaving, Diggory paused in the doorway. He turned back and placed his hand on Harry's shoulder. 'I have to be honest, I wasn't sure you'd pull it off, mate. I was afraid for you. Particularly with that story about your rock star friend all over the front page.'

Harry shook his head. 'You don't have to stop being nervous for me. I'll have enough people out for my scalp now.'

'You haven't seen the news – or been into town,' said Diggory, more earnestly than was usual for him. 'The whole place is buzzing. Seriously. I think there are enough people prepared to defend you for you not to worry about minding your back. They see you as their saviour. That story about the girl – I think the *Post* overestimated how important it was. There are far bigger things at stake here.'

Harry felt pride swell within him, to be immediately eclipsed by a wave of biliousness as he thought of James Cowley and the prospect of a bulging brown envelope. He opened the door for Diggory. 'Thanks for calling in. Do me another favour and make sure people don't get too carried away with it all. It might be just a temporary reprieve.'

'Come on, it's far more significant than that. Why not enjoy it? You deserve it.'

Harry began to close the front door, feeling weary suddenly, but Diggory was calling something from halfway up the drive. Harry cocked his head, hand to his ear.

'I don't suppose you heard but developers have put in a bid to buy the Chyangwens Hotel – make it into accommodation for two hundred students. That's your next battle.'

Harry stared at him in disbelief. 'The Chyangwens is a landmark, it's been there years. Are you sure?'

Diggory shrugged his shoulders. 'That's what I heard.'

Chapter 29

The editor of *News Time* was insistent that Harry should join the evening show the next day. She seemed most put out about having had to delay the interview by a day due to his close encounter with death.

Ludo had already conducted eight press interviews on Harry's behalf since the Council vote, but *News Time* insisted on Harry Manchester himself attending the studio. While Ludo had been variously called a hero, a leader, a campaigner, an anarchist and a role model, he had bent over backwards to sing the praises of Harry Manchester who had 'quite literally saved Poltowan and Poltowan University, for which both residents and students owe him a huge debt of gratitude'.

He had skilfully skirted any questions about how Harry came to end up in the water, mindful not to get drawn into any fanciful conspiracy theories. He had been tempted to answer that, knowing Harry, he had just wandered into the river and not realised until his feet were wet, but knew his friend would not thank him for that.

Ludo focussed on the positives – such as Dawn Goldberg's ashen face when the committee had announced their decision, her shocking white skin against her gold-tinted hair. Ludo had felt a fleeting twinge of pity as he watched her brash façade disintegrate before his eyes, her flinching gaze that of one who had suffered a terrible and unexpected shock.

He pictured once more Jason Redthorne, who had appeared to point accusingly at the Vice Chancellor before walking out of the meeting. He recalled seeing Steve Kent and James Cowley both standing dumbfounded, mouths gaping, so sure had they been of victory, before emitting a torrent of unimaginative expletives in the general direction of Darren Toddington, who stood tall, proudly – if not smugly – surveying the scene before him.

Ludo smiled as he recalled the sheer joy on the faces of the students, while many residents dabbed at their eyes as the words 'maintain the cap' were read out, hugging each other with relief before a spontaneous and deafening outburst of applause broke out. And all the while Harry had been fighting for his life in the icy waters of the Poltowan River. It made Ludo shudder to remember.

Harry was still feeling slightly jaded so Ludo had insisted on accompanying him to *News Time*, and had even offered to drive. Harry still felt guilty about his outburst, but not *that* guilty, and the thought of letting Ludo drive his Mercedes had been a sobering one. He acquiesced to letting Ludo join him on the trip to South West Media's studios, but Harry took the wheel himself.

It should have been less than two hours to Plymouth, but the volume of traffic saw the two of them crawling along the A30 for a good forty-five minutes, stuck behind a series of agricultural vehicles. Harry quickly grew frustrated and uptight, punching buttons continually to get traffic updates and engaging in shouting matches with the voice-recognition system, much to Ludo's amusement.

Harry had spoken briefly to Jo, gathering that she already knew what he was going to say. She had protested then that she would not just let him slip out of her life, not now, and he had been thrown into a momentary panic, defaulting instead to practicalities.

He had called the landlord of the penthouse who had agreed to void the lease with just two week's notice, gleefully informing Harry that he had received two enquiries that morning following the news that the cap on student numbers would remain in place. Harry had also spoken to the landlord of Jo's former flat and he had advised Harry of a neighbouring property that was currently vacant. When he had called Jo back to let her know, she had veered from pure rage to a flood of noisy tears and back again, before hanging up.

Sylvia had seemed better since his accident, as if looking after him had given her a new sense of purpose. She was brighter and more alert, and he had even heard her talking to the birds that morning, something she didn't indulge in when one of her black moods struck.

She had agreed to him coming home. Although he had spent the first two nights in the spare room while he recovered, he assumed this was a temporary arrangement. No need to hurry things. She had not said she was proud of his campaign victory, but she had held his hand for a prolonged period of time when they talked about it at the hospital, and he had heard her telling Nell on the phone 'despite your best efforts, Harry's cause proved triumphant'.

He had received two missed calls on his phone from Nell, firstly to apologise for *The Guardian* article, and secondly to wish him well after his dreadful accident. The poor woman had sounded close to tears, but Harry's emotional resources had already been exhausted and he had not returned her call. His instinct, unlike Sylvia's, was that Nell had made a careless mistake; that was all. Knowing she had recently experienced at first hand how disruptive the growing student population could be to residents' lives, he hoped she would applaud the decision that had been made, even if she did have to toe the line at work.

The car began to inch forward again before coming once more to an abrupt halt. Harry hit the wheel with the palm of his hand, prompting Ludo to glance sideways at him. Harry had lost weight over the last few weeks, his cheekbones more defined, jaw squarer. He was not bad looking, considered Ludo, if you allowed for the receding hairline and the glasses. Harry caught his eye.

'What? What is it?'

'Nothing. Chill out, Harry. Just checking you're OK.'

'Traffic.' He hit the update button again.

'We've plenty of time, Harry. Try not to get worked up, not now.'

Harry sighed heavily.

'You should enjoy this moment. This is what you've been working for all this time. You're a local hero. Go and milk it with that Jenny Crumble – she was so patronising last time.'

'Trundle. Jenny Trundle,' said Harry.

'Good job you're without a phone this time, eh?' Ludo gave a hearty belly laugh, remembering Harry's last studio appearance. 'That ringtone, man – I mean, it was bad, but there was no need to throw the thing in the river!'

Harry remained tight-lipped, eyes fixed firmly on the road ahead.

Ludo turned to look out of the window. He sensed that there was more to Harry's troubled state than his recent accident. They slowed to a halt again and Ludo asked hesitantly about Jo.

Harry shook his head and looked out of the side window at the driver to his right. 'It would never have worked out. I've told her I'm — sorry.'

The word was woefully inadequate. He fell silent and Ludo waited for him to continue. 'I love Sylvia — never stopped loving her. I see that now.' Harry pushed his glasses higher on the bridge of his nose. His spare pair were looser than his others and were already irritating him. 'Jo deserves better than me.'

'Sounds like she's pretty stuck on you.'

'Bastard,' said Harry loudly as a lorry cut him up, forcing him to brake. He blasted his horn for several seconds, gave the driver a dirty look. 'Sylvia and I are going to try and make things work.'

Ludo simply nodded.

'I need some stability. I need to be at home. I want things back the way they were.'

Ludo shifted in his seat, increasingly uncomfortable with Harry's solemn mood. 'That's fair enough. I mean, Sylvia... she seems like an impressive lady too. Very switched on. And beautiful bone structure.'

Harry gave him a sidelong glance as the traffic began to gather speed once more.

'Honestly, Harry, you're the hero of the hour – no wonder all these women are falling over themselves for you.'

'It's not that simple,' he said, ignoring Ludo's attempt at levity. 'They don't know me. No one really knows anyone in the end, do they?'

Ludo thought of Rockstr's revelation and began to pick at the rough skin on his left hand. She had sworn to him that there was nothing else she hadn't told him, and that she had always planned to come clean. It was early days, she said, and they needed some time together. He pulled a strip of skin clean off his thumb before glancing once more at Harry's blank features. 'Hey. You're on the gogglebox shortly. People want a bit of that Harry Manchester magic, that quick wit, that boundless optimism.'

Harry loosened his shoulders and elongated his neck. Ludo was right. He needed to get a grip and focus on the campaign, channel some of Ludo's enthusiasm.

'I'm wondering how best to handle the Rockstr question.'

Ludo tried to manoeuvre his long legs in the footwell. 'Tell the truth is all you can do, Harry. You didn't know. She's done her time, learned her lesson. And she's trying to make a good life for herself. That's all there is to say. We all make mistakes – it's how we deal with them that matters.'

Harry kept his eyes on the road ahead, not commenting.

'We won the campaign – we kept the cap,' continued Ludo. 'You survived a near-death experience. You've got your pick of women. Come on, man, lighten up! Go on TV in this mood and people will wonder what the hell you're so down about.'

James Cowley, thought Harry with a sickening jolt. That was what. The stealthy leads on people wanting to rent to students; the brown envelope that would soon arrive with hundreds of pounds inside it; his own hypocrisy just so he could stay afloat; so he didn't fail Sylvia or Jo, or watch his business go bust. Yet he had already let everyone down.

∾

They pulled up at the TV studios twenty-five minutes later, Harry guiding his car into a space near the entrance doors. Ludo glanced out of the window. 'Six quid an hour here, mate, you sure you don't want to find somewhere else to park?'

'I'm not taking any chances.'

Ludo hopped quickly out of the car and stretched his slim body to its full height, his hairy navel exposed over the top of his boxers as he gazed up at the looming South West Media sign. Harry extricated himself from the driver's seat and unhooked his suit jacket carefully from the back of the car. He looked at Ludo as he closed the door. 'You need to get a belt.'

They were whisked in as perfunctorily as before, with Harry being manhandled into make-up and Ludo left alone in the optimistically named Green Room, which was furnished with a seventy-five-inch flat-screen TV, a faded red sofa and a coffee machine.

Ludo took Harry's face in his hands before he was led off down the corridor, playfully slapping his cheeks. 'Come on, man, liven up. Just for ten minutes, then we can get you home again. Don't let the people down – they'll be tuning in to see your happy smiley face. Make sure you deliver. This is a good news bulletin, OK? And show that Jenny Crumble what you're made of too.' He thought he saw the twinkle return fleetingly to Harry's blue eyes.

Ludo paced the room, sucking distractedly on his electronic cigarette while the machine hissed and clunked its way towards providing him with a cup of bitter coffee. His phone began buzzing, Rockstr's name lighting up on the screen. At first he couldn't make out if she was crying or laughing. He moved around the small room, holding his phone in the air to try and get a better signal.

'What is it… what?' He heard the name Kris Jorgensen and then a muffled cry and a repetition of the same name. 'Slow down, Rocks, what are you saying?'

Suddenly the line became clear. Rockstr had been invited to play a set at Bootleg Records in London after its A&R man, Kris Jorgensen, had seen the video of her concert at The Oaks.

'His friend's nephew is at Poltowan Uni – he shared some of the video on Facebook and Kris watched my other videos on there too, the solo acoustic stuff. Said he was really impressed.'

'I bet he was,' said Ludo under his breath.

'Oh my God, can you believe it, Ludo? I actually have a chance to prove myself. I actually have a chance to, like, get a record contract. I go to see them next week.'

Ludo's mind was racing, torn as he was between pride and excitement and a creeping fear that things were changing; that things had already changed.

'That is deadly, Rocks, truly. I'm stoked for you, really I am.'

'And you know, it was you who did it! It was you who made this happen!'

'How'd you work that one out?'

'You got me the gig for the campaign, for Harry. You got

your mates to film it, like, professionally. You got me in front of all those people. It was my big break.'

'Well, hold your horses, don't get ahead of yourself. I mean, it's great, don't get me wrong, lady, but just don't get too excited until you hear what they say, eh?'

Rockstr sounded deflated. 'You're right. I'm just so—'

Harry's face suddenly loomed large on the oversized TV screen. 'Rocks, I'll call you back, Harry's on *News Time*. Switch it on now.'

He hung up and stood a foot away from the TV as Jenny Trundle introduced 'Harry Manchester, champion of the people of Poltowan'.

The sick feeling in the pit of Harry's stomach remained, his gut twisting itself tighter and tighter as he thought of all his supporters at home, of the hordes of students who had protested and then danced and cheered in his field.

He forced a smattering of mirth and wit into his responses, smiling cheerfully at Jenny Trundle's leading questions and batting away her interrogation about the river incident. 'It was something and nothing, Jenny, really. I'm just sorry I wasn't at Poltowan Town Hall to witness a truly historic occasion that saw the will of the people triumph.'

'But it's been quite an eventful week, with the revelation about Rockstr, whom you chose to front your campaign and headline your concert at the weekend, being a convicted drug dealer? Were you aware of her record?'

Harry felt instinctively for his watch. 'I was not aware beforehand, but Rockstr has served her time and has come to Poltowan to focus on rebuilding her life. She is a very talented girl who made a mistake – it's that simple. And she has paid for that mistake. Must she keep on paying?'

Jenny found herself drawn to the intensity in his blue eyes, wondering how she had not noticed them before. An impatient voice sounded in her earpiece. 'And… are you disappointed that the Strategic Planning Committee have said they will look at the cap decision again in eighteen months – does it mean fighting this campaign all over again when that time approaches? Is this a false dawn, Harry?'

Ludo bit savagely at his thumb nail, seeing a shadow of fatigue fleetingly darken Harry's features, like a cloud across the sun.

'Not at all.' He leaned forward, unmoved by Jenny Trundle's long legs and fluttering eyelashes. 'This campaign has served to wake up the community, to wake up the people of Poltowan – both students and residents – to how important and special our town is, and to how valuable the university can be if it is managed correctly.'

'Managed correctly?'

Harry looked intently at her for a moment, choosing his words carefully. 'It's a great responsibility to manage an educational institution in a town like Poltowan. So yes, absolutely, it must be managed correctly.'

'Are you implying that you would perhaps welcome a change in leadership at the university?'

Harry offered her, and the watching thousands, a wry smile via camera two. 'I don't think we can be complacent about the leadership there. It should be constantly challenged, constantly scrutinised – and certainly held accountable. If that means change, so be it.'

Jenny looked at his long fingers, the Rolex sitting just outside his starched cuff, his broad shoulders. He had a powerful aura about him today, an air of success. She opened her mouth with every intention of pursuing the point but was blindsided by Harry.

'Hopefully, people can now see how the town and the university could be made to thrive together, in tandem. We will continue to build on that foundation of knowledge, undoubtedly, but I believe there is a new awareness now, an energy towards preserving the status quo in Poltowan, that will not be denied. The Council are welcome to look again in eighteen months but they will only encounter an even more entrenched opposition to altering the scale of the university. We have unstoppable momentum.' Harry nodded on hearing his own words, his doubts dissolving under the white-hot studio lights.

Jenny Trundle smiled, her head angled to match Harry's, eyes narrowed in concentration. 'Even with developers beginning to see the town as an investment opportunity?' She glanced down at her notes. 'I believe a change of use for the historic Chyangwens Hotel is currently under discussion?'

Harry nodded. 'As I said, Jenny, the people of Poltowan are an unstoppable force.' He leaned towards the camera meaningfully. 'This week's decision to keep the cap is just the beginning.'

∽

In the Green Room Ludo punched his fist in the air, emitting a loud whoop followed by an incomprehensible stream of Irish jargon.

In her halls, Rockstr blew vivid pink kisses at the television and clenched her small hands in solidarity.

In the candlelit penthouse flat, Jo's eyes began to fill again as she glanced from Harry's face on the flat-screen TV to his vinyl records, stacked alphabetically in the corner. He would be back soon to pick up his things. She could not countenance a future without him, even if that meant she had to wait a long time.

At The Oaks, Sylvia stood in the middle of the room clutching the small bottle of pills and watching Harry's slightly pixelated face. She placed the bottle at the back of the cupboard for safekeeping before adding beetroot and turnips to her 'to do' list.

In her swanky kitchen, Dawn Goldberg crashed her wine glass onto the marble island, blaspheming loudly at both Jenny Trundle and Harry Manchester, before abruptly rejecting a call from Andy Hornblower and dialling Dennis Flintoff, who sat waiting for his phone to ring.

'They're treating him like a hero – a bloody estate agent and they're treating him like a god! And he's lapping it up!'

'We have over a year to push this thing through, once and for all,' said Dennis authoritatively, tensing his abs as he spoke. 'And just think, you haven't even announced your plans for a world-leading engineering research centre yet.'

She had to concede he was right. Harry Manchester might have won the piddling battle, but he had certainly not won the war. As her father would often say, it was all about playing the long game.

In a terraced house in Tremaine Road, Nell watched with a mixture of pride, love and regret as Harry's blue eyes sparkled kindly from her television set, a flood of remorseful tears rolling soundlessly down her cheeks. She picked up the phone to call Sylvia, hesitated, and replaced the handset.

In his contemporary seafront house just along the coast from Poltowan, Jason Redthorne grudgingly commended Harry Manchester's efforts, wondering if they could perhaps work together in future. Despite being at odds over increasing the number of students, they at least appeared to be firmly united in their dislike of Dawn Goldberg.

In a pub on Littlemore Street, James Cowley looked around him as fellow local business owners shook their heads, ranting at the TV, before draining their glasses in disgust. He stood up and ordered another pint, allowing himself a small smile. A lot could happen in eighteen months.

Acknowledgements

A huge thank you to the family and friends I dragooned into reading my early drafts, namely: Sheila Smith, David Smith, Fiona Rundle, Neil Hosken, Beth Davies, Tina Ashford-Rowe, Tonka Watson, Rowland and Caroline Abram and Nicky Trump. Their thoughtful and honest feedback, and their kind words, were hugely helpful.

A big thanks to editor extraordinaire, Lynn Curtis who was meticulous and questioning when it mattered. Also to Josie Staveley-Taylor, a very talented illustration student at Falmouth University, who worked wonders with my woolly brief to bring this book cover to life.

And to Jamie Rowe, a family friend and masterly epic fantasy author based in Brisbane, who shared a wealth of insider tips about the publishing process.

Endless gratitude to the family and friends who have listened to me chatter on about this book for many, many months. That'll teach you to ask how the next book is going.

I'm also grateful to Alexa Whitten of The Book Refinery, who painstakingly typeset my manuscript and patiently answered my endless questions.

And thank you - or meur ras - to Cornwall, which has always felt like home.

About the author

Nicola K Smith is a freelance journalist and writer living in Cornwall, regularly contributing to a number of national newspapers and magazines. She studied English Literature at Loughborough University.

Nicola was chosen as 'most promising student' on Curtis Brown Creative's '*Starting to Write Your Novel*' course, and *A Degree of Uncertainty* was conceived under their tutelage. This is her first novel.

You can find her at:
Twitter: @NicolaKSmith
Instagram: nicolaksmith740

Please take a few minutes to review *A Degree of Uncertainty* on Amazon.co.uk and spread the word, or even better, buy it for your friends!